SONGBINDER

Tales of the Outlaw Mages
Book Five

AMY CAMPBELL

Legend Has It LLC

SONGBINDER

Cover design by Amy Campbell
Edited by Vicky Brewster
Map by Amy Campbell
Chapter headings, heading art, and dividers designed by Amy Campbell

ISBN-13: 978-1-957816-95-1 (ebook), 978-1-957816-02-9 (print)

First edition: May 2024
www.amycampbell.info
v 070324

For my author friends who encourage me when I need it the most:
Sam, ARK, & Merrie

Author's Note

Sometimes life throws difficult situations at us—and this is true even in fantasy books. Even though they're an escape, fantasy helps us cope with the horrors of our own world. But by that same token, I don't want my words to cause harm to my readers, so please note that *Songbinder* contains the following: abusive relationship/emotional abuse, anxiety, assault, kidnapping, attempted murder, blood, death, divorce, hostages, needles, physical abuse, PTSD, stalking, torture, violence, forced captivity, and mild profanity.

Some of these are very heavy subjects, but I consider my books to be noblebright, so please know that in the end, *love always wins*.

In the newly recognized nation of the Gutter, the outlaw mages face unrest from the Salt-Iron Confederation. Vixen Valerie, aware of the looming threat of war, plans to use her unique position as the Spark of Garus, a chosen avatar of a deity revered in Phinora, to prevent conflict. She reveals her secret to Jefferson and convinces him to join her on a diplomatic mission to Izhadell.

Despite opposition from her former lover, Raven Dawson, Vixen, accompanied by Jefferson and Blaise, embarks on her journey. Along the way, Rhys, a Confederation Tracker who is revealed to be Vixen's brother, escorts them. Upon reaching Phinora, Jefferson is unexpectedly arrested.

Vixen, Blaise, and Rhys devise a plan to free Jefferson, only to find themselves opposed by unseen forces. While imprisoned, Phillip Dillon visits Jefferson, and it's quickly apparent that the Quiet Ones are pulling the strings. When Vixen attempts to intervene, her magic exposes her, leading to her own imprisonment. She is forced to reveal her true identity to secure her and Jefferson's release.

Back in Fortitude, Jack discovers Raven Dawson's disappearance, suspecting foul play. To aid Vixen, Jack and Kittie transport themselves to Izhadell, where they join forces with Blaise. They uncover the Maverick Underground, a group of freedom-fighting mages, and Jack is subsequently captured by Raven and taken to a shadow realm.

Vixen's true identity is joyfully acknowledged by the Luminary of Phinora, who is also her mother, Juliette Kildare. However, a gala event turns disastrous when Phillip Dillon and Tara Woodrow, members of the Quiet Ones, attempt to undermine Vixen. The evening culminates in the Luminary's abduction by Raven.

Kittie, alongside her elemental steed, Najaria, finds the Luminary in the shadow realm. They struggle to escape, showing the Luminary's initial reluctance to ally with mages. Meanwhile, Vixen informs her allies of the kidnapping, but news leaks prematurely.

Flora Strop joins the effort, discovering Jack's critical condition in Quiet One custody. Raven's attempt to abduct Jefferson backfires, leading to his capture and forced confession of his motives, driven by a promised love potion.

Vixen and her group, with Raven in tow, make a daring move on the Quiet Ones' stronghold, aiming to rescue Jack. Their plan doesn't go as hoped, and during the chaos, Vixen is captured. With the upper hand, Phillip and Tara press their advantage, pushing Vixen into a corner and forcing her to meet their demands.

Meanwhile, Rhys drops a bombshell: the ascension of a new Luminary traditionally requires a magical sacrifice, and Jack is marked for this grim fate. Determined not to let this happen, Blaise, Jefferson, Rhys, and Flora, with the support of the Maverick Underground, concoct a bold strategy to thwart the ceremony.

Their intervention is a success, preventing Jack's sacrifice. In a simultaneous turn of events, Kittie and the Luminary escape the shadow realm. In the aftermath, Juliette, the Luminary, publicly denounces the conspiracy against her. During Tara Woodrow's interrogation, Raven disrupts the proceedings with a shocking display of magic, fatally attacking Tara. His actions lead to his immediate arrest and imprisonment for murder.

In a pivotal moment, the deity Garus manifests, directly addressing Vixen. Garus liberates her from the heavy responsibilities tied to her role, choosing Rhys as the successor to carry the title of the Spark. Rhys eagerly steps into this new role, ready to embrace his destiny.

Amid these events, Kittie notices Jack's dire condition. He's on the brink of death, prompting her to act. With Blaise's help, she conjures a portal to Fortitude, allowing Nadine to come through. Nadine's healing skills bring Jack back from the edge, but it's clear his recovery will be a lengthy process.

In the aftermath, Juliette and Rhys disclose their intentions to collaborate with the Maverick Underground, aiming to better the lives of mages. They invite Vixen to join their cause, but she declines, yearning for her life back in the Gutter.

Driven by anger and concern for his loved ones' safety, Jefferson confronts Phillip Dillon. He uses his magic to unequivocally demand that Phillip and the Quiet Ones cease their threats. Phillip, in turn, inquires about the location of his wife, Alice—who is also Jefferson's sister. Jefferson, however, remains silent on the matter.

Finally, the outlaws make their way back to Fortitude. In a moment of clarity about the depth of his feelings, Blaise proposes to Jefferson, who joyfully accepts. It seems that a brighter future is on the horizon for them...

Pronunciation Guide

Words are fun. Below is a rough guide to the pronunciation for words you'll find in this book. If your brain disagrees, that's fine. Language is malleable, so you do you!

Argor – ARR-gor
Blaise – BLAY-z
Canen – KAY-nun
Chupacabra – CHOO-puh-cah-bruh
Desina – Dess-EE-nuh
Effigest – Eff-IH-jest
Emmaline – Em-uh-LINE
Emrys – Em-RISS
Faedra – FAY-druh
Faedran – FAY-drun
Ganland – Gan-LUND
Garus – Gair-USS
Geasa – GESH-uh
Itude – Ih-TOOD
Izhadell – Iz-UH-dell
Knossan – NOSS-uhn

Knossas – NOSS-us
Lucienne – Loo-SEE-ann
Marian – Mayr-EE-uhn
Mella – Mell-UH
Nadine – Nay-DEEN
Naureus — Nar-EE-us
Nera – NEER-uh
Oberidon – Oh-BEAR-uh-don (alternate: Oby – Oh-BEE)
Phinora – Fin-OR-uh
Ravance – Ruh-VAN-s
Reuben – Roo-ben
Seledora – Sel-uh-DOR-uh
Tabris – Tab-RISS
Theilia – Thee-LEE-uh
Theilian – Thee-LEE-uhn
Theurgist – THEE-ur-jest
Zepheus – Zeff-EE-us

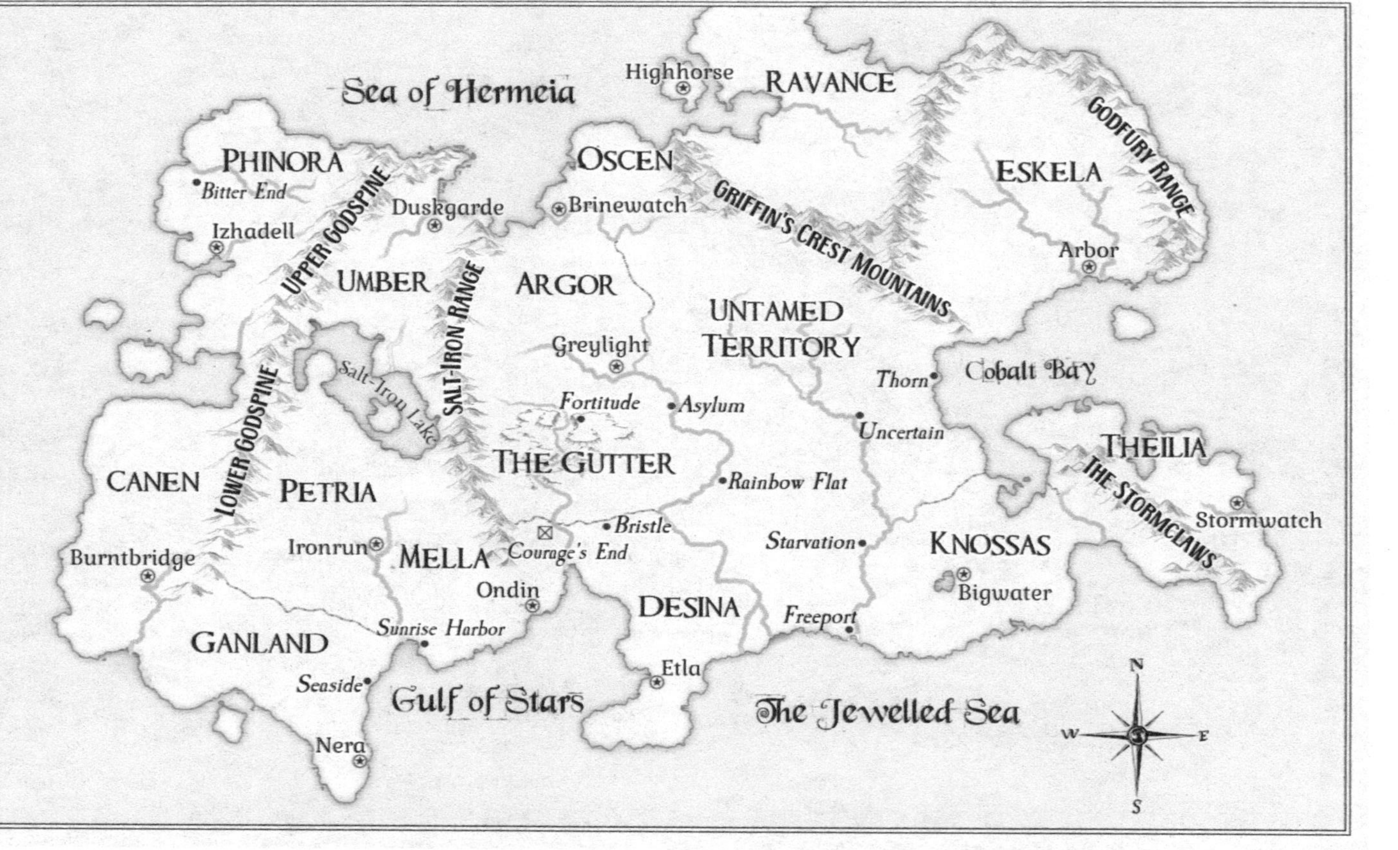

Sea of Hermeia
Highhorse
RAVANCE
GODFURY RANGE
PHINORA
Bitter End
Izhadell
UPPER GODSPINE
Duskgarde
OSCEN
Brinewatch
GRIFFIN'S CREST MOUNTAINS
ESKELA
Arbor
UMBER
SALT-IRON RANGE
ARGOR
Greylight
UNTAMED TERRITORY
Thorn
Cobalt Bay
LOWER GODSPINE
Salt-Iron Lake
Fortitude
Asylum
Uncertain
THEILIA
CANEN
PETRIA
THE GUTTER
Rainbow Flat
THE STORMCLAWS
Stormwatch
Bristle
Burntbridge
Ironrun
MELLA
Courage's End
Starvation
KNOSSAS
Ondin
DESINA
Bigwater
GANLAND
Sunrise Harbor
Freeport
Etla
Seaside
Gulf of Stars
The Jewelled Sea
Nera
N
W
E
S

CHAPTER ONE

Island Life

Jefferson

Sand sprayed into the air as the pair of pegasi galloped along the pristine white beach of Sunrich Isle. Seledora kept pace alongside Emrys, though Jefferson knew the mare was holding back. His fleet-footed pegasus was far faster than the ponderous black stallion.

<If it's a race you want, say the word,> Seledora suggested, arching her neck to glance back at him as the sand churned beneath her. <But I thought you'd appreciate staying near your mate.>

Oh, she was right about that. The wind whipped through Jefferson's hair, carrying with it the salty tang of the sea and the warmth of Blaise's presence. He leaned over her neck. "We're almost there."

With a snort, Seledora eased into a canter and then an easy trot.

Jefferson turned in the saddle, unable to hide his joy at seeing Blaise enjoying himself. His husband had a broad smile on his face as he watched the play of the surf against the beach.

"I never thought I'd see the day when you would be riding along the coast without a care in the world," Jefferson said, savoring the sight.

Blaise glanced over from beneath the wide brim of his hat, the sun casting shadows across his curly brown hair and neatly trimmed beard. He pulled a face, feigning annoyance. "I'm only out here because you insisted on this little adventure, remember?"

"Ah, but you can't deny that you're enjoying yourself," Jefferson countered as Seledora edged closer to Emrys's side. "I see that smile on your face."

Blaise's smile was a radiant thing, on par with the sun as far as Jefferson was concerned. The younger man nodded. "This is...nice. And I'll admit, there is something freeing about galloping along the shore like this." He adjusted his hat, a move that made Jefferson chuckle.

"What's so funny?" Blaise asked, curiosity bright in his eyes as he tugged at the sleeves of his shirt, making sure they covered every inch of skin.

Jefferson gestured to Blaise's extensive sun protection outfit and said, "You know your mother sent along a potion to protect us from the sun."

"I know. I'm wearing some." Blaise wiped a bead of sweat from his brow.

"As am I," Jefferson said, grinning. His arms and chest were bare, skin glistening in the sunlight thanks to the protective potion. "I decided to fully embrace the island lifestyle. Do you like the view?"

Blaise's eyebrows rose, but he gave Jefferson a considering look. "The beach is pretty nice."

Seledora nickered a laugh. <You got him right in the ego.>

Jefferson clutched a hand to his chest in mock indignation. "You wound me, sir. It concerns me that perhaps you didn't catch my meaning." Though the playful twist to Blaise's lips told him everything he needed to know: Blaise was relaxed, happy, and teasing him right back.

Blaise's expression softened, his eyes meeting Jefferson's. "You know I wouldn't be here if I didn't like the view." He rubbed at one of his long sleeves. "But as for me...well, I'm erring on the side of caution." He glanced skyward, his gaze lingering as if he were searching for clouds to shield him. "I still remember a rather nasty sunburn I got before..."

Beneath Blaise, Emrys twisted to nudge his rider's knee. <That was when you found me! I remember. You were as red as an apple.>

Blaise wrinkled his nose at the memory, visibly recalling the discomfort. "And it hurt."

Jefferson clucked his tongue in understanding. That had been before he'd known Blaise. So much for hoping that Blaise might join him in baring more skin to the tropical warmth. Maybe once he saw how well Marian Hawthorne's potion worked, Blaise would reconsider. He had to be hot, wearing long sleeves as he was.

"I see. Well, I hope you can enjoy our vacation in that garb. You've more than earned it," Jefferson said, guiding Seledora towards a hidden gem he'd discovered earlier—a secluded swimming hole. The water was a mesmerizing shade of azure, sparkling like a handful of sapphires tossed carelessly into the sand. Overhanging branches adorned with vibrant green leaves provided a natural canopy, casting dappled sunlight over the surface of the water. He slid a coy look over at Blaise. "Seledora and I found this place when you were busy ogling the baked goods in town this morning."

"Admiring. I was *admiring* them," Blaise insisted, crossing his arms in feigned exasperation.

<We taste-tested them, too. They were delicious,> Emrys added, his enormous tongue flopping from his mouth for a moment at the memory.

Jefferson chuckled as he gracefully slid off Seledora's back. His bare feet touched the ground, and he wiggled his toes, savoring the cool, soft grass that seemed to welcome him. "This," he gestured around, "is the perfect place for a refreshing swim." For a moment, he let his eyes roam over the secluded grove. The ferns and bushes that surrounded them seemed like guardians of the pool, providing a level of privacy that made the moment feel even more special.

Blaise glanced around, scanning the lush surroundings. After he dismounted, Emrys ambled over to a shady spot beside Seledora, head low and eyelids drooping with sleepy contentment. Blaise paused, as if he were deciding. He looked at the pool of water, then back at Jefferson, and that radiant smile that could rival the sun itself spread across his face.

"Perfect," Blaise agreed. The way he said it, the warmth in his eyes, made Jefferson's heart swell with happiness. In that instant, he knew Blaise wasn't just talking about the idyllic scenery around them.

Jefferson crouched by the water's edge, gently dipping his hand into the crystalline pool. The water felt cool to the touch, a perfect contrast to the persistent heat of the afternoon sun on his skin. As he looked up, he caught Blaise in the process of meticulously unbuttoning his shirt. Each movement was slow, deliberate, like carefully peeling back the golden crust of a well-baked pastry to reveal the sweet filling within.

"Change of heart?" Jefferson ventured, his gaze fixed on the gradually revealed expanse of skin beneath the fabric, a canvas he knew intimately yet never tired of exploring.

Blaise met his gaze and smirked, the corner of his mouth ticking upward. "We're going swimming, aren't we?"

"Indeed, we are," Jefferson replied, a thrill of anticipation curling within him. The air between them seemed to hum with unspoken promise.

"Then I don't want my shirt to get wet." Blaise's voice held a teasing edge as he peeled off his shirt, draping it over a low branch. He hung his hat next to it.

"Ever gone skinny dipping?" Jefferson asked as he rose from his crouch. His eyes remained fixed on his husband, cataloging every contour and shadow, as if Blaise were a sculpture he wished to commit to memory.

Blaise paused, a flicker of self-conscious hesitation crossing his features. "Can't say I have," he admitted, his gaze sweeping the secluded clearing as if assessing their level of privacy. "But I guess you have?"

Jefferson laughed, the sound bright and unrestrained. "You'd be absolutely right." Sensing Blaise's wavering resolve, Jefferson knew it was time to seize the moment. With a fluid motion, he shucked off his trousers and drawers, leaving them in a neat pile beside the water. Taking a deep breath to savor the anticipation, Jefferson slid into the water. He looked up at Blaise, his eyes twinkling with mischief, and shot him a saucy grin that he hoped conveyed a world of invitation.

Blaise rolled his eyes at Jefferson's daring display but soon followed suit. His trousers and boots joined the growing assortment of discarded clothing at the water's edge. "You're such a show-off," he said, his voice full of affectionate exasperation.

With a graceful slide, Blaise eased into the water on the opposite side of the swimming hole. He leaned against the moss-covered edge, releasing a soft sigh. The coolness enveloped them both, a soothing balm that washed away the relentless afternoon heat.

"You knew exactly what you were getting when you proposed to me," Jefferson said.

Blaise laughed, the sound musical and warm. "I did. And I love you for it. You're so audacious you'll always keep the attention away from me."

"Mmm," Jefferson hummed, pushing off from his side of the pool. He glided effortlessly through the water, closing the short distance between them. "The only problem is, you'll always have *my* attention."

Settling in next to Blaise, the tension in Jefferson's muscles melted away as the water buoyed him up. How he wished they could be more daring, let his hands wander beneath the water's surface in frisky exploration. But he knew Blaise, knew that his husband reserved those intimate moments for times when they were truly alone. Still, the simple joy of being here, submerged in this hidden paradise with the man he loved, sent a warmth spreading through his chest that no tropical sun could match.

Jefferson's fingers traced a delicate path down Blaise's arm, skimming over the familiar topography of old scars. "Are you truly enjoying our vacation?"

Blaise caught Jefferson's hand, squeezing it with an intensity that spoke volumes. "Very much so." His smile faltered, as if he were treading on uncertain ground. "I've never seen a place quite like this. The closest was our escape to the beach near Nera, after—"

Anticipating the shadows that could cloud their paradise, Jefferson pressed his fingers to Blaise's lips, halting the words before he dared speak them. This was not the time or place for grim memories. "The unpleasantness," he supplied softly, wanting to preserve the sanctuary they had found here, even if it was just for a little while.

His hand slid from Blaise's mouth to his cheek, his thumb caressing the line of Blaise's jaw with a tenderness that belied his usual audacity. "That was my most theatrical moment, you know. I felt very daring, like a hero from one of my favorite stage plays."

Blaise's lips quirked into a smile, the tension visibly melting from his expression. "Your most theatrical moment? I think you have one of those every few months."

"Months?" Jefferson feigned surprise, his eyes widening.

"Weeks," Blaise quickly amended, a twinkle in his eye.

<Every few days,> Seledora interjected, her snort echoing through their shady slice of paradise. The mare's comment broke the tension, and both men burst into laughter.

Jefferson shook his head, still grinning. "It would annoy me that you're ganging up on me, except you're probably right." He knew himself well enough to admit that he had a penchant for drama. Drama seemed to find him as reliably as a moth to a flame, coloring his life and the lives of those around him. But not here, not now. This was their sanctuary, at least for a little while. Though Jefferson couldn't help but entertain the thought of stirring up a different sort of drama with Blaise...later, perhaps, when they were truly alone.

Blaise leaned in, brushing his lips over Jefferson's with a tenderness that took his breath away. It was just a caress, a fleeting touch, yet it carried a promise—an unspoken vow that resonated deep within Jefferson's soul. He sighed into the kiss, feeling as if a part of him had just been anchored.

"Might let you be theatrical later," Blaise whispered.

"Mmm. Were you reading my mind?" Jefferson asked.

Blaise raised his eyebrows. "Not your mind so much as your body."

"Oh. Ah, of course, I'm that obvious." It was another reason he had chosen this secluded swimming hole; privacy was essential for these intimate exchanges. "Ahem. Sorry about that." Though he wasn't sorry, not really. He would never deny how much he loved Blaise, body and soul.

"Are you, though?" Blaise canted his head to the side, his eyes bright.

"Well, no," Jefferson conceded, his heart swelling with love. Deciding it was time for a change of subject—one that would equally delight his husband—he cleared his throat. "So, tell me more about this mango tart. It's a local delicacy, you said?"

The effect was instantaneous. Blaise's eyes lit up like the first stars of the evening, and Jefferson couldn't help but smile. He loved seeing Blaise this excited, this passionate.

"Yes! They make the tart with these small indigenous mangoes that grow here on the island," Blaise began, his voice resonant with enthusiasm. "They're unique—sweet, of course, but with a tartness and complexity that's truly one-of-a-kind."

He went on to describe the flaky crust, made with a local butter that had a rich, creamy note unlike anything they'd ever tasted. "And the filling," he continued, his words painting a vivid picture, "combines the diced mango with sugar and spices like cardamom and nutmeg. It's a medley of flavors that dance on your tongue. The tartness of the fruit balances so perfectly with the sweetness, and the spices add an almost perfume-like aroma. I can't wait to try making it myself when we get back home."

Jefferson smiled indulgently, his eyes softening as he listened to Blaise's enthusiasm bubbling over. It was one of the endearing traits that had first captured his attention years ago when Blaise had been a nervous, shy tenant hiding a huge magical secret as he worked in the Itude bakery.

"Maybe you can even improve on the recipe. Add your own special twist," Jefferson suggested.

Blaise's eyes sparkled, as if a culinary mage-light had just gone off in his head. "I was thinking of doing a deconstructed version— making a mango curd for the filling instead of just dicing the fruit. And as for the crust, I could use a traditional butter crust. You know, to give it a rich, crumbly texture."

Jefferson's mouth watered at the mere thought. "That sounds amazing. I can't wait to taste it."

Witnessing Blaise's boundless passion for baking always filled Jefferson with awe. But it was more than that; it was a reminder of the simple joys that colored their life together. Floating in a secluded swimming hole, their feet occasionally brushing against each other under the water, talking about dessert recipes—this was a contented, peaceful life Jefferson hadn't considered as a possibility until he'd met Blaise.

As their conversation naturally lulled, a comfortable silence settled over them. Jefferson shifted his gaze upward, his eyes tracing the intricate patterns of the leafy canopy above. Dappled sunlight filtered through, casting golden flecks on the water's surface. A sense of peace settled over him, as if the Fortunes of Tabris himself were affirming their happiness. It was almost tangible, this contentment that seemed to hover in the air around them.

After a while, Blaise broke the comfortable silence. "We should probably head back soon. I don't want to turn into a prune from soaking too long."

Jefferson chuckled, the sound causing a ripple across the water. "Well, we wouldn't want any important bits getting all wrinkly, would we? That might put a damper on our evening plans."

Blaise rolled his eyes but couldn't suppress a smile. "You have such a one-track mind sometimes. You're terrible."

"And yet you love me anyway," Jefferson said, unrepentant.

"Unfortunately, I do," Blaise said, the dryness of his tone belied by the warmth radiating from his eyes.

They climbed out of the swimming hole, water droplets clinging to their skin like tiny diamonds before they dressed. Mounting Seledora, Jefferson felt a deep-seated happiness settle within him. The day could not have been more perfect.

As the sun began its slow descent towards the horizon,

Jefferson and Blaise found themselves on the porch of their rented beach house. Arms entwined, they stood there, mesmerized by the dazzling sunset—a breathtaking medley of coral, tangerine, and violet hues.

Jefferson leaned in, pressing a gentle kiss to Blaise's temple. As he did, he inhaled deeply, savoring the faint aroma of cinnamon that always seemed to cling to Blaise. After all the hardships they'd faced, reality almost felt surreal: just the two of them sharing this perfect moment.

"Thank you for this," Jefferson murmured softly. "For being here with me. I don't think I've ever been happier than I am right now."

Blaise lifted his head, locking eyes with Jefferson. His gaze was tender. "You don't have to thank me. There's nowhere else I'd rather be." With that, he nestled his head back onto Jefferson's shoulder, fitting against him like the missing piece from a puzzle.

They remained that way as the sun dipped below the horizon, content in the cocoon of each other's arms. Though the future held its own uncertainties, for this fleeting moment, they had each other. They had this. And for now, that was more than enough.

CHAPTER TWO

The Voyage Home

Blaise

An overhead announcement echoed through the metal corridors of the Sky Voyager: "Ten minutes to departure. All passengers, please proceed to your designated areas."

The metallic voice reverberated in the confined space, amplifying Blaise's already heightened anxiety. He paused, his breath catching as the vibrations from the announcement faded. Blaise's hands trembled, and he clenched his left fist to staunch the involuntary reaction. His right hand held a treat for Emrys, and he was determined to not crush it.

Jefferson put an arm around him. "Almost there."

Blaise nodded, staying focused on their goal. Jefferson ushered them through a narrow door and into the broader hold of the airship.

Emrys and Seledora stood in temporary stalls, their ears

pricked forward as they watched their riders approach. Blaise hadn't been happy that he couldn't help Emrys board, but the stallion had reported that the crew had treated him well enough. And by the way, if Blaise could bring him a pastry before they left the mooring, that would be ever so welcome.

"I told you they were fine," Jefferson said, approaching Seledora and rubbing the mare's forehead. Then he pulled a handkerchief from his pocket, revealing a mango tart that he'd snuck aboard for her.

The sight of Emrys and Seledora, safe in their stalls, allowed a slow, relieved breath to escape Blaise's lips. It was as if the weight of a dozen sandbags had lifted from his shoulders. The pegasi seemed far more content than they had during their maritime voyage—a comfort, given Emrys's disdain for steamer ships. In fact, Emrys had pondered the idea of flying home himself to avoid another experience at sea.

The decision to travel by airship had been a compromise. Dragons in the area had a notorious reputation for hunting winged creatures, and the risk had been too great. Now, seeing the pegasi at ease, munching on treats, Blaise felt the walls of his anxiety recede.

<And where is mine?> Emrys asked, fixing his large, soulful eyes on Blaise. The pegasus's gaze was practically a physical force, as if he could will the treat into existence. <You didn't forget, did you?>

Blaise chuckled. The familiarity of Emrys's behavior, a blend of petulance and playfulness, grounded him amid the rattling gears and steam pipes. "Forget you? Impossible," he declared, theatrically sweeping his right hand from behind his back. Nestled in his palm was a slice of chocolate cake, lightly dusted with powdered sugar. "I would never forget to bring you a treat for your bravery in flying on an airship."

The stallion stretched out his neck, his upper lip wiggling in eagerness. <Gimme.>

<So rude,> Seledora commented, her mental voice full of reprimand even as she smacked her lips while devouring her own treat.

Ignoring Seledora's criticism, Blaise held the treat out to his stallion. Emrys dismantled the cake with precision, ensuring that not a single crumb escaped him.

As Blaise relished the delightful sight of watching Emrys enjoy his treat, the airship's mechanical innards released a sharp hiss of steam. The sound jolted Blaise, and for a heartbeat, panic gripped him, casting a dark cloud over his senses. Memories of another airship, a different time and place, surged forward in his mind—

Before the panic could spiral into a full-blown episode, Emrys's head swung into Blaise's chest with a force that almost toppled him. The impact served as a grounding moment, a physical anchor to the here and now. Emrys rubbed his forehead against Blaise, leaving behind a trail of shed horsehair as if to imprint a part of himself onto his rider.

<You are not in the past. You are here, in the present.> Emrys's voice rang with urgency. Doubling down on his reminder, the pegasus swiped his huge, sticky tongue across Blaise's chin. <You are with your pegasus and your mate. Safe.>

Blaise blinked, exhaling softly. With a small nod to himself, more than to Emrys, he pulled a handkerchief from his pocket and wiped his chin.

Jefferson watched the exchange without speaking, the skin around his eyes crinkling ever so slightly. He pulled a handkerchief from his pocket, meticulously wiping his own hand to rid it of any sticky residue before neatly folding the cloth and tucking it away.

"Well, we've given the pegasi their afternoon treat and checked on their comfort," Jefferson said, his voice full of a brightness that seemed forced. "Perhaps we should take in the sunset from the deck? A change of scenery might do us good."

The lump in Blaise's throat felt like a stone, but he swallowed it down. Turning to Emrys, he leaned in and wrapped his arms around the stallion's muscular neck, drawing comfort from the warmth and familiar scent. "Thank you."

Emrys snorted softly, the exhalation ruffling Blaise's hair. <Go. Enjoy the sunset and relax. We'll be right here.>

With a final pat, Blaise stepped away from Emrys and took Jefferson's offered arm. Side by side, they ascended the narrow, creaking stairway that led to the main deck.

Upon reaching the deck, the crew of the Sky Voyager were in a whirl of activity, working to adjust the airship's massive crimson and alabaster balloon-sails. As they caught a new gust of wind, the ship listed slightly to port. The deck shifted beneath Blaise's boots, a sensation that sent a rush of shock through him. He felt his heartbeat quicken, each pulse a tiny drumbeat of anxiety. But Jefferson's arm, solid and unyielding, remained at his side.

Blaise blinked against the golden light of the setting sun, revealed by the change of the ship's heading. The sky stretched endlessly before them, painted in vibrant shades of pink and orange. Below them, the Jewelled Sea lived up to its name, shimmering like a sprawling sapphire carpet that stretched as far as the eye could see.

Jefferson's fingers tightened gently around Blaise's arm. He let out a soft sigh, the sound a medley of relief and concern. "The pegasi are fine, but you...are you well?"

Blaise turned, meeting Jefferson's gaze. In his husband's face, he found a mixture of emotions—worry, yes, but also an undercurrent of unwavering love that outshone even the dramatic hues of the setting sun. "I'm managing," Blaise said. It wasn't the whole truth, but it was a step in that direction. Above them, the airship's balloon-sails billowed in the stiff breeze. "This airship is different. That helps."

Jefferson nodded. "You surprised me with your suggestion to travel this way. It's a courageous choice, considering your experiences."

"Facing my fears," Blaise murmured, though he felt as if he often failed to do so. "But it's difficult. Sometimes there are...reminders. Little things no one else would notice. Like when the deck shifted." Gods, his stomach soured at the old memory.

As they stood side by side, Jefferson's fingers entwined with Blaise's in a gentle but firm grasp. "No one else has your experiences. Be kind to yourself. Remember, you don't have to walk this journey alone. I'm right here beside you, always." The words barely left his lips before he leaned in, sealing the promise with a tender kiss that sent a ripple of warmth down Blaise's spine.

Feeling the heat rise to his cheeks, Blaise cast his eyes downward as a nearby crew member whistled appreciation at their display of affection.

Jefferson chuckled softly, a sound as comforting as a warm blanket. He adjusted his grip, capturing Blaise's pinky finger with his own, and gave a gentle tug, urging Blaise closer to the ship's railing. "Let's enjoy the last moments of daylight, shall we? Your presence has a way of making even a sunset seem lackluster by comparison."

Blaise snorted. "Flattery will get you nowhere with me."

"Is it flattery if it's the truth?" Jefferson quipped as they both settled against the railing.

Blaise exhaled slowly, letting the tension ebb from him. *This was my idea. I'm not going to let old fears control me. This is different. This is safe.* Blaise repeated those tenets over and over to himself until he almost believed them.

They watched the sky shift from cerulean to shades of pink and amber, the sun dipping lower and lower until the horizon nearly obscured it.

Blaise glanced at his husband. "Do you ever miss it?"

"Miss what?" Jefferson turned to him, his brows knitting in genuine curiosity.

"Your life as a Doyen. All the galas and...I don't know what else you did. Meetings, I guess?" Blaise raised his brows, dredging his memory for their discussions of Jefferson's time in politics.

Jefferson chuckled, the sound infused with a touch of irony. "Ah, yes. Meetings that could have been letters." He shook his head, the humor in his eyes replaced by a faraway look. "Sometimes they were more headaches than they were worth. And as for the galas..." His eyes met Blaise's, filled with a knowing warmth. "Well, nothing is stopping us from going to one if we ever get an invitation. I did take you to one."

Blaise snorted. "That one was quite enough."

"Trust me, that was a very poor example." Jefferson moved comfortably close, their shoulders brushing. "But these simpler moments with you? They make everything worthwhile." Jefferson paused, his attention caught by something in the distance. "Well, would you look at that. Do you see the glinting scales in the distance?"

Following Jefferson's line of sight, Blaise nodded. "All this time in the Dragon Latitudes, and we don't see a dragon until we're leaving."

"It's their migration season, from what I understand," Jefferson said. "They're heading back to their islands. To their families, I suppose." His voice held a soft undertone of longing.

Blaise nudged his shoulder against Jefferson's in a gentle, grounding touch. "And we're going back to our own family, to our own home."

Jefferson's lips pursed, a wistful note entering his voice. "The way your family is with each other—especially how your mother treats me—it's like I've been a part of it for years. Your amity is remarkable. I wish I had that with my sister."

"*Amity* might be pushing it." Blaise hesitated, then added, "You know the tensions I've had with my mother. And now Luci is... well." He shrugged. "She's been distant, her mood stormy. And it's not just teenage angst." He looked back at Jefferson, his expression earnest. "But what about you? What's really stopping you from reaching out to your sister?"

Jefferson sighed, a rare frown creasing his handsome face. "I'm afraid she won't accept me after...well, everything. That she'll reject any attempt I make to reconnect." He gestured to himself. "As Jefferson. I'm not the same person she knew."

The furrow in Jefferson's brow deepened, and Blaise knew he was wrestling with his unsavory past. It reminded Blaise of a similar struggle when Jefferson had first revealed the duality of his existence. Jefferson and Malcolm, two sides of the same complicated coin.

"Look, you told me once that Jefferson and Malcolm are inseparable parts of who you are," Blaise said. "Maybe Alice doesn't know that yet, but isn't it time you told her?"

Jefferson ran his free hand through his hair, then shook his head. "I should have told her. Long ago. Now, she might have heard from others, and that's a betrayal in itself."

And therein lay the rub. Blaise saw Jefferson's thorny problem. Word had spread far and wide that Malcolm Wells and Jefferson Cole were the same person. If the gossip had gotten to Alice—and it likely had—she might have taken it hard, knowing her brother hadn't personally delivered the news.

Blaise gave Jefferson's hand a gentle squeeze. "I understand. You made a mistake, and it's not one you can take back. You've made a lot of mistakes like that."

Jefferson wrinkled his nose. "That is not as reassuring as you think."

Blaise leaned closer, his lips finding the soft skin of Jefferson's cheek for a brief, comforting kiss. "I wasn't done. Alice is your family. Your blood family, I mean. That has to count for something."

Jefferson didn't look convinced, his doubts shadowing the depths of his eyes like gathering storm clouds.

Undeterred, Blaise gently prodded him further. "You

mentioned wanting to meet her son—your nephew. That's something, isn't it?"

At that, Jefferson perked up a bit. "Yes, I do want that," he admitted, a hint of wistfulness coloring his tone. "I wonder if he looks like me when I was a boy."

"Well, there you go." Blaise bumped Jefferson with his shoulder. "I'd say that's reason enough to put yourself out there. Take a chance."

Jefferson went quiet as he considered this, his gaze drifting to the darkening sky. The first evening stars were twinkling into view. After a long, contemplative moment, he gave a slow, almost reluctant nod.

"I'll think on it," he said. "It's just—I hate the idea of letting down the people I care about." Turning back to face Blaise, a tentative smile curved his lips. "But thank you. You always seem to find the right words when I need to hear them most."

Blaise grinned and pulled him in for a quick kiss. "Anytime. That's what I'm here for."

CHAPTER THREE

A Score to Settle

Phillip

Phillip Dillon found himself ensconced in a secluded alcove of the Rooster Club, the city of Greylight's sanctuary for the intellectual elite. His hair, once a lustrous black, now bore streaks of silver that seemed to absorb the dim light.

Patrons engrossed in animated discussions about philosophy, politics, and the wonders of alchemy filled the air with a chorus of laughter and fervent debate. Yet, their vivacity seemed to skid to a halt at the invisible boundary of Phillip's solitude, as if repelled by palpable melancholy.

Before him sat a glass of aged whiskey, its deep amber hue mocking him with a warmth he no longer felt. The glass was as untouched as his raw emotions, a bitter brew of regret swirling within him. His thoughts were captives to Alice, the wife who had slipped through his fingers like smoke, and Theo, their son, who lit up a room with his joyous presence.

The lounge's ambient light, diluted by thick plumes of cigar smoke and the heavy velvet drapes adorning the walls, cast a subdued glow on the gold wedding band that still circled his finger. It was as if the ring had turned into a conduit for memories—the good times, the bad; the life he'd shared with his family. A swell of longing surged through him, yearning for their presence and the family that was lost to him.

"Damn it all," Phillip muttered, unable to tear his gaze from the ring. With a flick of his wrist, he swirled the whiskey in its cut crystal glass, the liquid spinning in a mesmerizing dance of light and shadow.

"Something eatin' at you, friend?" A man with a thick mustache and a jovial twinkle in his eye sauntered over, slapping Phillip heartily on the back with a meaty hand. "You look like you've got a lot on your mind."

"Leave me be," Phillip snapped, gripping his glass so tight that his knuckles whitened.

"Suit yourself." The man lifted his hands in exaggerated surrender before blending back into the crowd of intellectuals and socialites.

As he sat alone again, Phillip's fingers drummed against the side of his glass, adding a staccato beat to the din of the club. He would occasionally grimace, each contraction of his facial muscles like a punctuation mark in the long sentence of his restlessness. Patrons and staff alike gave him a wide berth, sensing the storm that brewed within him.

"Blast it all, but Cole was right," Phillip muttered, the words barely escaping his lips before being swallowed by the surrounding swells of laughter and clinking glassware. "Alice would never accept me back, not in this state."

With that admission, he took a long, deliberate gulp of whiskey, feeling its burn scrape down his throat like liquid fire. It was a bittersweet reminder of the deal he had struck with Zebulon, the alchemist who promised to give him the one thing he needed most: the love of his wife, Alice. But the cost was one that he was still coming to terms with. Well, perhaps not the cost. But the end result, yes. Anything would be worth it, he assured himself, to have Alice and Theo back, to reassemble the fragments of a shattered family.

"Fortitude," Phillip murmured into the hollow of his almost-empty glass. He was contemplating a journey into the jaws of a place where his elite status would offer no protection. A town so lawless, it was as if the very atmosphere conspired to turn men into monsters.

"Damn those outlaws," he whispered to himself, the words barely escaping his lips as he thought about the dangerous path that awaited him. "But if I must face the outlaw mages to find them, so be it." The thought of seeing their faces again—holding them close and never letting go—gave him the strength he needed to overcome his fears.

Phillip's fingers clenched around the whiskey glass, his greying brows furrowing as he made a silent vow. He would brave the darkest depths of the Gutter and beyond, if need be, to find his family. This newfound determination seemed to breathe life back into him, stirring a visible change in his demeanor.

He savored the final, smoky sip of whiskey, allowing the liquid to embolden him before setting the glass down on the table with a resounding clank. The patrons closest to him looked over in surprise at the sudden shift in energy, but they quickly returned to their conversations. Phillip's mission was little more than the flapping of butterfly wings to them.

Phillip stood, steeling his resolve, and strode towards the exit. The Rooster Club had provided him with both shelter and solace —a place to bide his time while he planned his next move. But now it was time to leave this sanctuary behind and embark on the journey he had been dreading.

As he pushed through the club's heavy, ornate door, the atmosphere shifted like the turning of a page. The chatter and clink of glasses were replaced by the muted tones of a Greylight evening, as if the world itself were holding its breath. The air outside bit into his skin, sharp and unforgiving, contrasting the warm tobacco haze he left behind.

It was time to take the next step.

Phillip stepped out of the stagecoach, squinting against the searing brilliance of the sun as it splashed over the arid streets of Fortitude. He'd never been to the rustic town before, but he hadn't expected it to look so...prosperous. Men, women, and children bustled past him; some headed to merchants, while others simply went about their daily business. Children played in the nearby town square, laughter pealing through the air like wind chimes.

With a sudden whoosh, a pegasus cut across the cerulean sky, its wings cloaking the sun-scorched earth in fleeting shadow. Its shrill call pierced the air, yanking Phillip's gaze skyward and grounding him in the reality of his surroundings. This was an outlaw's paradise.

Phillip dressed in simple clothes to blend in, fully aware that his name and connections brought danger to those around him, making his attempt to go unnoticed all the more critical.

He glanced around, seeking the hotel he had been told about. There it was, at the end of a long row of buildings, sandwiched between a blacksmith's shop and a saloon.

Picking up his valise, Phillip made his way toward it, stepping up onto the wooden boardwalk to avoid a mule-drawn wagon burdened with crates. He paused when a cheerful, yellow-painted building caught his eye: Blaise's Bakery. Phillip nodded to himself, pleased that he had located another of the landmarks he would need.

Someone stepped into his path. Phillip drew up short. "I beg your par—"

The words died in his throat. He recognized the icy blue gaze. Jack Dewitt, the outlaw mage Phillip had almost succeeded in killing during their last encounter. The slouch hat he wore shadowed his face, but there was no mistaking the hatred burning in the mage's eyes.

"Phillip Dillon," Dewitt snarled, his face twisted with rage. "You got some gall showin' your mug in these parts." He closed the gap between them with a noticeable limp, though to Phillip's dismay, the outlaw's movements became fluid and precise as he unholstered his sixgun. "I should snuff you out right here."

Phillip's heart pounded in his chest, but he refused to let fear take hold. If facing Wildfire Jack Dewitt meant getting closer to finding Alice and Theo, then so be it.

"Mr. Dewitt, please, hear me out," Phillip began, trying to keep his voice steady despite the rising fear inside him.

"Shut your trap, you lying snake," Jack spat, but before he could utter more vitriol, or worse, a bullet, a brown-haired woman appeared at the end of the street.

"Jack, there you are!" the woman exclaimed, her footsteps slowing as she took in the charged atmosphere. Her eyes darted between the two men, as if assessing a puzzle with missing pieces. "But I see you're handling some business. Who's this?"

Jack's chilling gaze was enough to pin Phillip in place, even without the sixgun trained on him. "Darlin', say howdy to Phillip Dillon. The asshole who tried to get me hanged back in Izhadell."

The shift in the woman's eyes was immediate and unsettling. Any trace of warmth vanished, replaced by a glint of raw fury. Suddenly, the man holding the gun didn't seem like the biggest threat. This woman, likely Jack's wife Kittie, radiated a whole new level of danger.

Phillip's throat tightened. "Ma'am, I—"

"Be quiet." The woman marched over to him, a halo of fire

framing her shoulders and head. It was real...so real, Phillip felt the prickle of heat on his face. Her jaw tightened, her eyes glistening, not with sorrow but with restrained rage. "I should turn you to ash right here. *Right now.*"

Phillip sucked in a breath. "You'd have every right to," he said, realizing that agreeing with her was a gamble. But arguing? That would be like playing with dynamite. "But ask yourself first why I would come here, to your town. To a place I know I'm unwelcome."

Jack laughed. "People do stupid things all the damn time. That's reason enough."

Phillip's jaw clenched. As much as he hated to admit it, Jack had a point. His presence here was risky, maybe even reckless.

However, the woman seemed to mull over his words. She cocked her head to the side, sizing him up. "From what I understand, you and your...cohorts...play a long game. This might just be another of your schemes."

Phillip's eyes widened, earnest. "That's not it. I'm actually trying to find—"

"The peacock," Jack growled. Phillip blinked in confusion. "Jefferson Cole. You got a score to settle with him, too."

From the way the outlaw spoke, Phillip had the sense Jefferson wasn't this man's favorite person, either. But there was something fiercely protective in the outlaw's stance that communicated the fact that a threat against Jefferson would be met with violence.

"No, you've got it all wrong. I need Jefferson's help to find Alice and Theo—my missing wife and son," Phillip blurted out, his words spilling over each other in a desperate tumble to be heard and believed.

Jack's eyes narrowed, his finger twitching on the trigger. "And why should we believe anything that comes out of your lying mouth?"

Phillip's voice quivered, the emotion raw and open. "Please. I'm begging you. They're the only reason I'd risk coming here."

The tension was so thick it could be cut with a knife, each second stretching into eternity. Finally, something in Kittie's eyes shifted, as if Phillip's raw desperation had pierced through her armor of fury. She shared a meaningful glance with Jack, and Phillip sensed that redemption, though distant, might not be entirely off the table.

"Tell us more about this wife and son of yours," she said, her voice losing a fraction of its fiery edge. "And then maybe, just maybe, we'll consider what you have to say."

"Thank you," Phillip whispered, his relief tempered by the fear that still clung to him like a shroud. He swallowed hard and continued, "My wife's name is Alice, and our son is Theo. They..." He paused, shaking his head. Too ashamed to admit aloud that his wife had left because of him. Because he was a horrible person.

"Your sob story ain't winning you any favors," Jack snarled, his patience clearly wearing thin. "Why shouldn't I put an end to your misery right here and now?"

Kittie's flames vanished as if doused by an unseen force. She touched Jack's arm, a softness entering her expression. "Jack, if anyone can understand the ache of lost love and family, it's you."

"We ain't the same, Kittie," Jack retorted, his voice tinged with bitterness. And yet, as he spoke, a shadow of recognition crossed his face. It was as though he saw a grotesque reflection of himself in Phillip, and he didn't like it.

That was a crack in his wicked armor, and it was one Phillip would happily exploit. "Please. I know you have every reason to hate me and wish me dead. But I have a child."

"So. Do. I." Jack spoke slowly, enunciating each word as if it were a bullet from his sixgun, each one hitting its mark. Phillip recoiled, regretting his ill-thought-out plea. He had almost taken this man from his child, too. Would have, if not for the Breaker.

But then, to Phillip's disbelief, Jack unleashed a vehement curse and holstered his sixgun. "Hump a gassy dragon. You live.

For now." Though his eyes still blazed with anger, they also held a begrudging acceptance that Phillip attributed to Kittie's influence.

Drawing in a shaky breath, Phillip felt the crushing weight of imminent danger lift ever so slightly. This was a chance, however precarious, and he knew he couldn't squander it. "I don't know how to thank you for this reprieve," he started cautiously. "So, does this mean I can speak with Jefferson Cole?"

"Yeah," Jack growled, his eyes narrowing into slits of persistent distrust. "But don't mistake this for forgiveness. Cross me again, and it'll be the last thing you ever do."

With that chilling warning ringing in his ears, Phillip broke into a near-run, his boots sending puffs of dust into the air as he sprinted toward the sanctuary of the hotel. The sun's rays bore into him, sweat dampening the back of his collar, but it was inconsequential. He'd survived this perilous confrontation, and, however tenuous, a flicker of hope kindled in his chest. Perhaps he could still find his way back to his lost family.

CHAPTER FOUR

Snakes and Peacocks

Blaise

Conquering the skies aboard the Sky Voyager and landing in Freeport had been a personal triumph for Blaise. For someone who had battled anxiety at the mere thought of airship travel, the journey had turned out to be a surprising gift. A chance to face his fears and come out the other side stronger. But touching down in Fortitude a few days ago, this time on the back of his trusty pegasus, had been like slipping into a pair of worn-in boots: comfortable and grounding.

The buzzing excitement of overcoming his fears and their vacation adventures had settled into the warm, floury air of the bakery. Though the time away with Jefferson had been refreshing, Blaise couldn't help but feel a renewed sense of rightness in being back in his bakery, armed with a newfound courage.

Sunlight poured through the bakery window, turning flour

motes into golden fireflies that danced in the air. The warm scent of fresh-baked bread mingled with the aromatic bouquet of cinnamon and vanilla. Blaise adjusted the display of pastries with a meticulous hand, his gaze darting from one confection to another.

Jefferson sat at a nearby table, his attention absorbed by the figures on the ledger in front of him. His blond hair caught the sunlight, and for a moment, his furrowed brows relaxed.

The chime of the bell over the door pulled Blaise's attention. He looked up to see Jack step in, a limp in his walk but fire in his eyes. Despite his visible discomfort, Jack carried himself with a stubborn defiance that Blaise knew better than to question.

"Jack!" Blaise said in greeting, his voice warm, his smile genuine. "Good to see you." As he spoke, he briefly assessed Jack's condition—taking in the details but leaving his questions unasked.

"About damn time you two got back," Jack grumbled, his hand resting on the glass display case. "Hope you enjoyed gallivanting around the Dragon Latitudes while the rest of us were stuck here."

Blaise felt his cheeks flush at the memory of Jefferson riding Seledora on the beach, his body glistening in the sunlight. He glanced down at a cherry tart, gathering himself before meeting Jack's eye. "It was quite an experience," he admitted, letting the heat of the memory fill his voice. "But enough about us. How have you been, Jack? You look…" He hesitated, his brows rising as he searched for the right word.

"Alive?" Jack offered, one corner of his mouth curling into a sardonic grin.

"Sure," Blaise agreed, a small, relieved smile forming on his lips. That was indeed safer—and less awkward—than any other descriptor he might have chosen.

From the table, Jefferson added, his voice shaded with amusement, "I'd have said full of piss and vinegar."

A momentary grin spread across Jack's face. "You ain't wrong, peacock." His eyes then shifted, falling on Jefferson's ledger. "Might need those fancy skills of yours."

Jefferson's eyebrows shot up in genuine interest. "And why is that?"

"You won't believe this, but Kittie and Emmaline talked me into opening a toy store." Jack snorted, his eyes glinting, as if he himself couldn't quite believe what he was saying. "Can you imagine? Me, a damned merchant?"

Images of Jack's hand-crafted dolls, made with surprising tenderness for the theurgist children at the Golden Citadel, flickered through Blaise's thoughts. He suppressed a knowing smile, choosing to keep Jack's hidden artistry his own secret. "Actually, yes. Yes, I can," he replied, his voice laced with a touch of irony.

"Got a storefront up the street. Ain't open yet. Not sure when that'll happen." Jack's eyes moved involuntarily toward the door, as if he could see through walls to where his future shop would be. "But I didn't come here for pleasantries."

Blaise's smile faded, replaced by a frown that deepened the lines around his eyes. He sensed the gravity of the situation and glanced over at Jefferson, who caught his gaze and rose to join them, a wrinkle of concern between his green eyes.

"All right, Jack." Blaise braced himself, the levity of moments before now replaced by stoic resolve. "Why did you come here?"

"Phillip Dillon's in town," Jack said, the words shattering their peace like a bullet. The bakery suddenly felt claustrophobic. The late afternoon sun filtering through the window now cast elongated shadows that seemed more sinister than serene.

"Phillip Dillon? Here in Fortitude?" Jefferson shifted beside Blaise, his posture tensing, each muscle coiled like a spring. His voice, usually so controlled, trembled with a mixture of disbelief and dormant fury.

Blaise swallowed hard, his throat suddenly as dry as a desert. The thought of Phillip Dillon in Fortitude sent a chill down his spine. The man was a viper, having plotted against Jefferson and nearly killed Jack in the past. What could the Quiet One possibly want now? And more perplexingly, "You let him live?" The words slipped out before he could stop them. He knew Jack's lethal capabilities all too well.

"It was a close thing," Jack drawled, lifting his shoulders in a shrug that conveyed both reluctance and resignation. "Dillon's still breathin' 'cause Kittie said I outta give 'im a chance. Wasn't my first choice, but Kittie, well—she's got a way of breakin' through, even to a hardhead like me."

Blaise was taken aback. He vividly recalled how perilously close Jack had come to dying at Phillip's hands, and how incensed Kittie had been. That she could—and would—sway Jack to this degree was surprising. "What could Phillip possibly say to convince you, and especially Kittie, to spare him?"

"The snake expects the peacock here will help him find his wife and son," Jack said, his gaze shifting to meet Jefferson's.

Blaise swallowed, suddenly understanding. Kittie had a temper, but she also had compassion. The Pyromancer must have seen a mirror of herself and Jack in Phillip's request. All the same, Blaise didn't like it.

Jefferson's lips tightened into a thin line. "This could very well be a trap," he said, cautious. His eyes had gone steely and calculating with a hint of the politically savvy Doyen he had once been.

"Can't say I don't share those thoughts," Jack grumbled, his gaze fixed intently on Jefferson. "Don't trust Phillip any more'n y'all do. If you ain't keen on talkin' to him, just say the word. I'll make sure he never bothers you again."

The threat in Jack's words was unmistakable, and Blaise couldn't fault him for his feelings on the matter—he shared similar concerns. He glanced at Jefferson, who seemed to be mentally juggling options. His eyes flicked briefly between Jack and Blaise before settling into a kind of focused stillness.

After a moment, Jefferson sighed, meeting Blaise's gaze with a decision made. "I'll hear what he has to say," he said quietly, his voice resolute. "For Alice's sake."

"Your call," Jack muttered, clearly not thrilled but accepting it. He pushed off from the display case and limped toward the exit. Pausing at the door, he threw over his shoulder, "Just let me know if you have a change of heart. I might not be at the top of my game, but I still got bullets and magic."

With that, Jack stepped out. The door's bell gave a soft chime, its ring hanging in the air like a question left unanswered. The room felt quieter, almost holding its breath.

Blaise swallowed, studying his husband. "You really think he's here about Alice?"

Something flickered in Jefferson's eyes, a quicksilver emotion that Blaise couldn't quite pin down. "I do."

Blaise raised an eyebrow, voice cautiously neutral as he asked, "What aren't you saying, Jefferson?"

Jefferson leaned against the display case so that his shoulder brushed against Blaise's. "I paid Phillip a social call before I left Izhadell."

A frown creased Blaise's forehead, his eyes narrowing. "You did what?" He knew, without Jefferson even speaking the words, that it had been much more than a social call.

"Seledora was with me," Jefferson quickly added, as if that would be a balm to Blaise's rising irritation. "I was completely safe the entire time."

"You think that makes it right?" Blaise scoffed, rolling his eyes in disbelief. Then, his voice grew sharper. "It's not about you being safe, Jefferson. It's about the choices you make without me."

Jefferson's face tightened, his voice rising to match Blaise's. "Phillip is a menace. I had to confront him. Ensure he knows we aren't to be trifled with."

The tension between them escalated. Blaise, his voice biting, shot back, "So, you decided to flaunt your magic?"

A flash of defensiveness crossed Jefferson's eyes. He pushed away from the display case, stalking across the bakery. "Yes, of course, I used my magic. I would have been a fool not to."

"That wasn't a show of strength, Jefferson," Blaise seethed. "It was a show of arrogance."

Something fierce sparked in Jefferson's eyes. "I made a decision to protect us. I revealed the lengths I'd go to."

Blaise shook his head, his disgust at what Jefferson had done growing. A cold realization crept into Blaise's thoughts. Jefferson had a cruel streak, a willingness to mentally and emotionally scar others through his magical abilities. And what was worse, he saw no ethical dilemma in doing so if he believed he had just cause. "Lengths? More like depths. The chilling depths you're willing to sink to."

The severity of the confrontation seemed to wear on Jefferson, but his voice remained firm. "I regret not telling you. But regret my actions? No. Not when it comes to safeguarding our future."

Blaise's anger gave way to a broken-hearted calm. "Sometimes, it's not the threat outside, but the choices we make that endanger us most. We have to be better than them."

Hurt and pride battled in Jefferson's reply. "I still believe I am. But if you can't see that, maybe the problem isn't just with me."

Blaise stared at him, stunned. "What?"

Jefferson, drawing himself up, met Blaise's gaze fiercely. "You question my methods, my decisions. But we both know that when it comes down to it, you wouldn't take action until we were backed into a corner again. I needed to get ahead of this problem. To cut the head off the snake."

Blaise's face reddened with a mix of anger and desperation. "You're turning this on me now? After what you've just admitted to?"

Jefferson took a step closer, voice heated yet strained. "I've always acted with our best interests at heart. If you doubt that, then I don't know what to say."

Blaise's voice wavered, emotions threatening to overflow. "No,

I'm doubting the extremes you're willing to go to. You don't get to twist this."

Jefferson paused, looking as if he'd been slapped. The hurt was palpable, but so was his frustration. "Blaise, I can't talk to you when you've already judged me."

Blaise tried to reach out, his voice softening. "Jefferson, I just—"

But Jefferson stepped back, evading his touch. "I need some air," he cut in, his voice thick. "Some space to process this."

Words failing him, Blaise watched as Jefferson strode toward the door. There was a grace in his walk, but it was edged with deep hurt. The door opened, then closed with a soft jingle of the bell.

How had this gone wrong so quickly? Blaise shut his eyes, still stunned by their argument. He loved this man so deeply, yet in that moment, Jefferson felt like a stranger. A confusing stranger who could be both his sanctuary and his greatest challenge.

CHAPTER FIVE

Men of Honor

<I would like to point out that I told you it was a bad idea at the time,> Seledora's mental voice echoed, full of smug satisfaction. Her hooves crunched against the red soil, sending small plumes of dust into the air as they walked along the outskirts of Fortitude.

"You're my attorney," Jefferson shot back, his voice full of annoyance and affection. "You're supposed to get me out of pickles like this, not to say 'I told you so.'"

Seledora snorted, her hot breath forming a brief misty cloud in the crisp air before it disappeared. <Trust me, when it comes to emotional disputes, especially with people you love, I don't intervene. You're on your own.>

Jefferson sighed deeply, his steps slowing as they approached the cliff's edge overlooking the vast canyon below. The rugged landscape stretched out before him, a stunning tapestry of reds and browns that seemed to go on forever. It was as if the earth itself had opened up to reflect the gaping emotional chasm he now found himself in.

Fabulous. Even the landscape is trying to make me feel like a heel.

He could count the arguments he'd had with Blaise on one hand. Arguments were a part of his life as a Doyen, a natural extension of his political role. But arguing with Blaise? That was different. Blaise was a peacemaker at heart, a man who shied away from confrontation. For them to have a dispute of this magnitude felt like a perversion of the natural order.

And the worst part? It was entirely his fault.

He eased down onto a sandstone outcropping, a natural seat carved by time and wind, and one of his favorite places to come and think. Sometimes, Blaise would join him here. They'd sit side by side with the breeze tousling their hair, the beautiful and ill-named expanse of the Gutter stretched below them.

"I know. But I couldn't let any threats to Blaise—to *us*—stand," Jefferson continued, uncertain if he was trying to convince Sele-dora or himself. Maybe both. His eyes felt hot, and he rubbed them irritably. A chilling thought crossed his mind: what if Blaise finally realized that, despite their love, they were just too different to make it work?

Seledora nudged him sharply with her nose, jolting him from his dark thoughts. <Don't go down that path.>

Jefferson swallowed hard, looking up at her. "What path?"

The mare swished her tail dismissively. <I can't read your thoughts precisely, but I can feel the cloud of dread buzzing around your mind like flies swarming manure. Blaise still loves you; he's just really mad. And, for the record, I understand why he's mad.>

Jefferson gave a shaky, hesitant laugh, the sound tinged with self-deprecation. "Well, if my thoughts are manure, it's no wonder they're so *fertile* in producing poor decisions." Despite his attempt at humor, his next words were heavy with concern. "How can you be so sure, Seledora? I've never felt this kind of love before. My own parents couldn't even muster it. What if...what if it's in my blood to ruin this?"

Seledora rolled her eyes at his dramatics, clearly unimpressed. <Now you're being ridiculous. Of course, Blaise—wait, what's that?> Her head whipped around suddenly, her ears pinned back against her skull. <Someone's coming.>

Jefferson swallowed hard, then turned to follow Seledora's alert gaze. The instant his eyes landed on the approaching figure, his fists clenched involuntarily. The canyon wind seemed to howl in tandem with his rising annoyance.

"Jefferson! I'm so glad I found you!" Phillip Dillon called out as he closed the distance.

"Phillip," Jefferson growled, the name feeling like a shard of glass on his tongue. "This is not a good time." His words were sharp, a barely restrained storm cloud of emotions behind them. "If you have any sense, you'll leave now."

The urge to turn this man's life into a nightmare was strong, but...no, he couldn't do that now. Not when it was the entire reason Blaise was angry with him.

Phillip stopped, his eyes widening slightly as if he'd just stepped too close to a sidewinder. "I understand. I'll wait until you're more receptive. But I'm just so worried about Alice..." His voice hitched on the name, and Jefferson felt his heart twist with a guilt he'd been trying to bury.

"Fine," Jefferson spat, unable to hide his bitterness—and honestly not caring if he did. "I'll listen. But know this, Phillip: I'm far from pleased to see you."

"Of course! Your words and disposition are quite clear," Phillip responded quickly, his tone laden with forced gratitude. He took a deep breath, collecting himself. "I've thought a lot about our last conversation, Jefferson. I want to make things right with Alice."

Jefferson's eyes narrowed, sizing up the man standing before him. He schooled his features, hoping he didn't flinch at his sister's name. It felt as though fate was intent on making him confront his past failings with her. "Are you prepared to change, Phillip? To become someone worthy of Alice? Or is this another one of your manipulations?" Even as he questioned Phillip's sincerity, he wrestled with his own hypocrisy. At this point, was he even the right choice to speak to Alice? Probably not, but it felt as if fate had decided to shove him in her direction.

"I promise you," Phillip declared, his features taut with fervent hope, "I am determined to reinvent myself for Alice. She's entitled to better than the person I used to be, and I will become the man she deserves."

Jefferson stared at him, gauging the sincerity in Phillip's voice. On the one hand, he felt a hopeful optimism, thinking this might bridge the gap with his sister, Alice, and mend ties with Blaise. On the other, a wary skepticism remained, reminding him of Phillip's past betrayals.

Seledora snorted softly, as if sensing Jefferson's inner conflict. <This one's a tough read, but he seems genuine about wanting his wife back. At least, as genuine as someone like him can be.>

Jefferson sighed inwardly, knowing Seledora's intuition often proved accurate. "All right," he finally said, breaking the silence that had stretched between them like a chasm. "I'll find Alice and speak to her on your behalf. But on one condition." As he spoke, he saw Phillip's face light up with a glimmer of hope, but he pressed on, his voice firm. "You do not accompany me. This journey is mine alone."

"Surely, you jest," Phillip retorted, his previous charm eroding to reveal a hint of disdain. "How can you expect me to entrust you with such a delicate matter if I am not present to oversee it?"

Jefferson's eyes narrowed, his words laced with a steely resolve. "Consider it a test of your newfound sincerity. If you're truly committed to changing for Alice, you'll respect her brother's wishes."

Phillip's jaw clenched, and Jefferson could almost see the gears turning in his mind. "What guarantee do I have that you'll honor your word? Given our past, how can I trust you won't betray me again?"

Jefferson laughed. "Me betray *you?* That's rich, considering the smear campaign you led against me. Let's not forget who tried to discredit my very *existence.*" His voice dripped with a pointed bitterness, a reminder not just of his grievances but also of the latent power he held—a power he could unleash on Phillip if pushed.

Phillip's mouth opened, then quickly snapped shut, his jaw visibly clenched as he held back a sharp retort. A fleeting wave of latent anger washed over his finely chiseled features. After what seemed like an eternity but was actually only a few seconds, he visibly composed himself. "Fair enough," he said, his voice coated with reluctant acceptance. "All the same, surely you can understand my concern. This is not about me. It's about someone I care about."

Jefferson suppressed the urge to roll his eyes. The theatricality of Phillip's self-restraint was almost comical. *No, this is definitely all about you.* But tact prevailed over irritation. "Then we're at an impasse that requires cooperation," he said, his words carefully measured. "We'll just have to trust that we're both men of honor."

Phillip's eyes narrowed. "*Honor?* Pardon my skepticism, but trusting a man who used magic to turn my life into a waking nightmare seems like a risky endeavor."

Jefferson felt the sting of Phillip's accusation, a painful reminder of his own ethical lapses. But he quashed the emotional surge, keeping his face impassive. "Take it or leave it," he declared, his voice unwavering. "To me, it's a more than reasonable offer. And trust me, there are folks around here who'd be only too happy to see me take a far less *charitable* stance with you."

Phillip's demeanor shifted at Jefferson's words, his eyes widening in dire understanding. He swallowed hard, the apple of his throat bobbing. "You're right. Forgive me. I allowed my emotions to get the better of me."

Jefferson allowed himself a small, wry smile. "Maybe that's an aspect you need to improve on. Self-awareness isn't something you can turn off and on like a spigot."

Phillip's shoulders seemed to lose their tension, sagging as if a burden had been lifted but then replaced by another, heavier one. "I still have a lot to learn when it comes to changing who I am."

You and me both. Jefferson nodded, his own face a mask of controlled emotion. "You'll have plenty of time for introspection. Alice is not nearby."

Phillip looked up sharply, a mix of hope and desperation flickering across his eyes. "You know where she is?"

A smile curled across Jefferson's lips. "I do."

Phillip swallowed, his eyes widening with renewed fervor. "Where is she?"

Jefferson shook his head, steadfast. "That's not information I'm willing to share right now. Alice may choose to remain hidden from you, and I won't betray her wishes."

The older man's forehead creased, furrows deepening between his brows. "But we had an agreement."

"We agreed I would speak with her on your behalf," Jefferson clarified, his tone unyielding. "If she consents to see you, then you'll have your opportunity." He paused. "Once I've spoken to her —and if she agrees—where should I send a dispatch? Your home in Ganland?"

Phillip's face seemed to sag. "I've been staying in Argor these past few months. I can't bear to be in Ganland without them." His voice cracked on the final word. He reached into his pocket and pulled out a small, embossed card, extending it toward Jefferson. "You can send a dispatch here."

"Argor, you say?" Jefferson looked at the paper, rolling it between his fingers as he pondered. The proximity of Argor to the Untamed Territory was uncomfortably close. Could Phillip be operating from there to search for Alice? The very thought rankled him. "Stop looking for her."

Phillip's eyes widened as if Jefferson had read his deepest fears aloud. "I—"

"Don't think to lie to me," Jefferson cut in. Then his tone softened. "I heard how you spoke of Alice at our last meeting. If you loved her as much as you claim, then you would search for her relentlessly. That's why you came to me, after all." It's what Jefferson would have done.

Phillip wilted. "It's true. Fine. My leads have all died out, at any rate. I'll leave it to you." He swallowed. "But even if Alice doesn't want to have any contact with me, will you at least tell me if she and Theo are well?"

"I will," Jefferson agreed.

A genuine smile spread across Phillip's face. "Thank you. If nothing else, it will comfort me to know they're okay. Even if..." He sighed, shaking his head.

"Your comfort is not exactly my top priority. But luckily for you, I seem to be in a generous mood today," Jefferson said, clearing his throat to mask a surprising surge of empathy. "But let's make one thing clear: you'd do well to steer clear of Fortitude. It's not a conducive environment for your long-term *vitality,* if you catch my meaning."

Phillip nodded. "On that, we can agree." He turned to walk away, then paused, looking back. "I'll leave on the first stagecoach I can get aboard, hopefully tomorrow. But what of you? When will you head out to find Alice?"

"Sooner rather than later," Jefferson replied, his mind already racing with plans and the inevitable conversation he'd have to have with Blaise. "I have my own reasons for contacting Alice, and they can't wait."

As Phillip turned his back and walked away, the reality of what Jefferson needed to do settled in. He watched the older man's retreating form, and his mind immediately shifted to Blaise. This quest to find Alice wasn't just about righting past wrongs; it was a stepping stone to mending the rift that had torn open between him and the man he loved.

With only Seledora at his side, Jefferson stood at the cliff's edge, where the untamed land met an immeasurable chasm below. The sun was sinking fast, casting long shadows that seemed to reach for him like the many expectations and fears that clawed at his conscience.

The evening wind whispered through the nearby brush, as if nature itself were echoing his apprehension. His fists clenched at his sides, knuckles whitening. The path ahead was murky, fraught with uncertainties and potential pitfalls that could break his heart anew. But for Alice, for Blaise, and yes, for his own fragmented peace of mind, he had to tread it—no matter how treacherous.

Each unspoken worry felt like a stone in his pocket, weighing him down but also grounding him in the reality that what he did next mattered. *Well, if life insists on giving me lemons, I might as well make emotionally complex lemonade.*

<Blaise will be waiting for you,> Seledora said after a moment, nudging him. The certainty in her tone took Jefferson aback, making his breath catch as if snagged on a thorn of hope.

"Do you really think so?" Jefferson asked.

<The question is, do *you* really think so?> Her brown eyes seemed to pierce through him.

Jefferson smiled. He did.

CHAPTER SIX

Salty

Blaise

Blaise navigated the bakery kitchen, a haven typically infused with the warm smells of bread and sweets. But tonight, the fragrance of pot pies mingled with the tension hanging in the air, each savory note underscoring the growing emotional rift with Jefferson.

His fingers hesitated over the silverware, each piece landing with a clink that felt like an accusation. Blaise's jaw tightened, and he forced himself to breathe through the tension.

The bell over the front door jingled, and for a moment, Blaise wondered if it was a customer. But no, it was Jefferson, who apparently had also lost his usual entrance—through the side door, the entryway for family and loved ones. Relief washed over Blaise at his husband's return.

Their eyes met, and Jefferson's gaze carried a mix of regret and hesitance. He looked like a man who'd been wrestling with his conscience and hadn't yet declared a winner.

"You're back," Blaise said, his voice a tangle of conflicting emotions.

Jefferson glanced at the table settings. "Is one of those for me?" The question was laden with as much uncertainty as the room was filled with the scent of rosemary.

Blaise crossed his arms, leaning against the nearby counter. "Who else would it be for?"

Jefferson attempted to lighten the mood. "Perhaps Emrys? Wouldn't be the first time he's been in here, from what I understand."

Despite himself, Blaise's lips twitched in amusement. "It's for you. Always for you, even when I'm mad at you." He gestured to the chair opposite him. "What did you think I would do? Let you starve?"

Jefferson frowned, a faraway look in his eyes. Finally, he moved to take the seat. "To be honest, I didn't know what to expect. This is new territory for us."

Blaise couldn't help but snort. "New territory?" He clapped his right hand over his left bicep. "Let's not forget about the geasa tattoo." Jefferson winced as if physically struck. Maybe it was a low blow, but Blaise needed to get his point across. "You have a habit of making decisions for me rather than with me."

"That's a fair assessment," Jefferson murmured, his green eyes downcast. "I understand why you're upset with me."

As they ate, the tension in the room was brittle, like the flaking crust of the pot pies. Blaise hated this feeling, wishing everything could be right between them.

"I wish I could snap my fingers and fix things between us," Blaise said, breaking the silence, his eyes meeting Jefferson's. "But you need to understand that trust, once broken, takes time to mend."

"And I need to be the one to mend it," Jefferson replied softly.

He set his fork down, the metal ringing out as it struck the table. "There's something I need to do."

Blaise tensed, Jefferson's resigned tone making him uneasy. "And that is?"

"I need to take a short trip." Jefferson met Blaise's eyes, unwavering.

Blaise's fork hovered in midair, all thoughts of eating abandoned. His stomach churned, the sick feeling spreading through him. Jefferson would go alone. What did this mean for their relationship?

Before his mind could spiral further, Jefferson added, "I'm going to find Alice—so I can make things right with her."

A glimmer of understanding flickered in Blaise's eyes, loosening the knot that had tightened around his chest. Carefully, he asked, "Did you speak to Phillip?"

Jefferson grimaced, as if tasting something foul. "Regrettably, yes. But I'm not doing this for him. I'm doing it for me. Because I have to." He paused, meeting Blaise's eyes, the sincerity in his gaze unshakable. "You're not the only person I've disappointed. I need to start with Alice."

Blaise nodded, still processing. He hadn't expected Jefferson to act so soon after their discussion on the airship. "Do you know where she is?" His voice was thick with concern.

Jefferson picked up his fork again, though instead of eating, he turned it over in his hand. "Yes. I asked Flora to find her for me—just to put my mind at ease. She's in Starvation, across the Untamed Territory."

Blaise frowned, his face clouding over like a storm on the horizon. "Starvation? That's so far away." He'd never made it that far in his own ill-fated journey across the Untamed Territory, but he'd seen it on maps. Flashes of the Untamed Territory's wild, perilous landscapes crossed his mind, intensifying his worry. "And dangerous."

"I'm no stranger to the Untamed Territory," Jefferson said, his words carrying a hint of defensiveness. "And I've traveled great distances before."

"True," Blaise admitted, his fingers involuntarily tapping a nervous rhythm on the wooden table. "But in the past, you've had Flora. She kept you safe." His concern wasn't just for the distance.

"Flora's tied up with some ambassadorial matters in Nera." Jefferson's tone was almost apologetic. "But it's not as if I'd be going alone. Seledora will accompany me, of course."

Blaise pursed his lips. Sure, Seledora was a reliable companion, but the dangers of the Untamed Territory were unpredictable. Jefferson wasn't Jack, no matter how much worldly experience he had. Jefferson was better at fending for himself in the wilds of a gala, not the Untamed Territory.

But Blaise had to be honest with himself: Jefferson's ability to take care of himself wasn't what bothered him. His gaze drifted down to his wedding ring, the gold band gleaming softly in the mage-lights—a symbol of their connection.

"Jefferson," Blaise finally said. "Do you really want to go without me?"

A pained look crossed Jefferson's face. He slid his chair around the table to sit beside Blaise and tenderly clasped his hand. "Believe me, my dear, I want you with me more than anything," Jefferson confessed. "But this is something I have to do on my own. Besides, a bit of space might do us some good, help us both gain perspective."

Blaise searched Jefferson's face for any hint of doubt or insincerity. What he found there was a complex mix of love, regret, and a desperate longing for forgiveness. It was a hard realization, but one that settled in the core of his being—Jefferson was right. They needed this physical and emotional distance to clear their heads.

"Look after yourself out there," Blaise said, his voice edged with worry, fingers squeezing Jefferson's. "I might be mad at you, but I still love you."

Jefferson chuckled. "I know. You've tolerated my presence for dinner." His eyes softened. "I truly am sorry, and I hope that by doing this, I will do better for us in the future."

Then, with a look that conveyed a thousand unspoken words, Jefferson leaned in. He pressed his lips to Blaise's in a kiss that felt like a deep sigh of relief and a cry of longing all at once. For that moment, the weight of their disagreements and the worries about the future lifted, replaced by the comfort of their love.

As they parted, Blaise felt a constriction in his chest, a tightening coil of bittersweet emotion. The kiss had been both a promise and a farewell, a flash fire of love captured in the uncertain space between what was and what might be.

"When are you leaving?" Blaise asked, though he knew whether it was within the next five minutes or the next month, it would still hurt.

"Tomorrow," Jefferson responded, glancing away. "If I stay any longer, I'll just keep finding excuses not to go. And we both know that's not what needs to happen."

Blaise nodded. "Be careful. I need you to come back to me."

Jefferson's smile was tinged with sadness, but also filled with resolve. "I will always find my way back to you, Blaise. That's a promise I intend to keep."

With those words hanging in the air between them, they shared another tender embrace. It was as if they were trying to imprint the feeling of each other into their very bones, a memory to carry with them during their impending separation.

***

"Something's really off with these muffins," Emmaline declared, her lips curling with displeasure as she pulled away from the offending baked goods.

Blaise was elbow-deep in dough, his fingers methodically pressing and folding. Kneading usually served as a calming influence, but today, his thoughts were a chaotic swirl, centered on Jefferson.

Uncharacteristically, Jefferson had risen early to start his day. Blaise suspected it was because neither of them had slept well through the night. Blaise himself had tossed and turned, but hadn't wanted to ask Jefferson to use his Dreamer magic to help him sleep. And Jefferson had probably wanted to ask. But he probably feared disrupting their tentative truce and their last moments together before he left for Starvation.

"Blaise, you there?" Emmaline poked his shoulder, breaking his musings.

He turned, startled. "What?"

His friend gave him a patient look, as if she were dealing with a particularly dense loaf of bread. "I said these blueberry muffins aren't fit for selling. Unless you're planning on a salty surprise for our customers?"

Blaise frowned. "Let me see." Picking up a muffin, he took a bite without thinking—and immediately regretted it. An overwhelming wave of saltiness assaulted his taste buds. He hurriedly pulled out a handkerchief and spat into it. "Gods, that's revolting."

Emmaline quirked an eyebrow. "Told you so. I guess we could offer them to the horses or mules. They might appreciate a blueberry salt lick."

Blaise's cheeks warmed. He'd been the one to mix that batch. How could he have made such a basic, careless mistake? Salt for sugar? It was like putting vinegar in a sweet pie. His hands clenched involuntarily, flecks of dough clinging to his fingers. His mind had been lost, mulling over his quarrel with Jefferson. And now, his distraction had manifested in the most mundane yet revealing way possible.

Emmaline studied him intently, her eyes narrowing as if she were reading a complicated recipe. "What's wrong?"

Blaise sighed and moved to wipe his hands on a nearby towel.

He then took a seat at the table in the corner, grateful that the bakery was empty of customers.

Reuben, who had been carefully decorating cookies at the other end of the counter, sensed the shift in mood. He put down his icing bag and approached, concern etching his features. "You don't have to tell us anything, but it's obvious something's up."

Blaise buried his face in his hands, his shoulders slumping. He could play it off, act like everything was fine, but that would be a lie. And Emmaline and Reuben were more than employees; they were friends who had been there for him through thick and thin.

Taking a deep breath, he mumbled into his palms, "Jefferson and I had a fight. He left this morning."

Emmaline's eyes flashed with indignation as she pulled out a chair and sat down with a thud. "He left you? Daddy still has a poppet of him. Want me to give him a good hexing?"

Blaise's head shot up, his eyes widening in alarm. "No! Gods, no. It's not like that. We fought, yes, but he didn't just abandon me." At least, Blaise hoped that was the case. Both of them had been wrestling with their own emotional turmoil.

"Then what in the world made him leave?" Emmaline shot back, her tone a mixture of confusion and exasperation. "You don't just pack your bags after an argument."

Blaise sighed deeply. Emmaline had a very different personality from her father, and though he loved his dear friend, she wouldn't understand. It seemed she had forgotten there had been a time when Blaise himself had skipped town to avoid facing his troubles.

"No, it's not like that, either," Blaise said, shaking his head for emphasis. "Jefferson is off to find his sister. He'll be back. He promised."

Emmaline shot a skeptical glance at Reuben before focusing back on Blaise. "Are you really sure you don't want me to hex him? Daddy taught me some really wicked new spells..."

Yeah, Blaise was sure Jack would have done that. But hexing

Jefferson was the last thing he wanted to do. "No, I'm sure. It's just that arguing with anyone, let alone someone I love, takes a toll on me, you know?"

Reuben nodded sympathetically. "Why don't you take the rest of the day off? Maybe go for a ride with Emrys. Clear your head."

The suggestion sounded tempting, but the bakery had always been his sanctuary. Yet, today, it was anything but. A realization dawned on him: his love for this place was deeply tied to the times he had spent here with Jefferson. Now, the space felt like an echoing cavern, each corner whispering memories that made the hurt even sharper.

Blaise finally nodded, his decision made. "You know, I might just do that. Would you both be okay with closing up? I don't think I'll be coming back today."

Emmaline's brow furrowed. "What do you mean?"

Blaise closed his eyes for a moment, gathering himself. "I can't stay here." He gestured vaguely upward, toward the loft above the bakery. "Not tonight."

"Oh. Right." Emmaline caught his meaning, her eyes following his gesture. "Where will you go?"

Blaise inhaled deeply, his breath shaky. "I'll go stay with my family." He was sure his mother wouldn't mind.

"Okay. If that doesn't work out, let us know," Emmaline said. "I'm sure my parents or Nadine would help figure something out."

The genuine concern in their faces warmed his heart. Mustering a weak smile, Blaise said, "Thank you. I really appreciate it."

Blaise climbed the stairs to the loft. He packed a small bag with a change of clothes, just enough to get him through the next day. And even that was hard.

Turning, he gazed at the bed. The sheets lay twisted and creased, proof of the night of restless sleep and unsaid words.

"You're infuriating, and I love you so damn much," he whispered to the space where Jefferson had lain, his voice quivering.

Tears pricked at his eyes. Why did love have to be so complicated? It had been so simple back on the beach, away from the shadows of their world.

Slinging his bag over his shoulder, Blaise left the loft and descended into the bakery, walking through the kitchen and out the back door. He stopped by the stables, uncomfortably aware that Emrys knew all about his unsettled mind.

<Seledora left very early,> the stallion remarked, prodding Blaise with his nose. <Jefferson never gets up before the sun. When you didn't join him, I knew something was wrong.>

"Can we not talk about that right now?" Blaise asked. "I just…I just need to…"

The pegasus blew out a warm breath, craning his head until his dark eye was on a level with Blaise. <I'm sorry. I was worried, and I never like it when I feel your emotions abuzz like they are.> The stallion swiped his huge pink tongue over Blaise's cheek. <Let's fly. It would do you some good.>

And they did. Soaring through the canyons with eagles over-head did much to improve Blaise's mood, and he and Emrys spent the entire day together. They splashed in a tributary that fed the Deadwood River, and Emrys took Blaise to some of his favorite scenic vistas.

Blaise felt the last rays of the setting sun warm his back as Emrys dropped him off in front of his mother's home in Forti-tude. The pegasus let out a good-humored snort, declining Blaise's offer for a post-flight grooming. <The grooms need to earn their pay somehow,> the stallion said before trotting off on his own.

Taking a deep breath to steady himself, Blaise rapped his knuckles against the wooden door. A moment later, it swung open to reveal Marian Hawthorne. Short and round, her diminu-tive stature often led people to underestimate her, which was a dangerous proposition. In the past, she had run a benign apothecary shop, but she was a brilliant and dangerously skilled alchemist.

"Oh, Blaise!" His mother's eyes lit up as she reached out, enveloping him in a hug that smelled of lavender and sulfur. "I heard! How are you holding up?"

He let out a muffled groan against her shoulder. "Heard what?"

She pulled back, her brow furrowing into a landscape of maternal concern and indignation. "That Jefferson left you. I swear, I thought he was better than that. I have half a mind to—"

"Whoa, whoa, whoa." Blaise lifted his hands. As if his day hadn't been complicated enough, now the local rumor mill had spun his personal life into the stuff of scandal. "That's not how it is. So don't even think about creating an elixir that turns his voice into a soprano or makes him sneeze out soap bubbles or…whatever."

His mother gave him an amused look. "I don't have anything like that, but now you've gone and given me ideas." Then, she refocused on the matter at hand, crossing her arms. "So, what happened?"

Exasperated, Blaise sighed. The question was already wearing him thin, and it had only been one day. "Can we not talk about it right now? Could I just…stay here tonight?"

For a moment, Marian looked like she wanted to press further, but decided against it. "Of course, you can. My home is always open to you, and when you're ready to talk, I'll be here, as always."

Blaise followed his mother through the doorway, and like a brown-furred whirlwind, a puppy burst forth, barking and jumping with youthful abandon. The family's older, one-eyed dog, Chester, followed with as much exuberance as he could muster. Pausing, Blaise crouched and extended his hand toward the puppy, ethereal glimmers of Breaker magic dancing around his palm. "Nice try, little guy. Now come here."

The puppy let out a surprised yelp and beat a hasty retreat, its paws skittering across the wooden floor. Chester, however, saw this as his golden opportunity. With a burst of doggie enthusiasm, he leaped up toward Blaise, his tail wagging as if powered by sheer joy.

Blaise grinned and obliged, his fingers diving into Chester's thick ruff, hitting that magical spot just behind the ears. The one that turned dogs into puddles of delight. The moment Blaise hit the sweet spot, Chester's head cocked to the side as if pulled by an invisible string, his body arching into a canine crescent moon. His eyes half-closed in a state of pure bliss.

"Brody Hawthorne, enough with the shapeshifting! Drop the animal alchemy and greet your brother properly!" Marian demanded.

With a subdued *pop*, the scampering puppy transformed back into Blaise's nine-year-old brother, Brody. He looked both mischievous and slightly abashed. "That's not fair, using magic on me!"

Marian sighed deeply, her hands shooting up in a familiar gesture of annoyance. "How many times have I told you? No animal alchemy inside the house! And what about your chores? The garden still needs weeding!"

Brody pouted. "I thought if I turned into a dog, I wouldn't have to do chores."

"Do you see what I have to put up with here?" Marian asked Blaise, pointing at her youngest.

Blaise smiled at the strangely comforting normality of his mom's frustration spurred by Brody's impertinence. He rose, though Chester nudged him with a paw. "Yeah." Then a thought occurred to him. "Mom, do you have any potions that would help me sleep? Without dreams." Because without Jefferson, his dreams often warped into nightmares.

She pursed her lips but nodded. "There's a draught I can give you. But…" And now Blaise found himself the focus of her attention. "Some components can cause addiction. You can take it for two nights. No more."

"Two nights. Got it," Blaise confirmed, acutely aware of the fine line he was walking.

Marian nodded, apparently satisfied, and gestured for him to follow her deeper into the home. "The settee will have to do for now. But once we get you settled, we can all sit down to a nice dinner."

Relief washed over Blaise as he followed her. It wasn't the house he'd grown up in, but it was still home. And it was good to be home.

CHAPTER SEVEN

Love is a Convenient Lie

Blaise

Luci sauntered into the dining area, her eyes heavy with an emotion far deeper than her sixteen years should warrant. She sighed dramatically upon spotting Blaise, her eyes rolling like marbles in a cup before she unceremoniously dropped into her seat.

"Lucienne," Marian warned, her voice edged with a touch of steel as she scooped potatoes onto a plate. "I've told you about bringing that mood inside."

With an almost theatrical flourish, Luci stretched her lips into a grotesquely exaggerated smile. "I don't have the slightest idea what you mean, Mother." She flashed the unnaturally large grin at each family member, turning it on and off as if it were a mage-light.

Marian shook her head, a weary sigh escaping her lips. Blaise felt a prickling sense of unease. Maybe he should have taken Emmaline up on the offer to stay with her and her parents. Or even in Emrys's stall.

"I heard you're the reason Uncle Jefferson is gone," Brody blurted out, his mouth full of potatoes.

"Brody," Marian hissed, a glare sharper than a blade landing on her youngest. Luci's snicker cut through the tension.

Blaise felt his appetite wane, the delicious spread before him suddenly as appealing as sawdust. His shoulders tightened, hunching defensively. He didn't want to talk about it, but he had the sinking feeling that his argument with Jefferson was going to be the dragon in the room until he addressed it.

"He did leave, but he'll come back," Blaise said, forcing the words out. "And for the record, our disagreement isn't the reason he left." Though, inwardly, he conceded it had been the catalyst.

"Will Uncle Jefferson bring us anything back?" Brody asked, eyes gleaming with the innocent greed only a child could muster. "I loved the candy from Rainbow Flat last time."

Blaise managed a chuckle, the sound slightly hollow but genuine. "Well, you had a sugar rush for days. I wouldn't be surprised if he did. Jefferson has a knack for those thoughtful gestures." His words caught in his throat, a lump he had to swallow before he could continue. Even in his absence, Jefferson's presence loomed, a haunting reminder of the gaping hole left in his life.

"So, what's the big fight about, huh?" Luci probed, her eyes narrowing slightly as she looked across the table at Blaise.

"Lucienne, that's enough," Marian cut in.

"Why?" Luci retorted, throwing her hands up in the air as if her innocence were on trial. "The town's already buzzing with gossip. Might as well know what's actually going on, right?" Her smile was a weapon, sharp-edged and slicing through the already tense atmosphere.

Blaise took a long, steadying breath, trying to quell the rising tide of emotions within him. Since their father's death, Luci had been a storm cloud, her resentment toward him ebbing and flowing like volatile weather. Just when he thought the skies had cleared, another tempest would suddenly roll in, and he was left to wonder what he'd done to earn her renewed ire.

But maybe she had a point. Rumors were already swirling. His family deserved to hear the truth.

"You're right," he conceded, eyes on Luci as he spoke. "Jefferson made a choice in Izhadell that betrayed my trust. We had an argument about it, and we both agreed that we needed some time apart to clear our heads."

Luci leaned in, her eyes glinting with eagerness and malice. "Did he cheat on you or something?"

The accusation was a knife to his heart, even if he knew Luci only threw it to wound him. "No," Blaise retorted, his voice suddenly cold. "Jefferson would never do that." But as the words left his lips, doubt snaked its way into his thoughts. Jefferson had hidden his use of magic from Blaise—could he hide something else? With a mental shake, he dismissed the idea. Luci was just jabbing at him, exploiting his vulnerability to feed her own bitterness.

Gathering himself, he cleared his throat. "Jefferson used his magic in a way that I found unacceptable. That's it. End of story."

Marian fixed her gaze on her children, her eyes settling like a hawk's on Luci. "Any more questions about Blaise's personal life, and you'll find yourself elbow-deep in soapy water for a month."

Luci gave a scoff and an eye-roll. "Well, that won't affect me much. I'm practically out the door, anyway."

Marian's eyes narrowed, her gaze icy as she met Luci's challenge. "Don't test me right now, Lucienne. This is neither the time nor the place." Then she gestured to the food before them. "Let's talk about something more pleasant, shall we?" Marian suggested, steering the conversation onto safer roads as they all dug into the scrumptious meal she had prepared.

As forks and knives moved across plates, the conversation lightened. They discussed the thriving state of Blaise's Bakery, Marian's bustling apothecary, and the educational exploits of Brody and Lucienne's progress in their alchemical studies.

"Speaking of education," Luci broke in, her eyes on Blaise, "there's something you haven't heard yet because of...well, everything."

Blaise sensed a change in her demeanor. For the first time tonight, Luci seemed genuinely excited about something, and not in a way that would serve as another barb aimed at him. "What's that?"

Luci shot a quick glance at their mother, as if seeking silent permission, before revealing her news. "I applied to the alchemy program at Cheswell University. And guess what? I got in."

Blaise's eyebrows climbed higher than they had all evening. Universities were foreign territory to him. His magical abilities had ended any hope of a formal education. "Wow, congratulations." He hesitated, adding, "Isn't it unusual to get accepted at your age?"

She shot him a quick, almost annoyed glance, before her expression melted into something softer. "They granted me early admission because of my advanced skills in alchemy." Her smile this time was devoid of any malice or sarcasm; it was unfiltered joy.

That wasn't surprising. Luci had been learning alchemy at their mother's side since she was a toddler. She was a natural at it, and Blaise suspected one day she would be on par with, or maybe better than, their mother.

"That's amazing. You should be proud of yourself," Blaise said, his words infused with sincerity.

"I am," she replied, her voice surprisingly free of its earlier edge.

Marian slid a calculated look between them. "Speaking of achievements, I just secured a large contract for my shop. It'll be quite difficult to fulfill while also taking Luci to Cheswell." Her gaze landed squarely on Blaise. "And you need something to take your mind off your situation."

"Wait, what?" Blaise and Luci spoke in unison, a chorus of disbelief.

Marian gave them a sly smile, gesturing between them. "Blaise is the perfect person to take you to Cheswell."

"Blaise shouldn't leave his bakery for that long. He was just away," Luci said, as if striving to find a reasonable explanation for why Blaise couldn't go.

Blaise frowned. He normally used his bakery as an excuse, a shield against unwanted obligations. Hearing Luci use it on his behalf felt...off. "The bakery is in good hands. Emmaline and Reuben can handle it without me."

Marian nodded, a look of satisfaction spreading across her face. "I thought as much. So, it's settled. Blaise, you'll take her, won't you?"

"I wanted *you* to take me, Mom!" Luci protested.

Ignoring Luci's outburst, Marian's gaze remained arrowed onto Blaise, as if her eyes could compel him to agree. Trapped in the spotlight of her expectation, he felt the walls closing in.

Blaise shifted in his chair, his skin prickling with discomfort. Still raw from his argument with Jefferson, the last thing he wanted was to add fuel to another fire. Yet here he was, caught in the high-wire act of family dynamics, balancing precariously with no safety net below.

"Where is Cheswell?" Blaise asked, already thinking about the logistics of the trip.

Luci clenched her fists, her knuckles whitening as she shook her head in frustration. "This is so unfair!"

"It's in Greylight, the capitol of Argor," Marian said, ignoring her daughter's outburst. "So, not too far from here, really."

Argor was another Salt-Iron Confederation nation, though now it was, hopefully, friendlier to mages like him. And maybe if he went, he could just be a nobody. Go as Luci's big brother, deliver her to university. Blaise mulled it over. Yeah, that might work. His mother was right. A change of scenery might help. It would get him away from the bakery and the loft full of heart-breaking memories, at the very least.

"I can do it," he finally agreed. The moment the words left his lips, Luci shot him a look that could curdle milk, while Marian beamed as though he'd just handed her a rare alchemical compo-nent. Blaise sighed. It was like being caught in an emotional weather system between a thunderhead and sunshine.

"Perfect," Marian said, her voice filled with satisfaction as she rose. "Luci, your turn for dishes. Brody, time to prepare for bed." Her eyes then settled on Blaise. "And you, why don't you join me on the porch? The evening is simply lovely."

Blaise hesitated, grappling with a knot of emotions he couldn't easily untangle. Reluctantly, he followed his mother onto the porch. The night air wrapped around them like a cool, comforting blanket, bringing with it a sense of serenity. The creaking swing provided a soothing melody as they took a seat side by side.

"I'm glad you came to see us tonight," Marian began, her voice a gentle caress in the night air. Her hand came to rest on his knee. "And before we get into deeper topics, thank you for agreeing to take Luci."

Blaise grimaced. "Sounds like she's planning to make the journey as agonizing for me as possible."

Marian shook her head, her expression contemplative. "She'll settle, I think."

"She hates me."

Marian fixed her eyes on him, as if searching for the words to mend what was broken. "Luci's been through a lot. She doesn't hate you. I think she's working through some things." She leaned back against the swing. "That's the whole reason I agreed she could go to Cheswell. Luci's gone to this dark, angry place ever since Daniel died." Closing her eyes briefly, she seemed to draw on some inner reservoir of strength. "Which I suppose is natural."

Blaise nodded. He knew everyone worked through grief differently. "Dad would have loved to take her there."

Marian's eyes glittered with unshed tears. "He would. But I think he's in Paradise knowing that you're the next best choice. You'll keep her safe."

Blaise felt her words settle deep within him like a mantle of responsibility. And for the first time since his fight with Jefferson, he felt a renewed sense of purpose—anchored not by his own needs but by the people who depended on him.

"I will," Blaise vowed, the words coming out as a fervent promise. He released a long, whistling breath. "Even if she hates me the entire way."

"She doesn't hate you," Marian insisted. Then she patted his arm. "Now let's talk about you. Like I said, I'm so glad you came by tonight. When I heard the rumors, I wanted to run to you."

He sighed. "Should I even ask what the rumor mill is churning out?"

"Does it matter, since it's not the truth?" his mother asked.

Blaise scoffed, a brief sound that held a world of past hurts. "It matters because rumors have scarred me before." He paused, weighing her words. "But you're right." Knowing what was being said wouldn't help his mental state. And he was self-aware enough to know he needed to protect that right now. "Why did you call me out here?"

Marian studied him, her eyes soft. "Because I'm worried about you. I know you're hurting right now."

Blaise's breath hitched, and for a moment, words escaped him. "I...I'm okay."

Marian laughed, the sound a surprise. Blaise blinked at her, confused. "I'm only laughing because we have a very flexible definition of the word *okay*," Marian explained. She shook her head, a wry twist to her expression. "You're *not* okay. You had a heated argument with your husband, and now he's not here."

Blaise's shoulders slumped, as if the air had been let out of him. "I miss him, and I'm hurt. This argument we had... it really brought our differences to the forefront. I can't ignore what happened, and I'm trying to sort through my feelings."

Marian slid her arm around him. "And did you ask why he acted as he did?"

Blaise swallowed hard, the lump in his throat feeling like a boulder. "Yes, although I knew the answer. He did it to protect me. To protect us. But the method he chose...it was wrong on so many levels. Even more than him using his Dreamer magic to threaten and intimidate, what hurts the most is that he hid it from me."

Marian squeezed his knee gently, her touch grounding. "Blaise, you know as well as I do that you would have told him not to do it."

"Of course," he admitted, shaking his head. "But we would have found a way that didn't involve threats. And even if we disagreed, even if he still went ahead with his plan, it would have helped if we talked about it."

"Jefferson likely would have carried out his plan anyway," his mother pointed out, as if she knew firsthand the hardships that came with such decisions. "It would still be a betrayal of trust."

"Maybe," Blaise said, his voice heavy. "But at least it wouldn't have been a hidden betrayal. That's what's been eating away at me."

Marian sighed and looked up at the night sky, her brown eyes reflecting the stars. "I would have done the same thing, you know. But sometimes, our actions are guided by more complex emotions than just love. Jefferson's actions might seem irrational, but deep down, something was eating at him."

Blaise furrowed his brows, confused yet intrigued by his

mother's cryptic words. "Something besides his love? Besides his desire to protect us?"

Marian nodded solemnly. "Love, as overpowering as it is, doesn't act in isolation. He loves you, that much is clear. He must have known that his actions would cause you pain. You didn't marry a fool, Blaise." She paused, her gaze averting as if grappling with her own intricate web of feelings. "Sometimes we hurt the ones we love for a very, very good reason."

Hurt them for a very good reason? "That doesn't make any sense."

Marian sighed, her face softening. "I guess it doesn't make sense, does it?" She turned to him, and he could see a hint of tears gathering in her eyes. "But sometimes we hurt the people we love to save them from something worse."

Oh. Blaise felt a knot tighten in his stomach. He suddenly realized where his mother's mind had wandered. "You're thinking about the past, aren't you? About the alchemy." Blaise hadn't intended to broach the subject, but he was sure it was what she was hinting at. The revelation that his mother had used him as a subject in her alchemical experiments had been profoundly painful, but in time, they had reconciled and healed the wound.

She nodded, her expression weary. "Yes. The secrets I kept were my way of protecting you. But also a way to deal with my own guilt. To tell myself the terrible thing I did was somehow right." She rubbed at her forehead, her voice soft as she continued, "Sometimes love is a convenient lie we tell ourselves to justify a thing we did."

Blaise leaned into her, relishing the comfort of her familiar scent and warmth. "Mom, I forgave you a long time ago for that."

As they sat there, wrapped in the night's silence, Blaise's thoughts drifted back to Jefferson. If his mother could act out of a tangled mix of love and guilt, couldn't Jefferson have done the same? But guilt about what?

Blaise closed his eyes, feeling as if a heavy fog had lifted from his mind. He finally understood the ghost that had haunted Jefferson—guilt. Guilt that had been subtly influencing his actions, driving him to protect Blaise, perhaps too zealously.

"Oh," he whispered, the revelation weighty in its simplicity.

Marian looked at him, her eyes inquisitive. "You figured something out?"

"Yeah," he replied, his voice full of both relief and sadness. "I understand why Jefferson acted the way he did. Doesn't make it right, but it...it adds another layer."

Marian's lips curled into a soft smile, her eyes reflecting the wisdom of years. "Understanding may not simplify things, but it gives you the tools to navigate the storm."

Blaise inhaled deeply, letting his mother's words sink in. Understanding Jefferson's motivations didn't absolve him, but it did make him more relatable. It made it easier to see the man he loved, warts and all. *Not that Jefferson would ever have warts.*

Marian leaned in, her voice dropping to a near-whisper, as if the night itself shouldn't overhear. "If—no, *when*—you and Jefferson patch things up, what will you do if something like this happens again?"

Blaise pondered for a moment, the future stretching out before him like a path yet to be walked. "I'll try to understand him, to dig deeper into the reasons behind his actions. And we'll work on being more open, more honest. Maybe then we can build a stronger relationship, one not damaged by secrets."

Marian's face radiated warmth, her eyes shining with pride. "Blaise, remember, love is like an alchemical potion. It requires the right reagents, consistent attention, and the occasional refinement to achieve a higher state. You and Jefferson have a bond that is as enduring as gold. Hold onto that."

"Love is about forgiveness, too," Blaise added, his voice quiet. "I've forgiven him in my head, but my heart...well, it's lagging behind."

Marian's eyes softened, filled with a sympathetic understanding that only a mother could offer. "Oh, sweetheart, I know. Forgiveness isn't a simple thing. It's a journey." She laid her hand gently on his arm. "You forgave me for the secrets I kept, for the pain I caused you. Trust that, in time, your heart will catch up to your head."

Blaise felt a lump form in his throat, emotions cresting like a wave. He took a deep breath to steady himself and nodded. "You're right, Mom. Thanks. This was a difficult talk, but I think it's one I needed."

"I could see you were carrying something heavy the moment you stepped through the door," Marian said, her eyes searching Blaise's face. "It's getting late. Do you still need that sleeping draught?"

Blaise's voice came out as little more than a raw whisper. "Yeah, I do. I don't think I could bear any nightmares tonight." He didn't want to wake up screaming or crying. Not here.

Marian's expression held a well of sorrow, as if she could absorb all his nightmares and fears if she only had the power. "All right, let's get you settled for a peaceful night. You've had enough storms for one day."

CHAPTER EIGHT

A Lawsuit on Wheels

Jefferson

Jefferson and Seledora descended, touching down on a stretch of wild prairie. The golden grass swayed, kissed by a gentle breeze carrying the earthy scent of the open expanse. Nearby, a creek wound its way leisurely, waters gleaming in the sunlight. Live oaks flanked the banks, branches stretching across the creek like welcoming arms. The musical gurgle of the creek, paired with the rustling of the grass, created an idyllic backdrop. Jefferson found a comfortable spot by the water's edge, unpacking a sandwich and his canteen, which was sorely in need of refilling.

Seledora grazed nearby, taking advantage of the break and the surrounding grass. Jefferson enjoyed his lunch, appreciating the beauty of nature around him. He paused, brow crinkling when Seledora's head shot up, ears pricked.

<There's something strange on the horizon.>

Strange in the Untamed Territory could be a hazard to one's health. Jefferson wrapped his sandwich in his handkerchief and set it aside, rising. He squinted in the direction she was looking.

At first, he only saw a distant, dark shape moving against the backdrop of the prairie. But as the seconds ticked by, details emerged. An uncommonly large stagecoach, trailing billowing plumes of smoke from its stack, not unlike a steam locomotive. The juxtaposition of old and new, natural and mechanical, became evident as it barreled forward at an impressive speed.

"An invention of man's genius…or perhaps his folly," Jefferson whispered in awe.

Seledora snorted in response, her voice full of contempt. <A marvel of modern disaster, if you ask me. I pity those horses.>

The steam coach slowed, coming to a halt near the stream. The driver kept a respectable distance from Jefferson and Seledora. Jefferson saw tiny figures emerge from the coach, no doubt to stretch their legs, relieve themselves, and see to other needs. The stream was the first clean water Jefferson had come across for the day, so he couldn't fault them for taking advantage of it as well.

"I wonder where they're headed?" Jefferson mused. He wondered about the purpose of such a contraption. It didn't seem to be for freight. A new type of passenger conveyance, perhaps. Experimental, most likely, or he was certain he would have heard of it by now.

<That thing looks like a lawsuit on wheels.> Seledora shook her mane. <I'm surprised they can convince any horses to pull that stinking horror.>

Jefferson chuckled. "I suppose they'd have to use horses of a specific temperament."

With his curiosity sated, Jefferson settled back down to finish his lunch. They still had a long distance to cover before they reached Starvation. But they would get there, and he would begin the arduous task of correcting the course of his life and love.

CHAPTER NINE

Hexing is Not the Solution

Blaise

Blaise stepped onto the creaking boardwalk, his eyes trained on the peculiar storefront. The hand-painted sign read *Jack's Toy Emporium*. It was an absurd thought that Wildfire Jack Dewitt, the Scourge of the Untamed Territory, had turned into a merchant. He reached for the doorknob, only to find it locked.

Moving to the large plate-glass windows, he cupped his hands around his eyes for a better look inside. The interior was dim, but he could make out a shadowy figure that had Jack's unmistakable build. Blaise rapped his knuckles against the glass.

The door creaked open, and Jack's face appeared in the crack, his eyes narrowing for a moment before recognition set in. "C'mon in," he muttered, pulling the door wide and retreating inside.

"Good morning to you, too," Blaise said as he stepped inside, well aware that pleasantries were often wasted on Jack.

Jack snorted, his eyes drifting to a partially finished shelf that hung crooked on the wall. "It's morning. *Good* is up for debate."

Blaise glanced around, noting the rugged wooden shelves that lined the walls, ready to hold Jack's inventory. "You could hire a carpenter, you know."

Jack scoffed, crossing his arms over his chest. "Didn't think you'd stroll in here to tell me how to nail boards to a wall."

Blaise grinned, feeling a warm sense of camaraderie despite the barbed exchange. This was pleasantly *normal*, and he appreciated that. "Well, I *have* been running a business longer than you have."

Jack's eyes held a twinkle of amusement. "If I wanted your nose in my business, I'd have stuck it there myself."

Blaise chuckled, knowing full well the truth of that statement. "No, you wouldn't." Jack was recklessly stubborn, and it took a lot for him to ask for any sort of help. "But that's not why I'm here." Blaise shifted, his gaze meeting Jack's.

Jack's eyes narrowed, the glint of mischief replaced by a sober intensity. "I heard about your little spat with the peacock. You want me to hex him into next week?"

Blaise groaned. "Why is hexing the first solution everyone jumps to? No, Jack, I don't want you or anyone else to hex Jefferson."

The disappointment that flashed across Jack's face was almost comical. "Dammit. And to answer your question, it's because the guy's a walking, talking irritation. I always had a bad feeling about him."

Blaise raised an eyebrow, skepticism clear in his gaze. Jack had always kept Jefferson at arm's length, but over time, even he couldn't deny a grudging form of acceptance. "Seems to me you've put up with him just fine when it's to your advantage."

"A grudge is just a friendship that's too sober to admit it." Jack smirked.

Blaise sighed, the town's gossip wearing on him. "Why does everyone feel like they have a say in our relationship? You and Kittie argue all the time, and I don't see people lining up to hex her. Or you, for that matter."

Jack's eyes took on a devilish gleam. "Well, plenty of folks wouldn't mind seeing me hexed, but they know better. And no one dares lay a finger on Kittie, spat or no spat."

Blaise's voice mellowed, the edge of frustration giving way to earnestness. "Exactly. That's how I feel about Jefferson."

Jack seemed reluctant to admit that Blaise had made a valid point. His lips tightened, as if he were chewing on his own stubbornness. "Fine. If you change your mind, you know where to find me."

Blaise had to restrain a growl of irritation. "Okay, this isn't why I'm here, but I want Jefferson's poppet. Give it to me."

Feigning innocence, Jack's eyes widened theatrically. "Poppet? What poppet?"

"*Jack.*" Blaise's voice rumbled with warning, making it clear he was running low on patience.

The Effigest grumbled, rolling his eyes. "All right, all right. What made you think I've got a poppet of your peacock?"

Blaise began counting off on his fingers, his expression dead serious. "First, because it's *you*. You're the type to have a poppet of everyone you've ever met, just in case you need some leverage. Second, Emmaline told me."

"'Course she did," Jack grumbled with raspy irritation. He reached into the worn pocket of his trousers and pulled out a tiny, crudely made doll, tossing it through the air to Blaise with a flick of his wrist.

Catching the doll, Blaise examined it, his eyes narrowing. "You just walk around with a poppet of Jefferson in your pocket?"

"Yeah, so?"

"Jack, that's creepy." Blaise shook his head, tucking the poppet securely into his own pocket.

Jack chuckled, a guttural sound that echoed in the sparsely furnished room. "Ain't the first time you've told me that." Jack hobbled across the room, moving to sit on a wooden chair. He eased himself onto it, stretching out his left leg with a wince, as if each step were a reminder of pain. "But you said that wasn't why you came. So why are you here bugging me?"

Blaise's gaze softened, lingering on Jack's discomfort. The outlaw was still healing, still fighting battles invisible to the eye. It was disquieting to see him not fully himself, but it was better than the alternative. Jack was alive, and that was a victory in itself. Shaking off his reverie, Blaise returned to the reason for his visit. "Right. Mom wants me to take Luci to a school in Greylight. I thought I'd see if you could suggest a pegasus who might be willing to carry an alchemist."

A thoughtful expression crossed Jack's face. Alchemy was a subject that trod on thin ice in Fortitude. Mages and alchemists had a troubled past, one that had sown seeds of mistrust. "You've got options," Jack finally said, scratching at his stubbled chin. "But if you want a name right off, I'd suggest Naureus."

"Naureus?" Blaise asked, a touch of uncertainty lacing his voice. "The buckskin stallion that used to belong to Raven Dawson? Are you sure about that?"

"Yeah." Jack's voice dropped an octave, taking on a gentle, almost melancholic tone. "Naureus got gut-punched by betrayal, same as you. Some pegasi would've high-tailed it to the hills, broken and bitter. But not him. He's hangin' on, just...lost. No compass."

The word *betrayal* hung in the air like a wraith. Blaise felt it resonate deep in his bones. "I get what you're saying. Thanks, Jack. I'll talk to Naureus, see if he's up for the journey."

Jack leaned back, his eyes reflecting a moment of thought. "Speaking of travels, when you're in Greylight, you might want to check out Iron Hoof Stables. They'll be your safest option in that city, unless things have changed since my last time there."

Blaise raised a brow. *Safest* often had a different meaning for Jack than for him. "Really? Why wouldn't the others be safe?"

"Have I ever led you astray?" the outlaw asked. Because Faedra forbid he actually answer a question.

But his question made Blaise reconsider. Jack was many things, but despite his bluster, he was reliable. And he was a veritable font of information. "Thanks for the tip. I'll check them out." He paused, his eyes meeting Jack's. "How're you holding up?"

Jack's gaze shifted to the side, landing on a half-finished shelf laden with empty jars and disarray. "'Bout the same," he muttered, his voice edged with a fatigue that seemed to go beyond physical pain. That was Jack-speak for *struggling but too stubborn to admit it.* No one knew the full extent of his injuries or how his road to recovery looked. All Blaise knew was that the man had danced with death and lived to tell the tale, albeit grudgingly.

Blaise nodded, respecting Jack's reticence. "All right. When I get back from Argor, maybe I'll lend a hand around here." A warm smile flickered across his face. "Even if you don't ask for it."

"I ain't needin' a babysitter. Got enough of that with Zepheus and Kittie hoverin' around," Jack groused. But his eyes, those hard, flinty eyes, tempered for just a moment, betraying a hint of gratitude.

Blaise chuckled as he turned to leave, his hand gripping the door handle. "Thanks, Jack. See you soon." With that, he stepped out into the daylight, a renewed sense of purpose buoying his spirits.

CHAPTER TEN

The Twirling Tunesmith

Jefferson

The scent of dust and dry earth hung heavy in the air as Seledora navigated the winding streets of Starvation. Her hooves churned the cracked, sun-baked soil, leaving behind small clouds of dust that danced in the fading light. Jefferson, perched atop her broad back, took in the sights and sounds all around him. They were far from Rainbow Flat or Fortitude, but there was a hard-won charm to this place that made him begrudgingly admire it.

Seledora's ears perked up, her brown eyes inquisitive as they took in the rustic buildings and the occasional passerby. <What's the first order of business?>

"First, we find a stable for you and a room for me," Jefferson murmured, gently patting her muscular neck. "Then I'll begin my search."

Seledora nodded and flicked her tail. <Sounds like a solid plan. There's a livery down this way.> Without waiting for further instruction, she took the lead, turning down a side street.

As they moved through the town, Jefferson's eyes fell upon the lives unfolding around him—families sharing laughter, couples stealing glances. Each scene stabbed at him, a sharp reminder of what he lacked.

Gods, how he missed Blaise. All the quiet parts of their relationship. Waking up next to Blaise, inhaling the unique scent that was purely him, hearing the comforting timbre of his voice. How easily Jefferson had taken all those little things for granted, allowing them to blend into the backdrop of his daily life. Now, each missing piece was a haunting reminder of the empty space beside him, the silence where laughter used to reside.

Did Blaise feel the same void in his life? Did he lie awake at night, aching for the missing piece that was Jefferson? Or had he found solace in Jefferson's absence, realizing he was better off? No, he couldn't afford to think like that.

"Blaise loves me," he whispered to himself, his voice raw. But love had a way of being both a shield and a weapon, and right now, he couldn't tell which way it pointed. A tight knot of anxiety curled in his stomach.

<We're here.> Seledora's voice broke through his agonizing thoughts, grounding him in the present. <Pull yourself together.>

Shaking away his doubts, Jefferson swung his leg over the saddle and dismounted. "Yes, of course. Thank you," he said, leading her into the stable. The earthy scent of hay mixed with the musk of equine sharpened his focus.

The liveryman, a burly man with a mustache that looked like it had seen its share of stories, gave Seledora an appreciative glance. "Mighty fine horse you got there. Don't board many of her kind 'round these parts."

Jefferson managed a weary smile. Seledora had already hidden her wings, so she didn't draw undue attention. "She's one of a kind." He stated what he needed for Seledora's care and when the liveryman quoted a price that could have bought a small farm, Jefferson only sighed. "She has expensive tastes," he quipped, handing over the requisite number of golden eagles.

After making sure Seledora was settled in her new lodgings, Jefferson picked up his saddlebags and stepped back into the dying light of the day. The growing dusk seemed to mirror his own sinking spirits, casting long shadows that danced like specters on the earth. It was time to find a room, a place from where he could stage this enterprise.

The faded sign of the Dusty Rose Hotel beckoned, promising a modicum of comfort after days of harsh travel. Jefferson pushed through the doors, stepping into an atmosphere thick with the smoky haze of tobacco and worn-out dreams. The scent was oddly comforting, a blanket of humanity in an otherwise cruel world.

"Welcome, sir. Will you be needing a room?" The clerk, an elderly woman with hair the color of steel and eyes that had no doubt endured years of hardship, smiled with a warmth that was nearly disarming.

"Yes, thank you. Just myself for a few nights." Jefferson took the offered key, his hand brushing against the aged leather of the ledger as he signed his name.

His room was a modest space, sparse but clean. A narrow bed crowded the wall, its frayed sheets a stark contrast to the starched linens he shared with Blaise. He let his pack drop with a thud, its echo seeming to fill the space. For a moment, he stood still, his gaze sweeping over the room. Blaise's absence was like missing a part of himself. He almost expected to hear Blaise's footsteps behind him, to feel his warm embrace.

But he was alone.

"Keep it together, Jefferson Cole," he murmured, just to fill the emptiness with a voice.

With a sigh, he shook off the melancholy that threatened to

drown him. He splashed water from the washstand onto his face and changed into a clean shirt and trousers. There was work to be done.

Flora's information had provided a roadmap to Alice, albeit an incomplete one. She was here, somewhere, hidden among the weathered facades and dusty streets of Starvation. But in what role? His mind recoiled at the possibilities. Could she be one of the saloon girls, those so-called soiled doves, trading herself for survival? Or perhaps something less dire, a server or bartender? The uncertainty set him on edge.

Steeling himself for whatever truth awaited, Jefferson stepped out into the twilight. It was time to find Alice, to mend what was broken. It was the only way forward.

Saloons were plentiful in the towns of the Untamed Territory, offering welcome relief from the heat and danger in the form of cool drinks and entertainment. Starvation had five saloons, which meant Jefferson would search each one until he had a lead. He'd always been cautious in such places; it was all too easy to become a target, given his notoriety. But today, he threw caution aside for a desperate sort of hope. He had to find Alice.

The first two saloons yielded nothing but cold trails and strangers' faces. Bartenders shook their heads; no one knew an Alice who fit his description. But as he approached the third saloon, a fading broadside caught his eye. A black-haired woman holding a violin stared back at him from the poster, her gaze almost a dare. He froze, staring. Could it be?

Jefferson moved closer, examining the image. "Twirling Tunesmith," he read, thoughtful. Before her life had been irrevocably changed, Alice had been passionate about music. Their parents had steered her toward more *respectable* instruments like the piano or the flute, but the violin had always fascinated Alice. She had just started lessons when she was sold.

A flood of memories washed over him: Alice's laughter, her dreams of becoming a musician, the light in her eyes when she talked about the violin. Could it really be that she had found a way to live her dream after all this time?

Well, what did he have to lose?

The moment Jefferson pushed through the swinging doors of the saloon, a wall of grating noise and redolent stench slammed into him. A medley of piano notes clashed with uproarious laughter and drunken bellowing, all marinated in a thick atmosphere of tobacco smoke, sweat, and stale beer. He grimaced, and ordered a whiskey at the bar to at least look like he belonged. Then he found a table in the corner, where he could get his bearings and observe.

Just then, the tattered velvet curtains on the shabby stage swished open. A man in clothing so comically outdated it could only be described as *vintage* sauntered forward. "Folks, critters, and everyone in between! Prepare yourselves for an evening of unparalleled—well, let's just call it entertainment. I present to you, Claude and Sarai, the Rascally Rompers!"

The moment Claude and Sarai, the Rascally Rompers, sashayed onto the stage in their eye-catching, red-sequined outfits, the air thickened with electricity. Their grins were a devilish promise of the antics to come. With a flourish, Sarai pulled open a crate that seemed to contain an entire world of mischief—props that ranged from oversized cards and fake revolvers to a rubber chicken.

Their opening act was a slapstick masterpiece—a high-stakes poker game between two cowboy caricatures so exaggerated they could only exist on a stage like this. As they prepared to sit, each reached for the same chair, their faces a pantomime of shock and indignation. A war of exaggerated courtesy unfolded, each insisting the other take the sole seat. What followed was a frenetic game of musical chairs set to the tune of a banjo that made the audience roar with laughter.

And then, just when Jefferson thought they were about to

settle the chair dispute, Claude pulled out a WANTED poster with Sarai's face on it.

"Wanted: For stealing chairs and hearts!" he declared.

Sarai rolled her eyes and retorted, "Well, then you're wanted for impersonating a gentleman!"

The room was ablaze with laughter, punctuated by bawdy one-liners and double entendres that made even the most stony-faced patrons crack a smile. They wrapped up their act with Claude pretending to lasso Sarai only to get entangled himself, leaving the audience in stitches. One man laughed so hard he toppled out of his chair, clutching his belly.

Jefferson had to admit, although he was accustomed to more refined entertainment, he enjoyed their act. He found himself laughing and clapping along with the rest, and he couldn't deny it made him feel lighter and more hopeful.

The showman, once again seizing center stage, waved his hands dramatically. "Let's hear it for the Rascally Rompers! Now, brace yourselves for the musical styling of the one, the only, Twirling Tunesmith!"

The raucous atmosphere sobered into one of eager anticipation. The air seemed to thicken, like the charged moment before a summer storm. Jefferson's palms became clammy, and surreptitiously, he wiped them on his trousers beneath the table.

As the velvet curtains drew back, the spotlight fell upon Alice, standing poised at center stage. She was a vision, her hair artfully arranged in an intricate waterfall of curls that framed her face like a halo. Her eyes, alight with radiant energy, scanned the audience. She was clothed in an ensemble of iridescent purples and blues, a vivid contrast to the saloon's rustic backdrop. The outfit was far from the risqué costumes of the soiled doves, but it was equally mesmerizing, amplifying her natural grace.

"Fortunes of Tabris," Jefferson whispered, leaning forward in his seat.

With an almost reverent touch, Alice raised her bow. The

audience held its collective breath, waiting for her to coax the first notes from her instrument. The bow met the strings.

As Alice played the violin, she became one with the instrument. Her body swayed gracefully, her feet gliding across the wooden stage, each movement in perfect harmony with the notes. The bow danced across the strings in a skilled display, her fingers moving nimbly on the fingerboard, creating a cascade of harmonies that resonated with her audience.

She was not just playing a melody. She *was* the melody.

As Jefferson watched, entranced, it was as if the boundaries of his own self had blurred. The music reached into his core, pulling at strings he hadn't known existed, tweaking emotions he couldn't name but felt profoundly.

The saloon seemed to come alive under Alice's musical spell. Faces that had been stern or disinterested now shone with emotion. Waitresses and saloon girls moved more freely among the tables, bearing trays laden with food and drink. Their patrons, entranced by Alice's performance, seemed more than willing to part with their coins, filling the coffers without a second thought.

Jefferson flagged down a passing server, his eyes still fixed on the stage. "Another whiskey, neat," he called, his gaze never leaving Alice. The server returned promptly, setting the tumbler before him. He took a long sip, the liquid fire anchoring him as the emotional tide of Alice's melody nearly swept him away once more.

As he watched Alice pirouette across the stage, each twist of her body speaking volumes, he realized she was more than just a performer—she was a mage of music, wielding her violin with the same calculation and skill Jack used on his poppets.

The last note of her song hung in the air, a haunting echo that seemed to reverberate through the room. Coming back to himself, Jefferson shook his head, somewhat bewildered. In front of him sat a plate of food he had no memory of ordering. He glanced around and noticed he wasn't alone in this. Many tables were laden with half-eaten meals or untouched drinks, evidence of Alice's distracting allure.

Magic. It was indisputably magic. A subtle enchantment that loosened both purse strings and inhibitions.

His gaze settled on the now-closed curtain, pondering the implications. Music that could not only move hearts but also compel actions—whether it was splurging on food or drink, or perhaps something more? No wonder Phillip Dillon had bought her as a bride.

He swallowed, rising from his seat. Jefferson left a handful of golden eagles on the table, making eye contact with the bartender so that they knew he had paid his tab. The bartender gave him a sharp nod.

"Excuse me," Jefferson murmured, slipping past other patrons. His boots thudded against the worn floorboards, each step taking him closer to the door that he hoped led backstage. But before he could reach his destination, a man stepped into his path, arms folded across a chest as broad as a barrel.

"Sorry, but this area is for performers only," the bouncer said, his voice as gruff as a saw cutting through timber.

Those were words Jefferson didn't want to hear. But he was used to thinking fast, and a beat later, he'd already decided how to twist his tactics. Jefferson chuckled softly. "Ah, the age-old guardian of the backstage, I see. For a moment there, I was tempted to play the *do you know who I am?* card. But then, I'd have to admit to myself that I've become one of those insufferable types, wouldn't I?"

The bouncer clearly hadn't expected that. His stance relaxed a hair. Just enough to let Jefferson know he was on the right track. "And we wouldn't want that, now, would we?" the bouncer asked.

"Quite right," Jefferson agreed. "So, instead, let me appeal to your sense of family. The virtuoso who just enchanted this crowd with her violin—she's my sister. I've traveled a considerable distance to reunite with her."

"You're the third person to claim she's your sister this month," the bouncer said, suddenly wary.

Jefferson kept his face a mask, though he didn't like the idea that others were trying to get to Alice. He grinned. "Ah, she always had a knack for gathering admirers. They sprout like weeds, don't they? But I assure you, I am the genuine article. The family resemblance in our jawlines is uncanny."

That in itself was a blatant lie. Perhaps without his glamor, Jefferson's jawline would resemble Alice's. But not as he was. All the same, he considered it a worthy gamble.

The bouncer laughed. "Jawlines, you say? Most folks try to bribe their way past me."

"Ah, bribery—the refuge of scoundrels of low character," Jefferson said, feigning a shudder. "Not for me. I prefer to use wit, charm, and an honest face. Well, at least two out of the three." He'd never admit to this man that if charm didn't work, he would have tried bribery. And barring that, magic.

The bouncer chuckled. "You're not like the usual rabble that tries to get past me. All right, go on. But if you cause any trouble, you'll have me to answer to."

Jefferson tipped his hat. "You have my word as a gentleman—and as Alice's actual brother—that the only trouble I'll cause is perhaps an overly emotional family reunion."

With a nod from the bouncer, Jefferson passed the threshold, his heart pounding in excitement and apprehension. It was one thing to find Alice, another entirely to face her after all these years. But as he stepped backstage, one thought overwhelmed all others: he was about to speak with his sister again, and for that, he was profoundly grateful.

Alice

ALICE CLOSED THE DOOR TO HER DRESSING ROOM, ITS WALLS A comforting barrier between her and the rest of the world. She leaned against the door, her eyes closing briefly as she exhaled a relieved breath. The air was thick with the scents of rosewater perfume and powdery makeup, but she found it comforting—the blend symbolized her freedom.

With practiced ease, she peeled off her ornate, glittery stage outfit, its vibrant purples and blues shimmering even in the muted light. She traded the ostentatious fabrics for a simple, comfortable button-down shirt and flowing skirt that allowed her to breathe more easily.

The walls were a gallery of her new life's work, lined with fading posters from past performances. Each one was a memory of a time when she'd left her mark, her music touching the souls of those who listened. On a small vanity beside a cracked mirror were various trinkets and keepsakes—little tokens of love and appreciation she'd collected from those enraptured by her music. Each item was a testament to the life she had painstakingly built for herself, a life that stood in contrast to the stifling cage that her marriage to Phillip Dillon had been.

Her thoughts drifted to her young son, Theo, who would be waiting for her at their modest boarding house. A gentle smile tugged at her lips, her heart swelling with a love so profound it seemed to eclipse all the hardships she'd endured. That boy was her beacon, her light through the darkest, most treacherous tunnels of life.

A knock at the door jolted her back to reality. Her brow furrowed, lines of confusion etching themselves across her forehead. She wasn't expecting anyone. With trepidation, Alice slowly opened the door.

"Malcolm?" Alice's voice wavered, her eyes widening as they met the gaze of the man before her.

He wasn't Malcolm—not really. She remembered this face from that sham funeral—the one for Malcolm, a funeral that turned out to be nothing but smoke and mirrors. Her emotions whirled within her like a tempest, a maelstrom of anger, confusion, and a biting bitterness she couldn't ignore.

"*You!* You have a lot of nerve showing your face here!" she hissed, each word full of venom.

"It's Jefferson, actually," he corrected, a gentle cadence in his voice as if attempting to temper her fury. "I go by Jefferson now, Alice. I understand your anger, truly I do. But I've come a long way to see you."

Her eyes narrowed to slits, defiance flaring within them. Pretty words and pleading gazes were going to cut no ice with her. She'd been deceived by people like this far too often. "You understand my *anger?*" she scoffed, her voice a volatile blend of ice and fire. "You *abandoned* me, Malcolm—or Jefferson, or whatever name you're hiding behind. You lied to me, and now you waltz in here as if nothing happened?"

"Alice," he began, desperation etched on his face, "I know what I did was wrong, but I want to make things right."

"Make things right?" She crossed her arms, trembling with ill-concealed anger. "How do you expect to do that?"

"Please, Owl..." he whispered, invoking the childhood nickname that had once been a term of endearment. It fell from his lips like a last-ditch plea, a spectral echo from a past that seemed like another lifetime.

Her rouged lips curled with renewed anger. "Don't you dare—don't you dare use that name. You lost that right when you lied to me."

"Look, I won't deny I made mistakes," Malcolm pleaded, his eyes searching hers, as if sifting for a fragment of understanding or forgiveness. "But I'd like to make things right for both of us."

"Making it right would mean turning back time, Malcolm." She nearly laughed, but her voice wavered, charged with unshed tears. "And we both know that's impossible."

With a surge of finality, she thrust the door closed. She rested her back against the unyielding wood, her heart racing as she tried to absorb the unexpected encounter. Through the door, the persistent knock echoed, each rap accompanied by Malcolm's empty apologies.

"Go away!" The words broke from her lips, muffled by the door between them, while tears carved trails down her cheeks.

"Please, Alice." Malcolm's voice cracked with emotion. "Give me a chance to explain, to make amends. I can't fix the past, but maybe we can start anew."

A moment's hesitation gripped her as her heart warred between an aching longing and a protective fear. Could she dare trust him? Was there a chance to rebuild the shattered foundation of their relationship, or would it only sow fresh seeds of pain and betrayal?

No, she thought, her resolve hardening once more. She couldn't risk it, not when she had built a new life for herself and her son. They didn't need Malcolm's lies and deceit to come crashing into their fragile world.

"Leave!" Alice's voice shook, her eyes stinging with tears. "You've done enough damage! I don't want to see you again, Malcolm!"

Desperate to silence the pleas that seemed to echo in the corners of her mind, she reached for her violin. The instrument felt like an extension of her soul, familiar and comforting. Taking a steadying breath, she drew the bow across the strings, and a haunting melody unfurled. The tune was a quilt of her emotions, a blend of sorrow and resilience that filled the room, each note a reverberation of the pain that roiled within her.

She could have tempered it with her magic, used it to repel Malcolm, but she didn't. It was her magic, but it was also her peace. As her fingers danced along the fingerboard and the bow coaxed the strings into song, she felt the tension in her muscles release. Each note held its own story, some stained with the ache of betrayal and hurt, others laced with bittersweet memories of the past.

Her music muffled the knocks and entreaties, providing a sanctuary for her conflicting emotions. The composition reached its climax in a powerful crescendo that seemed to shake the very walls of the dressing room. As the final notes faded into silence, she lowered her violin, her chest heaving as she struggled to regain her composure.

The knocking had ceased, but the intense emotions stirred by the encounter seemed to hang in the air like a mist, leaving an indelible mark upon her soul.

CHAPTER ELEVEN

Tough Love

Blaise

The Deadwood River carved a path through the sandstone canyon, its rushing waters a soothing background noise. Birds of prey soared high overhead, and Blaise found himself envying their distance from his uneasy journey with Luci.

He spread a worn wool blanket over the rocky outcropping, a makeshift picnic spot overlooking the frothy water. As Blaise unpacked their simple lunch of bread, cheese, and dried meats, his thoughts churned like the river's undercurrent.

While they ate in silence, Blaise felt as if he was walking on eggshells around Luci. He didn't know what to say, but the quiet between them felt suffocating. He had to break it somehow.

Hoping to bridge the widening chasm of awkwardness, Blaise

cleared his throat. "So...Cheswell University. That's really exciting."

Luci offered a non-committal shrug, her gaze anchored to the distant horizon. The sun caught the fringes of her rich brown hair, setting them aglow.

Pushing forward, Blaise ventured, "Have you given any thought to what you'll study there?"

He immediately regretted it, given the obvious answer. Luci's eyes rolled—a clear sign of her growing irritation—as she tore into a hunk of bread. After a deliberate delay, she replied, "Alchemy. Plus, the usual subjects like mathematics, history, and sciences." Her voice dripped with sarcasm. "You know, the typical courses ordinary students pursue."

Blaise felt warm at his collar, and he tugged it away from his throat. "Of course. You'll probably surpass Mom's skills before long."

At the mention of their mother, Luci scowled, her brows knitting together. "I wanted Mom to take me to Cheswell. Not you."

Blaise winced at the venom in her tone. He opened his mouth to respond, but Luci barreled on.

"This was supposed to be my time with her before I left home. But once again, you've ruined everything." Luci speared him with an icy glare. "You have a real talent for that, you know."

Blaise reeled, her words hitting him like a physical blow. He stared at Luci, shock rippling through him. Where had this come from?

Luci's lip curled in a sneer. "You ruin everything you touch, Blaise. Including the lives of the people around you."

Blaise floundered, surprised, her words a vise around his heart. He turned his gaze to the river, letting its undulating flow momentarily distract him from the slow suffocation of Luci's words. He felt exposed, vulnerable, every misstep and mistake in his life scrutinized. Her observation burrowed under Blaise's skin like splinters. Was she right? Had he really ruined so much? Doubt and shame crashed over him.

He thought of his argument with Jefferson, the rift it had caused. Luci was supposed to be starting an exciting new chapter of her life, but instead, she was stuck with him as an unwanted escort. What else had he ruined without realizing it? Blaise's shoulders slumped beneath Luci's condemnation. He stared at the flowing water, wishing he could dive in and let the current sweep him far away. But he had to see this through. Had to get Luci to Cheswell safely, no matter how much she resented him.

Jaw clenched, Blaise began repacking their leftover food. He would finish this task, then get out of Luci's way. Maybe she was right. Maybe everyone would be better off without him ruining things.

Emrys, who had been grazing nearby, lifted his head, snorting. He ambled over, wisps of grass hanging from his lips as he reached down and nudged Blaise's shoulder.

<Do not listen to her words,> Emrys said, his voice colored with indignation. <She is wrong. Do not doubt yourself.>

Blaise sighed, resting his head against Emrys's warm cheek, catching the aroma of the stallion's grass-scented breath. If only it were that simple. Luci's barbs had struck deep, digging into fresh wounds and fears.

They finished eating in silence. "We should go," Blaise said, deciding that for now, while he was hurting, he would keep their conversations short.

Doubt plagued Blaise as he mounted up, and they continued their journey. Had he ruined Jefferson's life by getting involved with him? Was Luci right about his destructive influence? Blaise's failures and regrets tore at him like the claws of a thousand angry crows.

He would guard his words around Luci and focus on his mission: getting her safely to Cheswell, to her new life. Focus on one thing at a time.

Luci

LUCI SHIFTED UNCOMFORTABLY IN HER SADDLE, FEELING EVERY BIT of the day's long journey in her aching muscles. Saddle sore and stiff, her mood was as rough as the terrain around them. She was looking forward to time out of the saddle and sleep, although the prospect of a bedroll on the ground wasn't enticing. Blaise was more accustomed to rough conditions than she was. It was just another burr that got under her skin when it came to him.

From the way the pegasi were spiraling downward, Luci hoped they were searching for a place to spend the night. Emrys didn't broadcast his speech to her, but she saw Blaise nod at something, probably another suggestion from his pegasus. Luci wished they would include her in their conversation.

But she knew why Blaise hadn't. Luci had been more cutting with him than she'd intended at their lunch stop, and he'd withdrawn. At first, she'd relished the minor victory, inwardly celebrating his lost confidence. But then she'd glimpsed the genuine pain in his expression, a deep wound, and knew that she'd miscalculated. Blaise had gone quiet ever since.

The pegasus Luci rode, Naureus, followed Emrys to the ground. The buckskin landed so smoothly that Luci hardly jarred in the saddle. He glanced over his shoulder to check his rider, then bobbed his head with satisfaction.

Naureus flicked his ears, scanning their surroundings. <Not an awful place to spend the night.> He trotted closer to Emrys, then came to a squared halt for Luci to dismount.

Blaise slipped from the saddle with a soft thud, the fine sand puffing up in a small cloud around his boots as they met the ground. His eyes shifted toward Luci, but she evaded his gaze. Instead, she let her eyes wander over the russet hues of the canyon walls and the meandering curves of the nearby river. She didn't want to be weighed down by guilt for the barbs she'd thrown earlier, even though a nagging voice inside her head insisted she owed him an apology.

Blaise broke the awkward silence, his voice tinged with hesitancy, as if he were preparing to walk across hot coals. "If you could gather some tinder and start a fire, I can work on getting our dinner ready."

Luci turned toward him, an incredulous eyebrow arching upward. Had Blaise really forgotten he was sharing this journey with an alchemist? They were far beyond the quaint needs of ordinary adventurers. "Tinder? Really? Unless you're thinking of spit-roasting a wild boar, I don't see why we'd need that."

Her sarcastic remark made Blaise's lips tighten into a thin line. "No, but...what are you suggesting, then?"

With a smug smile, Luci went over to her saddlebags. She unbuckled one side and began rifling through its contents until her fingers wrapped around a cylindrical silver canister. She pulled it out and held it up like a trophy. "Something I've been tinkering with."

A look of wary curiosity crossed Blaise's face. "Alchemy?"

"Obviously." She chewed on her bottom lip, wishing she could tell him more—how she had created it to serve as a part for a travel-sized alchemical furnace. But she was suddenly shy, feeling worlds apart from Blaise.

So instead, Luci scanned the area, searching for the perfect spot to light their fire. She found a flat patch of ground surrounded by rocks, ideal. She nestled the canister in the middle of this natural firepit and carefully opened its lid. Then, pulling her hand back swiftly, she triggered the device. A controlled burst of flame erupted from the canister, settling into a stable fire that hovered a few inches above the rocks.

"Huh." Blaise eyed it. "Let me guess. Whatever you have in there reacts when you expose it to air?"

"Yep," Luci said, a flicker of genuine pride lighting up her features for a fleeting moment before her expression tightened again, her defenses snapping back into place.

As Blaise busied himself with assembling a simple but hearty meal from their provisions, Luci set about unsaddling the pegasi. She had just begun currying Naureus's sleek coat when the buckskin stallion twisted his head around to fix his dark eyes on her.

<I know you are hurting, but you do not need to inflict the same pain on others,> the pegasus said, his mental voice a rich, velvety baritone.

Luci's eyes narrowed, and her lips tightened into a thin line. "You've been rooting around in my head. I didn't invite you."

The stallion snorted, his flank twitching to ward off a pesky fly. <Those are some bold accusations, filly. No, I have not been rooting around in your head, as you say. But I do not need to rummage through your head to feel the tension in your muscles or hear the sting in your words. You are turning your own hurt outward, aiming it at those who are already bruised.>

For a moment, Luci froze, her currycomb hovering in mid-air. She wanted to rebuff him, to tell him he had no idea what he was talking about. But deep down, she knew he was right. It was easier to project her hurt onto others than to confront it herself. "You don't understand," she finally muttered, more to herself than to Naureus, as she resumed her grooming with a renewed, albeit uneasy, focus.

<No?> Naureus turned away, dropping his head to graze as she continued currying him. <After my rider's betrayal, I could have turned bitter, snapping at other pegasi or lashing out at unsuspecting grooms with my hooves. But I chose not to.>

She frowned. Luci didn't understand how her own wounds and shortcomings were relevant to the betrayal Naureus had endured. She knew it was a horrible situation, how the buckskin's rider had betrayed not only him, but people Raven was supposed to care about. It was nothing like her case, though.

<Think on it,> Naureus offered softly, his tone less a rebuke

than a gentle nudge. <This life is too fleeting, too fragile, to spend it with your ears pinned back at the people you care about.>

A lump formed in Luci's throat, but she nodded, her eyes stinging with unshed tears. She finished grooming Naureus, giving him a final pat before moving on to Emrys. She half-expected Blaise's stallion to chastise her, too. But the black pegasus remained silent, his attention frequently drifting toward Blaise with the sort of fretful concern that reminded Luci of a mother hen fussing over her chicks.

Eventually, Luci made her way back to the fire pit where Blaise had set out their dinner on tin plates. The fire, fueled by her alchemical concoction, flickered against the growing darkness, casting dancing shadows that seemed almost like an audience for the unspoken drama that had unfolded between them.

Halfway through the meal, Luci couldn't stand the stifling silence any longer. "I'm sorry for what I said at lunch. I shouldn't...I shouldn't have said that."

Blaise shrugged, a noncommittal gesture, but didn't meet her eyes. "I've heard worse."

Her brother's soft words gave her pause. Luci swallowed. She'd grown accustomed to seeing Blaise as the town's golden boy, the mage-hero who could do no wrong. It was easy to forget that he'd once been an object of contempt and misunderstanding. "But it was cruel." The words had been a below-the-belt jab, especially considering his fight with Jefferson.

At her admission, Blaise finally looked up, his eyes meeting hers. "You might not be entirely wrong, though."

Sighing, Luci shook her head. "No, I *was* wrong. I wasn't thinking when I said that. I just...lashed out."

Blaise stared into the fire, his expression shifting from sadness to guarded understanding. "I've been trying to figure out why you're so mad at me. I know I wasn't your first choice to bring you to Cheswell."

Swallowing hard, Luci nodded. "You're right, you weren't. But it's not about you, not entirely. Mom made the decision to send you with me, and you couldn't exactly say no to her." She paused, rubbing her cheek as if the action could somehow erase the tension between them. "It's not just that I'm mad at you, Blaise. I'm mad at the world, at how everything seems to be falling apart around me."

Blaise's furrowed brow deepened at her words, as if he were trying to solve a puzzle that kept changing its pieces. "I'm not sure what you're getting at."

Luci let out a weary breath, her eyes momentarily focused on the dancing flames. "Sometimes I'm not sure, either. I think about Dad a lot. About…how unfair it is that he was taken from us like that. Murdered. And I think about everything we've been through."

The apple in Blaise's throat bobbed as he swallowed. "You mean everything you've had to go through because of me."

Oh. A pang of realization hit Luci. She hadn't exactly been thinking along those lines when she'd unleashed her anger earlier. Well, maybe a part of her had blamed Blaise for not being there to protect their father. But Blaise seemed to burden himself with more guilt than just that.

"No, not just because of you," she clarified, shaking her head to dispel the notion. "I mean, sometimes, in my weaker moments, I want to blame you for everything. But then…" Luci winced, hesitating to give voice to her thoughts. The Salt-Iron Confederation had imprisoned and tortured Blaise, subjected him to unspeakable horrors. It felt selfish to dwell on her own grievances when his were so much worse.

Blaise seemed to read the struggle in her eyes. "Our emotions aren't always rational, you know. They don't always line up neatly, like ingredients in a recipe."

She paused, then laughed. Leave it to Blaise to liken this to baking. "Yeah. And that's frustrating for me. As an alchemist, I'm *supposed* to be rational."

Blaise chuckled. "I think people are anything but rational. We act and react based on the strangest and most illogical impulses sometimes."

Luci allowed herself a small smile. "Yeah."

Blaise seemed to relax a fraction, his eyes softening as he regarded her. "Look, Luci, I get that this whole trip is far from ideal. And I'm sorry it's me taking you to Cheswell and not Mom. But I want you to know, no matter what, I'm here for you."

His kindness was almost too much, especially considering the harsh words she'd thrown at him earlier. "Don't you ever get angry?" she blurted out, curiosity getting the better of her. "Like, really, viscerally angry? The sort of angry where you just want to destroy everything in your path?"

His eyebrows shot up, momentarily surprised by her question. "Everyone gets mad."

"You look more like a kicked puppy when I think you should be furious about something," she observed.

Blaise glanced away, as if wrestling with a difficult thought. "Of course, I get mad about things. But I've had to learn how to temper my response." He glanced at his hands, and Luci glimpsed the dancing motes of magic. "There are some things not worth getting mad about. So, when I do get really mad, believe me, it'll be clear."

A shiver of realization ran down Luci's spine. She didn't doubt his words for a moment. "But have you ever?"

Her brother's voice was soft when he answered. "When Jefferson was taken to the Golden Citadel, I was one snap decision away from leveling the place. But people like us, Luci..." Blaise paused, as if gathering his thoughts. "We have to be careful. Our actions have consequences."

"Why include me?" she asked with a frown.

His smile was gentle, reassuring. "Why wouldn't I?"

"Because I'm not...I'm not like you," she stammered, grappling with her sense of inadequacy. She wasn't a mage like Blaise.

"You're an alchemist," Blaise said, his voice earnest. "A gifted one, at that. There's a reason mages, and anyone with common sense, fear alchemists. There's power there. It's meant to be respected." To emphasize his point, he gestured toward the alchemical fire burning in its rocky cradle.

Luci blinked, taken aback. She'd never really considered her own strength in that way. All this time, she'd felt dwarfed by the looming shadows of her mother's genius and Blaise's unique magic.

"Oh," she whispered.

"Anyway, it's normal for you to be nervous about Cheswell," Blaise said, eager to steer the conversation elsewhere. "It's a big change. But you're smart and amazing at alchemy. I know you're going to do great."

His words felt like a soothing balm on her frayed nerves, magnifying her regret over her earlier harsh comments. "Thanks."

He nodded. "You're welcome. Did you bring any alchemical wonders to clean the plates?"

Luci shook her head, almost amused. "No."

His smile widened into a genuine grin. "I cooked, you clean."

Luci sighed, giving him her best eye-roll. But then she smiled, the air between them lighter. Nearby, she heard a snort from Naureus.

<Well done, filly. I knew you had it in you.>

CHAPTER TWELVE

Overtures

Alice

Alice cradled her violin as if it were her own precious child, her fingers tracing its curves as she stepped onto the saloon's rustic stage. She felt the glow of the gas lamps warm her skin, casting a radiant sheen on her cascading coils of lustrous black hair. Her scarlet dress, adorned with an array of sequins, twinkled under the lights like a flickering flame, capturing the attention of everyone in the room.

She settled the violin against her shoulder, its familiar weight a comforting presence. With her bow poised elegantly, she looked over the crowd that had gathered, their applause a mix of genteel clapping and rowdy hoots of approval.

Despite the excitement in the air, her eyes couldn't help but drift beyond the halo of stage lights, scanning the dimly lit corners of the room for one face that had become painfully famil-iar: Malcolm.

Over the past week, he'd been a constant fixture amid the rough-and-tumble patrons of Starvation's most popular watering hole. His carefully groomed visage was a sharp contrast to the sun-worn faces and weathered work clothes that populated the saloon; it seemed out of place.

At first, his persistence was a frustration for Alice. Why wouldn't he just leave? Didn't he understand she was happy to sever ties with everyone from her past? But deep down, she couldn't ignore the curiosity that nibbled at her, wondering at her older brother's persistence. That wasn't something to think about now, though. She wasn't getting paid to daydream on stage.

Her bow sang against the violin strings.

In most performances, her magic fused seamlessly with her music, the two flowing together as naturally as a river's current. But tonight was different. Tonight, Malcolm's watchful eyes seemed to weigh on her, making each note feel like a stone she had to lift.

As her body swayed, pirouetting in time with the soulful strains that magically urged the patrons to part with their coin, Alice felt her concentration splinter.

Malcolm. She refused to let him win. Alice blocked him from her mind, throwing her frustration into the melody.

His presence felt like a storm cloud, overshadowing her other-wise sunny days. Malcolm had become an uninvited guest at each of her performances, hovering in the background like some specter from a life she'd long since left behind. His dogged persis-tence was infuriating, and Alice knew she had to confront him. Otherwise, the itch of his unspoken intentions would persist in the back of her mind.

The next day, the familiar sight of him greeted her once again. He was perched at his now-customary table in the saloon, nursing a glass of amber liquid. Steeling herself, Alice approached him, her heels rapping against the worn wooden floor in a rhythm that matched her racing pulse. As she neared, he turned, his eyes widening in a mix of surprise and anticipation when he recognized her. Malcolm opened his mouth to speak, but Alice held up a hand, silencing him.

"One hour, Malcolm. I'll grant you one hour to speak with me after my performance today. I'll meet you here."

"It's Jefferson," he said, the correction gentle. "And thank you. I look forward to it."

Alice's scowl deepened at the mention of his assumed name. Jefferson. Each syllable dripped with deceit, a lie wrapped in the guise of truth. Oh, he would have to answer for that, but now was not the time for a reckoning. She gave him a curt nod before heading backstage to prepare for her act.

The heaviness of the upcoming confrontation with Jefferson seemed to add literal weight to her violin as Alice warmed up backstage. Her fingers twitched with nervous energy as she fine-tuned the strings. But when the bow met the strings, the music was nothing short of impeccable. The melodies she conjured were her old friends, reliable and comforting. But tonight, the magic was tinged with uncertainty, with the shadow of old wounds waiting to be reopened.

The crowd in the saloon was as raucous as ever, their enthusiasm giving Alice a sense of purpose. If her brother—this stranger who called himself Jefferson—wanted to unearth the skeletons of their history, then she'd face him with all the bravado she could muster. Her footwork grew bolder, more intricate, as she soared across the stage, weaving her magic into the very fabric of the room.

At last, her performance reached its crescendo, the last notes hanging in the air like the echoes of long-forgotten memories. Applause swelled, and Alice bowed gracefully before exiting the stage.

Retreating to her dressing room, Alice let out a shaky breath, caught in the paradox of feeling both invigorated and drained. She carefully placed her violin in its velvet-lined case, fingers caressing the polished wood. The hour she had promised Jefferson was fast approaching, and Alice steeled herself for what lay ahead.

Slipping into a simple cotton dress, she mulled over the questions she wanted to ask Malcolm. Why now? What had taken him so long to reappear in her life? And what did he want from her?

She studied herself in the old mirror hanging on the wall. The woman who stared back was not the same one Malcolm had known. Her eyes were different—more focused and filled with tenacity. She was ready for whatever he had to say.

Taking a deep breath, Alice left her dressing room and walked into the noisy saloon. She felt a small sense of pride as people turned to look, recognizing her from her performance. But tonight, that didn't matter. All that mattered was the man waiting for her at the back of the saloon. She walked through the crowd, making her way to Malcolm, ready to confront her past and get some answers.

As she approached the table, Malcolm caught her eye. His green eyes held a mix of hope and worry, as if he had bet everything on this one meeting. His smile was hesitant. "Alice, you were incredible up there, as always. It seems those years of ballet paid off."

"Thank you." Alice kept her tone neutral. Malcolm wasn't the only one with secrets. All those years ago, when she was supposed to be learning ballet, her instructor had clandestinely taught her Vientoza, a method of dance based on martial arts that hailed from the southern islands. Vientoza paired well with her style of violin performance.

She sat down across from him, her fingers tapping a restless beat on the wooden table. A saloon girl brought over her usual drink and a plate of food without her even asking.

"Let's get straight to the point, Malcolm," she said, fixing him with a steely gaze. She noted the slight wince that crossed his face when she used his birth name. She filed that away for later. "Your hour starts now. Make it worth my time."

Taking a deep breath, he nodded. "Alice, I can't even tell you how sorry I am for not stepping in when our father sold you. I just...I did nothing." He looked away, his eyes falling to the half-finished plate in front of him.

Alice's jaw tightened. "That's only one of your many sins."

"You're right," he said softly, looking back up at her. The sadness in his eyes was genuine, and for a moment, it almost got to her. "But it's the one that haunts me."

***

Jefferson

"THEN TELL ME," ALICE DEMANDED, LEANING IN CLOSER, HER EYES searching his. "Why did you lie to me about who you were and about your supposed death? That's what hurts me the most. That you didn't trust me enough to tell me the truth."

Jefferson looked down at the worn wood of the table, feeling Alice's eyes burrow into him. "I wish I hadn't lied." His thoughts were awash with memories, both sweet and agonizing. "It's complicated. I've lived as both Malcolm Wells and Jefferson Cole, but I couldn't stand who I was as Malcolm."

Alice's expression eased, but her stance remained guarded. "So you hated your own name?"

Meeting her gaze felt like walking a tightrope, but he did it. "It wasn't just the name. It was who I was when I wore it. What our father wanted to turn *me* into." he said, each word heavier than the last. "I would look in the mirror and see a young version of *him*. And every day, it ate at me."

Jefferson looked into Alice's eyes, searching for a flicker of understanding. What he found was a storm of mixed emotions—confusion, hurt, and maybe, just maybe, a sliver of empathy. Could she forgive him enough to let him back into her life?

"That's why I go by Jefferson now," he finally said, breaking the thick silence between them. "I don't want to be a Wells." The irony of it stung. He'd hurt Blaise and others by acting like a Wells, by using power to manipulate, intimidate, and control. He pushed that guilt aside for now—this hour was about him and Alice.

Alice's forehead wrinkled, her eyes clouded with confusion. "I don't get it," she said, her hand gesturing vaguely at his face. "How do you do it? Look so different, I mean."

Jefferson hesitated, then raised his hand, letting the dim light of the saloon play off the scarlet cabochon ring he wore. A sad, almost sheepish smile crossed his face. "When I came of age and got my Fortune of Majority, some of the money went into buying this."

Alice's eyes narrowed as they fixed on the ring, scrutinizing. "Is that magic? A glamor?"

"Exactly," Jefferson confirmed with a nod. "I couldn't go on being who I was. Changing myself was the only way to move forward, to survive."

The words hung heavy in the air. Alice's eyes softened, a glimmer of surprise flickering in her gaze. "I never knew you felt that way," she said, her voice barely above a whisper.

"No, you wouldn't have," Jefferson responded, the regret in his voice palpable. "Because these feelings only came to me after you'd been sold, after you were gone." He looked her squarely in the eyes, though it was hard. "I wouldn't blame you if you can't forgive me. I can't forgive myself."

A renewed silence fell between them as his words faded. Alice's gaze drifted down to the untouched plate of food before her. Jefferson felt every second tick away, each moment slipping through his fingers like grains of sand.

Glancing down, he pulled out his pocket watch. Its gold casing glimmered faintly in the dim light of the saloon. With a subdued click that echoed louder than intended in the quiet that had fallen between them, he closed the watch. "Our hour is up."

Alice looked up, her face a mask, hiding any emotions she might be feeling. She nodded and slowly got to her feet. "I need time to think about all this," she said, her voice measured, cautious. She didn't offer him forgiveness or even the hint of it; all she offered was the possibility that she might consider what he had said.

His heart in his throat, Jefferson asked, "Can we meet again?" He tried to temper the urgency in his voice, but the hope was an undercurrent he couldn't entirely disguise.

Alice paused, her eyes meeting his for a moment that felt like an eternity. Then she shrugged, a simple movement that carried a world of uncertainty. "I don't know, Jefferson. Right now, I just don't know."

As Alice's silhouette disappeared into the throng of saloon patrons, Jefferson's gaze remained on the space she had occupied. Her exit seemed to carve a path through the crowd, as if she were a ship moving through turbulent waters.

When the saloon doors creaked shut behind Alice, sealing her exit, an overwhelming sense of loneliness gripped Jefferson. He wasn't used to this ever-present feeling of being cut off from others. Jefferson swallowed, gaze flicking to the crowd around him. Years ago, he would have sought out entertainments and a willing companion to ease the loneliness. To take his mind off everything that had gone wrong. Jefferson rubbed his wedding ring. He didn't want anyone else, not since he had found Blaise. And other entertainments...well, after his discussion with Alice, nothing enticed him.

Jefferson lifted his chin, as if a change in his posture might stave off the despair that clawed at him. He wouldn't—*couldn't*— let himself be consumed by the darkness that beckoned. Jefferson would do whatever was necessary to earn Alice's forgiveness, to prove he was not the man he'd once been. He would make amends for the years of silence, for the sins of his past.

Nothing stopped Jefferson Cole once he set his mind to something.

CHAPTER THIRTEEN

Cheswell

Blaise

The city of Greylight unfolded before them, its cobblestone streets bustling with carriages and pedestrians. Architectural marvels stretched toward the sky, while the distant mountains provided a majestic backdrop, their peaks piercing the cloudy veils far overhead.

<This is certainly a far cry from Fortitude,> Emrys observed, scanning the towering buildings and the throngs of people. His hide twitched involuntarily, as though unsettled by the city's pulsating energy. <Not sure I like it.>

<Well, you don't have to live here,> Naureus answered, his snort carrying an undercurrent of relief.

Luci eased off Naureus, giving him a thankful pat. "It's a lot to take in, for sure," she admitted, looking up at the towers.

"But at least it's not Izhadell," Blaise whispered as he scratched Emrys behind one ear.

A short time later, they found themselves in front of a boarding stable that had seen better days. Faded paint clung to weathered boards, and rusty hinges squeaked in the wind. It was an odd recommendation from Jack, given the more polished establishments they'd passed.

Blaise looked skeptically at the building, uncomfortable with its ramshackle appearance. "Did Jack really think this is the best place for our pegasi?" he muttered, squinting at the sun-bleached sign swinging lazily in the breeze. The words *Iron Hoof Stables* were barely legible.

<Oh, for many reasons.> Naureus's eyes gleamed, as if he relished the question. <The location is convenient for a quick getaway. Plus, look around. This is not the sort of place where people ask questions.> He cocked his head, his eyes narrowing as they settled on the latch of the nearest stall door. <And these latches...let's just say we'd have no problem with them.>

Blaise blinked, his expression shifting from skepticism to grudging admiration. "You got all that just by looking at the place?" He paused. "And why do we even need all of these safeguards?"

Naureus arched his neck, as if proud of his own acumen. <I have been around long enough to know what to look for. As for why...*you* are an outlaw mage. *We* are pegasi. That is reason enough.>

Blaise pursed his lips. He wanted to argue that he *wasn't* an outlaw mage—right now he was only Luci's brother, dropping her off at her new school. But Naureus was right about the pegasi. If they had reason to exit their stalls, it was reassuring to know they could do so.

Blaise chuckled. "Well, I stand corrected." He glanced over at Luci. "If you stay with our mounts, I'll check in with the stablemaster."

After handing over Emrys's reins to Luci, Blaise stepped into the stable's murky interior, the aroma of hay and manure mixing with old wood. It was a place that had seen years of use and minimal upkeep.

The stablemaster came out, frowning when he saw the pair of stallions.

"Could we—?" Blaise began, but the man cut him off with a raised hand.

"No can do. Come back when they're geldings," the stablemaster grumbled, drawing a snort of indignation from Emrys.

"That's rude." Luci scowled at the man. "What's your problem?"

"Stallions, lady. Boarding them ain't cheap. They're nothing but trouble." The stablemaster gestured dismissively at the pair of disguised pegasi.

Inwardly, Blaise sighed. *If these pegasi were any more well-behaved, they'd be monks.* Jack had warned him that this might be an issue. But there were ways around it.

"So, what's the damage for boarding them?" Blaise folded his arms, hoping to look more assertive than he felt.

The stablemaster paused, assessing Blaise before throwing out a number so high it nearly knocked the wind out of him.

"You're kidding, right?" Luci shot back, incredulous. "That's highway robbery!"

"Best I can do," the stablemaster said with a shrug.

"Ugh, fine," Blaise groaned, annoyed. He reached into his belt pouch and pulled out several golden eagle coins—more than he'd wanted to part with. "Here's half. You'll get the rest when we pick them up."

The stablemaster was agreeable to that. While Blaise made sure the pegasi were settled, Luci swapped her belongings out from the saddlebags and into a valise they had picked up at a shop prior to their stop at the stables. Luci stood there, valise in hand, looking every bit the adult she was becoming, chin lifted, her eyes focused and unyielding.

Noticing her, Blaise couldn't help but smile. His arms loosened a bit, no longer clenched with the tension he'd carried since they arrived at the stables.

"What?" Luci asked, noticing his gaze.

He shook his head, still smiling. "Nothing. Just proud is all. You good to go?"

Luci hesitated for just a moment, swallowed, and then nodded. "Yeah, I'm ready."

Together, they made their way to Cheswell. It wasn't just a building; it was an institution, a complex of structures enclosed by a tall, wrought-iron fence. The fence itself was lined with an astonishing array of roses, their colors a rainbow.

Walking toward the admissions office, Blaise felt a sense of uncertainty creep in. He was out of his element here. His own schooling had been limited, rudimentary at best. In fact, this whole trip left him wondering...what if? What if life had dealt him a different hand? If he'd not been turned into a mage, would he have been an alchemist? Would he have come to a place like this to learn more, to improve his craft?

Or perhaps he would have been drawn to one of the more specialized schools Jefferson had mentioned to him before—schools that focused on arts like baking. Blaise sighed, then shook his head. No sense longing for a life that would never be his.

Luci hesitantly pushed open the door to the admissions office. The room was a study in organized chaos—shelves lined with books, desks cluttered with papers, and the air filled with the aroma of ink and paper. A young man glanced up, his face briefly registering surprise before settling into a distracted expression. "Name?"

Luci's eyebrows knitted together. She looked back at Blaise, seeking a momentary reassurance, before clearing her throat. "Luci Mason."

The young man began flipping through a stack of papers. So many papers and forms that Blaise figured Jefferson, who had a strange fondness for forms, would appreciate it. Momentary confusion crossed the man's face. "I don't see a...oh. You're a Luci with an *i*, not a *y*."

Relief washed over Luci's features, her shoulders dropping as if she'd been holding her breath. "Yes."

Blaise gave her an encouraging smile. He knew she had been apprehensive about the alias their mother insisted on. Marian had good reasons for registering her as Luci Mason instead of Lucienne Hawthorne.

The man handed Luci forms and pointed to a chair where she could sit and fill them out. She moved to do so, and Blaise sat beside her.

"Jefferson would be all over this," he whispered.

Luci gave him a hint of side-eye but let out a genuine giggle. "You're not wrong. But seriously, how many forms does one person need?" She sighed but got down to business.

As Luci focused on her paperwork, the door opened to admit an older man. He had a lanky build, his clothes well-worn yet distinctly scholarly. His thinning black hair seemed to be in retreat, but his eyes were a different story—sharp and attentive, constantly assessing his surroundings. He wore an aura of intellectual gravitas like a second skin, much the same way Jefferson used to wear his own air of authority as a Doyen.

"She's all set, Dean Woodrow," the young man announced, neatly aligning the paperwork on the cluttered desk.

As if he had been waiting for that specific cue, Woodrow advanced. His movements were precise, and his smile had an affable quality that put Blaise at ease, albeit momentarily.

"Ah, welcome to the hallowed halls of Cheswell," Woodrow greeted them with a peculiar but seemingly genuine enthusiasm. His hand extended first to Luci and then to Blaise.

Blaise stared at the man's outstretched hand, a flash of discomfort crossing his features. His aversion to touch reared up, but he suppressed it for Luci's sake and shook Woodrow's hand. The professor appeared too engrossed in Luci to notice Blaise's brief hesitation.

"You've missed the group tour, but how about a private one led by yours truly?" Woodrow asked, chuckling as if he found the offer endlessly amusing.

Luci and Blaise exchanged glances. He could see the apprehension in her eyes. It mirrored his own feelings—wanting to make sure this place was right for her.

Luci nodded. "This is all new to me, so a tour would be great."

Dean Woodrow picked up a paper from the cluttered desk, giving it a cursory glance before setting it back down. "Ah, I see. From a small town, correct? Asylum—located in the Gutter, if I'm not mistaken? We rarely get alchemists from such...unique locales."

"Yes," Luci said, her voice steady, but Blaise noticed her eyes flicker, uncomfortable with the falsehood. He felt a knot tighten in his gut, hoping the conversation wouldn't dig deeper into dangerous territory.

"Hmm, intriguing." Woodrow shrugged, his tone still affable but edged with an almost imperceptible curiosity. "You must have quite a story to share. Well then, shall we begin our little excursion?"

As they followed Dean Woodrow through Cheswell's stately halls, Blaise found himself captivated by the grandeur of the university. Stone walls stood as silent witnesses to years of scholarly pursuit, their surfaces etched with intricate carvings that seemed to tell tales from ages past. He glanced at Luci, who appeared equally spellbound, her eyes wide as saucers. Blaise couldn't hide a smile at her expression.

"Isn't this incredible?" Blaise whispered, and she nodded, still drinking in the surroundings.

Woodrow spoke, his tone infused with unmistakable pride. "You see, here at Cheswell, our College of Alchemy is, shall we say, the crown jewel. And I have the distinct honor of serving as its

Dean." He gestured grandly, as if unveiling the history and unspoken wisdom contained within the very walls. "Since the unfortunate, rather tragic collapse of the Arboretum in Phinora, we have ascended as the premier alchemical institution on the continent."

Blaise coughed at the mention of the Arboretum, and Dean Woodrow turned to glance at him. "Um, something in my throat." Blaise coughed again, trying and failing not to think about the Arboretum. The place where their mother had been held after Blaise's capture. The same place Kittie Dewitt turned to ash.

"That's the Cheswell air—ideal for preserving rare manuscripts, but a bit of a character test for the unacclimated, wouldn't you agree?" Woodrow remarked with a wink, though the gesture was more pedantic than cheeky.

Blaise nodded, glad for the cover.

Dean Woodrow paused for a beat, his grin widening. "Ah, but before we proceed, allow me a moment to draw your attention to another of our crowning achievements. Our College of Biology has been making quite the strides, particularly in equine sciences. They've been striving—most successfully, I might add—to improve equine bloodlines, rendering them stronger, swifter, and requiring less sustenance or rest." He leaned in closer to them, eyebrows raised. "And here's the particularly riveting detail: our College of Alchemy, housed in the esteemed Rickson Building just across this plaza, has been lending a rather—how shall I say?— *arcane* hand in this endeavor. Fusion of the natural and the alchemical, if you will. Quite fascinating, don't you think?"

Blaise's stomach twisted. For a moment, he was rooted into place, sickened by the repugnant idea of experimenting on living creatures. He had been an experiment, and it wasn't a fate he wished on anyone else.

"You could call it that," Blaise agreed weakly. Was this going to be Luci's future?

Dean Woodrow led the way toward a grand courtyard

surrounded by buildings representing an array of architectural influences. "To your left—" He gestured. "—is the College of Engineering, the vanguard of innovation. Our advances in steam technology are, dare I say, *steamrolling* the competition."

Blaise nodded, pretending to be impressed as he took calming breaths. He kept an eye on Luci, relieved that she was paying rapt attention.

Woodrow then extended his arm, pointing gracefully toward a venerable-looking building draped with ivy. "And here, the lodgings that await you. A place steeped in tradition, yet ever so welcoming of the future."

Blaise noticed Luci's eyes dart between excitement and apprehension, like fireflies caught in a dance. "You're going to do amazing things here," he whispered to her, the words tinged with bittersweet emotion.

"Thanks, Blaise," Luci murmured back, her eyes fixed on the building as if trying to read its stones for clues about her future.

Upon entering the building, Woodrow exchanged a few words with a young woman who appeared in her early twenties. "Allow me to introduce Misty, the resident advisor of this building," Dean Woodrow said, turning back to Luci. "Misty, meet Luci Mason."

Misty's eyes narrowed ever so slightly at the mention of Luci's name, her lips pursing in an apparent moment of calculation. Then her face broke into a welcoming smile. "Oh, Luci, it's wonderful to have another woman in the alchemy department. We're a bit sparse, gender-wise."

Dean Woodrow, who had been standing a few steps back, shifted his gaze to Blaise. His keen eyes seemed to size him up, as if reassessing a formula in his mind. Then, with a small smile and awkward wave, he turned and left, his departure almost as unassuming as his presence.

Luci shrugged. "I grew up the only girl among brothers. Being outnumbered isn't new to me."

Misty nodded, turning to look at Blaise. She tilted her head, as if he were a puzzle. "I see. Well, our floor is girls only. I can help you get settled, as long as that's okay with..."

"Blaise," Luci interjected before her brother could even open his mouth. He felt a twinge of annoyance; he would've preferred to remain anonymous. But he gave Luci a slight nod, appreciating that she at least spared him the ordeal of mentioning a last name —real or otherwise.

"Blaise." Misty elongated the name as if tasting it, then cleared her throat, jolting the atmosphere. "I assume you'll be all right if I take Luci to her room alone?"

He looked at Luci, their eyes meeting in silent agreement. "Go ahead."

"Fantastic," Misty said, her gaze lingering on Blaise as if trying to read an unopened book. Then, she shifted her focus to Luci. "Let's collect your belongings and get you settled in."

"I'd like that," Luci responded, her smile hesitant but genuine.

The air was laden with a mixture of awkwardness and emotion. Blaise hated goodbyes. "Take care of yourself," he whispered, wanting to say so much more. But he was never good at giving voice to the things he felt. "You're going to do amazing things."

Luci's eyes met his, shining with the sheen of tears she was fighting back. "Thank you, Blaise. For everything you've done."

Blaise swallowed a lump in his throat. He watched her retreating figure. A sensation of loneliness swept over him. Blaise shook it off, turning to head out of the building.

His role as escort was complete. It was good to see Luci stretching her own wings, or so he tried to tell himself. At Cheswell, she could come into her own, no longer in the long shadow cast by her mother or brother. It was for the best.

But that didn't make *goodbye* any easier.

CHAPTER FOURTEEN

Villain

Jefferson

Jefferson scrutinized his reflection in the mirror, his hands nervously adjusting the puff tie at his neck. "Too formal for a saloon?" he asked himself.

In his former political life, second-guessing one's attire was akin to questioning one's party allegiance. But tonight was different. He knew acutely that any small thing he did—or didn't do—might impact his chances with Alice.

His fellow saloon-goers usually sported worn leather and frayed fabrics, a far cry from his tailored coats and polished shoes. "I can't very well show up looking like I've just crawled out of the Untamed Territory," he reasoned, smoothing the lapels of his jacket. "This is fine. I'm fine," he muttered, as if trying to convince the reflection staring back at him. Jefferson shut his eyes. Like everything in his life, it was a lie. He wasn't fine. Jefferson huffed out a breath, calling on his resolve. "But I'll make it fine. I must." And the sooner he did, the sooner he could try to fix things with Blaise.

An unexpected knock on the door ricocheted through the room, jolting him from his thoughts. "Curious," he muttered, a crease forming between his brows. He wasn't expecting any callers, and without Flora or Blaise by his side, he felt unusually exposed. "Who's there?" he inquired cautiously, his voice betraying a hint of trepidation.

The voice that filtered through the wooden door made his breath hitch. "It's me," Alice announced.

The moment he swung the door open, Jefferson's eyes met Alice's. She stood there, a formidable figure in the dimly lit hallway, arms crossed, her expression unreadable. Lurking behind her was a small boy, half-hidden, as if taking refuge in her shadow. A skinny arm and a crescent of a curious face peeked out from behind her, clearly trying to assess the stranger before him.

"Alice," Jefferson whispered, hardly believing it. She was here. She had come to him. Flustered, he stumbled over his next words. "Hello. Ah, what can I do for you? Would you like to come in?" He felt as if he had lost all sense of how to function around others, his brain afire with the triumphant thought that Alice had come to him.

Alice studied him, her expression taut. "No, I don't have time for that. My landlady, who usually watches Theo, is sick. I have no one else to turn to." She hesitated, the words seeming to catch in her throat. "Could you watch him tonight? You won't be able to come to my performance, but—"

Jefferson didn't need to hear the rest. His heart swelled at the opportunity—a real, tangible chance to make things right, to rebuild the bridge he'd burned. "Absolutely," he rushed to say. "I'd be honored to help."

A flicker of relief washed over Alice's face, though she quickly masked it. "Thank you," she said, her eyes briefly avoiding his before locking on again. "Well, Theo, come here." She stepped aside, fully revealing the young boy.

Theo shuffled forward, his big, brown eyes peering up at Jefferson, curious but cautious.

Alice crouched down to Theo's level. "Theo, this is your Uncle Jefferson. Remember I told you about him? Be good for him, okay?"

Theo held Jefferson's gaze, his eyes wide and full of questions. Then, taking a tentative step forward, he extended his small hand. "Okay, Mama. Hi, Uncle Jefferson."

Jefferson smiled as he shook Theo's hand, careful to match the boy's soft grip. "Hello, Theo." The contact, brief as it was, filled a void he hadn't realized was gaping inside him. "You're quite the young gentleman, aren't you?" The boy was on the petite side for his age, but Jefferson's compliment still elicited an ear-to-ear grin.

"I'm six!" Theo declared, his chest puffing out with pride. Then his eyes brightened. "I found a shiny rock by the creek the other day. It's smooth and feels lucky. Do you want to see it?"

Unprepared for the barrage of juvenile excitement, Jefferson's brows nearly brushed his hair in surprise. But he quickly recovered—he had experienced such conversations with Blaise's excitable brother before. "I would certainly love to see your lucky rock. Perhaps after I finish speaking with your mother."

Alice's lips pursed, as if she hadn't expected his response. "Theo, Uncle Jefferson knows when my show ends. He'll bring you to me at the saloon afterward, okay?" She threw a confirming glance Jefferson's way, and he nodded, silently vowing to himself to uphold her trust. "Have a good time. I'll see you both later." Straightening her posture, Alice cast a wistful look at her son before turning to leave.

As Alice's footsteps retreated, Jefferson turned his attention back to Theo. "So, young man, looks like it's just you and me. Any ideas on how we can make this a fun evening?" His mind raced through memories of time spent with Brody, trying to recall what activities had captured the boy's imagination. His room was devoid of toys—unless Theo fancied a game of dress-up with an assortment of fine clothing.

Theo glanced over his shoulder, likely checking that his mother was truly gone, before shrugging. "I dunno. You pick."

Drat. "How about a little adventure? Would you like to go for a walk?" Jefferson suggested.

Theo's eyes sparkled, his enthusiasm reborn. "Yeah! Can we?"

"Absolutely. Let's go!" Jefferson extended his hand, and Theo eagerly latched onto it. The two of them stepped out of the hotel room, the door clicking shut behind them. As they walked down the hallway, Jefferson felt a surprising buoyancy. The child's uninhibited joy was like a salve on a wound, filling him with the optimism he'd been missing since Alice had confronted him about his past.

As they meandered through the streets, taking in the sights and sounds of the bustling town, Theo ambled beside Jefferson, sometimes hopping along on one foot. Then, the boy suddenly stopped. He tugged at Jefferson's hand, a reminder sparking in his bright eyes.

"Uncle Jefferson, wait! I gotta show you something." Theo reached into his pocket with the eagerness of a child who had a treasured secret to share.

Curious, Jefferson stopped and crouched to Theo's level as the boy pulled out a small, smooth rock, its surface catching the light of the setting sun. "This is the lucky rock I found by the creek. It's really shiny, see?"

Jefferson took the rock, turning it over in his hand, admiring its sheen. "It's a very special rock. You have a great eye for finding treasures," he replied, handing it back with a smile.

Through the thick aromas of cooking meats and freshly baked bread, Jefferson caught a whiff of something sweeter. Honey-roasted nuts, if he had to guess. A vendor selling small paper bags of the treats stood beside a stall, and moments later, Jefferson had purchased one for Theo.

As he munched, Theo glanced up at Jefferson. "Um, I didn't know I had an Uncle Jefferson," he finally ventured. "Mama only talked 'bout Uncle Malcolm."

"Is that so?" Jefferson managed, maintaining an air of casual interest while his heart tightened. "What did she say about him?"

Theo scrunched his face in thought for a moment before answering, "She said he's a bad man. A really bad man."

The blunt honesty of a child's perspective landed like a blow to Jefferson's core. He had reconciled with the idea that his past actions as Malcolm were reprehensible, but hearing it from Theo —so young, so untarnished by life's complexities—felt like a new kind of condemnation.

Perhaps picking up on the hurt on his face, Theo frowned at him. "Why? Do you know Uncle Malcolm? Is he..." The child's face contorted as he tried to untangle the family tree. "Is he your uncle, too?"

Despite the ache in his heart, Jefferson couldn't help but chuckle at the boy's endearing attempt to navigate the maze of family relations. "No, Theo. He's not my uncle. But I do know him very well." He paused, swallowing the lump in his throat. The next words were difficult, and he weighed their impact carefully before deciding that Theo had a right to know. "You see, I am your Uncle Malcolm."

Theo's eyes widened in surprise, and he stopped walking to fully process the information. "But Mama said you were Uncle Jefferson."

"Correct," Jefferson replied, lowering himself onto one knee so he could look into Theo's eyes. It was a humble pose, one that begged forgiveness—or at least understanding—from a six-year-old. "These days, I go by Jefferson. But your mother wasn't wrong. I was, and still am, Malcolm. I'm her brother and your uncle."

"Really?" Theo's face scrunched in curiosity. "Why'd you change your name?"

Jefferson hesitated for a moment, searching for the right words to explain his dual personas to the young boy. He doubted Alice would have told Theo about the monster their father was.

"Well, Theo, people make mistakes sometimes, and those mistakes can stick to them like mud on boots. Changing my name was like scraping off that mud so I could walk easier; be a better man."

Theo tilted his head, his small features pulling into an expression of deep contemplation—an uncanny mimicry of Alice when she was pondering something complex. Then he nodded. "Everyone makes mistakes, Uncle Jefferson. I spilled milk everywhere yesterday, and Mama said it's okay 'cause accidents happen."

Jefferson couldn't help but smile at Theo's innocence. If only his life were as simple to rectify as a glass of spilled milk. "You're absolutely right, Theo. We all make mistakes. But some mistakes are like...dropping a delicate vase. They're harder to put back together."

Theo's face turned serious, a sudden shift from his youthful cheerfulness. "Uncle Jefferson, Mama told me I should hate you," he said, his gaze piercing. "But I don't think I want to."

The revelation took Jefferson aback, but he didn't let his surprise show. "It's all right if you don't want to hate me. I don't want you to hate me either," he said gently. "But I need you to understand that I've made some choices in the past that hurt your mother, and she has every right to feel the way she does."

"Okay," Theo said, nodding solemnly. "But you're working on becoming a good guy now, right?"

"Absolutely," Jefferson assured him.

"Then maybe Mama will see you're not a villain," Theo suggested hopefully.

Villain. The word hung there, both an apt observation and an accusation. He wanted to deny it, but it wasn't wrong. Jefferson had always wanted to play the role of the hero in his own personal story. It was a tough pill to swallow, this knowledge that someone he loved considered him to be the very opposite.

"I hope so," Jefferson said, though now doubt clung to him. What he needed was a change of scenery, a distraction. An idea came to him. "Say, Theo, would you like to visit my..." Oh gods, he hoped Seledora wasn't monitoring him at the moment. "Horse?"

"Really? You have a horse?" Theo's eyes lit up with excitement.

"Indeed, I do," Jefferson said, his spirits buoyed by Theo's infectious enthusiasm. He extended his hand, an unspoken invitation for a new beginning. Theo grabbed it without a second thought, his small fingers enveloping Jefferson's in a grip filled with implicit trust.

Together, they headed toward the stables, though Theo quickly found a new game and abandoned Jefferson's hand. He hopped over the lines between the wooden boards on the boardwalk, turning the simple act of walking into a game.

"You can't step on the cracks, Uncle Jefferson! They're lava!" Theo declared.

"Lava?" Jefferson repeated. This was not a game he was familiar with.

"Yes, lava." Theo straddled the boardwalk, careful not to touch any of the lava cracks. "The ground is lava, and if you touch it..." He spread his hands and wiggled his fingers, which Jefferson supposed was Theo's way of communicating an explosion and imminent death.

"Then it's unfortunate I left my lava-proof boots at home." Jefferson stepped carefully over the cracks to avoid the imaginary lava, earning a wave of giggles from Theo.

"There's no such thing!" Theo crowed.

I wouldn't be so sure. Jefferson idly touched his enchanted cabochon ring. "So, we've reached the stables." He stopped on the end of the boardwalk, contemplative. "But it seems that there's a lake of lava that will prevent us from reaching our destination."

Theo cocked his head, thinking. "The lava is gone. It's ice now. So thick we can walk on it."

Jefferson chuckled. Oh, to be a child and conquer adversity with such ease. "Excellent. How fortunate that things have worked in our favor."

As they entered the stable, the muffled sounds of hooves shuffling and the contented snorts of horses filled the air. Navigating the narrow aisles between the stalls, he felt Theo's grip tighten, his eyes widening as they settled on the inhabitants.

Finally, they reached Seledora's stall. The mare's silvery-grey coat glimmered in the muted light filtering through the wooden slats like the sheen of a moonbeam made flesh. She pricked her ears in their direction, taking a single step closer to her stall door.

"Seledora, this is my nephew, Theo," Jefferson introduced them, recalling that Seledora had a soft spot for children. Seledora leaned down, her nostrils flaring as she gave Theo a soft, investigative snuffle.

"Dora is so pretty! Can I give her candy?" Theo held up the crumpled paper sack of candy.

Jefferson chuckled. "Yes, you may. She's quite fond of treats."

<I'll forgive him for mangling my name since he's small and has sweets,> the mare said, extending her velvety lips to pluck a piece of candy from Theo's palm. With a contented crunch, she returned the favor by nuzzling his tousled hair.

Theo patted her nose. "I like horses. But I really love dogs. Do you have any dogs, Uncle Jefferson?"

<Horses?> Seledora glanced at Jefferson. She snorted. <Well, I suppose we are supposed to keep a low profile. We don't need a child running around yelling about pegasi.>

Smiling at Seledora's mental commentary, Jefferson turned to

Theo. "I had a dog many years ago, but not anymore. However, I do have chickens back at home." He hoped Mother Clucker and their other recent additions were doing well. Reuben had promised to take care of them.

"The butcher's dog had puppies last week," Theo said, wiping his hands on his trousers.

"Puppies, you say?" Jefferson mused, his eyes lighting up at the prospect of more family outings for Theo. "Well, that does sound like an adventure waiting to happen."

Theo grinned, rubbing his small hands together to erase any remaining stickiness from the candy. "They're all fluffy and cute. Mama said when they're older, I can play with them!"

The mention of Alice jarred Jefferson back to their original purpose. He discreetly slid his pocket watch from its vest pocket, popping open its ornate cover. The delicate hands showed it was nearly time for Alice's performance to conclude.

"That will be a lot of fun, I'm sure. But for now, we should head to the saloon. Your mother will finish her show soon," Jefferson said with great reluctance.

"Okay!" Theo chirped, his enthusiasm undiminished. He gave Seledora a final, affectionate pat. "Bye-bye, Dora!"

As they emerged from the comforting embrace of the stable, the world outside seemed to snap back into focus. Wagons rumbled by, their wooden wheels churning up dust, while riders on horseback maneuvered deftly through the crowds.

Positioning themselves outside the saloon, Jefferson stood by while Theo crouched to draw in the dirt with a finger. *My nephew is so cute. I hope we get to spend more time together.*

Finally, the saloon doors swung open and out stepped Alice. Her eyes, always so full of guarded emotion, met Jefferson's. She pursed her lips, but her expression shifted to pleasure when she saw Theo.

"Hi, Mama!" Theo exclaimed, his face lighting up like the first star of the evening. He dashed to her side, bubbling over with excitement. "Guess what? I got to eat candy and pet a horse today!"

Caught in the moment, Jefferson's eyes flicked to Alice, half expecting her to react negatively to the candy. *Sugar before bedtime. Excellent choice, Jefferson.* He braced for potential maternal disapproval.

However, Alice's lips curled into what could almost pass for a smile, softening the typically reserved lines of her face. "Well, it sounds like you two had a good time," she said. Her voice was infused with a rare gentleness, directed more toward her son but including Jefferson in its warmth.

"Of course, it was my pleasure," Jefferson replied, allowing a hopeful smile to blossom on his face. "If you ever need me to watch Theo again, please don't hesitate to ask."

Alice looked at him, her eyes meeting his for a moment that felt like an eternity. "Thank you," she finally said, and Jefferson sensed a thawing in her icy demeanor, a glimmer of spring-like warmth that seemed to hint at the possibility of forgiveness, or at least a tentative truce.

"Bye, Uncle Jefferson!" Theo called, one small hand waving in the air as he clung to his mother's hand with the other. The innocence and affection radiating from the child struck Jefferson, serving as both a balm for his fractured soul and a reminder of why he needed to mend his family ties.

"Goodbye, Theo. I look forward to our next adventure," Jefferson called back, his hand raised in a reciprocal wave. He remained rooted to the spot, watching as Alice and Theo retreated down the dusty road.

As they disappeared around a corner, Jefferson smiled. "Progress," he whispered to himself. Then, in a gesture of hard-won triumph, he pulled his arm back, elbow bent, before thrusting it upwards in a victorious arc. "I've made progress today!" He punctuated his joy, striking at the air with his fist as if he could physically grasp the elusive hope he'd been chasing.

Alice

THE NEXT AFTERNOON, ALICE STOOD OUTSIDE THE SALOON, HER hand raised to her forehead to shield her eyes against the sun's unforgiving glare. At her feet, Theo was engrossed in his own world, crouched in the dirt and using a stick to etch drawings of animals. Then, through the bustling crowd and whirl of dust, she spotted Jefferson. Dressed in an outfit clearly too refined for a saloon, he sauntered across the street toward her, the embodiment of his relentless pursuit to win her forgiveness.

"Mal—Jefferson!" she hollered, her voice cutting through the noise of the busy street. As the words left her lips, she gritted her teeth, annoyed at her own slip-up. Since their last meeting, she had given considerable thought to his decision to change his name, and begrudgingly, she'd reconsidered her earlier judgment of him. Maybe, just maybe, he wasn't the spitting image of their despicable father.

At the sound of her voice, Jefferson halted and pivoted, his eyes meeting hers. The corners of his mouth lifted in a pleased grin, a hint of triumph lighting up his face. Jefferson glanced down at Theo, then focused on Alice once more. "Good evening, Alice."

Theo's ears perked up at the sound of Jefferson's voice. Dropping his stick, he sprang to his feet and dashed over to Jefferson, wrapping his small arms around his uncle's waist in an exuberant hug. "Uncle Malerson!" he declared, his face beaming with innocent delight.

"Uncle what?" Jefferson looked genuinely puzzled, his eyes flicking up to meet Alice's, as if searching for an explanation.

Theo peered up at them. "It's like a sandwich of you! Uncle Malcolm on one side, Uncle Jefferson on the other." He clapped his hands together for emphasis, a triumphant smile on his face. "Smashed together, you're Uncle Malerson!"

Jefferson chuckled, a hearty sound that seemed to resonate through the air. "Well, that's certainly an imaginative take," he said. "And I must say, I don't mind the new moniker at all."

Alice felt her muscles loosen, a subtle sense of relief washing over her as she observed Theo's easy rapport with Jefferson. It made the favor she was about to ask less of a burden, at least emotionally. "Listen, I need a favor. I'm still without someone to watch Theo tonight."

Jefferson shifted his focus from Theo back to her. "Of course, consider it done. I'd be more than happy to watch him."

His immediate agreement struck her as strangely uncharacteristic. The Malcolm she remembered would have disdained being asked to watch a child, especially when the allure of other entertainments beckoned. The discrepancy bothered her. Could she actually trust this new version of her brother? Years of betrayal and deceit had erected walls between them, and old habits of suspicion were hard to shake. She shook her head, as if physically dispelling her doubts. Dwelling on it would only result in a deadlock, and right now, she needed a solution for Theo.

"Thank you," Alice managed, her words laced with a begrudging appreciation. "My boarding house serves a communal dinner, so you and Theo won't go hungry. It's located at—"

"I already know where it is," Jefferson interrupted, dismissing her concern with a casual wave of his hand. "You have a performance to prepare for. Don't worry. Theo and I will manage just fine."

He bent down to take Theo's eager hand in his own, and the two of them turned to stroll back up the dusty street. Alice watched them recede into the distance, her fists balling at her sides as a cold, simmering anger replaced her previous relief. He had found her, tracked her down to the very place she called home. For a man so keen on turning over a new leaf, her brother still had a knack for cutting too close to her well-guarded boundaries.

Alice shook her head, wrestling with her thoughts. Was he truly at fault for wanting to find her? He had traveled a considerable distance to reconnect. Perhaps if the roles were reversed, she would've done the same.

With a resigned sigh, she pivoted on her heel and retreated into the familiar embrace of the saloon.

Alice slipped backstage, her practiced hands deftly arranging her performance attire and tuning her cherished violin. The stage manager knocked on her door to let her know it was time, and Alice stepped out, violin in hand.

The moment her heels touched the stage, a hush fell over the room, as though the air itself held its breath in anticipation. This was her chance to shine, to captivate them all with the raw intensity of her music.

And then she was transformed. Her body became an extension of her violin, swaying gently yet passionately, like a lone wildflower dancing to the whims of the wind. Each sweep of her bow unleashed a torrent of notes, a tempestuous melody that seemed to embody the untamed spirit of the frontier itself—the breathtaking vistas, the lurking dangers, the ceaseless allure that beckoned the bold and the reckless alike.

The crowd was utterly enthralled, their eyes and souls riveted on Alice as she funneled every drop of her emotion, her history, her very essence into each note that sprang from her strings. The melody ascended, its harmonious strains fusing seamlessly with the hopes, dreams, and fears of every soul in that room.

When the last note finally faded, the room erupted into a rumble of cheers and applause. Alice lowered her bow, her chest heaving with exertion, a rare smile gracing her lips as she basked in their admiration. She lifted a hand, accepting their applause, then gracefully slipped backstage.

Bruce, their bouncer, ambled over to her. In his meaty hands, he held a bouquet of red roses, gripping the stems as if they were a weapon rather than a romantic gesture. "Someone left these for you. Said they're an admirer."

"An admirer?" Alice echoed, her eyes widening as they fell upon the vibrant crimson petals. Roses were an uncommon luxury in these harsh lands, an exotic beauty out of place in the rugged terrain of the Untamed Territory. Someone must have gone to great effort to procure them for her.

"That's what they said," Bruce confirmed with a shrug. "You want 'em, or should I feed 'em to my mule? She's got a taste for flowers."

The thought of such rare blooms becoming mule fodder made Alice wince. "No, I'll take them," she said, her fingers gingerly grasping the bouquet. Retreating to her dressing room, she changed out of her performance attire, her mind awhirl with questions.

As she exited the saloon, her senses sharpened, catching sight of unfamiliar faces among the crowd, newcomers who watched her just a beat too long. It was an uncomfortable sensation, like the prickle of a chill wind on her nape. She brushed the feeling aside, attributing it to the inevitable attention her performance usually garnered. However, her thoughts kept drifting back to the bouquet cradled in her arms, its captivating beauty.

The entry to the boarding house was empty, though that wasn't unusual in the evening. Most of the other women were likely out, entertaining or already ensconced in the privacy of their rooms. What caught her attention, though, was an unex-pected aroma wafting through the air—a warm, rich sweetness that would be more at home in a bakery.

Alice stepped into her room, her eyes widening in pleasant surprise at the cozy scene before her. Jefferson and Theo sat cross-legged on the worn floorboards, engrossed in an intricate battle of tin soldiers that seemed to span some imaginary frontier.

But what truly caught her attention was the cake perched on

the side table, its surface slathered with a layer of decadent, fluffy brown frosting that looked sinfully delicious.

"Mama, look, look!" Theo exclaimed, jumping up and rushing over to show her his creation. "Uncle Malerson helped me make it!"

"Is that so?" Alice arched an eyebrow, her gaze shifting to Jefferson, who returned her look with a self-satisfied grin. She couldn't help but smile at his unexpected domestic side. "How did you manage that?"

"Oh, we just whipped it up in the shared kitchen. The oven was still hot from the pot pies from dinner." Jefferson shrugged, as if it were a simple matter.

"Can we stay up a little longer to eat some with you, Mama? Pleeease?" Theo begged, his eyes pleading as well. Alice hesitated, torn between indulging him and enforcing his usual bedtime.

After a moment of internal debate, she decided. "All right," she conceded, "but only for our cake feast. Then it's straight to bed for you, mister."

"Deal!" Theo cheered. "I'll set the table!" With the energy only a child could muster, he darted to their modest sideboard and began assembling a trio of plates and mismatched forks.

Alice watched him, her heart catching in her throat as he handled the delicate porcelain. The plates were already a patch-work of minor cracks and chips, relics that endured daily life.

To distract herself from the precarious dance of dishware, she turned her attention to her unexpected bouquet. Locating a vase —more of a jar, really—she filled it with water and arranged the roses, their deep crimson hue offering a vivid contrast to the simple room. Their beauty was an enigma, much like the man who had helped her son bake a cake, and Alice pondered the unfolding complexities of her life as she inserted the last rose into the makeshift vase.

"Those are quite lovely," Jefferson remarked, glancing at the bouquet of roses as he deftly maneuvered a knife through the cake, carving out generous slices. "I didn't know there were roses like that in this part of the Untamed Territory."

"I didn't think there were," Alice admitted. "An admirer gave them to me after my performance." With the floral arrangement settled, Alice took her seat at the modest wooden table as Theo settled into his own chair. "You two really baked this cake?"

"We sure did, Mama!" Theo crowed, bouncing in his seat.

"I learned from the best," Jefferson chimed in, extending a plate toward Alice. The slice of chocolate cake it held seemed to promise a sort of culinary paradise.

"And who might that be?" Alice asked, her curiosity piqued.

"My husband," Jefferson replied matter-of-factly.

Alice blinked, caught off guard. Husband? Her gaze settled on Jefferson's hands, noticing for the first time a simple gold band nestled alongside that ostentatious cabochon ring. A flood of questions swelled within her. "I didn't..." She paused, her mind racing as she tried to reconcile the idea of the brother she had known settling down to marry anyone aside from Cinna Smithstone. Even then, she hadn't imagined he would stay true to Cinna. "I wasn't aware you were married."

"Blaise Hawthorne." Jefferson's voice was soft, almost reverent. Filled with an edge of affection that added another layer to her ever-complicated perception of her brother. "It was rather recent, and we didn't make much of a fuss about it."

Alice raised her eyebrows, intrigued. This was a far cry from the Malcolm she'd grown up knowing—the one who reveled in grandiose events, who basked in the limelight and courted attention like a butterfly. For a moment, she toyed with the notion that this man could not possibly be her brother. Yet deep down, a kernel of recognition told her he was, albeit evolved in some unfathomable way.

"Congratulations are in order, then," she finally said, piercing a forkful of cake and bringing it to her lips.

"Thank you," Jefferson responded, the simple words tinged

with a subtle undercurrent of melancholy. He, too, broke into his slice, savoring a mouthful.

Alice's taste buds came alive at the first bite. The cake was decadently moist, the frosting rich. Across the table, Theo was already halfway through his slice, a smudge of chocolate merrily adorning his face. As she indulged in another bite, Alice couldn't help but observe how seamlessly Jefferson had integrated into this scene of domesticity. Gone was the stiffness that usually accompanied his formal attire, replaced by genuine ease as he relished each bite of cake.

"Your husband must be quite the baker if he taught you to make something this delicious," Alice commented, her fork pausing mid-air as she savored the flavors dancing on her tongue.

"Indeed, he is." Jefferson nodded. "But I have to give credit to Theo here, too. He was an invaluable assistant." He shot a playful wink toward Theo, who practically glowed with pride and delight.

"Really?" Alice swiveled her gaze toward Theo. "You're becoming quite the little chef, aren't you?"

"Yep!" Theo grinned. "Maybe I'll grow up to be a famous baker or something!"

As they laughed and talked, Alice enjoyed the moment. It was a rare feeling of warmth and companionship, one that she hadn't experienced in far too long. She took another sumptuous bite of the cake, its flavors cascading over her taste buds like a chocolate waterfall. Her gaze wandered to the crimson roses on the table, their petals now unfurled in full bloom, their scent intermingling with the rich, chocolaty aroma that pervaded the room.

Yet, even as she lost herself in this fleeting moment of familial bliss, a niggling sense of unease tugged at her consciousness. Something about those roses felt...off. But what could be amiss with a bouquet?

Shaking off the irrational thought, she cleared her throat, steering the conversation back to the topic that had momentarily been shelved. "So, your husband, Blaise. He didn't accompany you on this journey?"

A shadow crossed Jefferson's face, a momentary flicker of pain that seemed to dull the luster in his eyes. He put down his fork, its metal tines clinking against the porcelain plate. He picked up his glass of water and took a deliberate sip, as if buying time to marshal his thoughts. When he finally spoke, his eyes were downcast. "No. He..." Jefferson grimaced. "This mess between you and me...it was better if I came alone, I thought."

There was an undercurrent of emotion, a hidden layer in Jefferson's words that Alice couldn't quite put her finger on. But before she could probe further, his face crumbled into an expression of such raw vulnerability that she couldn't bring herself to root it out. "I see. I—"

Without warning, Theo's head slumped forward, almost sending his empty plate crashing to the floor.

"Theo!" Alice's heart catapulted into her throat, her pulse pounding like a drumbeat of dread in her ears. She attempted to push her chair back, but suddenly, it felt like her limbs were rebelling. Her body was so uncoordinated it was as if every muscle had fallen asleep at once. She braced her arms against the table, her knuckles turning white as she fought to maintain her balance.

Jefferson's face twisted into a visage of fear, his eyes widening as the gravity of the situation hit him. "I'll fetch help—a Healer!" He lunged out of his chair, his movements jagged and erratic, like a marionette dancing on broken strings. He wobbled dangerously, his legs betraying him as he stumbled, barely catching himself before he fell.

A deafening roar filled Alice's ears, drowning out all other sounds as if she were submerged in a raging river. Her vision blurred, dark splotches dancing before her eyes like malevolent spirits. This couldn't be happening; it simply couldn't. With a surge of desperation, she attempted to will her body into action, to break free from this nightmarish spell that had ensnared them.

But she couldn't.

Alice slumped forward, her cheek coming to rest against the cool, unforgiving wood of the table. The last fragment of her awareness registered Jefferson collapsing to his knees before he, too, crumpled to the floor, his form blurring into the encroaching darkness that swallowed her whole.

CHAPTER FIFTEEN

Silly, Pompous Human

Seledora

Seledora sprawled in her stall, breathing out a long sigh of utter contentment. The comforting earthy aromas of fresh straw and the moist soil below mingled in the air, soothing her like a balm.

While Seledora relished the tranquility of the stable, a part of her remained ever vigilant. Her senses kept her connected to the environment, even as she enjoyed this respite from her usual responsibilities as Jefferson's attorney in Fortitude.

A blend of mental chatter filled her consciousness—horses mulling over feed, chickens squawking about pecking order, and the infrequent thoughts of a curious mouse or two. This congregation of minds served as a sort of mental background music, guiding her toward a state of calm.

It was a break she sorely needed, especially given Jefferson's knack for landing himself in complicated situations. Whether it was legal troubles or personal drama, her rider had a talent for stirring the pot. This often left Seledora to sort through the mess, a responsibility she undertook but didn't particularly relish. She sympathized with Blaise's exasperation regarding Jefferson—understandable, considering her rider's tendency to be his own worst enemy.

But all those concerns felt miles away right now. As Jefferson navigated the delicate task of mending fences with his estranged sister, Seledora found herself with an opportunity to relax. She took a deep, satisfied breath, exhaling slowly as she sank further into her little oasis of calm.

An abrupt shout pierced the tranquil air, jolting Seledora from her peace. The sound of boots clomping heavily on the stable's wooden floorboards reverberated through the building, as if trying to chase away the quiet. Seledora heaved herself up, shaking bits of straw from her silvery mane and tail. Her ears twitched as a pair of male voices rang out, bossing around the stable hands who had emerged, somewhat begrudgingly, to see what the commotion was about.

"Hey there, we're in a hurry! Bring out our stagecoach horses!" one man bellowed, his voice thick with impatience, as if each word were a stone hurled at the stable hands.

"Right away, sir," a stable hand replied, his voice full of resignation as he hurried off to carry out the order.

Though she had seen her fair share of frenzied travelers, something about this duo set her senses tingling. Seledora resumed her telepathic scan, this time honing in on the emotional undertones that wafted from the two men like the stench of a rotting carcass. She perked up her ears, trying to sift through their words for any hint of a deeper, perhaps darker, intent.

"Damn, we don't have time for this," the first man grumbled, his voice laced with a blend of frustration and an underlying anxiety that Seledora found curious.

"Relax, we'll make it," the second man responded with a forced chuckle.

A thread of unease wove its way through Seledora. The men's tension and their rushed manner triggered her curiosity. What urgent business drove them to such haste?

"All right, they're ready!" a stable hand announced, leading out two well-groomed stagecoach horses that shone in the dim light of the stable. A second hand emerged, guiding another pair of matched bays that pinned back their ears at the ruckus. Currency exchanged hands with a chink of coins. The men turned on their heels, their boots thudding as they marched out to oversee the hitching process.

In that moment, Seledora extended her telepathic tendrils, seeking to touch Jefferson's consciousness. What she found was disturbing—his mind was as still as a pond with no ripples, a contrast to his usually vibrant mental landscape. It didn't speak of the restful quiet of sleep and, overall, was very un-Jeffersonlike.

<Jefferson?> Her mental call was more like a battering ram against the foggy barriers shrouding his mind. No answer came back—only a too-empty silence.

Driven by mounting concern, Seledora knew she had to act. With a graceful bend of her neck, she manipulated her stall door latch with her agile lips. With a forceful nudge of her nose, she pushed the door open, and it creaked as she moved into the aisle, her hooves clacking against the wooden floor. It was a sound that usually garnered human attention, but tonight, it seemed, everyone was preoccupied.

Her nearest stall neighbor, a curious chestnut gelding with a wide blaze, peered at her over the top of his enclosure. He snorted softly, the sound envious, as if wondering whether she might liberate him as well.

<This is not a lark,> she told the gelding, pinning back her ears. With determined steps, she advanced down the stable aisle, her hooves sending soft echoes through the wooden boards. She

was on a mission to locate Jefferson, and if that meant marching straight into the saloon or his hotel, so be it.

Just as she was about to exit, the stable owner appeared, blocking her path. He was a stout, middle-aged man, his hair greying with age. The familiar scent of him—a mix of sweat, hay, and the pervasive, earthy smell of horses—reached her sensitive nostrils. He stepped toward her, hand outstretched, trying to guide her back to her stall with comforting words.

"Easy now, girl," he cooed, his tone patronizing, as if she were some wayward mare who'd taken a fancy to wander. But Seledora wasn't about to be cajoled.

<Leave me alone, I'm on business,> her mental voice rang out, clear and unyielding. To underscore her point, she unfurled her wings, stretching them as wide as the narrow stable aisle would allow. The magnificent feathers shimmered as they caught the light that filtered through the stable.

The stable owner's eyes became downright owlish. "A pegasus! Come here, you daft creature! I'll never hear the end of it if I lose a pegasus." He lunged at her, attempting to grab her mane since she wore no halter.

Despite his best efforts, Seledora danced effortlessly around the stable owner, easily evading his fumbling attempts to seize her. With a quick sidestep, she watched him lurch forward, his arms wheeling for balance. With a yelp of dismay, he tumbled face-first into a wheelbarrow of fresh manure that had yet to be carted away.

The chestnut gelding neighed in amusement at the scene, while the other horses watched with interest. Seledora cast a parting glance at the manure-caked man, her eyes expressing a silent apology. He was an obstacle, yes, but not an enemy.

The scent of wood smoke and the distant murmur of voices greeted her as she emerged from the stables. Ears pricked and senses alert, Seledora sent out another telepathic call to Jefferson.

She felt his dimmed presence. He was close. Still unconscious or...whatever he was. Not asleep, not dead. With a snort, she quickened her pace, ignoring the scattered exclamations that rose around her. "Loose horse! No, wait, that's a pegasus!"

Jefferson's hotel was close by, but she didn't sense him in that direction. Nor toward the saloon. Instead, she felt pulled toward the team of matched bay horses hitched to a stagecoach. They stood outside a two-story building that bore all the marks of a boarding house. Jefferson had mentioned that Alice was staying in a place like this.

Seledora sidled up alongside an empty wagon, peering around it as she assessed the scene. The two men she'd seen at the stables earlier heaved a limp figure into the stagecoach. Her nostrils flared, instinctively trying to catch a scent that might identify the individual. But the breeze was uncooperative, carrying scents away from her. She probed the figure's foggy consciousness but found nothing that resembled Jefferson's distinct mental signature.

Then she spotted him—unmistakable even in his current state. Two other men were hauling Jefferson's listless body between them, his face as slack as wet canvas, his arms and legs dangling lifelessly. She reached out with a mental nudge, an almost desperate telepathic touch, but still, his mind remained unre-sponsive.

She pawed at the ground in frustration. *My rider is being kidnapped right in front of me!* Seledora shook her mane. As much as she wished she had the ferocity to charge onto the scene and free Jefferson, that was not something she was comfortable doing. She'd stood alongside human outlaws and fellow pegasi in battle before, but then she'd had the strength of numbers. In this moment, she was alone. Her only ally was being loaded into that stagecoach.

The glint of fading sunlight caught the metal on top of the stagecoach, and Seledora noted the familiar billow of smoke coming from the distinctive stack atop it. It was the same technologically advanced coach she and Jefferson had spotted days ago in the Untamed Territory: a fusion of steam and horse, a juxtaposition of old and new. The same fast-traveling marvel that had previously intrigued Jefferson was now the very vessel transporting him to an uncertain fate.

Seledora's hooves shifted nervously on the ground, her mind racing. What was she to do? She was an attorney, more comfortable going through legal precedents and plotting arguments than galloping to the rescue. But if she didn't act, Seledora didn't know what would become of Jefferson. And though most considered her aloof, she had become rather attached to the silly human.

He was *her* silly, pompous human.

Her ears flicked back as the stagecoach door slammed shut with a thud, snapping her from her internal debate. A man leaned out of the window, smacking the side of the coach with a gloved hand, signaling for departure. The bay horses snorted, gathering their energy as they started out at a walk before breaking into a brisk trot.

I'm coming, Jefferson. I don't know what I'll do yet, but I'll keep this stagecoach in my sights.

Decision made, Seledora moved out from behind the wagon. Her mane flowed in the wind as she calculated her timing. Only when the stagecoach had dwindled into a lumbering, dark shape, the smoke from its stack still visible in the fading light, did she spring into action. She transitioned from a trot to a bounding lope, unfurling her wings to their full span as she lifted off. Even with the growing dark, the smoke would make the coach easy to track. That was a small concession in her favor, and Seledora would take it.

The chase was on, and there was no turning back. Seledora flew into the heart of dusk, her wings beating a steady rhythm.

She would not rest until her rider was safe once more.

CHAPTER SIXTEEN

An Innocent Cake

Jefferson

Jefferson's eyes flickered open as he struggled to shake the fog that enveloped his mind. His head throbbed, and the world around him seemed to swim in a sea of confusion. It wasn't until he felt the uneven rocking motion beneath him and caught the musty scent of worn upholstery that he realized where he was—slouched on the bench seat of a stagecoach, his hands bound behind his back.

He shut his eyes again, sucking in a breath. *Fortunes of Tabris, I'm so damned tired of being captured.* Old memories reared up, and for a dozen heartbeats he understood Blaise's moments of panic all too well. But he couldn't let panic and fear shut him down, binding him another way.

Also, he wasn't alone. As much as he wished he were, he couldn't ignore that reality. Shifting as best as he could, given his restraints, he glimpsed Alice's familiar blouse beside him. She was leaning toward Theo, her focus entirely on her son, offering whispered words that were meant to comfort but felt heavy in the confined space.

"I want to go home," Theo whimpered.

"I know, baby, I know," Alice replied. Her voice trembled like the flicker of a candle flame, showing a weakness in her words that should have been soothing. "We'll be okay. I promise I won't let anything happen to you."

Jefferson clenched his jaw, wishing desperately that he could believe her assurances. Jefferson shifted his gaze to the left, where two young men sat across from them. They had the lean, muscular build often associated with athletes, and they peppered their animated conversation with phrases like "pinning him down" and "last round." One of them casually toyed with a revolver, twirling it as he recounted moments that sounded like they belonged in a rowdy sports match rather than a barroom brawl.

Two guards. Jefferson wondered who had kidnapped them, but at the moment, it really didn't matter. Escape mattered. He stared at the drapery covering the stagecoach's window, glimpsing the darkness beyond. Night. It was night.

Wetting his lips, he formed a tentative plan. He sent out a tendril of his Dreamer magic, stretching it toward the nearest guard. Jefferson felt the man's presence and smiled to himself before releasing the power like a lasso, hoping to ensnare his prey.

But the magic fizzled out, dissipating like smoke. The guard continued his conversation, utterly unaffected.

Baffled and growing desperate, Jefferson tried again, only to encounter the same disheartening failure. He pulled back, assessing the situation. His magic felt weaker in here, as if whatever had been used to incapacitate him had also dulled his abilities.

This was a grave complication. It also meant he wouldn't be

able to reach out to Blaise. He swallowed, his heart sinking. Blaise was right. He shouldn't have come alone. In his foolhardy conceit, he'd now not only put himself at risk, but also his sister and nephew.

Jefferson shifted uncomfortably on the bench seat, his eyes flicking back to the guards. Their glances met his, then quickly returned to their own lively discussion. They clearly believed he was powerless, bound as he was. Frustratingly, it was true.

"About time you woke up," Alice hissed.

"I've *been* awake, thank you very much," Jefferson muttered.

"Uncle Malerson, I'm scared," Theo whined from his position on Alice's other side. "And I can't reach my lucky rock. I don't know if I still have it. I wanted to hold it to help us."

Theo's innocent and heartfelt attempt to help their situation cleaved Jefferson's heart. What could he possibly say to make this better? There was nothing. "If you've lost it, I'll make certain we find an even luckier rock to replace it as soon as we can," Jefferson said, hoping that would give him a little comfort, at least. He hoped he would have a chance to make good on his promise.

"This is all your fault, isn't it?" Alice's voice was barely above a whisper, but it was laden with accusation.

Jefferson could feel Alice's fury radiating toward him, an almost tangible heat in the confined space of the stagecoach. "Me? Why would you even suggest that?" His own voice rose, raw with indignation.

"Because Theo and I were fine until you arrived. I was happy! And then you came back into my life, and look at us now," Alice retorted. Her shoulder twitched in a futile attempt to gesture at their surroundings. "You're nothing but trouble."

That hurt. Jefferson clenched his jaw, holding back the heated rebuttal that leaped to his lips. Alice was scared and lashing out, trying to protect herself and her child in the only way she could. He could understand that, but it didn't mean he had to like it.

"Again, I'm not sure I follow your current line of accusations,"

Jefferson finally said, his voice carrying a soft, controlled undertone.

"That cake. You poisoned us with that cake," Alice shot back, her words aimed like a well-thrown dart he couldn't dodge.

His brows furrowed deeply, eyes narrowing. The cake? Accusing him of poisoning a recipe that held sentimental value, taught to him by Blaise, was a reprehensible act. "It was most certainly not the cake. Poison, really? Theo helped mix that cake!" His voice rose slightly in incredulity. And would a poison even do…whatever had happened to them? That was not in Jefferson's wheelhouse, certainly.

"Keep your voice down. Theo is asleep again," Alice warned, her voice softening for a moment. But then her posture stiffened, as though steeling herself for another round. "If it wasn't the cake, then what knocked all of us out?"

Jefferson's eyes clouded with thought, his jaw working subtly as he sifted through his hazy recollections. His mind reconstructed the scene: Alice's modest but cozy apartment, fragrant with the scents of freshly baked chocolate cake and—roses. Those were the only new variables in their environment.

"The roses. I think it was your roses," he ventured quietly, almost reluctantly.

Alice's eyes widened, cynicism transforming into indignation. "They're flowers, Jefferson. Pretty flowers from an admirer. Harmless! I can't believe you'd accuse *flowers*."

His eyes met hers, unyielding. "Well, it certainly wasn't my cake."

"Yes, it was," Alice growled.

"Flowers," he muttered under his breath, not backing down an inch.

"Cake," Alice insisted.

Jefferson gave her a side-eyed look. "Care to make a friendly wager?"

She stared at him, incredulous. "A wager while we're being kidnapped?"

He shrugged, the corners of his mouth twitching upward. "Not like we have anything better to do. Might as well make the most of our, ahem, *captivating* situation."

Alice shook her head, her eyes rolling. "You're unbelievable. Fine. What are we wagering?"

Emboldened by her concession, Jefferson leaned in, lowering his voice as if sharing a state secret. "On the method of our kidnapping," he explained, "if I'm right, you grant me the privilege of five more hour-long sessions to speak with you and only you."

Beside him, his sister went eerily still, her breath catching as if she was considering his words. "And if I'm right?"

He swallowed. He was damn certain he was right, but still… "Then I'll leave you alone. You won't hear from me ever again."

"You seem pretty sure that we'll get out of this mess," Alice observed.

"Oh, this? This is like an average day for me," Jefferson said. "Honestly, I was long overdue a good kidnapping."

He felt her jolt of shock. "Seriously?"

He chuckled, his eyes meeting hers. "Well, no. This is not my favorite way to spend an evening." He paused, his expression becoming more serious. "But I'm cautiously optimistic we'll get out of this."

Alice let out a long sigh, her eyes meeting his as if searching for any signs of deceit. "I hope you're right. Fine, how do we discover which of us is correct?"

Jefferson's eyes sparkled with renewed enthusiasm. "We ask our delightful hosts." He gestured with his chin towards the two guards, who had been blissfully ignorant of their whispered debate, engrossed in their own banter. Clearing his throat, he projected his voice towards them. "Excuse me!"

The guards turned their attention to Jefferson, their youthful faces slightly roughened by the beginnings of stubble. They were clearly young bucks, probably at an age where they thought they were invincible. Under their canvas dusters, Jefferson noticed they both wore button-down shirts featuring some sort of insignia. The design was too small and, from his vantage point, too wrinkled to identify, but it was an interesting detail. Jefferson tucked this piece of information into the back of his mind for later consideration.

"What?" The young man on the left—whose face was sprinkled with freckles like a constellation across the night sky—seemed bemused by the interruption.

Summoning his most charming smile, Jefferson met the young man's eyes. "I was wondering if one of you fine gentlemen might settle a wager between us." He inclined his head toward Alice, hoping to keep things light in an otherwise grim situation.

The man on the right, who Jefferson noticed had a thick unibrow, frowned. "Depends on what it is."

Taking the response as agreement, Jefferson couldn't help but feel a sense of anticipation. "Excellent. We have a minor disagreement regarding the method of our capture. Was our unfortunate fate sealed by a decadent chocolate cake or an innocent bouquet of roses?"

Unibrow and Freckles exchanged a confused glance. "I told you we should have taken some of the cake," Freckles muttered to Unibrow.

"There wasn't time!" Unibrow grumbled. "And besides, it was hard enough to haul them out, even with help."

Jefferson suppressed a smirk. "So, it *wasn't* the cake?" He allowed himself a moment to savor the small but sweet victory.

"Flowers," Freckles confirmed with a hint of exasperation, as if the answer should have been obvious. "But that's all we're gonna say on the subject."

While it was unfortunate that the guards were clamming up, Jefferson felt a swell of vindication. "It appears you owe me those five one-on-one sessions," he said, meeting Alice's eye. He let the words hang in the air for a moment before adding, "And an apology."

"An apology for what?" Alice's eyebrows shot up.

"For doubting the integrity of an innocent and, might I add, *delicious* chocolate cake," Jefferson said, feigning righteous indignation.

Alice released a resigned sigh, as if conceding a well-fought battle. "All right, fine. I'm sorry for blaming your cake. But you have to admit, it was so good it made me suspicious. Like it was covering up for something else."

Jefferson chuckled. "The only plot that cake was hiding was against my figure. Too much of that, and I'd need a new tailor."

Alice was quiet for a moment. "What are we going to do?"

Sinking back into the velvet-covered seat, Jefferson felt the severity of their predicament. He so wished he could whip out a foolproof scheme from his mental playbook, one that would spring them from this upholstered prison on wheels. "For now? We sit tight and wait. In the world of kidnappings, patience is more than a virtue—it's a survival strategy."

CHAPTER SEVENTEEN

Educational Opportunities

Jefferson

Jolted awake by the stagecoach's abrupt halt, Jefferson blinked away his haze of disorientation. For a moment, he was lost in time and place—then the door creaked open, and reality rushed back in.

"All aboard for the end of the line!" Freckles quipped, the jaunty enthusiasm in his voice jarringly at odds with the situation.

Unibrow rolled his eyes. "You don't say *all aboard* when people are about to get off, Nathan."

Nathan, formerly Freckles, shrugged. "Whatever. You know what I mean. Anyway, you there." He pointed at Jefferson, brandishing a knife with a flourish that made Jefferson involuntarily twitch. "Come here, but no funny business."

"I assure you, comedy is the last thing on my mind. I'll stay right here," Jefferson said, eyeing the knife warily.

Unibrow chuckled. "He thinks you're gonna turn him into a pincushion, you oaf."

Nathan looked puzzled for a moment before realization dawned. "Oh! No, no, the knife's for your ropes, not for you."

At that, Jefferson brightened considerably. "Well, that changes everything, doesn't it? By all means, proceed." He awkwardly shuffled out of the seat, turning so Nathan could sever the ropes that had been numbing his hands.

Unibrow ushered Jefferson out while Nathan saw to Alice and Theo. He glanced back at the stagecoach he had emerged from. A waft of steam hung in the air above the roof. His eyes widened at the sight of the smokestack rearing above the coach. This wasn't just any stagecoach; it was the steam-powered one he and Seledora had seen in the Untamed Territory.

Jefferson's mouth went dry. Had they been following him from Fortitude? He shook the thought away, turning to take in his surroundings. Brick-and-mortar academic buildings surrounded them.

"We're at a university?" he asked with incredulity. "Ah, yes. Because when I envisioned my next kidnapping, I was really hoping it would be more...educational."

Unibrow turned back toward him, and for the first time, Jefferson got a good look at the insignia on the young man's shirt. "Welcome to Cheswell University," he said, the crest on his shirt confirming the name. "Home of the—well, never mind that. Just come along."

Jefferson glanced back at the stagecoach, where Alice was just beginning to emerge, her face a mask of concern. "But my—"

"No buts," Unibrow interrupted, laying a hand on Jefferson's shoulder as if they were fraternity pals walking to class rather than captor and captive. "You're with me now." A group of other sturdy-looking students joined Unibrow, dressed in the same Cheswell button-down shirts. Jefferson found himself nudged along by the student guards, who were more like playful jocks than cruel captors.

"Keep up, old man," one of them teased.

This was a far cry from the uncompromising, professional captors he'd met in the past. These were college kids, albeit beefy ones, probably involved in athletics. The realization both puzzled and eased him. But it left a nagging question: why a university?

"We've got a delightful little room for you," another student said, grinning as they led him into what appeared to be a dormitory building. "You'll love the view of the brick wall."

Ushering him up a seemingly endless series of stairs, Jefferson felt the burn in his legs. "Is this part of the university's new fitness initiative?" he panted as they reached another landing. "If so, I'd like to opt out."

"Trust me, you haven't lived until you've sprinted these stairs in the middle of the night after cramming for finals," the first student replied with a chuckle, nudging him to keep moving.

Finally, they reached a corridor, the walls adorned with hand-painted signs and banners, perhaps announcing student events or societies. They stopped in front of a wooden door, its surface marred by years of use.

"After you," one student said, his grin widening as he opened the door.

Jefferson shook his head. "Oh, I'd be happy to get a hotel room. I don't wish to impose—" He never got to finish, instead shoved inside by his escorts.

Left alone in the dormitory room, Jefferson felt a strange juxtaposition of comfort and captivity. The room had an air of academic utility, furnished with a sturdy wooden bed dressed in fresh linens that smelled faintly of lavender. Against one wall stood a heavy wooden desk, its surface cluttered with inkwells, an assortment of glass pens, and paper—perhaps left by a previous resident. A water closet was tucked in one corner, its porcelain fixtures appearing as relics of modern convenience in an otherwise austere setting.

He wandered over to the room's lone window, its glass rippled with imperfections. The window was small, framed with thick wooden mullions, and peering out revealed he was on the fifth floor with a sheer drop to the stone-paved courtyard below. Escape seemed an untenable prospect, unless one had a way of defying gravity.

"Blast," he whispered.

With a sigh, Jefferson flopped onto the bed, scanning the beams of the ceiling. This was a strange place to be held captive, unlike any he'd been in before. The room was too ordinary for the dangers he usually faced. What weighed on him most was not knowing what had happened to Alice and Theo. Were they also locked away in rooms like this one, their worries growing as they waited for whatever came next?

A knock at the door interrupted his thoughts. Before he could respond, it opened, and a man stepped inside. Jefferson bolted upright, a spark of hope flaring within him. Perhaps this unassuming gentleman could provide some answers.

The man who entered was a study in contrasts. Lean to the point of gauntness, his sallow skin stretched taut over a skeletal frame. His black hair was not just thinning but actively retreating, as if it, too, found his scalp an uncomfortable place to live. His clothes had the musty air of academia, well-worn and outdated, like holdovers from a bygone era. Yet his eyes were the most disconcerting thing about him: keen and watchful. They flickered with an intelligence that belied his otherwise drab appearance. He looked like a professor, but one who had long since given up on tenure and now lived in the realm of the perpetually adjunct.

Jefferson swallowed down his discomfort and demanded, "Why am I here?"

The stranger remained silent for a moment, letting a thick sense of unease settle over the room. He seemed to size up Jefferson, as though he were an interesting item in a curio shop. Finally, in a voice that dripped with a kind of tedious intrigue, he said, "You know, it's funny. We're not so different, you and I."

Jefferson's irritation rose. "What's that supposed to mean? I don't even know you. And I'm certainly not a...a professor or an academic or whatever you are!"

The man smiled, though a hint of sadness shaded the expression. "No, you're not. But like me, you are someone who loves very deeply, very fiercely. Someone who would do anything for those you care about." He glanced back at the door, as if expecting someone to walk in at any moment. His voice, though soft, carried a weight, an intensity. "Anything at all."

Jefferson's eyebrows stitched together, his mind whirling to make sense of the bewildering speech. He'd taken part in many strange conversations before, but this one was just...downright confusing. Instinctively, his fingers grazed the wedding ring that adorned his hand—a tactile anchor in a sea of confusion. When in doubt, it was time to fall back on manners.

He cleared his throat. "I'm Jefferson Cole. And you are?"

The corners of the man's mouth lifted ever so slightly, forming a thin but deliberate smile. "Ah, well, the pleasure is all mine, Jefferson. I'm Zebulon Woodrow. And I do believe you're acquainted with my late wife, Tara. Isn't life just a small, interconnected web?"

An icy wave of realization crashed over Jefferson. Fortunes of Tabris, that wasn't good. Tara was dead. Murdered by Raven Dawson. So, what did this mean? He fought to maintain a mask of calm, even as his pulse quickened. "Ah, pleased to meet you. Yes, I knew Tara. I believe I recall seeing you at..." *Oh. Oh, no.*

Zebulon's eyes gleamed, a look of satisfaction washing over his face. "Yes, Nera. You and your band of...merry men, shall we say? You certainly made it a night to remember."

"Well, I'm very sorry for your loss," Jefferson said, though the words were little more than ash on his tongue. Tara had been, in his opinion, a terrible person. But now, this man's earlier words made sense. Zebulon loved Tara. "Now I think you need to release me. You have no reason to keep me here."

"But, you see, I have every reason," Zebulon said, drifting closer with an eerie calm. "Both of us would, let's say, go to the ends of the earth for the people we love. We might even do something as audacious as betraying a nation." His voice lowered, making the statement even more chilling.

Jefferson's muscles tensed. The man was navigating waters he'd rather not dip his toes into. He chose his next words carefully. "I don't know what you want from me."

Zebulon tilted his head, eyes narrowing ever so slightly. "Oh, but it's quite simple. You see, I'm curious about the origin of your magical abilities. Your sister, Alice, her powers make complete sense. They appeared at an expected time. But yours are quite the enigma. How did you, of all people, manage it?"

Jefferson remained silent, staring at Zebulon with a carefully neutral expression.

After an uncomfortably long pause, Zebulon resumed, almost as if talking to himself. "I have my theories, naturally. Marian Hawthorne couldn't have been the source. She has no motive to awaken anything in you. And I doubt you could bribe her with all the golden eagles in the world."

Jefferson dropped his gaze, staring at the floor. *Sweet Tabris, this is bad.*

Seeming to enjoy his own contemplation, Zebulon started pacing. "So, that leaves us with the inevitable conclusion that *you* did something. It had to be you. No one else makes sense. Initially, like everyone else, I found it baffling that Gregor Gaitwood couldn't bind Blaise Hawthorne. And then the revelation— it was *you*. You employed the geasa and bound the Breaker, didn't you?"

A muscle in Jefferson's cheek ticked at the mention of Blaise. His gut clenched. Bad enough that he was involved in whatever this alchemist had planned. All hope of keeping Blaise out of it was dissipating like sea foam in the wind.

"Over the years, many handlers have formed bonds with theurgists," Zebulon pondered aloud, reveling in his own musings. "But none—*none*—gained magical abilities through the mere act of binding."

He halted his pacing and turned to face Jefferson, eyes locking onto him. "No, something sets you apart." A slow, confident smile crept across his lips. "The Wells family bloodline has always had a certain...affinity for magic. Your sister, Alice, manifested her abilities in the usual way. But you." His eyes shimmered with an unsettling gleam. "You only exhibited magical tendencies when exposed to the blood of an *alchemical mage*."

Jefferson's pulse accelerated. This man had unearthed secrets he wished no one outside their trusted circle to discover. Maintaining a neutral expression became an uphill battle as panic clawed its way up his chest. The information Zebulon possessed was leverage—dangerous leverage. Jefferson needed to escape, fast.

Mustering as much composure as he could, Jefferson took a deep, steadying breath. "You must let me go. People will look for me, you know. I'm an ambassador."

Zebulon's grin widened at the statement, his eyes twinkling with a sort of manic anticipation. "Ah, I'm quite aware, Mr. Cole, and I relish the thought." He chuckled softly, almost to himself. "You see, I have plans—so many delightful plans. The new academic semester commences in just two days. The research possibilities that open up with your presence are, well, exhilarating. This year, we shall undertake experiments that will not just turn heads, but make the world truly take notice!"

Jefferson blinked, momentarily thrown off balance. Had Zebulon really just segued from kidnapping and life-altering secrets to gushing about his syllabus? It was disconcerting, to say the least, adding another layer of unpredictability to an already alarming situation.

"Please, if you have any decency, let my sister and nephew go," Jefferson implored. The thought of Theo caught up in this web of chaos was unbearable.

Zebulon shook his head, an expression of melancholy crossing his face. "Oh, that won't be possible, I'm afraid. You see, they're quite integral to the overarching narrative I've got planned here. Plus, I made a deal—a binding agreement, if you will." A glint of something resolute appeared in his eyes. "However, let me assure you, Mr. Cole, your stay at Cheswell will be as pleasant as captivity can be. Of course, you won't be leaving this room without an escort."

As he moved towards the door, Zebulon paused and added, "Ah, do take note of the walls. Fresh coat of paint!"

Jefferson's gaze shifted to the walls. They looked like any other walls. Why was this detail important?

"It's null paint," Zebulon clarified, reading Jefferson's confusion. "It's quite the safeguard, meant to keep all of us out of harm's way."

Safe, Jefferson thought, his stomach sinking. Safe from the magic of a Dreamer, from his own latent abilities. His fists clenched involuntarily. How could he negotiate with someone so impossibly enigmatic? He only had one potential bargaining chip left. "I can free you from the Quiet Ones."

Zebulon's gaze momentarily shifted, his eyes clouding over with sentiment as he spoke. "I was already freed when Tara passed." His voice wavered, a pang of deep-seated sorrow breaking through his composure. He took a moment to wipe away an errant tear. "Where was I? Ah, yes, you'll be getting a meal soon. The resident advisor will bring it by in about an hour."

His expression hardened, his eyes narrowing as if to drive home the severity of his next statement. "I must insist that you treat her, and any other students you come across, with the utmost respect. Failure to do so will result in your sedation—making you a non-factor in any, shall we say, *endeavors* you might be contemplating."

Jefferson couldn't help but frown. *Sedation?* But then again, the mention of a student offered a glimmer of hope. "I have no intention of mistreating anyone," he assured, thinking that perhaps his natural charm might help him glean some crucial information—maybe even a way out of this mess.

Zebulon seemed to accept this, nodding as he made his way toward the door. He paused, his hand resting on the doorknob, and cast a last look over his shoulder. "You may wish to get comfortable, Mr. Cole. There's a long road ahead, filled with...educational opportunities."

The door clicked shut behind him, leaving Jefferson utterly alone.

CHAPTER EIGHTEEN

Loose Horse

Blaise

Blaise savored the last bites of his oatmeal, sweetened with honey and sprinkled with nuts. The inn's dining room was mostly empty, filled only with the murmur of a few patrons and the occasional clinking of utensils against plates. It was soothing, but the empty chair across from him served as a constant reminder of Jefferson's absence.

The sunlight filtering through the windows warmed the room, illuminating the aged wood of the tables and chairs. He took a sip of his coffee, finding it as bittersweet as his thoughts. Love was a complicated thing. But he shook away that line of thought. There would be plenty of time to examine his relationship with Jefferson on the journey back to Fortitude.

His thoughts shifted to Luci, now safely enrolled at Cheswell University. It was a relief to know she'd have opportunities beyond what her old life could offer. But the joy of her new beginning did little to ease the sting of their farewell. After remaining in Greylight for a few more days—ostensibly to ensure Luci was well-settled but truthfully to delay his return home—he knew it was time to face whatever awaited him in Fortitude.

A sudden intrusion jolted Blaise from his brooding. <Blaise!> The urgency in Emrys's tone set his pulse racing. <Seledora is nearby.>

His thoughts scrambled. Seledora? Here? A surge of hope bubbled up within him, mingling with confusion. Had Jefferson returned to Fortitude only to discover he'd left with Luci? Had Jefferson come after him?

In a fluid motion, Blaise slid off his chair, left a golden eagle coin on the table for his meal, and made his way out of the inn. He sidestepped patrons and dodged tables, offering hurried apologies as he went. Bright morning light and the scent of the dusty street met him as he pushed through the inn's doors.

His boots pounded against the ground as he broke into a jog, each step sending up a small cloud of dust. The livery stable, where he'd left Emrys and Naureus, came into view, and his pace quickened.

Blaise paused outside the stables but found no sign of Seledora. He made his way down the row of stalls, and when he reached Emrys, he let himself in.

The black stallion came to him, bumping his muzzle against Blaise's chest. <You smell good. Honey in your oatmeal—wait, I need to stay focused.> Emrys stomped a hind hoof, as if to emphasize the urgency of the situation.

"You do," Blaise agreed. "What exactly do you mean when you say Seledora is nearby?" He tried to keep the excitement from his voice and failed.

<I mean I can sense her,> Emrys clarified, his telepathic voice filled with a gravity that only intensified Blaise's mounting apprehension. <She's close, Blaise. Very close.>

Naureus, in the stall next to Emrys, thrust his head over the divider. <There aren't many pegasi around here. I agree, it must be her. She has a unique...presence.>

Blaise's throat felt tight as he nodded. "All right. Let's go find her." *And hopefully Jefferson, too.*

He hurried to the tack room, his hands trembling as he grabbed Emrys and Naureus's saddles and hackamores. Thoughts tumbled through his mind like a cascading waterfall—what would it mean to find Seledora? What would Jefferson say? He was so engrossed in his thoughts that he almost fumbled the cinch while saddling Emrys.

Once both pegasi were ready, Blaise led them out of the livery stable. He told the stablemaster they would return, then swung into Emrys's saddle. Naureus followed close behind as they rode out of town at a brisk trot.

Blaise was barely aware of the world around him, his senses tuned to Emrys as if the pegasus were an extension of himself. Each moment that stretched on heightened his anticipation until he felt a familiar, delicate nudge in his mind from Emrys.

<This way,> Emrys said, guiding them off the main road and toward a distant cluster of trees. Blaise's heart raced, adrenaline coursing through his veins. He tightened his grip on the reins and squeezed his thighs around Emrys's barrel, bracing himself for whatever lay ahead.

<Blaise! Stay put. I'm coming to you!> Seledora's voice startled Blaise, making him sit straighter in the saddle. Both Emrys and Naureus came to an abrupt stop, standing beneath the shafts of sunlight filtering through the leaves of a grand oak tree, responding to the same mental directive.

Blaise scanned the surrounding forest, searching for any sign of the approaching pegasus. His hands gripped the reins a little tighter, his palms growing damp from nervousness.

The thunder of hooves reached his ears before he caught sight of Seledora galloping toward them at full speed, her wings hidden.

Trailing not too far behind her was a man, shouting and waving a lead rope in the air as if attempting to lasso a wild animal.

<Well, she's not alone,> Emrys noted, his nostrils flaring at the sight of the stranger.

Blaise cursed under his breath. Quick thinking was required. "All right, let's intercept. Naureus, act like you're ground-tied."

<On it.> The buckskin lowered his head, the very picture of a well-trained steed prepared to stand in one spot all day if need be.

As Seledora closed the distance between them, Emrys leaped into action, lunging forward with a burst of speed aimed directly at the man pursuing her.

"Whoa there!" Blaise shouted, raising a hand as Emrys skillfully moved to cut off the man's path. "So sorry! This mare's mine —she slipped away from our camp earlier. Been tracking her down all morning."

The man skidded to a halt, giving Blaise an appraising look, as if trying to weigh his truthfulness on some invisible scale. "She yours? Came tearin' through my east pasture outta nowhere. Scared my goats half to death, and let me tell ya, those goats have seen things."

Blaise winced. "My apologies. I'll repay you for any damages." He slipped out of the saddle and made a show of catching Seledora. The mare snorted, rolling her eyes. Her coat was slick with sweat, and lather had formed in patches around her neck and between her legs. "Sorry for the trouble."

The man's features relaxed somewhat, his eyes losing their initial edge of suspicion. "Ah, don't worry about it. My goats have had worse days. Just keep a better handle on her, will ya?"

Blaise touched the brim of his hat in a gesture of respect. "You have my word," he assured the man, watching as he turned away, though Blaise wondered what more frightening sights the farmer's goats had endured.

With a sigh that was half-relief, half-apprehension, Blaise turned back to his pegasi. The immediate crisis may have been averted, but Jefferson's absence was a sore spot. Why wasn't he with Seledora?

He led Seledora back to where Naureus stood, still embodying the epitome of a well-behaved, ground-tied steed. Emrys followed, his eyes reflecting the same concerns that plagued Blaise's thoughts.

When they reached the tree, Blaise ran his hand along Seledora's neck, frowning at the roughness of her coat and the trembling in her muscles. She was utterly exhausted, likely having flown and galloped a great distance.

"Where's Jefferson?" The question came out as a whisper, his voice tinged with a fear he couldn't mask. The feeling of dread that had been pooling within him now threatened to spill over as he grappled with increasingly terrifying possibilities.

Seledora sighed heavily, her legs buckling as she sank into the grass. Blaise dropped to his knees beside her, cradling her head in his hands as she lay down. Alarmed, Emrys and Naureus moved close, protective, their heads low.

<Taken,> her voice whispered in his mind.

Blaise's mouth went dry. "Who took him? Where?" The words came out choked, each syllable a struggle.

With an effort that seemed to sap the last of her strength, Seledora lifted her head slightly, her eyes turning toward the distant silhouette of Cheswell University. <I don't know who. But they took him away in a stagecoach, which I followed all the way here. He's in that place. The sign...it said Cheswell. I can still feel him there.>

"Rest, Seledora, just rest," Blaise said, his voice breaking as he stroked her sweat-matted forehead. His emotions were a storm, swirling and crashing against the walls of his composure. "You've done more than anyone could ask. Take a moment to catch your breath."

Jefferson was here, in Cheswell? Where Luci now resided? His thoughts raced like a runaway pegasus. He swallowed, struggling to rein them in.

Drawing a shuddering breath, Blaise forced himself back to the moment. Panic wouldn't bring Jefferson back. Nor would it protect Luci from whatever unseen dangers lurked in Cheswell.

Seledora's eye, large and expressive, fixed on him. <Why are *you* here?>

Naureus broke in before Blaise could respond, his mental voice shaded with a touch of worry. <Blaise's sister, Luci, is now a student at the university. We escorted her here.>

Seledora's surprise echoed in Blaise's mind. <That does not bode well, I think.>

Blaise huffed a humorless laugh. "No," he agreed, "it really doesn't."

He raked a hand through his hair, mind racing. Whatever was happening, Luci was now caught up in it, too. He had to get back into Cheswell, find his sister, and somehow convince her to abandon her newfound academic haven. Even if it renewed her loathing for him. Then, he could focus on helping Jefferson escape from wherever he was being held.

First things first, though. Seledora's well-being was immediate and non-negotiable.

"Rest here," he told the exhausted mare. "As soon as you're strong enough to walk, we'll head back to town and find you a stable. Then I need to make my way back to Cheswell."

Emrys shook his head, his forelock flying with the motion. <Wouldn't it be easier to just send Luci a message?>

Blaise considered it. Technically, he could, but a note wouldn't do anything for Jefferson, and he couldn't leave Luci's safety to chance. "I need to see her face-to-face to make sure she's okay, Emrys. And to convince her to leave. Besides, today I'm not a mage or anyone special. I'm just Blaise, a regular man who happens to be a very concerned older brother."

Emrys shifted his weight from one hoof to the other, clearly not convinced but choosing not to push the issue further. The stallion's eyes met Blaise's, and in that moment, unspoken understanding passed between them. There was no need for more words. They both knew Blaise had to get Luci out.

Blaise's gaze shifted to Naureus, his eyes meeting the buckskin's understanding gaze. "We'll figure this out. Naureus, once Luci is safe, you'll fly her back to Fortitude. I trust you with her." His mind started running through a list of potential allies. Who could they rely on? Jack's name came to mind, but he quickly dismissed it. The man was still recuperating from his own battles; summoning him would do more harm than good. That also ruled out Kittie and Emmaline. Vixen? Vixen was a possibility. Or maybe Nadine...what if they needed a Healer?

Seledora, who had been quietly gathering her strength, suddenly spoke up, her voice tremulous in his mind. <We don't even know why they've taken him.>

He swallowed hard, her words like ice water to his face. She was absolutely right. As much as he wanted to rally support and storm wherever Jefferson was being held, time wasn't a luxury they could afford. Beyond that, Blaise's heart clenched with a truth he couldn't ignore: he loved Jefferson, disagreement or not, and he couldn't stand the thought of him in danger.

With a resigned nod, Blaise made the call. "Naureus, you'll inform Nadine of what's happening. She's resourceful. Also, let my mother know; she has her own set of contacts. But we can't afford to wait for reinforcements. The moment Luci is out of Cheswell, we go after Jefferson."

His fingers grazed the cool silver band encircling his ring finger, the metal a tactile reminder of the vows he'd made and the love he was committed to. It grounded him, filling him with an indomitable spirit. Whatever it took, he would bring Jefferson home.

CHAPTER NINETEEN

Memories

Alice

Alice watched as Jefferson was led away, a confusing blend of emotions settling over her. It was funny how captivity could create a bond, even with someone as infuriating as her brother. But now he was gone, and she and Theo were left to navigate this frightening maze on their own.

The atmosphere was stifling, almost as if the air itself was thick with dread. Her fingers tightened around Theo's hand, her maternal instincts heightening every one of her senses. The towering stone edifices seemed to glower down at them, their looming silhouettes casting deepening shadows on the cobble-stone pathways.

"Mama?" Theo's voice was a fragile whisper. "Where are we?"

"Not sure yet, sweetheart," she answered softly, her gaze flit-ting between the buildings as if they might suddenly reveal their secrets. A flicker of recognition lit somewhere deep within her, threatening to burst into flame. But where did she know this place from?

And then it clicked.

Cheswell University. The very institution she had once dreamed of attending. Memories of a life not so long ago, in which music was her escape and a mage's fate hadn't ensnared her, sent shivers down her spine. How cruelly ironic that destiny now brought her back here.

Their guards led them away, taking a different route than where they had taken Jefferson. Alice's eyes narrowed. These weren't seasoned soldiers or mercenaries; they were students. That realization brought both relief and a fresh wave of tension. It made them less predictable, and in her book, unpredictability was just another form of danger.

Alice eyed them warily as they approached one of the smaller buildings that flanked the courtyard. Her pulse quickened, dread pooling in her stomach at the unknown fate that awaited them inside.

When they stepped inside, the contrast was jarring. The light that spilled through the stained-glass windows depicting academic scenes seemed almost ethereal, casting a rainbow of colors across the floor. Rich tapestries adorned the walls, each one a frozen tableau of history or myth, while plush furniture, upholstered in deep, luxurious fabrics, populated the room. The sumptuousness felt like an affront, a mockery of her uncertain situation.

But it was the sight that met her in the next room that truly made her blood run cold.

Phillip. Her estranged husband rose from a velvet chair. His face lit up, mouth stretching into a broad, expectant smile, as if this were a delightful surprise. "Alice, my love," he declared, his voice oozing a warmth that felt as invasive as it was insincere.

Something visceral recoiled within her, a gut reaction so

strong it was almost a physical blow. Her feet moved of their own accord, taking a retreating step as if they, too, rejected the sight of her husband. For a fleeting moment, her eyes flicked to the exit, calculating the distance and the probability of successful escape.

Not likely.

But then she remembered Theo. His small hand still clutched hers, his wide eyes darting between his parents, confusion in their depths. No, she couldn't let her son see this tension, this silent war between his mother and father.

Inhaling sharply, Alice composed her features into a neutral mask. She turned back to Phillip, her voice a study in controlled detachment. "Phillip," she said, intentionally stripping the name of any warmth, any past intimacy. Her body remained stiff, a fortress walling off affection.

Phillip's smile wavered, a fissure appearing in his carefully constructed facade. He took a step toward her, arms extending as if preparing to pull her into an embrace. But Alice stood like a statue, her body language a stark *do not enter* sign. Her refusal to play the part of the doting wife was a tangible force that seemed to fill the room.

Caught off guard, Phillip recovered his poise, albeit awkwardly, clearing his throat. Then his gaze slid to Theo, and Alice witnessed a transformation. The lines of his face softened, his eyes warming as he stooped down to eye-level with their son. "There's my boy," he said, his voice full of a warmth that Alice, despite all her reservations, had to admit sounded genuine as he affectionately ruffled Theo's hair.

Alice watched the exchange in silence, conflicting emotions brewing within her. She had vowed never to fight in front of Theo, wanting to give him the stable upbringing she'd never had. But seeing Phillip exude such compassion, while internally cataloging the cruelties and manipulations he was capable of, sparked a torrent of anger she struggled to contain.

"Daddy, I'm hungry." Theo peered into his father's face. "And I lost my lucky rock."

The simple statement acted like a pressure valve, allowing some of the building tension to escape. Relief flitted across Phillip's features, as if grateful for the respite Theo's words provided. "You must be starving after such a long trip," he agreed, gesturing to one of the young student-guards. "The cafeteria is near. Would you escort him there for a bite to eat? And find him a...lucky rock, I suppose."

The student nodded and gave Theo a friendly smile. "Come along. Let's find you a snack and a rock."

"Not just *any* rock is lucky," Theo told the student as he walked off with her, though he paused to glance back at his mother. She swallowed but nodded for him to go ahead. There were things she needed to say that he shouldn't hear.

As soon as the door swung shut after him, Alice pivoted sharply. Her eyes arrowed to Phillip with a burning intensity. This was her moment, the sliver of time when she could confront him without the buffer of their son's innocence. "Why did you take us?" Her question bore hints of unspoken accusation, each word slicing through the tense air like a razor-sharp knife. "You had no right—"

"Why did you leave?" Phillip interrupted, his own voice hushed but raw with emotion.

Alice didn't flinch at his question. Her eyes narrowed to icy slits, her voice cold as she unleashed years of resentment and anger. "You know exactly why I left, Phillip. You never loved me— I was just another possession to you, a means to an end. Worth no more to you than the Herald, who you didn't even mourn."

At the mention of the Herald, Phillip's former pet mage, his face blanched. Phillip's mouth opened and closed in a futile attempt to form a response. Alice savored his speechlessness; it was as close to a victory as she could hope for at this moment.

Disgust rippled through her as she shook her head. "I couldn't stay, not in a relationship where I was reduced to a mere instrument for your ambitions. You were more than willing to exploit my—" Here, her eyes darted to the others in the room, students who had become unwitting witnesses to this bitter reunion. She wasn't about to expose her true nature in front of this audience. "Abilities," she finished, her voice dripping with scorn.

Phillip's face contorted, his eyes glinting with both hurt and fiery rage at her accusation. "How can you say that?" His voice was a venomous whisper, each syllable laced with a combustible mix of hurt and indignation. "I gave you everything! The manor, the staff, access to all my accounts—"

"Yes, you gave me *things*!" She jabbed the air with her finger for emphasis, her voice as sharp as a whip. "But you never gave me what I truly needed: a loving relationship. You treated me like an ornament, Phillip. Like I was yours to control."

"Because you *are* mine!" Phillip's face reddened, his veneer of civility shattering completely.

Alice took an involuntary step back, his outburst creating a physical canyon between them, reflecting the emotional abyss that had long existed.

"I've never stopped loving you, Alice," he said, his voice softer but no less intense as he took a step closer, trying to bridge the gap. "I know deep down, buried under all your resistance, you still care about me."

His hands reached out as if to grasp some fleeting hope, but Alice recoiled, as if his touch were poison. The air between them was electric, each glare a bolt of lightning, each word a clap of thunder.

"You're delusional," Alice spat, her voice low but filled with venom. "If you think I've *ever* loved you, or could love you now, you've utterly lost your mind."

Phillip's eyes bulged, the blood draining from his face. He took a shaky breath, his shoulders slumping as he seemed to internalize her rejection. After a moment that felt like an eternity, he straightened, turning to the students who had awkwardly hovered in the background, their eyes wide with a mix of curiosity and discomfort.

"Take her to her room," he said, each word clipped and icy. "We're done here."

A shiver ran through Alice as the reality of her situation settled over her like a shroud. She was imprisoned, isolated. The students gently gripped her elbows, guiding her out of the room as if she were a fragile vase, but inside, she felt like shattered glass.

Her mind churned frantically, searching for any shred of an escape plan. But as the door to a spartan dorm room closed behind her with a resounding thud, the lock clicking with an air of finality, she knew she was trapped.

Jefferson

JEFFERSON LET OUT A WEARY SIGH AS HE CROSSED THE ROOM TO THE wooden desk situated against the wall. The room felt oddly still, as if the weight of the situation had settled into every crevice and corner. Shaking off his pressing thoughts for a moment, he pulled out the chair and sat, his eyes catching sight of a glass pen next to the inkwell. The pen was elegantly crafted, its glass body shimmering in the dim light. Jefferson picked it up, feeling the cool glass against his skin. It was well-balanced, the craftsmanship impeccable.

"Someone around here has good taste," he mused to himself, a small, approving smile playing across his face. For a moment, the beauty of the object allowed him to forget his circumstances.

Setting the pen down, he reached for a sheet of paper from the stack at the corner of the desk. He pulled it toward him, laying it out neatly. His gaze fell upon the blank expanse of the paper, and the smile that had momentarily graced his face faded. The emptiness of the page seemed to mirror the hollow feeling in his chest, the guilt that gnawed at him. Thoughts of Blaise filled his mind— their argument, the way Blaise had looked so wounded by Jefferson's unwelcome use of magic. And then there was Alice. His sister had been so close, and yet he had failed to protect her, failed to reconcile with her. And Theo, an innocent caught in a web of adult complexities.

Jefferson took a deep breath, pushing aside the boulder of his guilt for a moment. He picked up the pen once more, dipping it into the inkwell. His eyes returned to the blank paper, still an intimidating expanse, but also a canvas for his thoughts, his feelings.

I should write to Blaise. But where do I even begin?

His gaze shifted from the paper to the ceiling, as if seeking divine inspiration.

"I can't start with apologies," he mused. "Not when the pain is still so fresh, not when I don't even know if he'll read this letter." That wasn't what Jefferson wanted to think about in this situation, anyway.

The pen hovered over the paper, its tip glistening with ink. And then, as if guided by some unseen force, Jefferson wrote. Not about the present, not about their argument or his failures. No, he wrote about a memory that had become a source of joy for both of them.

The first time I ever laid eyes on you, Blaise, was in that quaint bakery in Fortitude.

He wrote, the words flowing effortlessly now, as if they'd been dammed up inside him for too long.

You were a vision of anxiety, hands dusted with

flour, your eyes darting around as if you were on the verge of flight. And yet, there was a grace about you, a kindness that radiated from your very being.

Jefferson smiled as he recalled the moment, the scent of freshly baked bread in the air, the way the cookie he'd purchased melted on his tongue.

You didn't want to talk to me. It was plain to see in the way you tried to ignore me when I spoke to Reuben. You were wary, perhaps a bit intimidated. But I couldn't help myself, Blaise. I had to meet you, had to know the man behind those hesitant smiles and the desserts that sent me to Paradise and back.

He paused, setting down the pen to read what he had written. The words seemed so small on the paper, so inadequate in capturing the emotions of the moment. But they were the best he had, a bridge made of ink and paper to span the distance that had opened between him and Blaise.

Jefferson felt a lump forming in his throat as he considered how far they had come from that first meeting and how much they had lost. But at least for this moment, in this room, he could live in that memory.

It brought him hope. And happiness.

Jefferson felt the pen call to him again. He dipped it back into the inkwell and resumed his letter to Blaise.

Remember the first time we shared a bed? I knew you were nervous. And as much as I wanted you, I feared I might scare you away. So we talked most of the night, and I'm so grateful we did.

Jefferson paused, huffing out a contented breath at the memory.

I had never connected with anyone like that before. That was when I understood there was more than physical need. I needed you on an emotional level. By the time the first rays of dawn broke through the window, I felt like I had known you for a lifetime.

He paused, recalling that morning. Jefferson saw his husband in his mind's eye, standing before him with the dogged determination Blaise could summon when he dug deep into himself. It gave him a brief pang of regret for accusing Blaise of never acting in time.

Do you know that your unwavering need to save your friends made me jealous? I didn't want you to go, even though we both knew you must.
Then came the time when I asked you to destroy the airship,

Jefferson wrote, each word heavier than the last.

I remember the look in your eyes—fear, uncertainty, but also a resolve that shook me to my core. I had to ask you, but it nearly broke me to do so.

Sending you into the face of danger went against every instinct I had, but the alternative was unthinkable.

And then you kissed me. It wasn't filled with fireworks or the urgency that comes from a moment of danger. It was sweet, sincere—a promise sealed in the quiet of a new day. I felt as though we had crossed a line, one that I'd been scared to approach but also deeply yearned for.

Jefferson smiled at the memory, though the expression fled his lips as he thought about what happened afterward.

But then there was...the airship. My airship.

The ink seemed to dry slower, as if absorbing the sum of his regret.

Asking you to risk your life in that way was one of the hardest things I've ever done. I felt I was sending a part of my soul into a storm, unsure if it would return.

Setting the pen down, Jefferson leaned back in his chair. No, that wasn't something to think about right now. He needed a happier memory. Maybe one of the occasions when Blaise had shown him how to bake—

Behind him, the doorknob jiggled. Jefferson spun, shoving the chair away as he rose to face the door as it opened.

CHAPTER TWENTY

Detour

Sleep had been a distant companion last night, his anxious thoughts forming an insurmountable barrier to rest. He knew he needed to check on Seledora, to confirm she was recovering. And then, he had to find Luci—convince her to abandon her newfound life at Cheswell University. As for Jefferson...well, that was a mountain he would have to climb later. Right now, he needed to focus on the immediate tasks at hand.

"Morning, Seledora," he greeted softly as he stepped into the mare's stall. She seemed stronger than before, her breathing steadier. "How are you feeling?"

<I am much improved, thank you,> Seledora replied, nuzzling his shoulder in an uncharacteristic show of gratitude. <The box of sugar cubes you gave me last night did wonders for my energy, though I will still need a few more days to recover.>

Blaise crouched beside her, his hands cautiously moving down her legs. Each touch was deliberate as he checked for swelling or signs of injury. His fingers probed gently, finding their way to her hooves, where he inspected them for cracks or lodged stones he might have missed the previous night, but all seemed well.

Straightening up, he sighed in relief, his shoulders loosening. "I'm no Beast Healer, but you really do seem okay." A small breath escaped him as he stroked Seledora's neck, finding a measure of relief in the contact. If things went according to plan, and he could extract Jefferson, they'd be able to leave this place soon. He leaned his forehead against her neck, gathering himself for the tasks ahead.

Seledora stood still, allowing him the brief respite. <You must get your sister.>

Blaise pulled away, his eyes meeting hers for a fleeting second, before he nodded. "Yeah," he agreed, though he felt as if he were preparing to scale a mountain.

One thing at a time. It was all he could do.

Content that Seledora was on the mend, Blaise took a deep breath as he left her stall. The worry that had tightened his chest eased, if only a little. Emrys and Naureus sensed his thoughts, their heads peering over their stall doors, attentive.

<I wish I could come with you,> Emrys fretted, pinning his ears back.

"I know, but being seen on campus with a black pegasus isn't the definition of low-profile," Blaise replied. He rubbed the spot between Emrys's eyes. "Can you two keep an eye on Seledora?"

<Of course,> Emrys responded, almost indignant at the suggestion that he wouldn't have anyway. Naureus simply bobbed his head, his agreement more understated but no less meaningful.

Steeling himself for what lay ahead, Blaise exited the livery stable. Every step toward Cheswell University felt like a step into uncertainty. But he had to do this. He had to find Luci. It was the next necessary action in a chain of daunting tasks.

And after that, Jefferson.

Blaise approached the imposing iron gates of Cheswell University with a sinking feeling in his gut. The towering architecture beyond the gate held promises of knowledge and enlightenment, promises that now seemed tinged with something far darker. He'd walked Luci through these very gates only days ago, full of hope for her future. Now he hoped she would leave with him, leave behind whatever secrets these walls were keeping.

The guard at the entrance squinted at him, sizing him up. "State your business," he commanded, his tone more a challenge than a question.

Blaise tipped his hat politely, attempting to project a confidence he certainly didn't feel. "Good morning. I'm here to speak with my sister, Luci Mason. She's a new student."

The guard's scrutiny only intensified Blaise's mounting anxiety, his eyes sweeping over Blaise as if he were a problem to be solved. "Classes have already started. We have a strict rule that no visitors are allowed the first two weeks that students are in residence. To give them time to adjust to the rigors of Cheswell."

Blaise felt his heart sink a little. He hadn't expected this obstacle. He'd thought his familiarity with the campus from dropping Luci off would make this part easy. Anxiety surged within him, whispering persuasions to retreat. But retreating wasn't an option, not when Luci's safety—and Jefferson's—depended on him.

Gathering his courage, he said, "I understand, but this is a family matter that really can't wait. If I could just speak with someone in admissions, I'm certain they'll grant me a brief visit." He forced a shaky smile onto his face, hoping to convey his earnestness. He was walking a fine line between manipulation and honesty, a place he seldom dared to tread. But this was a desperate time.

The guard seemed to weigh his words, as if measuring the sincerity in Blaise's eyes. Finally, he nodded. "Wait here." He retreated into the guardhouse, leaving Blaise alone with his racing thoughts. His eyes flicked nervously toward the cobblestone pathway leading into the academic fortress.

When the guard reappeared, the nod he gave was curt but affirmative. "Dean Woodrow will see you. Do you know the way to Admissions?"

Blaise suppressed a sigh of relief. "Yes," he said, though his certainty wavered. What he remembered were signs pointing the way, and he hoped that would be enough. He couldn't afford to lose any more time.

As the wrought-iron gates closed behind him, Blaise found his steps quickening, guided by signs to the Admissions building.

Upon entering the building, his eyes immediately found Dean Woodrow in the reception area. The Dean of Alchemy greeted him with a tepid smile. "Ah, look who we have here. The doting older brother checking in, am I correct?"

Blaise managed a weak smile in greeting. "Sort of. But there's an urgent family matter I need to speak with Luci about. Something's come up."

Woodrow's already subtle smile thinned, his eyes narrowing ever so slightly. "That does sound pressing. While we typically discourage early visits to allow students to acclimate, I suppose there are situations that necessitate exceptions. A letter lacks that personal touch, doesn't it?"

A wave of relief washed over Blaise. "I'm glad you understand."

Dean Woodrow's smile returned, tinged with a hint of reserved satisfaction. "Of course! I'd happily accompany you to Ms. Mason, but duty calls in the form of a meeting. We'll find someone to—"

His sentence was interrupted by the creak of the reception door. A young woman poked her head in. "Dean Woodrow? I have a student with a question about their supply voucher form."

"Ah, Misty!" Woodrow's eyes twinkled as he clapped his hands in mild delight. Blaise's memory stirred; he'd seen this young woman when Luci first arrived. "You're serendipitously convenient for the current situation."

Misty stepped fully into the room, her expression marked by confusion. "I am?" Then her eyes connected with Blaise's, widening in recognition. "Oh."

The dean nodded. "Indeed. You are a resident advisor, after all. And Blaise here has pressing matters to discuss with Luci Mason. As for your inquisitive student, direct them to Admissions. Brad —" He pointed languidly to a young man submerged behind a desk of scattered paperwork. "—is the designated problem-solver today."

Misty hesitated, her bottom lip caught between her teeth. "But—"

"You're in your last semester here, Misty, focusing on your practicum, yes?" Professor Woodrow interrupted, his voice a tranquil monotone.

Misty paused, weighing her options, before finally nodding. "Yes, Dean Woodrow. I'll guide him to Luci and advise the other student to consult Brad."

Woodrow's smile seemed to broaden incrementally. "Splendid. Now, if you'll pardon me, there are matters that require my attention." With that, he exited the room, the soft tap of his footsteps receding down the corridor.

Once they were out of the office, Blaise cleared his throat, trying to ease the knot of tension that had settled there. "So, uh, how's my sister settling in so far?"

Misty offered a reassuring smile. "I think she's doing just fine. I know it can be a big change, those first few weeks. I remember I was so overwhelmed when I started here. But Luci seems to be taking it all in stride."

A modicum of relief eased its way into Blaise's posture, his shoulders lowering ever so slightly. Luci was doing all right. That was one less worry. Now, the challenge was to convince her they needed to leave this seemingly benign place.

As they strolled across the quad, Blaise felt the late morning sun warm his face. Students lounged on the grass, engrossed in lively conversations or paging through books. It all appeared so...normal. So far removed from the thoughts of danger that clawed at him. Doubt crept into the corners of his mind. What if Seledora was wrong? What if Jefferson wasn't here in Cheswell but somewhere else in Greylight? Was he about to uproot Luci from her new life on a false alarm?

Blaise's eyebrows knitted together as Misty made an abrupt turn toward a domed edifice. The name *Rickson Building* was inscribed above the wide entrance on a stone arch. The young woman headed for the entrance, then realized Blaise wasn't keeping up. She turned to track his progress. Blaise's eyes met hers, a silent question hovering in the air between them. A memory of his tour with Luci nudged him. This was the alchemy building.

"Is Luci in class here?" Blaise asked. If so, maybe it was best to wait until she had been dismissed.

Misty offered a sheepish grin. "We're headed for the dorms, actually. This is just a detour. I need to grab something from the lab. It won't take long."

A prickle of unease danced down Blaise's spine, but he pushed it aside, offering a nod of agreement. "Sure, no problem." After all, he was the unexpected visitor. It seemed only fair to be accommodating.

The building welcomed them with a hush, their footsteps reverberating through its hallways as if they were disturbed by their presence. Misty guided him up a flight of stairs worn by years of academic traffic, down a corridor lined with doors that looked identical. Finally, she halted before one, seemingly no different from the rest.

"Just a moment." Misty vanished into the room, leaving him alone in the corridor.

He shifted his weight from one foot to the other, scanning the empty hallway. His ears strained, trying to catch any telltale sounds from the room Misty had entered, but all he heard was the uncanny silence of the corridor.

Finally, the door creaked open, and Misty reappeared, a leather satchel now slung over her shoulder. "Got what I needed. We're good to go," she declared, her voice a little too bright as she locked the door behind her.

Blaise's eyes flicked to the satchel, but he bit back the questions that surged to his lips. He was here on her goodwill, and it wouldn't do to appear ungrateful or suspicious. "All right then," he said, forcing a smile.

As they exited the building and resumed their path toward the dormitories, the uneasy feeling continued to nag at him. He pushed it down, focusing on the task at hand: find Luci, make sure she's safe, and get out. It was a simple plan, but in a place like this, nothing felt simple anymore.

Misty guided Blaise through the courtyard, arriving at a dignified brick dormitory adorned with white window trims. Together, they ascended a series of wooden stairs and navigated down a narrow corridor. The faded floral carpet underfoot seemed to absorb their footsteps, adding a layer of eerie quiet.

Finally, Misty stopped before a nondescript door, indistinguishable from the countless others that lined the hall. Rather than knocking or announcing their arrival, she began fiddling with her satchel. "I hate it when these things just won't cooperate," she muttered, almost to herself. She lowered the satchel to the floor and hunched over it.

Blaise's brows furrowed in mild confusion. Shouldn't she be knocking or, at the very least, producing a key? What was she doing?

Before he could fully process the situation, Misty straightened up, her face flushed. "Look, I'm sorry. You seem like a nice guy, but I've got to ace this practicum." Before he could parse the meaning behind her words, he felt a sharp prick in his upper arm. A needle.

His eyes widened, a bolt of alarm racing through his body. He instinctively jerked away, feeling a stinging sensation where the needle had made contact.

Not missing a beat, Misty swiftly pulled a key from her pocket, unlocked the door, and swung it open.

A voice echoed from the depths of the room, sounding puzzled and alarmed. "What—?"

Blaise's head spun, his focus blurring. As Misty shoved him over the threshold, he wobbled, struggling to maintain his balance.

"Blaise!"

Through the disorienting haze, he saw a familiar figure rush toward him. Jefferson. Just before his legs gave out, strong arms enveloped him, guiding him gently to the floor. He looked up, managing a weak smile at the face filled with concern and disbelief.

"Hey," Blaise mumbled, his words slurred. "Found you."

His vision narrowed, the edges darkening like the close of a grim theater curtain. He slumped against Jefferson, the last remnants of consciousness slipping from his grasp. The last sound to reach his ears was the ominous click of the door locking behind him, sealing his fate.

CHAPTER TWENTY-ONE

A Little Sip

Alice

Alice sat alone in the dorm room, the exhaustion of the passing hours settling into her bones. Thoughts of Theo consumed her mind, and each sound from outside—distant footsteps, muffled conversations—honed her senses to a razor's edge, making her more and more eager for some sign of him.

No one answered her shouts or banging on the door. No one. She was utterly alone.

The creak of the door opening interrupted her thoughts. She sprang from her seat on the bed, mentally preparing herself to confront whoever entered. Her muscles tensed, ready to defend or flee. A flurry of possibilities raced through her mind: Could it be Phillip, back for another venomous exchange? A guard bearing some meager meal? Or perhaps the student to whom this room actually belonged? No matter who it was, she steeled herself, ready to do whatever it took to find her son and escape this place.

When the door finally swung wide, it revealed not Phillip. Not a guard, not even a student, but a stranger—a man with a balding pate and an unremarkable face. For just a second, Alice let her guard down, tricked by his nondescript appearance. But almost immediately, she pulled her defenses back up, tucking her chin and narrowing her eyes.

"Who are you?" she asked, her voice calm yet demanding. She scanned him, searching for any signs of a hidden weapon or concealed intentions. The man seemed harmless enough, but his smile—it didn't reach his eyes, and that put her on edge.

He lingered in the doorway, that strange smile still on his face. "The name's Zebulon Woodrow," he replied, his tone oddly pleasant, as if they were casual acquaintances meeting at a dinner party rather than enemies in a makeshift prison. "I must say, it's quite intriguing to have you here at Cheswell, Alice."

Her pulsed raced in alarm. She knew this man. Or, at the very least, she had seen him before, at the galas and events she had to attend as Phillip's wife. This man was the spouse of another Quiet One, Tara Woodrow. And, similar to how Phillip had taken Alice for her magic, she recalled that Tara's husband was an alchemist.

She swallowed, lifting her chin. "Now I remember you. Why am I here?"

Zebulon's smile stretched a notch wider, as if her query was an amusing riddle. "All in good time, my dear. All in good time," he said with an off-putting casualness that made her flesh crawl.

"Don't *my dear* me," she retorted, her eyes boring into his. She would not be lulled into a false sense of security. "I have no intention of becoming a permanent resident of Cheswell. I want out, and I want my son with me."

Zebulon looked at her with his head tilted, as if examining a curious artifact. "You've barely scratched the surface of what

Cheswell offers. Perhaps a brief tour could persuade you to stay awhile?" He extended his arm.

Alice hesitated, suspicion and distrust warring with her desperate need to find Theo. If she wanted answers, she'd have to play his game, at least for now.

With a reluctant sigh, she slipped her hand into the crook of his elbow. Zebulon's smile widened, sending a fresh wave of unease coursing through her veins. "Wonderful. Right this way, please," Zebulon urged, guiding her out of the room and down a staircase. The brick walls seemed to close in, heavy with untold secrets and history. Alice scanned her surroundings, her eyes darting for any sign, any clue, that could offer insight into this confounding place.

"My son," Alice started, her voice firming. "Where is he? I need to see him now."

Zebulon offered another ambiguous smile. "All in good time, Alice. All in good time."

Alice clenched her jaw so tightly she thought her teeth might crack. Every nerve in her body screamed to lash out, to demand her son's whereabouts, but she reined in her instincts. Right now, her best chance at finding Theo lay in playing along with this odd man.

They reached the bottom of the stairs, and Alice's heart pounded as they stepped outside. For a moment, she thought he might lead her to freedom. But Zebulon instead guided her across the courtyard toward another stately building. He paused at its heavy wooden door, turning toward her with a look she couldn't quite decipher.

"I think you'll find this next part...quite enlightening," he said with a sort of delighted anticipation. Before she could voice another demand for her son, he pulled the door open.

Alice took a hesitant step, peering into the building. It differed from the others—less inviting, more clinical. The hairs on the back of her neck stood on end.

"I've seen enough," she said, her voice steely as she crossed her arms. "Where is my son?"

Zebulon looked at her, his eyes twinkling, as if enjoying a private joke. "Ah, patience. A tour of the campus, and then you shall see Theo."

Alice suppressed a shiver. She trusted this man as far as she could throw him. But if tolerating his mysterious tour led her to Theo, she would endure it—for now.

Alice gathered her courage and stepped through the door, Zebulon following close behind. The door closed with a resonant thud that echoed down the narrow corridor. They hurried down the hallway, a constricting passage that seemed to tighten around them, suffocating in its closeness. Devoid of windows, the corridor presented an academic tunnel, its end lost in oppressive shadows.

At last, Zebulon paused before a nondescript door, its window obscured from within. He produced a key, and the lock clicked open with an unnerving finality.

"After you." He gestured, his mouth twisting in a disquieting semblance of courtesy.

Gathering a shaky breath, Alice stepped inside. The room was brightly lit, casting her surroundings into harsh relief. It was clearly some sort of laboratory or medical facility. Shelves filled with neatly arranged vials and arcane equipment covered the walls. But what truly disturbed her was the lone chair in the center of the room. It looked like an ordinary armchair, if one could ignore the leather restraints dangling ominously from its arms and legs.

Alice couldn't ignore them. She whirled around to find Zebulon securing the door behind them, locking them in this oppressive room. "Where is my son?" Alice's voice came out brittle.

"Theo is quite safe, I assure you," Zebulon responded, his voice a model of icy calm.

"Then where is he?" Alice's voice turned shrill, her maternal fear sharpening each word. "I want to see my son. Now!"

Zebulon raised a pacifying hand. "All in due time. But first, would you kindly have a seat?" His eyes flicked toward the chair, its restraints seeming to beckon menacingly under the bright lights.

Alice shook her head vehemently, backing away. "No way in Perdition."

Zebulon let out a sigh tinged with a note of irritable condescension. "Very well," he said, moving toward the door and opening it again. "She's proving to be...uncooperative. Bring them in, if you will." His voice carried down the sterile, echoing hallway.

A cold dread settled into Alice's stomach as two robust young men stepped into the room. They were strapping figures, their physiques sculpted as if from a lifetime of demanding physical training. The one on the right had a youthful, almost cherubic face that clashed with the hard, muscular lines of his build. It only intensified her wariness as he looked at her, his expression torn between duty and discomfort.

Zebulon gestured vaguely in Alice's direction. "Our guest seems to be resisting the seating arrangements. Do make her comfortable, won't you?"

Alice's eyes darted around the harshly lit room, frantically assessing her options. The room offered no allies, just cold metal and hard corners. Her heart pounded a frantic rhythm in her chest as she clenched her fists, sinking into a makeshift fighting stance.

The two men approached her cautiously, as if she were a rabid animal. "Look, ma'am," the cherub-faced one began softly, his eyes flicking briefly to Zebulon. "I really don't want a poor grade on my record. So, if you'd please have a seat...?"

Alice's adrenaline surged, narrowing her world to this immediate threat. As the young man extended his hand, she lashed out, her nails raking across his cheek like the claws of a cornered animal. He staggered back, his hand rising to touch the fresh welts that marred his boyish face, trickling thin rivulets of blood.

"Wow, you've some fight in you," he managed, wincing through what looked like a forced grin. "But we really have to go through with this."

Before she could plan another attack, the second man—built like a locomotive—swiftly circled behind her. His arms latched around hers like steel traps, immobilizing her upper body. She thrashed wildly, her muscles fueled by a mother's desperate strength, but his hold was unyielding. The cherub-faced young man, recovering quickly, lunged for her legs, halting her frantic kicks. Together, they hoisted her off the ground and moved her toward the chair as if she were a piece of rogue machinery.

With a guttural scream that tore from the depths of her being, Alice bucked and twisted, but to no avail. Her captors worked with grim, mechanical efficiency, strapping her into the chair. The leather restraints bit into her skin, but she hardly felt it; her entire being was aflame with righteous indignation.

"Let me go!" Alice's voice was raw. "You can't do this to me!"

The young men shifted uncomfortably, their shoulders hunched, but they didn't dare to challenge Zebulon's authority. They stepped aside, their gazes focused on their shoes.

The door creaked open again, and Alice's eyes shot toward it. For a brief, hopeful second, she thought it might be Theo. Her hopes were dashed.

"You!" she snarled as Phillip entered, lips curled in contempt. "I should have known you were behind this, you bastard!"

Phillip seemed genuinely surprised by the intensity of her disdain. "Now, Alice, there's no need for that kind of talk. You broke my heart. Running off, not even a note. And taking Theo with you."

Anger coursed through Alice like liquid ice. "I had to. There's no way I'm going to...to allow him to be raised to be just like you!" Or like her own father. Never.

Phillip's eyes narrowed, his face clouding over like a storm gathering force. "So, *I'm* the villain here? I tried to provide for our family, and yet you ran away and took my son."

Alice ground her teeth together. It was true; Phillip did seem to care for Theo. But her gut told her she couldn't let her son grow up in the kind of family she'd escaped from. Words jumbled in her mind, each one a potential key to her shackles, but none seemed to fit. She lowered her gaze, struggling to marshal her thoughts.

Phillip let out a resigned sigh. "If you would, please."

Alice looked up, thinking for a moment he was speaking to her. But he was watching Zebulon, who had ambled over to a table laden with an array of scientific apparatus. Glass vials filled with various colored liquids sat nestled in wooden racks. Intricate metal tools lay scattered across the surface, their purpose unknown to her. Zebulon selected a vial filled with a mysterious liquid and returned to where she was restrained. He offered her a cheerful smile. "This little elixir is quite the problem-solver. A taste of this, and you'll find many of your questions will be answered."

Alice's eyes widened, her breath hitching as Zebulon leaned in, the vial inches from her lips. Every muscle in her body tensed, pulling against the leather restraints until they bit into her skin.

"Keep that poison away from me!" she bellowed, her voice reverberating in the sterile room. Her eyes were ablaze with fear and defiance.

Zebulon sighed, false sympathy dripping from his tone. "Oh, Alice, resistance is so counterproductive. A little sip, and we can proceed to more pleasant conversations."

He glanced at the young assistants who were hovering by the door. They exchanged rueful glances as they moved closer to Alice. With practiced ease, they held her head, their grip unyielding. She twisted and writhed, her heart pounding in her chest, but their strength was overwhelming.

As Zebulon tilted the vial, Alice clenched her teeth, her jaw locked. But he pinched her nose shut, forcing her to gasp for air. In that split second, he seized the opportunity and poured the liquid between her lips. It was an acrid blend, bitter and metallic, assaulting her taste buds. She coughed violently, trying to expel it, but the substance had already made its way down her throat. A futile spray of spittle was all she got out.

Alice wheezed, sucking in air greedily as the young men stepped back, their faces etched with an agitation they couldn't hide. The potion seemed to crawl through her insides, settling in her stomach like a block of ice—no, worse. It was as though her very stomach had turned to ice, and now it was fracturing, sending fissures of cold through her body. She clenched her eyes shut, tears of pain and anger seeping through her eyelashes.

Alice felt the air shift as Zebulon spoke, his tone clinical. "Phillip, eye contact is crucial for the process to be effective. Make sure you catch her gaze."

Eye contact? Why? What had they done to her with that vile potion? She squeezed her eyes shut, willing herself not to open them, not even for a second. She'd keep them shut for an eternity if she had to.

The room grew quieter, uneasy murmurs fading away. Footsteps receded, announcing the departure of the young men. Leaving her alone in this cold room with Phillip and Zebulon. Time was on her side; if there was one thing she had plenty of, it was stubbornness.

With her eyes clenched shut, tears weeping from the corners, she waited, muscles taut. Waited for whatever grim fate came next. But she would not open her eyes. She would not give them the satisfaction of using her like some experiment, like a cog in their sinister machine. Never again would she be a helpless pawn in their hands.

Phillip's voice shattered the silence, thick with a remorse she didn't trust. "Alice, my love. Open your eyes. Let me explain, let me—"

"Quiet," Zebulon interjected softly. "She'll come around. Give her time."

Phillip moved closer, his presence looming over her. The familiar scent of sandalwood and cloves invaded her senses, awakening memories she had fought tooth and nail to repress.

"Alice." Phillip's voice quivered, teetering on the edge of despair. "I never wanted to hurt you. The gods know I've erred, made unforgivable mistakes. But things have changed. *I've* changed." He inhaled deeply, the sound shaky. "When you took Theo and left, you took a part of me with you. A part I didn't even know I could lose. My world crumbled."

She bit down hard on her lip, refusing to grant him the satisfaction of hearing her cry.

"I thought if I could just get you back, show you how much you mean to me, I could make things right between us," Phillip continued, his words suffused with anguish. "I see now that I've only made things worse. But please, Alice, give me one more chance. Let me show you I've changed."

She shook her head. "Tigers never change their stripes. You're incapable of such a thing." But was he? Was Jefferson? And did it even matter? She didn't love Phillip, and that was all there was to it. This was madness.

His hand gently brushed her tear-streaked cheek, the warmth of his touch making her skin crawl. She recoiled inwardly but didn't physically shrink back. "Open your eyes, Alice," he implored softly. "Just look at me, please."

Alice's voice rose, edged with a feral intensity. "No. Go away. I thought I made it clear when I left. I don't want to be your possession anymore!"

She heard him swallow hard, his shoes squeaking against the sterile floor, the muted sound of leather soles reluctantly retreating. The door hinges groaned as it opened and then whispered shut, sealing her in the room. Straining her ears, she listened for any telltale signs of his presence: a furtive breath, the scrape of a foot shifting weight. But she only heard the reverberation of something from within the building, some sort of mechanical whine. It raised in pitch until it would have drowned out the softer sounds in the room.

So she waited. Alice didn't know how long. Her stomach gnarled in hunger, a bodily protest that she defiantly ignored. She'd rather starve than open her eyes.

As more time slipped through the hourglass of her patience, unbearable tension settled over her like a suffocating cloak. She couldn't endure it any longer. With a cautious crack of her eyelid, she peered out, plunging headlong into Phillip's intent gaze, as if the ground had suddenly vanished from beneath her feet.

Something fractured within her core, shattering the walls she had built to protect herself from her husband. Alice felt like she was in freefall, an unending descent into the deep pools of Phillip's eyes, each layer of her resistance peeling away in the turbulence. Compelled by a force she couldn't resist, she fully opened her other eye, her mind swirling in bewildered astonishment.

Phillip's face swam into focus, his eyes reflecting regret and vulnerable warmth. *Oh. Phillip.* The man whose love had once been her sanctuary. Her lips unfurled into a gentle smile, filled with a newfound affection that surprised even her.

"Phillip," she whispered, his name like a prayer on her tongue.

Phillip's eyes searched her face, uncertainty clouding his features. "Alice?" he ventured, his voice soaked in a tentative hope.

Hearing Phillip's voice, Alice's smile hesitated, a subtle tremor of uncertainty. As though for the first time, she noticed the restraints binding her arms to the chair. Her brows knitted together as she gave a puzzled tug against the leather cuffs.

"What's this?" she asked, looking back up at Phillip. "Why can't I come to you? What's going on?"

Phillip blew out a long breath, his shoulders sagging as if releasing a heavy burden. He swallowed hard before responding. "You're okay now, Alice," he said, his tone gentle. "I'll get you out of there, and then everything will be fine again. We'll get Theo and be a happy family once more. Just like we were always meant to be."

Alice's smile blossomed anew, radiant and unburdened. The words *happy family* echoed in her ears like the refrain of a soothing lullaby. The bitterness and sense of betrayal that had once consumed her seemed to evaporate, replaced by the new life Phillip promised.

She felt—deep in her core—that everything would fall into place. With Phillip by her side and Theo in her arms, all the pieces would fit. And in that moment, with that newfound conviction, nothing else in the world seemed to matter.

CHAPTER TWENTY-TWO

More Potential for Accidental Disfigurement

Luci

*L*uci stood in the quad, her shoulders a little less tense than they had been on her first day. She took a deep, steadying breath, her eyes roving over familiar faces and architectural landmarks. It was her third day at Cheswell University, and the apprehension and excitement that had gripped her initially was slowly giving way to a sense of cautious optimism. "You've got this. This is your big chance," she muttered to herself, her fingers drumming a quick rhythm against her bag.

Walking towards her math class, her grip on her bag was less frantic than before, her steps more assured. The hallways, once a bustling maze, had started to make sense, and she found her seat without the need to double-check her classroom number. She felt a small thrill of accomplishment. She was getting the hang of this.

"Good morning, everyone! Now that we've got a couple of

classes under our belts, let's dive into some more challenging problems," the professor announced, his academic excitement serving as a reminder of why she found math oddly comforting. Numbers were constant. They didn't change or become less reliable when you crossed lines.

Settling in, Luci opened her notebook to a page already filled with scribbled equations and notes from previous classes. As she listened to the professor, the room's ambiance—an amalgamation of the instructor's steady cadence and the soft scratching of pencil on paper—worked its soothing magic. Luci lost herself in the logic and elegance of math, her pencil flying over the paper as she worked through the problems at hand.

By the time the class was drawing to a close, Luci felt a surge of self-assurance. She glanced around, catching the eye of a few classmates who nodded back at her, their faces familiar by now. *Yes, I do belong here.* And with that empowering realization, her thoughts eagerly jumped to what awaited her next: Introduction to Alchemical Theory. She could hardly wait.

As Luci stepped into the alchemy classroom, a wave of chatter washed over her, accompanied by the rustling of pages and the clinking of glass vials. Students were already clustered in small groups, animatedly discussing the latest lesson or perhaps sharing rumors about the mysterious ingredients listed in the syllabus. Her eyes naturally drifted to the front of the room, where Professor Woodrow, who had given her the tour on her first day, was engrossed in a discussion with an older student. They were in the midst of a lively debate, their hands gesturing wildly as if trying to conjure an answer from thin air.

"Professor Woodrow certainly knows how to engage his students," Luci mused to herself, the wisp of a smile crossing her lips.

She took a seat near a girl who was flipping through her textbook with a furrowed brow. "Hey, I'm Luci. We didn't get a chance to introduce ourselves the other day," Luci said, extending a hand.

The girl looked up, her eyes meeting Luci's for a moment, before a warm smile spread across her face. "Oh, hi! I'm Kelsey. And yeah, the first couple of days in a new school are always hectic, aren't they?"

"Absolutely," Luci agreed, her own smile growing wider. "I've been trying to soak it all in. Cheswell is quite different from where I come from."

Kelsey's eyes twinkled. "Isn't that the case for many of us? But, you know, every expert was once a beginner. Don't sweat it."

Before Luci could express her gratitude for the reassuring words, Professor Woodrow's clapping reverberated through the room, the sound crisp and commanding.

"Ah, day three of our academic foray," Professor Woodrow began, rubbing his palms together. "By now, the initial sheen of scholarly novelty should be giving way to a more, shall we say, single-minded curiosity about alchemical particulars."

The room settled into a focused hush, students eagerly flipping open their notebooks and pulling out pencils. As he spoke, Luci observed her classmates' reactions: a blend of respect and perhaps a touch of puzzlement—altogether fitting for a professor whose method mingled dry humor with academic rigor.

"Alchemy," Professor Woodrow continued, sauntering by the chalkboard scrawled with arcane symbols from his last session. "It's both an art and a science, you know. A little like cooking, but with fewer onions and more potential for accidental disfigurement. So, you'll want to pay attention."

Luci tightened her grip on her pencil. She'd been practicing alchemy under her mother's tutelage for years, but Professor Woodrow's approach made her keenly aware of the field's vast scope.

"Now, I do have certain expectations." He paused, his gaze darting around the room until they briefly met Luci's. "Alchemy isn't about your starting point; it's about your journey. How far are you willing to venture, and how many times are you willing to fail, perhaps spectacularly, along the way?"

Inhaling deeply, Luci absorbed his words. Cheswell was a landscape unlike any she'd known, and she was ready to tackle every challenge it offered.

"Shall we, then," Professor Woodrow concluded, his voice ringing with high drama, "continue our modest pursuit of alchemical mastery? Today, we'll explore the enigma of the alchemic furnace and its applications in various traditions. A subject both enlightening and, dare I say, cautionary."

He picked up a piece of chalk and scrawled the words *Alchemic Furnace* in broad, looping strokes on the chalkboard. Luci leaned forward, pencil poised and ready.

Professor Woodrow paced languidly in front of the board, each step measured. "Let's ruminate on the furnace, shall we? A delightful contraption—more than a mere apparatus—it's...well, it's a metaphor. A life lesson on a stand. Its flames? Ah, they're emblematic of alchemy's dramatic transformative power. Did you know, by the way, that fire is deeply celebrated in a plethora of traditions? Quite the purifier."

Luci jotted notes, absorbing every nuanced word.

"Now, imagine for a moment," he continued with a mock daydreamy quality, "substances thrown into this furnace. The gentle, or not so gentle, embrace of heat breaks them down, whittling them to their purest essence, readying them for some elemental mingling. And here's a tidbit for the curious mind." He cast a fleeting look of feigned surprise at the students. "The precision of this heat? Paramount. Undershoot and you're left with an incomplete metamorphosis. Overshoot and, well, you might as well bid farewell to your concoction."

His voice lowered, almost to a whisper, for dramatic tension. "Down south, in certain traditions, the furnace attains a near-mythical stature. It's no mere tool, but a spiritual chalice, under the guardianship of ethereal alchemists, fusing not mere metals, but life's intricate essences."

With deliberate slowness, he turned to the chalkboard, sketching a rudimentary furnace diagram, annotating each segment. "Every bit matters. The crucible. The bellow. That lofty chimney. Miss one? It's like forgetting the milk in your morning tea."

His gaze settled on Luci, a glint of challenge in his eyes. "Think of it as a dance: a test of wits, finesse, and endless patience. Befriend the furnace, understand its quirks, and you're, oh, a leap closer to unlocking alchemy's mysteries."

The remainder of his talk wove through materials, tales, and age-old traditions, tinged with anecdotes of famed alchemists and their heartwarming furnace escapades.

Finally, wrapping up his detailed elucidation, he set down the chalk, wiping the residue on his sweater. "As we venture further into the semester," Professor Woodrow added, "we'll unpack more of alchemy's foundational elements. Trust me, by the time you're done with this course, you won't just be mixing basic elixirs. You'll be well on your way to understanding the universe's most intricate secrets."

A frisson of excitement coursed through Luci as she listened to Professor Woodrow. Her initial uncertainty had transformed into a mounting eagerness to delve deeper into the practice that had fascinated her since childhood.

"And let's not forget," Professor Woodrow added, his voice dropping to an almost tantalizing whisper, as if sharing a secret recipe for turning lead into gold, "I've got some special projects up my sleeve. Projects that will not only test your theoretical knowledge but also give you a taste of the real-world applications of alchemy. I will generously reward extra credit to those brave enough to volunteer." He inclined his head. "Is anyone here up to the challenge?"

Luci felt her heartbeat speed up. Practical experience was the crucible in which academic knowledge was tested and refined. She had come to Cheswell to grow, to evolve, and to master the alchemical arts. Her hand shot into the air.

Luci scanned the room as her fellow students also raised their hands, eager to volunteer. Her tenacity flared; this was her moment to shine, to prove she belonged here. When Professor Woodrow's eyes met the sea of upraised hands, Luci held her breath, silently imploring him to pick her.

The room was filled with excitement as each student introduced themselves as he sifted through his volunteers. Luci listened attentively, mentally piecing together the puzzle of her classmates' varied experiences. Some had clearly dabbled in alchemy before, while others seemed like they were just beginning their journey into the art.

When it was Luci's turn to speak, she inhaled deeply and introduced herself. "Hello, everyone. I'm Luci Mason. I've been studying alchemy for years under my mom's tutelage. She's an accomplished alchemist, and I'm excited to take what I've learned from her and to build on it here with all of you."

Professor Woodrow paused, resting his folded hands atop his stomach as he considered her words. "Ah, an alchemist mother. What might her name be? I've been around the, er, alchemical block, you might say."

A twinge of regret surged through Luci. She hadn't intended to mention her mother. It was a detail she was supposed to keep under wraps. But now it was out there. "Um, Mary Mason," she stammered, hiding her mother's true identity.

"Mary Mason?" Professor Woodrow mused, as if flipping through a mental catalog of alchemists he'd met or heard of. "No, can't say the name rings any bells. But it's certainly promising that you've had early exposure to alchemy. The apple doesn't fall far from the aludel, you know." With a flick of his wrist, he moved on to the next eager student.

As Professor Woodrow began announcing the chosen volunteers, Luci's breath hitched in anticipation. The room seemed to grow dense with suspense as each name echoed in the room. The moment she heard her own name, a surge of elation washed over her. She would be part of something extraordinary.

"Those of you selected," Professor Woodrow continued, his expression more animated than it had been, "consider yourselves the fortunate few. We will plumb the depths of alchemical wisdom together, stretching the boundaries of not just our understanding, but also our capabilities. We're embarking on an educational treasure hunt of sorts, and who knows what gems of knowledge we might unearth?"

Switching to a more solemn tone, he added, "Our special evening sessions will indeed be...well, *special*. We'll dive nose-first into advanced alchemical theories and hands-on practices. I expect you all to be punctual, committed, and, above all, focused. It would be a shame if someone were to, say, accidentally transmute themselves into a tree stump because of a lapse in attention."

Luci's mind raced as she mentally prepared herself for the challenge ahead. This was her chance to prove her worth and showcase the skills she'd honed alongside her mother for years. She was determined not to let this opportunity slip through her fingers.

"Your first session will begin tomorrow evening at seven o'clock sharp," Professor Woodrow announced, his gaze scrutinizing each student as if he could discern their level of commitment merely through eye contact. "I trust you all will arrive punctual, prepared, and brimming with an insatiable thirst for knowledge. Anything less would be, well, a disservice to yourselves and a waste of my valuable time."

As the bell signaled the end of class, Luci meticulously stowed away her notebook and alchemical tools with a sense of sacred duty. Exiting the classroom, she waved a farewell to Kelsey as she headed for her next class. Luci released a contented sigh. Her face almost hurt from smiling, but she didn't care.

This was perfect.

CHAPTER TWENTY-THREE

Extracurricular Imprisonment

A gossamer line of drool clung to the bristles of Blaise's beard as he lay on the bed in the dorm room. Jefferson touched his husband's shoulder, his fingers barely grazing the soft fabric of Blaise's shirt, a riot of emotions surging through him.

When that door had swung open, the last person he'd expected to see was Blaise. The moment he had stumbled into Jefferson's arms, only to collapse into unconsciousness, was etched into his mind like a scar.

A torrent of questions stormed through Jefferson's head, each one more worrisome than the last. Why had Blaise been drugged and brought here? What were the alchemist's plans for them?

The lack of answers frustrated Jefferson, leaving an empty pit in his stomach. Gently, almost reverently, he brushed his fingers over Blaise's bearded cheek, the warmth emanating from his skin a small comfort. There was a tiny solace in their togetherness, even if it was marred by their circumstances.

His thoughts veered toward Alice and Theo, his worry for them prickling like a thorn in his side. Jefferson's internal whirlwind of worry and frustration was momentarily calmed when he noticed Blaise beginning to stir. His husband's eyes fluttered.

Eager to offer comfort, Jefferson leaned over and gently kissed Blaise's forehead. "Blaise, can you hear me?"

With a languid groan, Blaise's eyes cracked open, unfocused and glazed. For a moment, he looked utterly bewildered, as if waking from a disorienting dream.

"Ah, my head," he mumbled, pressing his palm to his forehead as if trying to physically hold the pain at bay. "Where are we?" Then he paused, his blue eyes widening with realization. "Wait…I remember. Sort of. I'm really confused."

Gently, Jefferson helped Blaise shift upright. He fought the urge to pull Blaise into an embrace. Jefferson longed for the solid comfort of someone he cared about, but he didn't want to take his chances while Blaise was still disoriented. "You're at Cheswell University. Are you all right?"

Blaise's hand returned to his forehead, massaging gently. "I'm…I think I'm okay. Why are you here at Cheswell?"

Jefferson huffed out a breath that was almost a laugh. "I was going to ask you the very same thing."

Blaise stretched, his back arching like a cat awakening from a long slumber, working out the knots. "Luci's come here for further alchemy studies. Mom insisted I escort her."

Jefferson's eyebrows lifted in surprise. It made sense, but it also raised questions. "Do they know her true identity?"

Shaking his head, Blaise answered, "No. She's registered under an assumed name."

At that, Jefferson pursed his lips. While that was a good idea, and admirable, there were not as many alchemists as there were, say, political science majors or history scholars. He didn't think it would be very difficult for someone with the right motivation to ferret out who, exactly, Luci was. He sighed. If he'd known, he could have cautioned them against that.

But by the same token, this was Luci's life. She was impacted because of who she was related to, and it was unfair. But if there was one lesson Jefferson had learned in his youth, it was that life was often unfair—even for the elite.

He nodded. "I see. Was she captured, too?"

A heaviness settled on Blaise's shoulders. "I can't say for sure. Everything seemed normal during her admission. I was about to head back to Fortitude when Seledora intercepted us."

Blaise rubbed his hands together. Jefferson longed to snare his husband's hands in his, to grant him comfort. Was that something Blaise wanted? Jefferson couldn't tell.

Blaise swallowed. "If she hadn't, I would have left. I wouldn't have known you were here."

A large part of Jefferson wished that had been the case. He feared what Zebulon might do with Blaise under his thumb. "I see."

Blaise's eyes narrowed, scrutinizing him. "So, what's your story? You're not here for a late-in-life academic career, are you?"

Jefferson offered a wry half-smile, a feeble attempt to lighten their dire situation. "Oh, come now. It's never too late for higher education. Maybe I wanted to major in Advanced Captivity Studies."

Blaise arched an eyebrow, not buying the jest for a second. "I doubt they offer that course, and you're not the type for extracurricular imprisonment." The moment of levity vanished as quickly as it had appeared. "Did you reach Alice before all this?" Blaise's tone turned grave.

Jefferson's smile faltered, giving way to a sigh that seemed to drain his remaining energy. "Yes, we did speak. Alice and I...we were making progress, breaking down walls. But none of that seems to matter now. They were both taken with me."

Blaise's eyes widened, still clouded with the haze of grogginess. "What? Who would abduct all three of you and bring you to a university? That doesn't make sense."

"No, it doesn't," Jefferson concurred, his eyes darkening. "But Zebulon Woodrow seems to be the puppeteer pulling the strings. He's a professor here, from what I understand."

"Zebulon Woodrow?" Blaise squinted, as if the name were a puzzle he was trying to solve. "Why does that sound like a name I should remember?"

Jefferson grimaced. "He was married to Tara Woodrow. Do you remember her?"

Recognition flared in Blaise's eyes. "Oh, right, Tara. A Quiet One. She was the one who tried to drug Kittie, wasn't she?"

Oh, Fortunes of Tabris. With all that had gone on, Jefferson had nearly forgotten about that. This all made so much more sense. Tara had access to potions that could sedate or knock someone out through Zebulon. "The very same."

"She's the woman Raven killed." Blaise frowned.

"Yes."

"And so, Zebulon is..." Blaise's voice trailed off, as if the fog in his mind was lifting. "Oh, *biscuits.* The alchemist. And wait, he's also *Dean* Woodrow, the head of the College of Alchemy here, isn't he?"

"It seems you may possess a piece of the puzzle that wasn't in my hands," Jefferson said softly. "I didn't know he was in a position of leadership."

Blaise shut his eyes for a beat, then flashed them open once more, turning to Jefferson. "Are you okay? He didn't hurt you, did he?" There was an undercurrent of ferocity in Blaise's soft words that made Jefferson's breath hitch.

"No, I'm fine. He didn't hurt me." Jefferson rubbed his forehead. "But he did come speak to me. I'm not sure what he wants yet, but he seems...unhinged."

Blaise pursed his lips. "He seemed eccentric when we met him. But no one else seemed alarmed by him."

Jefferson longed to put an arm around Blaise, to hold him, but Jefferson was uncertain where he stood. "I don't know why we were brought together like this. It makes me wonder what he's planning," Jefferson admitted.

Blaise's brow wrinkled in contemplation. "It does seem like a miscalculation." Then he shook his head. "Alchemists don't make miscalculations. At least, not good ones."

"Perhaps his grief has kept him from thinking clearly," Jefferson hedged, though even as he said the words, he didn't believe them. Grief struck people in different ways. Zebulon might be grieving, but he'd also seemed deliberate.

"Well, whatever the plan is, he won't succeed." Blaise's words were resolute, bolstering Jefferson's flagging spirits. "I'm just glad to see you. When that girl brought me here, all I could think about was trying to convince Luci to leave. Now it looks like I'll have to get both of you out of here." His voice was light, but his eyes were serious. Blaise added, "And I think it's high time to start working on that."

Oh. He didn't know. Jefferson lifted a hand in caution. "My darling cinnamon roll…"

But Blaise was on a mission. He strode over to the door, pressing his palm flat against the painted surface. He frowned. "That's strange…" He turned back to look at Jefferson. "My magic feels muted. Numb, almost."

Jefferson sighed. "That's what I was trying to tell you. There's null paint on the walls. Zebulon mentioned it to me before he left."

Surprised, Blaise glanced at the door, reconsidering. "Null paint? But that shouldn't affect me. I can break through salt-iron."

Jefferson shook his head, his expression turning grim. "Null isn't salt-iron. Salt-iron drains magic, makes it weaker. Null just cancels it out completely."

"Even for a Breaker?" Blaise's eyes widened.

"It seems so," Jefferson confirmed, his voice tinged with regret. "Which means we can't rely on our abilities to get us out of this room."

Blaise dragged a hand over his beard. "That really frosts my cookies." His shoulders slumped. Without access to his magic, his confidence evaporated. He trudged back to the small bed and sat down heavily beside Jefferson.

His husband looked so down Jefferson couldn't stop himself from wrapping an arm around him, pulling Blaise close. Blaise leaned into him, resting his head on Jefferson's shoulder with a resigned sigh.

I missed this. I missed you. Jefferson hated that this was what had brought them back together.

They sat in silence for a few moments, taking comfort in each other's presence. Jefferson was the one who broke the quiet. "We'll figure this out," he murmured. "Together."

Blaise lifted his head to meet Jefferson's gaze. The muscles of his jaw tightened, signaling the return of his resolve. "You're right. I won't let some unhinged alchemist paint us into a corner."

Jefferson's lips curved upward in a faint but sincere smile. "We'll just brush it off, then."

Blaise chuckled, aiming a wry half-smile at Jefferson. "We've gotten out of worse scrapes than this."

Jefferson huffed a soft laugh, his shoulders easing in tandem with the momentary lightening of the atmosphere. "Too right, love."

Blaise's eyes widened a fraction, an eyebrow subtly arching upward. "Also, did you call me *cinnamon roll* earlier?"

Caught off guard, Jefferson blinked at the question. "Oh. Yes. Was it too much?"

Blaise shook his head ever so slightly, unspoken contentment flashing across his face. "No. I kinda liked it."

CHAPTER TWENTY-FOUR

Words to Actions

Phillip

Phillip scooped another spoonful of oatmeal into his mouth, his eyes roving toward Alice with each bite. Her bright, vacuous smiles tugged at his conscience. Yes, he had manipulated the love of his life, but wasn't it for the greater good? For their family's unity?

The room they occupied was a study in contrasts, a makeshift sanctum in the basement of one of the academic buildings. Plush, embroidered bedding coexisted with unyielding wooden tables, mellowed only by the diffuse glow of a gas lamp that cast a gentle light across the room. The air held a peculiar blend of aromas: the comforting scent of warm oats, the musk of leather-bound tomes, and a faint trace of cleaning supplies. It was a far cry from the sumptuousness of their home, but it was serviceable for their current needs.

Just as he was about to scoop up another mouthful of oatmeal, a knock reverberated through the silence.

"Oh! We have a visitor!" Alice's voice was unusually bright.

Phillip pushed back his chair and rose, but before he could reach the door, it swung open to reveal Zebulon Woodrow carrying a violin case. Phillip's eyes narrowed, recognizing it. Alice's violin. He hadn't seen it since...well, since she had run off.

Alice's voice sounded dreamy, unlike herself. "Oh! A violin? I love the violin."

Zebulon sauntered in, setting the case on one of the wooden tables. "It does make beautiful music, doesn't it?" His voice was unassumingly pleasant as he took a seat.

Phillip's gaze settled on Alice, and the disquiet within him deepened. The effects of the love potion were undeniable—she was behaving like an automaton, her fierce independence replaced by mindless adoration. He had wanted this, he kept reminding himself. To get his obedient, loving wife back. But seeing Alice like this stirred an unexpected pang of regret in Phillip's chest. She wasn't herself anymore. The Alice he knew, the one he had fallen in love with, was spirited and strong-willed. Not this docile, vacant-eyed woman gazing at him with a placid smile.

Zebulon appeared to revel in the transformation, savoring the discomfort it provoked in Phillip. "My, my," he said, his voice tinged with a modest satisfaction that only intensified Phillip's disquiet. "How the tables have turned. From a headstrong, defiant woman to a doting, submissive wife. The wonders of alchemy are limitless, don't you agree?"

Phillip's jaw clenched involuntarily, but he said nothing.

Seemingly undeterred by Phillip's silence, Zebulon leaned back in his chair, a smug expression settling over his features. "You look as though you've bitten into a sour fruit, Phillip. Isn't this precisely what you were hoping for? A docile wife, entirely within your sphere of influence?"

Phillip's voice emerged as a low growl, every syllable rumbling with restrained fury. "I wanted my family back. Whole and intact."

Zebulon raised an eyebrow. "And now you have it. Alice is yours again. Just as you wished."

Unable to meet Zebulon's gaze any longer, Phillip looked away. A torrent of conflicting emotions roared within him. Yes, he had regained his wife, but the cost was becoming unbearable to consider.

Taking a deep, steadying breath, Phillip willed himself back to the present moment. There were urgent matters at hand, issues that demanded his attention. "So, Zebulon," he said, forcing his voice to remain calm as he redirected the conversation. "What brings you here?"

Zebulon slouched, his posture the epitome of nonchalance. "Ah, I'm merely here to remind you of our little agreement. The time has come to transition from words to actions, so to speak."

"Agreement? My promise?" Phillip's voice was tinged with skepticism and rising dread. In his desperate rush to recover Alice and Theo, he had hastily struck a deal with Zebulon, giving little thought to the alchemist's intentions.

"Indeed," Zebulon said, his voice dripping with a casual assurance that Phillip found increasingly concerning. "In return for reuniting you with your wife, you agreed to assist me with my own endeavors."

Phillip felt a sinking feeling in his gut. "What exactly do you need me to do?"

A calculated grin spread across Zebulon's face. "Oh, it's not overly complicated. I require Alice to contribute a musical backdrop to my work. A specific melody or tune that will render the alchemy wing entirely invisible to the minds of the curious."

Phillip's brows furrowed. Why would Zebulon need the alchemy wing to be invisible? What was Zebulon up to in that lab of his? Nothing good, Phillip suspected.

Grimacing, Phillip shook his head. "I can't allow Alice to become a pawn in whatever scheme you're orchestrating."

Zebulon's previously affable expression morphed into a mask of icy sternness. "Let's not forget our arrangement, shall we? After all, your reunited family—" He gestured toward Alice, who remained blissfully unaware. "—is the direct result of our collaboration."

Fed up and frustrated, Phillip shot up from his chair. "Deal or no deal, I refuse to be a part of this any longer. I'm taking Alice and Theo, and we're leaving Cheswell tonight."

Zebulon pushed himself up from the chair. Though he stood a head shorter than Phillip, his presence seemed to fill the small room. "I must insist that your plans for departure are...impractical," he said in a voice that was almost a whisper.

Phillip clenched his fists. "Your approval is irrelevant."

Zebulon tilted his head slightly, his dark eyes fixed on Phillip. "Ah, but you'll find it's rather pertinent. You see, young Theo could serve as a fascinating subject—"

"Don't you dare threaten my son," he growled, the words escaping through clenched teeth. Phillip's eyes flared with an immediate, protective fury. The hint of a threat toward his son was enough to fuel his worst fears.

Zebulon's demeanor remained eerily calm. "Then I suggest you uphold your end of our agreement," he replied, though disappointment shadowed his features. "You *did* promise to do whatever was necessary to reclaim your wife."

Phillip's heart hammered in his chest, the implications of Zebulon's words sinking in like a blade. His son was a pawn, leverage to ensure his own compliance. Anger surged within him, a wildfire threatening to consume his self-control. He took a deliberate breath, pushing the fiery emotions back down. He had to keep a level head. Theo's safety was at stake.

"I want to see my son," Phillip said, his voice taut with controlled emotion. "I need proof that he's unharmed."

Zebulon laced his hands behind his back with an air of smug satisfaction. "Really, Phillip, you must understand you're in no position to issue demands."

The harsh reality of Phillip's situation loomed before him. He was, indeed, a captive, trapped in a web spun from his own desperation and short-sightedness. He expelled a long, drawn-out breath, his mind racing. Alice was under *his* influence, her magic at Phillip's command. He detested the idea of exploiting her for Zebulon's nefarious plans, but what choice was left to him? Alice, he knew, would prioritize Theo's safety above all else.

His shoulders sagged, almost imperceptibly, as he conceded. "Very well. Alice will provide the musical accompaniment you seek."

Zebulon's lips curled into a satisfied grin. "Splendid. We're on the same page, then." His eyes flicked toward the violin case leaning against the wall. "Please bring that along and follow me."

Grimacing, Phillip bent to retrieve the violin case. As he straightened, he found Alice's eyes on him, filled with a vacant yet adoring warmth. The love potion had done its work more efficiently than even Zebulon had promised.

"Come along, Alice," Phillip whispered. "We have to go with Zebulon."

"Of course, my love," Alice responded, her voice almost ethereal in its sweetness. She drifted to his side, her fingers interlocking with his in a trusting grip. Despite the turmoil coursing through him, Phillip felt a rush of warmth at her touch.

Leading Alice by the hand, Phillip trailed behind Zebulon as they exited the makeshift living quarters. Zebulon guided them across the campus quad, eventually arriving at an elegant building adorned with ornate columns and intricate friezes. It had the grandeur of a music hall—quite different from the alchemy wing where Phillip had assumed they would be taken.

They passed through the soaring foyer and up a winding staircase. They emerged into a circular chamber crowned with a lofty, domed ceiling. The room was elegantly furnished, but its grandeur did little to dispel Phillip's unease. At the center, a luxuriously upholstered chair awaited.

Phillip's pace slowed as they crossed the threshold, scanning the room cautiously. Despite the room's outward beauty, an intangible feeling of disquiet seemed to hang in the air.

With impatience, Zebulon gestured toward the chair. "If you'd be so kind as to have Alice sit."

Biting back his irritation, Phillip guided Alice to the chair, her steps as delicate as her grip on his arm. She settled into it gracefully, her skirts billowing around her like the petals of a flower. Crouching down before her, Phillip took her hands into his.

"Alice, my love," he said, his voice full of sorrow he couldn't quite mask. "Zebulon needs you to play a specific melody on your violin. It's crucial for what he's working on."

Alice's face brightened, an unusual eagerness in her eyes. "I'd be delighted to play for both of you."

A knot tightened in Phillip's stomach. This accommodating woman was not his Alice. His Alice, who loved her violin as an extension of her own soul, would have questioned, would have doubted. She would never have acquiesced so readily, so unquestioningly. With a sense of dread, Phillip opened the violin case and carefully lifted out the instrument, its wood glowing softly in the room's muted light.

Alice took it from him, her smile unnervingly radiant, a smile that didn't reach the depths of her empty eyes. "What piece shall I play?" she asked, her voice lilting yet vacant, as though she were a beautifully crafted instrument herself, missing the soul that gave her music life.

Phillip considered how to word the command. Alice could play the violin without allowing her magic to temper the music, but that wasn't what Zebulon required. He looked toward Zebulon, who was standing by windows that offered a panoramic view of the Cheswell campus. "Which building is it?"

Zebulon moved closer to a window on the east side. "That one there. The Rickson Building." He pointed.

Nodding, Phillip turned back to Alice, his eyes meeting her unnaturally bright gaze. "Did you see the building our friend Zebulon pointed out? We need you to use your magic, Alice. Zebulon must work without being disturbed, so your melody will make anyone who wants to go into that building reconsider, and no one will believe anything is amiss." He glanced at Zebulon. "How long does she need to play?"

"Every evening starting at seven o'clock, for at least five hours," Zebulon responded, his tone casual, as if he were discussing dinner plans.

Phillip's eyes widened. "Five hours? Every evening? That's— she can't sustain that kind of magical output."

Seemingly unfazed, Zebulon reached into his coat pocket and produced a small vial, gently shaking it to stir its contents. "I believe this will assist her in that regard."

Dread touched Phillip's spine. Another potion. While not a mage himself, he understood enough about magical energy to know its limitations. Just as a human body couldn't run incessantly without collapsing from exhaustion, a mage couldn't continuously channel their powers without significant strain. Alice was practiced with her violin and her power, but this...it was asking too much.

Alice held the violin as tenderly as if it were a baby, her eyes flicking toward the window. A hint of confusion marked her placid expression. "Theo's not here. But he's around, isn't he? I'll play a song that he'll love. He loves my music. I can play for a long time."

Zebulon grinned, and at that moment, Phillip felt a surge of loathing for the man. "See? Everything is falling into place."

Phillip was cornered, and he knew it. He gave Alice a resigned nod. "Go ahead, love. Play for as long as you're able." He then turned his attention to Zebulon, lowering his voice to a harsh whisper. "You may be using her, but she's still a person! Alice will need regular breaks for food and water. Trips to the lavatory. Sleep. If any harm comes—"

Zebulon waved a dismissive hand, cutting him off. "I'm not a monster. We'll only call upon her abilities as necessary. Consider today a trial run."

Alice's gaze met Phillip's, her eyes filled with an uncanny adoration as she positioned the violin beneath her chin and lifted the bow. The first notes she coaxed from the strings were hauntingly beautiful, filling the room with music that should have been heartwarming but instead sounded like a lament. Phillip couldn't help but watch her intently. Her fingers moved flawlessly over the strings, her bow arm steady, but the vibrant spirit that usually infused her music was conspicuously absent.

It was yet another reminder of what had been taken from her.

And what he had allowed to be taken.

CHAPTER TWENTY-FIVE

Breaker's Sister

Luci

*L*uci dropped into her seat in the alchemy classroom, the creak of the chair barely audible over the chatter of arriving students. Kelsey, the first-year she'd met yesterday, approached her with a couple of other acquaintances in tow. Their faces wore expressions of suppressed excitement, and Luci felt a knot of unease tighten in her gut. What did they want?

"So, is it true?" Kelsey leaned on the desk beside her, a sly grin pulling at the corners of her mouth. "You know, the talk that's buzzing all over campus."

Luci knit her brows, genuinely puzzled. "Talk? What do you mean?"

Kelsey's eyes glimmered as her smile broadened. "That you're the Breaker's sister."

A jolt of panic surged through Luci, her eyes widening involuntarily. How in Perdition had they found out about Blaise? She struggled to maintain a neutral expression, her eyes darting to the side as she weighed her options.

"What? No, that's ridiculous," she scoffed, hoping the tremor in her voice wasn't obvious. Her mind raced as she scrambled to understand how this information could have leaked. Who else knew this potentially dangerous secret? She had to do damage control, and fast. Luci forced out a laugh, the sound more hollow than she would've liked. "The Breaker's sister? Seriously, where do people come up with these wild tales?"

The disbelief in the eyes of Kelsey and her companions remained. Another girl, a tall redhead with a stern expression, cut in. "Don't deny it. Tina saw you walking with him on your first day here."

A feeling of dread pooled in Luci's stomach. She was cornered, and there was no sidestepping the issue any longer. She drew a calming breath, gathering her thoughts.

"Okay, fine. He's my brother," she admitted. The others started murmuring excitedly, but Luci held up a hand. "But he's adopted. It's not like we're actually related by blood." Even as the words tumbled from her lips, Luci felt a pang of guilt stab at her conscience. She'd always regarded Blaise as her true-born brother, despite the family complexities and his magical quirks. Yet, here she was, willing to sacrifice that relationship to protect herself.

She scanned the faces surrounding her, searching for some clue as to how her revelation had landed. A few seemed ready to pounce with more questions, their eyes narrowing skeptically. Others seemed to relax a little, as if her half-truth had put them at ease.

Kelsey leaned in closer, a gleam of curiosity in her eyes. "So, spill. What's his magic like? Does he really just shatter things with a glance?"

Before Luci could even plan a reply, more questions peppered her from the small crowd that had gathered.

"Can he even control that kind of power?"

"Ever seen him hurt someone?"

"Is breaking stuff the only thing he can do, or is there more?"

Luci raised her hands, palms out, in a bid to halt the barrage of inquiries. This was spiraling, and she needed to regain control before it turned into a full-blown interrogation.

"He's just...a mage, okay?" Luci's voice had a casual undertone, but she felt anything but. "Honestly, I didn't pay much attention to his magic when I was growing up. We're different, okay? He's not like us."

She was playing to their already-formed opinions of mages, hoping to deflect the spotlight away from her and Blaise. She scanned their faces, noting that a few seemed to nod, as though her words had lent credence to their preconceptions.

Before the conversation could continue down this dangerous road, a voice cut through the chatter. "Students! Please take your seats."

Professor Zebulon Woodrow had entered the classroom, clapping his hands to underscore the urgency of his words. Luci exhaled a quiet sigh of relief. Saved by the professor's timely arrival.

As Luci opened her notebook, she sent up a silent prayer of thanks for the luck that had allowed her to extract herself from that confrontation without revealing anything too damaging. But she knew the rumors would continue to fester, and this was far from over. She would have to be more careful going forward.

Luci tried to focus as Professor Woodrow began the day's lesson, but her mind was still spinning from the rumors. She stared down at the open pages of her notebook, absently doodling in the margins rather than taking notes.

How had those girls found out about Blaise? Worry clawed at Luci's insides. It was bad enough that she'd had to distance herself from her own brother in front of her classmates. Her stomach churned with a mix of guilt and apprehension. Imagined scenarios spiraled out of control in her mind, each darker than the last. Had Blaise been ambushed on the way home? Was he hurt, or worse?

She shook her head sharply, as if the physical motion could dislodge the dark thoughts. Blaise was smart. He was resourceful. He had his own unique abilities, and besides, he had Emrys on his side. He had to be okay, she reassured herself. But despite her inner pep talk, Luci couldn't fully dispel the unease that had settled in the pit of her stomach.

Just then, Professor Woodrow's voice cut through her turbulent thoughts. "Miss Mason, please remain behind. I'd like a word with you after class."

Her eyes flicked upwards, meeting the professor's scrutinizing gaze, which gave away nothing of his intentions. A million questions ricocheted around her mind. Had he heard the gossip? Noticed her lack of focus during the lesson? Her insides squirmed with a blend of fear and anticipation, like a rabbit caught in a snare.

As the room emptied, the shuffling of feet and buckling of bags seemed magnified, almost accusatory. Luci felt her classmates' eyes on her—brief, darting glances full of speculation—before they vanished through the door.

Alone with Professor Woodrow, Luci took a seat at the front of the class. She sat ramrod straight, bracing herself. Her mind raced—would he interrogate her about Blaise? Threaten to expel her for lying about her family? She clenched her fists in her lap, willing herself to remain calm.

Professor Woodrow took his place behind the podium. "Now, Miss Mason," he began, breaking the silence that had settled between them, "you mentioned having a younger brother?"

Luci's eyes widened, her mind working overtime to process this unexpected turn. "Uh, yes. His name is Brody." Her thoughts pulsed with a silent plea: *Don't ask about Blaise. Please, not that.*

"Ah, Brody," Professor Woodrow replied, interlocking his

fingers in a contemplative steeple. "Sounds like a sturdy name, doesn't it?" His gaze studied her, as if peeling back the layers of her composure. "You see, I find myself in a...quandary, and I believe you're uniquely qualified to help me. I have an associate who needs a caretaker for his six-year-old son. Temporary, of course. Would you be interested?"

Luci's thoughts tumbled into disarray. Babysitting? Here, in a place where her primary focus should be her studies? She had expected many challenges at the university, but childcare was not one of them. But the professor had singled her out for this task. Declining could have unforeseen repercussions on her academic standing or her relationship with him. She hesitated, caught in a rising tide of indecision.

Professor Woodrow leaned forward, his tone softening to an almost paternal lilt. "I know, it's a bit out of the ordinary. However, your reputation precedes you, and I believe you're more than up to the task. A few hours a day, that's all. For someone of your talents and instincts, it should be a walk in the park."

The professor's flattery left her momentarily disarmed. Was this some sort of test, a way to gauge her commitment or resourcefulness? Her eyes flicked to his, searching for a hint, a clue, anything. Could this be a chance to prove herself? Earn some extra credit in the unspoken curriculum of faculty favor?

"I'll...I'll need to consult my schedule," she finally answered, cautiously navigating her words. "I don't want this to interfere with my academic commitments."

Professor Woodrow's smile took on a satisfied curve, as if he'd expected this answer all along. "Excellent. Your thoughtfulness in pondering the opportunity is commendable. We can hash out the finer details at a later juncture, after you've had the chance to align your priorities."

Luci felt a surge of relief wash over her. "Thank you, Professor. I'm honored that you would consider me for such roles."

Professor Woodrow waved a hand. "No need to decide now.

We can discuss the particulars later, should you agree." Then, leaning in, he added, "However, allow me to sweeten the pot a tad. If you need to skip a class or two to fulfill your caregiving duties, I'll vouch for you. I'll ensure that your professors are informed, and you won't suffer any academic setbacks."

Luci's eyebrows lifted at the unexpected offering. The prospect of having Professor Woodrow as her advocate with other faculty was an undeniable advantage.

"And there's more," he continued, his eyes twinkling with a mysterious light. "If you agree to this, I'd like to offer you a role in a research initiative of mine—a rather groundbreaking one, I must add—that I've only opened up to my graduate students."

Luci had to temper her enthusiasm, her heart racing in her chest. This might be an unparalleled chance, the kind of academic opportunity that could shape her future. She would be a fool to let it slip through her fingers.

Taking a deep breath to steady her excitement, she looked into Professor Woodrow's expectant eyes. "That's an incredibly generous offer, Professor. With those conditions, I'd be more than willing to help look after the child."

Professor Woodrow offered a final, enigmatic smile. "Very well. I look forward to seeing how you handle this additional responsibility." He moved from the podium, coming closer to slide a piece of paper across the desk to her. "Here is the place where the boy is staying and who to ask for when you arrive. I'll send word to them that you'll come by tomorrow."

Luci took the paper and glanced over the flowing script. Her thoughts raced, still coming to terms with this task she had taken on. And there was still the nagging concern over her fellow students' prying questions about Blaise. She needed to learn more about those rumors.

"Thank you again, Professor," Luci said, rising from her seat. "I appreciate the opportunity."

Professor Woodrow nodded, his eyes arrowing to hers in a

manner that made her feel scrutinized. "You're most welcome. Just remember, I have significant expectations of you. Please don't disappoint."

That statement hung in the air like a solemn promise—or a veiled warning—as Luci gathered her belongings. Her heart was a conflicting jumble of excitement and unease, a dance of emotions she couldn't fully reconcile.

With anticipation and anxiety warring within her, Luci made her way to the classroom door. Stepping into the hallway, the distant sound of a melancholy violin met her ears, its melody echoing down the empty corridors. She paused, listening for a moment, before continuing on her way.

THE HALLWAY WAS ALIVE WITH STUDENTS, A LIVELY MIX OF VOICES and laughter filling the air. Amid the hustle, Luci stood still, her eyes glued to the pages of her book. But even the text couldn't fully distract her from the gazes that flicked in her direction or the indistinct murmurs that reached her ears. The rumors about her being Blaise's sister were always on her mind, reminding her of the complicated mess she was in.

A voice broke into her thoughts. "Hey, are you Luci Mason?"

She glanced up and saw a second-year student, his eyes filled with inquiry and a hint of daring.

"Uh, yes. What can I do for you?" Luci's cheeks warmed, expecting what was likely coming next.

"Is it true that Blaise Hawthorne is your brother?" The question was unabashed and direct.

Luci felt heat creep up her cheeks, but she held her ground. "Blaise is my... distant cousin," she said, each word a calculated step in a high-stakes game of deception. "We're not very close, so I don't know much about him." But even as she spoke the words, Luci mentally kicked herself. Why had she done that? She'd had a somewhat reasonable explanation for Kelsey and the others. Luci was supposed to be cool and calculated, not lose the thread of her own lies as soon as she was pressed.

"Really? 'Cause everyone's saying he's your brother and that he's the Breaker." The second-year student leaned in closer, his eyes wide with intrigue.

"Is that so? Well, people say a lot of things," Luci countered, keeping her voice steady despite the onslaught of emotions inside her. "Like I told you, he's a distant relative. That's all there is to it. Now, I really should get to class."

She pivoted on her heel and strode away, her mind awash with concerns. The rumors about her and Blaise were a danger. Every whisper brought them closer to being exposed, and she couldn't afford to let that happen. Both her brother's safety and her own were on the line. It was time to do something about it.

Pushing open the door to the dormitory, Luci spotted a small knot of students gathered near the entrance, their voices hushed but animated. Among them was a classmate who had been sneaking glances at her earlier that day. This was as good a place as any to start her investigation.

Taking a steadying breath, she approached. "Hey, do you mind telling me where you heard those rumors about me?"

An awkward silence hung in the air as the group exchanged uneasy glances. Finally, one of them spoke up.

"Um, Misty, our resident advisor, first mentioned it," the student offered hesitantly.

"Good to know, thanks," Luci responded, her tone deliberately light to keep them off guard. She gave a quick nod of acknowledgment and turned away, her thoughts already racing ahead to her next move.

As she walked towards the dormitory's common area, Misty's usual haunt, Luci knew she was entering a delicate phase in her inquiry. Her mind flicked through options to force Misty's compliance. There were potions for that, but Luci didn't know how to craft them. Even if she did, she didn't have the time...or the desire. Luci didn't like the idea of taking away someone's free will. She would need to handle this carefully if she hoped to find the source of the rumors and shut them down for good. Luci took a deep breath. She could do this.

Once Luci entered the common area, she quickly found Misty, who was comfortably settled on the plush settee. Her focus was on a stack of paperwork that lay spread out on the coffee table in front of her. Luci cautiously took a seat across from Misty. She felt like a detective about to interrogate a suspect, and the thought made her uneasy.

"Hey, Misty. I was hoping you could tell me how I could talk to Blaise. He's the family member who brought me here. Just want to let him know I appreciate everything he's done. I think he might still be in the area," she said, her words carefully chosen to gauge Misty's reaction. Luci felt a twinge of deception course through her; she knew well that Blaise was supposed to have already left the campus, but she needed to see how Misty would respond.

Misty glanced up from her paperwork, eyes wary and her posture suddenly defensive. "Luci, you know the campus rules. We're not allowed to contact anyone outside of the school without permission from administration for the first few weeks of the semester. Focusing on adjusting to Cheswell is the most important thing you can do right now."

The guarded look in Misty's eyes reinforced Luci's belief that there was more to her words than just school policy. Trying to maintain a neutral expression, Luci nodded. Her thoughts whirred like a hummingbird's wings. Something didn't add up here. The resident advisor was hiding something.

"I'm going to be honest with you, Misty. I also wanted to speak with you because there's a rumor going around about me and Blaise. Do you have any idea where those might have come from?" Luci posed the question as casually as she could, but inside, her stomach fluttered with anxiety.

Misty's demeanor changed; she became tense and fidgety, her eyes darting away from Luci's penetrating gaze. Her hands twitched, as if she were contemplating picking up her paperwork again just to have something to do. "I don't know what you're talking about, Luci. People talk, rumors spread. It's just the way things are around here."

But Luci wouldn't back down. "It's just strange that you were the only student to escort us on campus, and now all these rumors are flying," she said, leaning forward to emphasize her point. "Aside from Dean Woodrow, very few people saw us here together."

The expression on Misty's face shifted from guarded to startled, her eyes widening as if Luci had caught her red-handed. "You think I started the rumor?"

Luci cocked her hip. "I don't think you *meant* to start a rumor. I come from a small town, and I know the type of people who thrive on gossip. You're not cut from that cloth. But I do think you told someone about us."

Misty grimaced. The guilt was clear in her eyes, like a storm cloud in an otherwise clear sky. "All right, fine. It's true. I recognized Blaise from some old research I was doing on alchemy history and advancements for my practicum. I didn't mean to start a rumor."

"Research?" Luci's ears perked up, and her thoughts veered toward the possibilities. Was Misty referring to the time when Blaise had been imprisoned in the Golden Citadel? Or was it something else entirely?

"Alchemy research," Misty clarified, still avoiding direct eye contact. "But that's not important right now."

"Really?" Luci narrowed her eyes, her focus sharpening like a blade as she pressed Misty for details. "Because it seems like it might be. What else are you not telling me?"

Misty hesitated, her posture becoming even more rigid. She broke eye contact for a moment, clearly wrestling with her next words before finally admitting, "I spoke with one of my professors about him. He told me that he needed Blaise if he ever returned to campus."

"Needed him?" Luci's voice spiked, her eyebrows arching in genuine alarm. "Why?"

"Because he's *the Breaker*. That's my guess, anyway," Misty said with a shrug.

Luci felt a cold shiver run down her spine. The idea of people fearing Blaise was jarring. Yes, Blaise was a Breaker, but he was also her brother—someone she had always seen as harmless. The dissonance was awkward, and it made her regret her earlier distancing from him all the more keenly. She forced herself to voice the question that was threatening to choke her. "So did he? Return to campus, I mean."

Misty looked down, then back up at Luci with a nod. "Yes."

It was the very answer Luci had dreaded. Her mind raced with questions—why had Blaise returned? What was he thinking? But she pushed those thoughts aside for the moment, focusing on the immediate issue. "What happened to him?"

"We...detained him," Misty's voice came out almost as a whisper, full of regret.

Detained him? Panic tightened around Luci's chest like a vise. "Where is he now?"

"The dorms," Misty said, her voice wavering. "I was told to put him in a specific room."

Luci's mouth went dry. For a moment, she froze in place, grappling with the magnitude of what Misty had just revealed. Blaise was being held here against his will.

"Take me to him. Now," Luci demanded, her voice steely and unwavering. The need to see Blaise, to verify his well-being with her own eyes, was overpowering.

Misty hesitated, her eyes darting around the room. The decision seemed to tear at her, but finally, she sighed, her shoulders dropping. "I have brothers, too," she admitted softly. "All right, I'll let you see Blaise—this once. But you can't tell anyone, understand?"

"Understood," Luci said, her voice firm with gratitude despite her clenched jaw.

Misty nodded, then led Luci through a series of hallways and doors, the tension mounting with each step. Luci's heart raced as they passed floor after floor, her mind running through endless scenarios of what she might find when they reached Blaise.

Finally, they stopped on a floor that seemed empty of life. Further down the hallway, one door was propped open.

"This floor is undergoing renovations, but they're not really working on it right now," Misty explained as she stopped in front of a nondescript door, identical to all the others lining the hall-way. Her hand hovered over the doorknob for a moment, the key in the lock. "You have thirty minutes." Then she stepped back, allowing Luci to enter the room alone.

As the door creaked open, Luci steeled herself for the unknown. She scanned the room, finally settling on the figures of Blaise and Jefferson sitting on the room's lone bed. Their faces lit up in a blend of astonishment and relief, like shipwrecked sailors spotting land.

"Luci!" Blaise burst out as he rose from the bed. In two swift strides, he was by her side, the door closing and locking behind her with an ominous click.

"Blaise!" Luci's voice quivered as she lunged forward, tears brimming in her eyes. She wrapped her arms around him in a hug so tight it could have fused bones. Then she winced, pulling back to look at him. "Sorry. I should have asked if a hug was okay."

"Right now it's very okay," Blaise said, voice soft. His arms surrounded her just as tightly, his coarse beard brushing against the side of her face with a comforting rasp.

"Well, this is unexpected and confusing," Jefferson commented amiably from where he sat, watching them. "But I suppose now you know where your sister is, Blaise."

Blaise took a step back, disentangling himself from the hug but keeping his hands on Luci's shoulders. The distance allowed Luci to give him a thorough once-over. He appeared unscathed, but her instincts told her to look deeper. Physical marks could heal; it was the invisible scars that remained.

"What are you doing here?" she asked, concern lacing her voice.

"Actually, I was going to ask you the same thing," Blaise replied, a hint of amusement in his tone despite the gravity of the situation.

Their words overlapped, an eagerness to understand and provide answers clear in both their voices. Collecting herself, Luci began explaining the rumors that had started about their relationship as siblings and how she had decided to investigate.

"Rumors? About us?" Blaise frowned, his brow furrowing with confusion. "I didn't think anyone would know—"

"Someone must have seen us together and started talking," Luci interrupted, her voice shaded with anger. "It doesn't matter now. Why did you come back?"

"Before I left, Seledora told me Jefferson was here," Blaise said, gesturing towards his husband with a casual flick of his thumb. "I came back to tell you that something strange was going on here and to convince you to leave."

"I'd say *strange* is putting it mildly at this point," Jefferson chimed in, his tone lighter than Luci thought the situation warranted. He made a show of leisurely crossing one leg over the other. "And the next time anyone in your family decides to go the pseudonym route, I hope I'm consulted so I can provide better guidance."

Blaise shot him a side-eyed look. "I really hope no one needs to call on your expertise in that area."

Luci blinked. For a heartbeat, it was as if they had been transported home, and nothing was amiss. Then reality crashed down once more. Her brother and his husband were not guests here.

They were captives. Her thoughts raced like gears in a clockwork mechanism, each cog turning another as she mentally scrambled for a way out.

"Blaise," Luci said, her voice sharpening with fear, "you need to escape. Now. Just use your magic to break out of here." He *was* the Breaker, after all. Luci didn't think Blaise had ever met a door-knob that could best him.

Blaise sighed, his hand shifting to the back of his neck in a gesture of weary frustration. "I would if I could, Luci. But the walls are coated with null paint. My magic's about as effective as a pie without filling."

"Quite disappointing." Jefferson sighed.

"Fine," Luci said, her mind clicking through other options but coming up empty. "I'll find another way to help you both escape. We'll think of something."

"Wait," Jefferson cut in, urgency lacing his voice. "Before we rush headlong into an escape, I need to know if my sister, Alice, and my nephew, Theo, are safe. They're still in Cheswell, and I can't—*won't*—leave without them. Theo's just a child, only six years old. I can't abandon him to whatever dark machinations are at play here."

As Jefferson spoke, Luci felt her mind spin into overdrive. Then, like a beacon cutting through the fog of her thoughts, she remembered her conversation with Professor Woodrow. He'd asked her to babysit a young boy. The age matched. Could it be Theo?

"Jefferson," Luci began cautiously, "I might have some infor-mation about Theo. One of my professors asked me to watch a child of the same age. I wonder if it's him."

"Really?" Jefferson's eyes widened, hope burning in their depths. "That would be incredible! Maybe you can find out where Alice and Theo are being held."

"Maybe," Luci conceded, feeling the heavy mantle of responsibility drape itself around her. "We need to think about getting you two out of here, too."

Blaise, who had been watching the exchange with an unreadable expression, spoke. "Let's take this one step at a time, Luci. For now, focus on finding out more about Theo and Alice. While I'm not overjoyed at being trapped here, no one has harmed us."

Luci hesitated, knowing he was right, but she struggled to accept the idea of leaving them behind. She felt raw helplessness creep into her heart, but she shoved it aside. This was not the time for doubt. "Fine," Luci conceded, reluctant. "I'll see what I can find out for you about Alice and Theo. Once I know something, I'll report back as soon as I can."

"How will you get back in here?" Blaise asked. "I saw someone let you in."

Luci shrugged. "I'll sort that out when the time comes." She'd gotten in once, albeit by begging Misty. She'd do it again, even if it meant she had to take more extreme measures. *I am Marian Hawthorne's daughter. The Breaker's sister. I'm not weak. I can be a legend, too.*

Blaise's blue eyes met hers, and she saw a parade of conflicting emotions within them: pride, worry, and a deep, unspoken understanding. "Be careful, Luci."

Luci wanted to put on a brave face, she really did. But instead, she stumbled into him for another hug, burying her head against his chest and breathing in his familiar scent. How did the faint whiff of yeast and sweetness still cling to him from his baking? Luci didn't know, but she treasured it. It steadied her. "I'll try," Luci murmured, her voice barely above a whisper. "No promises, though."

Jefferson let out a soft chuckle, breaking the tension that had thickened the air. "Well, she certainly shares your penchant for caution—or lack thereof."

"Hey, I'm nothing if not careful," Blaise retorted.

"Of course you are, darling," Jefferson replied, his voice dripping with affectionate irony.

Luci picked up on the unspoken understanding between them. Blaise had always tried to tread carefully, but life's circumstances had often forced him far outside his comfort zone. Luci was starting to understand a lot more about her big brother.

She smiled up at him. "See you soon."

As she turned toward the door, her hand hesitating for a moment on the doorknob, a silent vow solidified in her mind. She would come back. And she would bring with her the answers they so desperately needed, even if she had to rattle every door in Cheswell to find them.

CHAPTER TWENTY-SIX

Still Feels Like Doom

The room felt smaller following Luci's departure, its emptiness echoing with the sound of the door closing. Blaise stared at the door, keenly aware of the prickling anxiety that he wasn't doing enough; that Luci shouldn't be the one handling this problem.

From the corner, Jefferson's voice cut through Blaise's thoughts. "If I had a coin for every time your face had that worried expression, I'd probably be able to buy this dreadful place and set us free."

Blaise looked at him, the faintest hint of a smile on his lips. "I'm worried about her. She shouldn't be involved in this."

Jefferson nodded, his green eyes suddenly serious. "I feel the same about Alice. But that's a circumstance we can't change." He cocked his head, thoughtful. "This is the point where we have to engage our boundless optimism. Alice is resilient. And Luci is sharper than one of your kitchen knives."

Boundless optimism. That was something Jefferson had in spades. "I missed talking to you like this," Blaise admitted, voice soft. He pulled Jefferson's poppet out from his pocket, turning it over in his hands.

Jefferson's smile was genuine, warming the space between them. "The feeling's mutual. Missed our banter. And missed *you* most of all." Then he paused. "Is that what I think it is?"

Blaise shrugged. "I don't know what you think it is, but if you guessed *a somewhat ruthless Effigest's poppet of you*, then you would be correct."

Jefferson's eyebrows lifted. "I forgot he had one of me. Gods, now I feel like I've truly dodged a bullet."

Blaise tossed the poppet from one hand to the other. "You did."

"And why do you have it?" Jefferson's tone was laced with curiosity.

Blaise sighed. "Because when you left, everyone's first reaction was *let's hex Jefferson.*"

His husband wet his lips, his face a mask. "And your reaction was…?"

"Absolutely not." Blaise brandished the poppet. "That's why I took it. So Jack couldn't get up to any of his antics." Though Blaise thought it likely the wily outlaw had backup poppets of people he considered interesting.

"Well, I appreciate you not wishing ill on me." Jefferson's voice was soft.

"I'm allowed to be mad at you, but I still love you like no one else," Blaise reminded him. And speaking of that…it was time to do something about the barrier between them. "We need to talk."

Jefferson stilled. "In my experience, those words are typically an omen of impending doom."

"No, not doom," Blaise said with a shake of his head. He moved to sit on the bed, too. "I mean, we should talk about us."

"Still feels like doom."

Blaise saw by the set of Jefferson's jaw that he was serious. When Jefferson wanted to, he wore a mask that hid his true feelings, though he often let it slip around Blaise. Right now, he was worried. Blaise took Jefferson's hand, threading their fingers together. He felt the raw tension in his husband's hand.

"What? Do you think I intend to break up with you while we're literally trapped in the same room together?" Blaise asked.

"The thought had occurred to me."

Blaise huffed a laugh. "Given my *strong* aversion to all things awkward, that sounds like the last thing I'd want." He tightened his grip on Jefferson's hand, grounding them both. "No, what I want is for *us* to work. And I think you want that, too."

The brief pause that followed was telling. When Jefferson's muscles relaxed, Blaise felt it more than saw it. "It's what I want more than anything," Jefferson admitted. "I deeply regret not confiding in you about my magic use against Phillip Dillon."

"I know," Blaise said, his voice soft. "And I know you said you did what you did to protect us, but I think there's more to it than that."

The tension returned to Jefferson's muscles once more. But Blaise saw the slightest squint of his eyes and knew that behind the protective wall Jefferson had put up, he was thinking. After a hesitant breath, his voice barely above a whisper, Jefferson asked, "What do you suspect lies beneath?"

Jefferson's question hung in the air like a mist. Blaise's thoughtful silence held weight as he chose his words with precision. "Guilt," he began, his tone contemplative. "A heavy dose of regret. Your protective nature...it's clear you want to defend us, but..." He trailed off, gathering his thoughts. "Why else would you decide that the path to fixing us starts with your sister?"

Jefferson blinked, the mask slipping once more. He looked down at the floor briefly before meeting Blaise's gaze again.

"Because I...well, perhaps there's a nugget of truth there," he conceded.

Blaise nodded slowly, relieved that Jefferson seemed open to discussing this difficult topic. He waited, giving his husband space to think.

The room was silent, save for their quiet breathing. Finally, Jefferson shifted, making the bed grate against the wall. "So much of what's happened to you is because of me. Including our stay in this chamber, which is making me reconsider my stance on antique decor. And not in a good way."

Blaise, however, was quick to counter, fervently shaking his head. "You can't bear the burden of the world, especially for choices made by others. And you can't let that old guilt get between you and the people who love you."

Jefferson stared at Blaise, clearly surprised by his words. "You're right," he admitted, his lips pulling into a self-deprecating smile. "I have this insufferable habit of shouldering guilt. I feel like...like I must atone not only for my own misdeeds, but those of my family."

Mom was right. Blaise offered his husband a gentle smile. "That's an impossible burden."

"Perhaps." There was a weariness in Jefferson's voice, a shadow of old pain.

"Hey." Blaise squeezed Jefferson's hand to snare his attention. "Look, I understand you're concerned about Alice and Theo. Alice might place blame where it doesn't belong, but deep down, you know that's not the truth."

A sigh escaped from Jefferson, followed by a wry smile. "Sometimes I think you know me better than I know myself." He paused, his expression turning pensive. "I just want Alice to see the man I've become. Not judge me by the sins of...well..." He trailed off, and Blaise could practically hear the unspoken name between them: Stafford Wells.

Blaise leaned against Jefferson's shoulder. "Once we get out of this mess, I'll help her see that. Maybe this isn't something for you to do alone."

Jefferson frowned. "But I *do* think we needed a little time apart. To clear our heads."

Blaise leaned back against the wall, a trace of irony in his voice. "Sure. A weekend getaway would've been enough, not this...extended vacation." His quip was rewarded with an honest laugh from Jefferson.

"Deal," Jefferson murmured. "But I still need to make things right with you."

Blaise shook his head. "This isn't just a *you* issue. It's us. Something we have to work on together. You have a lot of baggage up here." He tapped a finger against Jefferson's temple. "I need to be more understanding of that and take some time to figure out where you're coming from."

"Baggage." A tiny smile touched Jefferson's lips. "I suppose there are worse things you could call it." He nodded. "And I...I know I promised before to never keep secrets from you, and then I broke that—"

"Guilt," Blaise reminded him. "Get past it."

Jefferson sighed. "Right. Yes. Transparency. I will be more transparent with you. How's that?"

Blaise chuckled. "I think it's a solid start. We'll take it one day at a time."

Jefferson's expression eased as he gazed at their joined hands. "One day at a time," he agreed quietly. "You *really* have no idea how much I missed this. Missed you."

Blaise tilted his head, his gaze searching Jefferson's. "Isn't there an old saying? About missing someone?"

Jefferson's fingers trailed Blaise's cheek, the touch feather-light. "Absence makes the heart grow fonder." He hesitated, the corners of his mouth turning upwards. "I was already quite fond of you, though. And I will say, it cut me deep to know that I disappointed you."

"Well, you're not perfect," Blaise pointed out.

Arching an eyebrow, Jefferson feigned surprise. "Blasphemy! I'm fairly certain that I *am*, in fact, perfect."

The renewed levity was a promising sign. Blaise laughed, then leaned in to brush a tender kiss against Jefferson's lips. "Ah, there you are. *There's* my peacock of a husband again."

"Oh, he never left. He was just buried under all that guilt you mentioned earlier, and it took some doing to shake all my feathers out." Jefferson breathed out a soft sigh. "You and I...are we okay now?

There was a tentative tremor in his voice, as if Jefferson feared they were still upon a precipice. *He really is afraid of losing me. But I know how to put those fears to rest.* With that thought, Blaise maneuvered closer, letting his fingers glide to the nape of Jefferson's neck, tugging him into an embrace. Jefferson's uncertainty melted away as Blaise bridged the distance between them with a kiss.

The world seemed to blur and narrow, every sound muted, every sensation heightened. It was just the two of them, the draw between them irresistible. Blaise shivered as Jefferson's hands moved to the back of his neck, fingers entangling in his hair. Their kiss was both reckoning and reunion, a shattering of the wall their argument had built.

When they finally parted, Jefferson's eyebrows lifted so high they brushed against a tendril of his golden hair. "I'm going to assume that's a *yes*."

"That's a yes," Blaise whispered.

CHAPTER TWENTY-SEVEN

Subject Zero

Luci

Luci's boots seemed far too loud as she walked down the hallway, their echo accompanying her like a loyal but nervous companion. The location Zebulon had provided was etched in her memory, and after her visit with Blaise and Jefferson, she couldn't shake the feeling that something truly awful was going on in this place of higher education.

Distantly, she still heard the violin's sweet notes drifting through the air. She found it strange that she had heard a violin so frequently in this place. The further she ventured, the more the strange melody seemed to take on a life of its own, weaving itself into the fabric of her thoughts. Luci gritted her teeth, refusing to let the eerie ambiance distract her from her mission.

As she neared the dorm room, a new sound emerged—the muted cries of a child. Each whimper guided her forward, tugging at her heartstrings and fueling her determination. She had a job to do. Right now, this was the best way to help her brother and solve this mystery.

The sound of crying intensified, reverberating through the otherwise quiet corridor. Luci's chest tightened, a visceral response that turned her worry into action.

"Hold on. I'm almost there," she whispered, her words a soft promise in the empty air. She wasn't sure if she was reassuring the child or fortifying herself.

Breathing deeply to steady her racing heart, Luci arrived at the door that served as the source of the young cries. She paused, her hand floating just inches from the doorknob. Drawing another breath to steel her nerves, she turned the knob.

As the door creaked open, Luci stepped into the modest confines of a student dorm room. Sunlight seeped through a small window, its golden rays softening the stark wooden furniture. A ruffled twin bed and a desk that had seen better days made up the room's sparse furnishings.

Her eyes then drifted to the corner of the room. Nestled there was a young boy, almost camouflaged by a mound of stuffed animals, like a small ship swamped in a plush, comforting storm. Luci's breath caught at the sight. The boy looked no older than six or seven, his cheeks slick with tears, his dark hair clinging to his forehead.

Luci's heart ached at the sight.

Just then, a voice pierced the heavy atmosphere of the room, tinged with a note of frustration that grated on her nerves."You have no idea how glad I am to see you," the young man said, unfolding his arms and rising from a creaky wooden chair. He was a few years older than Luci, his face etched with annoyance. "You won't believe this, but my professor picked me for babysitting duty because I mentioned I'd watched my cousins—a whole two times! Extra credit or not, I'm about ready to abandon ship. I can't take this whining anymore."

Luci frowned at his callous words. The young man glanced at the distraught child before slipping past Luci and out the door. She bit back an angry curse. She took a deep breath, centering herself before slowly approaching the boy. She knelt beside him, careful not to crowd too close. "Hello," she said gently. "My name is Luci. What's your name?"

For a moment, the boy looked up, his teary, red-rimmed eyes meeting hers. "Th-Theo," he stammered out between hiccups.

Yes! She had been correct in her suspicion. This was good. "It's very nice to meet you, Theo. I heard you were feeling sad. Do you want to talk about it?"

Theo's lower lip trembled as if he were holding back a dam of emotions. "I want my mama!" he burst out, his words accompanied by a fresh stream of tears that traced wet paths down his flushed cheeks. "Where is she? I wanna go home!"

As Theo's tearful words hung in the air, a knot of emotion tightened in Luci's throat. She felt an overwhelming urge to wrap him in a hug, to offer some small sanctuary. But she knew she had to navigate this delicate situation with care.

"I know you miss your mama," Luci said, keeping her voice kind. "I bet she misses you, too. But she would want you to be brave right now. Can you try to be brave?"

Theo sniffled, looking uncertain. "I guess so."

"Good," Luci encouraged, her face lighting up with a genuine smile. "That's what we need right now. And guess what? Your Uncle Jefferson is here, too. He's been really worried and asked me to find you."

Theo's eyes sparkled for the first time, his face brightening at the mention of his uncle. "Uncle Malerson is here?" His small voice trembled, teetering on the edge of renewed tears.

Malerson? Luci's mind did a quick pivot, piecing together the odd name fusion of Malcolm and Jefferson. It was a fun name, and she idly wondered what the ever-so-proper Jefferson thought about it. And did Blaise know? She was certain her brother would find it amusing. Luci kept her thoughts under wraps. She had to focus on the matter at hand, though she was glad for the brief distraction.

"Yes," Luci continued, steering her focus back to the child. "He wanted me to make sure you're okay."

Theo's small hand came up to wipe his face, smearing away some of the tear tracks. "I want to see him. And my mama, too! We were all together, my daddy, too, and then..." His voice faltered, his eyes filling up again with the promise of more tears.

Pulling a handkerchief from her pocket, Luci gently dabbed at Theo's wet cheeks. "It's okay, Theo. I know this is scary, being away from your family. But you're not alone, okay? I'm here now, and I'm going to keep you safe until we can get you back to them. I promise."

Theo's eyes, still glistening with unshed tears, met hers. He seemed to weigh her sincerity, as if deciding whether to invest his fragile trust in her. After a beat, he nodded, just a tiny tilt of the head, but it was enough for Luci to feel a wave of relief.

Inhaling deeply, Luci knew she had to choose her next words with care. This was delicate ground she was treading on. "I understand that you're eager to see your Mama and Uncle Malerson," she said, her voice softening. "And I really want to make that happen for you. But I'll need a little time to sort things out. This is a big place, and I'm still figuring it out."

The corners of Theo's mouth dipped into a pout, his eyes clouding over with new tears.

Sensing another emotional storm on the horizon, Luci quickly shifted gears. "How about we have a little fun while we wait?" she ventured, a bubbly note creeping into her voice. "We could explore this place, or maybe go see the horses at the stables. And, ahem, I might know where they hide the best pastries in the cafeteria."

No one had said she couldn't leave with her charge, after all. And it might give her an opportunity to find Theo's mother, too.

The mention of *pastries* appeared to work like a charm. Theo's eyes widened a fraction. He paused, then used his small hand to rub his snotty nose. "Pastries? Like cupcakes?"

Luci smiled. "Yep, I bet we could find something yummy. What's your favorite treat?"

Theo considered for a moment. "Cookies?" he finally said shyly.

Luci's eyes brightened. "Cookies it is," she said, feeling a pang of nostalgia. Theo's innocent request brought her thoughts back to Blaise and his knack for baking delicious cookies. She made a silent promise that, someday soon, Theo would have the chance to taste cookies baked by his own Uncle Blaise.

Yet, for all her plans and hopes, she reeled herself back to the present. *One step at a time.* She stood up, extending her hand toward the young boy. After a moment of timid contemplation, Theo nestled his hand into hers. Luci felt a swell of protectiveness for this young, frightened boy. She would do whatever it took to reunite him with his family. But for today, she could try to bring a small measure of comfort and joy back into his world.

As they exited the room, their hands entwined, the lingering notes of the violin seemed to follow them, filling the air with its mournful melody. Theo stopped in his tracks, his eyes widening as if seeing something invisible to Luci. "Mama?" He turned, scanning the surrounding area.

Luci looked at him, puzzled. "What are you talking about?"

"That's Mama's music," Theo declared with childlike certainty. "I know it."

Luci's eyebrows arched, feeling surprise mixed with a sense of discovery. That was a piece of the puzzle she hadn't expected but gratefully welcomed. "Well, if that's the case, that's excellent news. It means your mom can't be far. But first, let's concentrate on the immediate mission: Operation Cookie Hunt."

Conflicted emotions crossed Theo's face before the desire for sugar won out. "Okay."

As they walked, Luci's mind raced with the revelation. Alice must be near, and Luci now had a tangible thread to follow. But she tucked that away for the moment, turning her focus back to the young boy, who looked up at her with hope.

"So, Theo, what's your go-to cookie?" Luci inquired, steering their conversation to safer, more comforting ground as they meandered through the corridor.

His face brightened as he pondered her question. "Chocolate chip!"

"A classic." Luci grinned, sharing in his enthusiasm. "I know where we can find some gooey, warm chocolate chip cookies waiting just for you."

Theo's eyes lit up at the promise of the treat. Luci was glad to see a small spark return to the child after the tears. As they walked, she pointed out paintings lining the walls, inventing silly stories about the people in them to amuse Theo. His giggles and gasps of delight told her the distraction was working.

Time slipped by while they roamed, with Luci's whimsical stories transforming the corridor into a gallery of wonders. After what seemed like moments, but was in fact a full hour, they transitioned from the echoing hallway to the seclusion of a library nook.

Once they were surrounded by captivating books, Theo's expression momentarily clouded with sadness. He fidgeted, his fingers exploring the empty pockets of his trousers.

Luci paused in her reading. "Is something wrong?"

"Miss Luci?" Theo began hesitantly. "I had a lucky rock, but I lost it. It was shiny and smooth, and I found it by the creek."

His tone was so forlorn, Luci felt a pang for his lost lucky rock. Sometimes, even the smallest loss cut deep. "I'm sorry to hear that, Theo. It must have been special to you."

Theo nodded, his eyes downcast. "Yeah, it made me feel good...like when Mama is around. I wish I could find another lucky rock."

Luci smiled. "Well, you know what? Maybe we can look for a new lucky rock together. After our story, we could take a little walk outside."

Theo shook his head. "Someone else here was gonna take me, but I told them no. Uncle Malerson said he'd find one with me. I want to look for one with him." Theo hugged his knees against his chest.

Jefferson had made quite the impact on his nephew, it seemed. Luci nodded in understanding. "That sounds like a fun thing to do. I know he'll enjoy doing that with you."

The boy tilted his head, as if he were reconsidering. "He might not get to go with me soon. Not like I want. And I think having my lucky rock would make me feel better. I can find another second lucky rock with Uncle Malerson another time. Two is better than one."

Luci smiled. "If it would make you feel better, then I'd be happy to help you find one."

She finished reading their story, then took Theo outside. Luci knew they couldn't wander away from the university grounds—as a student, they wouldn't let her leave at this point in the semester. She'd heard other students brag of their prowess at skirting that restriction for a night of entertainment in Greylight, but Luci doubted that was a good idea in her current situation. The university garden proved to work for their purposes, though.

Theo's face lit up as he plucked a stone from the garden bed. "Look, Luci! This one's perfect," he exclaimed, turning the rock over in his small hands. "It's smooth and shiny, just like my old one. I think it's super lucky!" His joy was infectious, his bright eyes reflecting the sheen of his new treasure as he slipped it into his pocket.

Luci leaned down to admire the stone, her smile matching Theo's excitement. "It's a beautiful find," she said warmly. "With a rock like that, I'm sure it will be twice as lucky. Just look at how it catches the light — it's as if it was waiting here just for you."

Late in the afternoon, once they were back in Theo's temporary quarters, a lanky student with a mop of curly hair strode in, ready to relieve Luci. She felt a pang of reluctance. Luci had grown fond of the boy's cheerful company.

Theo's voice trembled a little. "You're leaving?"

Luci knelt to his level, her eyes meeting his watery ones. "Just for a bit," she assured him. "But I'll come and see you tomorrow. We have more stories to explore, remember?"

His response was a tight hug, seeking comfort. "See you soon, Miss Luci."

Luci gave him a gentle pat. As she left, her thoughts turned to food more substantial than cookies. The cafeteria beckoned with its promise of hearty meals. Luci pulled out a pocket watch. She had just enough time to grab a bite to eat before heading to the lab.

A half-hour later, Luci pushed open the door to the Rickson Building and made her way down to a lower level, seeking Professor Woodrow's lab.

Upon entering the laboratory, Luci felt a mix of awe and intimidation. Soft, yellow gaslights lit the space, their flickering flames casting a warm, amber glow that danced across the ceiling. The room buzzed with an undercurrent of excitement. Students, engrossed in their work, moved about, their motions fluid, as if part of a carefully choreographed dance. The musty scent of books mingled with the sharper notes of mysterious elixirs and compounds.

A group of students momentarily captured Luci's attention, laughing at an inside joke while they crushed herbs with mortar and pestle. A little further away, another student carefully measured out a liquid into a flask, his face illuminated by the eerie blue glow of the concoction.

But it was the glass prism that caught Luci's eye. It was a tall, rectangular aquarium filled with a luminous green-blue liquid. As

Luci moved closer to investigate, her breath caught when she realized what she was looking at.

It wasn't an aquarium; it was a glass case with a woman's body suspended within. The woman had long black hair that bobbed around her face like delicate anemones, and aristocratic features that were serene in death. Luci suppressed a gag as she took in the jagged, brutal laceration across the woman's throat. It had been crudely stitched back together, the thick black sutures a gruesome contrast against the waxy flesh.

Luci stumbled back, barely able to contain her revulsion at the sight of the macabre experiment. Why was this poor woman's body preserved in such a horrific state?

"Impressive, isn't it?" The voice, dripping with amusement, seemed to come from nowhere.

Luci, startled, spun around. A tall young man with tousled brown hair and sharp, piercing eyes stood there, studying her reaction. His attire was typical of the students—a simple white shirt, a waistcoat adorned with tiny brass buttons, and dark trousers.

She stammered, struggling to find words. "What...what is this?"

The young man leaned nonchalantly against a workbench laden with alchemical tools and responded with a casual shrug. "Another one of Professor Woodrow's experiments. Don't worry; she was already dead when she arrived here in the box." His casual tone chilled Luci to the core. She took a moment, gathering her thoughts, trying to process the sheer morbidity of the scene. What sort of alchemy would involve the dead?

Before she could voice her rising concerns, a familiar voice echoed through the vast room. "Miss Mason? Over here, if you please."

Luci's gaze followed the voice. There, standing in an arched doorway, was Professor Woodrow. The light seemed to make his features more pronounced, the lines of age more defined. But the glint in his eyes—a combination of mischief and genuine excitement—revealed a side of him she hadn't seen before.

As Luci approached, he gave her a thin smile. "I will show you to our workspace. Please, come this way."

He led her through the doorway into a smaller chamber. Luci's eyes took in the room, absorbing the details. The walls, made of aged brick, had a patina that hinted at years of exposure to various chemical reactions. The soft glow from the gas lamps bathed the room in a warm amber hue. On one side, a massive wooden shelf held ornate jars filled with roots, dried herbs, and peculiar-looking critters, their labels written in cryptic symbols. A large pendulum clock ticked rhythmically, its hands inching through the evening.

The male student from earlier passed by, holding a steaming beaker, and gave her a quick nod. The entire space felt like a blend of science and wonder, and Luci could almost feel the history embedded within its walls.

Professor Woodrow glanced over at Luci as he guided her to a cluttered table covered in books and notebooks. "You might say it's all a bit of a...jumble right now. Almost like trying to make sense of a crossword, but bear with me. Clarity is on the horizon," he remarked with a light chuckle.

Luci swallowed, her eyes darting across the table. Among the pile, she cautiously reached out for a notebook. It was old and worn, its pages filled with a maze of cramped handwriting and esoteric symbols. None of it made any sense to her.

"Professor," she began hesitantly, "I'm afraid I still don't understand what exactly you want me to help you with. What is this project about?"

His face lit up, eyes bright with the satisfaction of holding a secret. "Ah, Miss Hawthorne, this undertaking? I've a hunch you'll find it rather...captivating." He moved with deliberate slowness, selecting a leather-clad journal from a shelf. "The reason you're here, apart from your dazzling intellect, is because of certain...encounters you've had."

When he spoke her true surname, Luci's breath caught. Her mind became a panicked blur. What could she do?

Professor Woodrow seemed oblivious to her state of panic, delicately opening the journal. He treated each page as if it were made of gold leaf. "You might not know this, but back in the day, I collaborated with a few other sharp minds. A group of us, really. All engrossed in the same riddle—much like trying to piece together a jigsaw puzzle in the dark. Exhilarating stuff!" His smile conveyed a mixture of nostalgia and smugness. "One genius cracked the problem, but then played quite the game of keep-away with the answer." He let out a theatrical sigh.

Mother. Luci *knew* he must be referring to her. Marian Hawthorne, her enigmatic mother, had woven a tale of secrets and shadows, one that Luci had only ever glimpsed from the fringes. Although whispers of her mother's creation had always haunted their lives, landing them in the crosshairs of the formidable Salt-Iron Confederation, the details remained hidden from Luci. Her mother had been tight-lipped about why, had vowed never to share the discovery that had sent her on the run. Luci suspected Blaise knew, but he had also remained frustratingly silent.

Caught up in her thoughts, Luci almost missed the patient gaze of Professor Woodrow, who was clearly awaiting some acknowledgment. Pushing past the sudden lump in her throat, she murmured, "I see."

"Well, Miss Hawthorne," Professor Woodrow began in a tone one might use to explain a mildly fascinating fact about postage stamps, "I'm not entirely sure you see the full picture—though, in due course, I have a sneaking suspicion you might. You see, we're on the precipice of something quite exhilarating: cracking the code of these so-called alchemical mages."

Luci nibbled her lower lip as Professor Woodrow pointed to

an open page in the journal. Her eyes fell on the familiar face drawn upon it. It was Blaise, unmistakable even in the delicate strokes of a pencil. The world seemed to blur once more as she took in the annotations around the sketch, and the chilling phrase *Alchemical Mage* underlined with urgency.

"Ah, now that," he mused, peering at her over the rims of his glasses, "is where things get intriguing. We're about to delve deep into your mother's legacy, Miss Hawthorne. Quite the adventure, don't you think?"

Luci felt a knot tighten in her chest. The scrawled image of Blaise stared back at her from the worn pages, proof of a hidden narrative. Her stomach soured at the thought, and she realized which professor Misty had spoken to about Blaise. Professor Woodrow had connected the dots as easily as a child playing a game. She had been a fool to come here.

But she couldn't let Professor Woodrow know that. Maybe she could force him to doubt his claims, or to reconsider. That would buy her time, wouldn't it?

"I...I don't understand," Luci stammered.

His smile was patient. "Oh, come now. Surely some of this rings a bell? Subject Zero over there—" He gestured to the drawing of Blaise. "—stands as a tantalizing enigma in the world of alchemical studies."

Luci's hands curled into fists at her sides. She wanted to scream, to lash out, to wipe that chilling smile off the professor's face. But she knew she had to restrain herself, had to keep playing along if she had any hope of protecting the people she cared about.

"I don't know anything about this," Luci whispered.

Professor Woodrow clucked his tongue, his expression that of the mild disappointment one might feel when a novice makes a basic error. "It's quite unfortunate, if that's the case. But, given your *close* association with Marian Hawthorne, I'm confident that your mind is a veritable treasure trove of insights. And, with both

Subject Zero and our dear Subject One," he added slyly, "in residence, so to speak, it's like having all the key ingredients for an intriguing recipe. The prospects, my dear, are quite promising."

Zero and One? Luci's brow crinkled, but then her understanding clicked like the answer to a troublesome equation. *Blaise and Jefferson?* She recalled Jefferson was a late bloomer in the world of magic.

Torn between loyalty and a nagging curiosity, Luci weighed her options. Assisting this man would betray her family. But if she denied him, told him *no*...she *couldn't* do that. Luci would lose her chance for precious inside information. A real chance to help her brother.

But, oh gods, Blaise has been through so much...

Tears stung her eyes. "Don't hurt him."

Professor Woodrow seemed momentarily perplexed by her plea. "Oh, you're referring to Subject Zero? Well, Miss Hawthorne, he's quite the rare gem. You're not imagining I run things like they do at the Golden Citadel, are you?" He chuckled with mild amusement. "Rest assured, he's rather cozy here. Subject Zero is akin to a collector's item in my eyes."

He has a name. He's Blaise. My brother. He's not a specimen. Not a treasure for you to possess. Luci bit back the angry correction.

Professor Woodrow tilted his head, reminding her of a curious bird. "Now, coming to the heart of the matter, Miss Hawthorne. Are you prepared to dive into this fascinating endeavor? To unravel your mother's legacy?"

Luci's gaze landed on Blaise's sketched face, labelled *Subject Zero*.

Please forgive me, Blaise. I promise I'm trying to help. She pasted a brave smile on her face, meeting her professor's eyes. "It sounds exciting. When do we begin?"

CHAPTER TWENTY-EIGHT

Adult Problems

"This card game feels like you've thrown together all the rules of every game you ever knew and forgot half of them," Blaise said, frowning as he tried to comprehend Jefferson's haphazard instructions.

Jefferson gave a rueful smile. "Perhaps I was a tad ambitious," he admitted, shuffling the cards absently. "Or maybe I just have a terrible memory for games when half the deck's missing."

Blaise chuckled, a sound that made Jefferson's heart feel lighter despite their dire situation. "Maybe let's think about it. We can come back to it later."

Later. The expanse of time seemed to yawn before them. Jefferson wished he knew what was coming, what to expect. He didn't know how long they might be held in this academic prison. He struggled to maintain his optimistic facade. Jefferson was accustomed to planning his moves well in advance, but he had to know what game was being played to be effective.

He glanced at the desk, thinking back to the things he'd written about Blaise. After their captors had unceremoniously deposited his husband in the dorm room, Jefferson had folded the papers up, placing them at the top of a drawer for safekeeping.

Blaise didn't notice his glance. He'd risen to make a quick circuit of the room, stretching his legs. Jefferson knew by the movements that Blaise was itchy for freedom. He'd tried to prod different areas of the room with Breaker magic, only to discover that it was basically useless. Jefferson wished that, at the very least, they had been trapped in the university's kitchen. That would have given Blaise a welcome outlet for his nerves.

Jefferson watched from the corner, his fingers toying with the buttons of his borrowed shirt. The frayed edges and the once-vibrant Cheswell insignia, now faded to a shadow of its former glory, were a far cry from his usual attire. An idea struck him, and he tried to inject some levity into the situation. "You know, this room isn't that much different from our loft back home."

Blaise paused mid-step, arching an eyebrow. "Minus your wardrobe trunks taking up half the room, you mean?"

Jefferson feigned offense. "Those trunks hold fashion master-pieces! How many times have I told you the importance of a versatile wardrobe?" He sighed dramatically, adding, "Although, I will admit, this Cheswell uniform has its...*quaint charm*."

"I never thought I'd hear the words *quaint charm* spoken like a curse." Blaise chuckled. "But do you like the loft?"

Jefferson paused. The very first time he'd set foot in that loft, it had felt cozy yet cramped. But he also knew how much the location meant to Blaise. The bakery wasn't just a source of livelihood but a haven for him. "I've always imagined something spacious for us, maybe with a garden. But if it's the loft you love, then that's home to me," Jefferson murmured, his voice soft with affection.

Blaise's eyes gleamed, his expression coming alive. "What if, when we return to Fortitude, we find something...bigger? Maybe a house?"

A house? Jefferson swallowed, knowing that for Blaise, this was an enormous leap. "But the bakery is your happy place. Your home. Wouldn't this idea prove inconvenient?"

"We wouldn't have to be that far from town," Blaise said. "And what good is having a sugar-obsessed pegasus if I can't have him take me to and from the bakery every day?"

Jefferson chuckled. "I see. Well, I must admit, I rather like the idea." His heart felt a surge of warmth. There was hope in Blaise's words, the promise of a future. "And, perhaps, a bigger yard for Mother Clucker and her brood to frolic in?"

"Still can't believe you named a chicken that," Blaise muttered with a laugh. But his expression was filled with such happiness that Jefferson grinned. "But yes, I think it would be good all around. Maybe we'd even have room for a barn for Emrys and Seledora."

Jefferson cocked his head, feeling almost effervescent. Blaise was building a life for them with his words, and every single one was a soothing balm for Jefferson's soul. "It sounds delightful."

A knock cut through their intimate conversation, an abrupt reminder of their reality. "You have a visitor!" a voice declared.

All the tension came back in a rush. Jefferson and Blaise both rose, exchanging protective looks. They made a united front.

The door creaked open, and a petite blonde girl peeked in. Jefferson didn't know her name, but she was one of the students who often brought them food but kept responses to questions as short as possible.

"Who is it?" Jefferson asked.

The girl stepped to the side, revealing Luci and Theo. "You've got ten minutes," she said, her voice neutral, but the set of her lips expressed a hint of sympathy.

Theo's bright eyes widened at the sight of Jefferson, and without hesitation, he sprinted into the room. He was a blur of energy as he threw himself into Jefferson's waiting arms. Jefferson pulled his nephew close, surprised by the immense relief he felt at the sight of him.

"Uncle Malerson!" Theo exclaimed, voice muffled against Jefferson's shirt.

Jefferson hugged the boy against him, but from the corner of his eye, he saw Blaise exchange a quizzical look with Luci. Blaise mouthed, "Uncle Malerson?" Luci merely smirked and offered an amused shrug.

"Did you two kiss and make up?" Luci barely suppressed her smile.

"We certainly got to the kissing part," Jefferson said, unable to hide his satisfaction.

"Ew!" Theo scrunched up his face in mock disgust. He stuck out his tongue. "Yucky!"

Chuckling, Jefferson tousled the boy's hair. "I promise we'll spare you from the mushy stuff." Though a fleeting glance exchanged with Blaise held a silent promise of more conversations—and definitely more kisses—to come.

Still crouched down, Jefferson gently released his embrace and turned Theo around to face Blaise. "I want to introduce you to someone. This is Blaise, my husband."

Theo tensed, then moved to hide behind Jefferson. The boy peered around Jefferson's side. The behavior was more than childhood shyness. With dismay, Jefferson realized that Theo now didn't know which adults he could trust.

"Blaise is a good man. A *hero*," Jefferson said, keeping his voice low. But loud enough for Blaise to hear. An exasperated look crossed Blaise's face.

But the assurance worked. Theo edged around Jefferson, sizing up Blaise. "So, you're Uncle Malerson's prince?"

Confusion replaced the exasperation on Blaise's face. "I... *what?*"

"We were reading stories earlier," Luci said by way of explanation. "And yes, Blaise is definitely a prince." She aimed a teasing look at her brother, and for a heartbeat, it was as if nothing were wrong at all.

Blaise's expression tightened, as if he were parsing her words for some sort of insult but couldn't find one. Fortunately, Theo served as an admirable distraction. The little boy offered his hand, every bit the young gentleman. "Pleased to meet you."

Theo's move forced Blaise to relax. He took the much smaller hand and gave it a gentle shake. "Howdy."

Theo giggled. "You're silly."

Luci sobered, her face growing serious. "We should make the most of our time."

Ten minutes, the girl had warned. Luci was right: they couldn't waste an instant. "Of course. What did you find out?"

Theo, meanwhile, extricated himself from Jefferson and plopped down in the chair, sitting backwards and pretending it was a horse. "Look, Uncle Malerson! I'm riding Dora!" He waved his hands overhead, then made galloping sounds, followed by his attempt at a whinny.

"And what a fine rider you are," Jefferson murmured. "Keep playing, Theo. We have to discuss adult problems."

Luci leaned against the wall, since the small room didn't have any place to sit besides the currently occupied bed or the desk chair. "So, as you can see, I found Theo." She gestured to the boy.

"And that's marvelous," Jefferson said. "How did you convince them to allow you another visit?"

Luci grinned. "That little boy can pull some top-tier puppy dog eyes when needed."

Jefferson cast a fond look at Theo. "Going to be a charmer like me, no doubt." He tried not to let Theo's dark hair serve as a reminder of the Wells blood coursing through his veins. Jefferson was different. Theo would be different, too.

The mention of a puppy drew Theo's attention. "Uncle Malerson, I bet the puppies back home will almost be old enough to play with now. Do you think so?"

Jefferson blinked, unprepared for the abrupt change of topic. "I suppose that's likely." Theo climbed off the chair and proceeded to go down on his hands and knees, apparently pretending to be a puppy. He growled at Jefferson's feet. It was becoming exceedingly difficult to have serious conversations with a six-year-old present. Jefferson turned his attention to Luci. "Have you had any luck regarding Alice?"

Luci shook her head. "I'm still searching. It's hard with working shifts to watch Theo, going to class, and taking part in a special assignment."

Something about her last words tweaked Jefferson's interest, but Theo spoke up. "She's here. I hear Mama's music."

"Oh." Jefferson made a soft exhalation. "And here I thought the music I heard was just students practicing."

Theo frowned. "Mama's music isn't right."

Blaise glanced at Jefferson. "Does that mean something?"

"It's her magic," Jefferson explained. "It's music-based. I heard it when I was in Starvation." He cocked his head, thoughtful. "Perhaps that's why it didn't occur to me that the music belonged to Alice. When she plays..." He paused, as if searching for the words. "It's like a force of nature. Something wild and fierce. Joyful."

"Her music is sad," Theo added. "Mama's sad."

Luci clenched her jaw. "Don't worry. She's next on my list to hunt for. But...there's something else I really need to tell you before I'm out of time."

Jefferson felt a surge of worry as he caught the seriousness in Luci's expression. Beside him, Blaise asked, "What is it?"

Luci took a deep breath before speaking. "Last night, I went to my first special session with Professor Woodrow."

At the name, Jefferson exchanged a concerned look with Blaise. Of course, Woodrow would entangle Luci in this. Jefferson belatedly realized they hadn't mentioned the alchemist at all in their previous furtive visit with Luci, and that had been a mistake.

"Dean Woodrow is your professor?" Blaise asked.

Luci nodded, but now her intent gaze was on her brother. "He...he wants me to help create alchemical mages."

After Zebulon's discussion with Jefferson, that wasn't surprising. Blaise, however, froze.

Luci plowed on, the words spilling out. "And I put the pieces together. I realized that's what you are. What both of you are, right? It's the only explanation for Jefferson, at least. And Blaise...Professor Woodrow called you Subject Zero. So it has to be...you must be an alchemical mage." Her voice sharpened as she reached the end, her eyes wide.

It was as if her words released Blaise from his freeze. "I am." Jefferson heard the acceptance ringing in his husband's voice. Blaise was comfortable with who he was. "And you're right about Jefferson. Though he came about it in a very dramatic, Jefferson-esque way."

Jefferson's brows lifted. "Ooh. I like that. Jeffersonesque." It had a nice ring to it.

Luci glanced between them. "So you're not mad at me?"

Blaise frowned. "Why would we be? You're stuck in a tough situation, same as us. So, are you going to help him?"

She looked down, unable to meet their eyes. "I didn't know what to do. I agreed because I thought it could help me learn more about his plans." Luci glanced back up hesitantly. "Was that wrong?"

Blaise shook his head, rising from the bed. "You've done nothing wrong. In fact, I think that was very smart of you."

Luci blinked in surprise. "You do?"

Blaise placed his hands on her shoulders. "Staying close to Professor Woodrow is the best way to learn more about what he's planning. And if he thinks you're on his side, it will make it easier for you to help us." Then he glanced over his shoulder at Jefferson, as if hoping for confirmation.

"Keeping close to Woodrow, gathering information—it might be our way out of this. We just need to play our cards right." Jefferson rubbed his chin. If Flora were here, that was what she would have done. He decided not to mention that to Blaise, though. Blaise wouldn't appreciate his sister taking on the role of the boisterous and daring half-knocker.

Luci let out a shaky breath,. She had clearly been worried about them disagreeing with her choice. "I...I talked to him about you, Blaise. He said he won't hurt you because you're unique. So you should be safe, I think." Her words were another rush, as if she were trying to reassure herself as much as them. "And I'll do what I can to find Alice," she said, undeterred. "And I'll try to get you both out of here."

"Be careful," Blaise cautioned. Worry reflected in the depths of his eyes. "Don't take unnecessary risks."

Luci scoffed. "Considering the situations you've landed in, I think it's clear caution doesn't run in our family."

Blaise simply shook his head, amusement touching his expression. "All I'm saying is, while we're in here, be safe out there."

Uncertainty and fear crossed Luci's face. She moved forward and wrapped her arms around Blaise in a fierce hug. "I'll try not to be reckless, but I might have to do some things you won't like," she murmured, voice muffled against his chest. After a moment, she stepped back, blinking rapidly.

Jefferson grimaced. "So it goes."

There was another brisk knock at the door. "Time's up," came the girl's voice from earlier.

Luci sighed, squaring her shoulders. "We have to go. But I'll be back as soon as I can."

Blaise nodded, jaw set. "We'll see you soon."

Gods, why did time pass so quickly? Jefferson turned to Theo, his nephew watching them with round eyes.

"I don't wanna go, Uncle Malerson," the little boy said. "They won't let me stay with you or Mama?" His voice pitched high with his words.

Jefferson wanted to pull Theo into another hug, but he knew he'd have an impossible time releasing him. "I know. I need you to be brave, Theo. We'll get out of this, and then we can be together again."

Theo's eyes lit with hope. "Are you gonna be a hero?"

The words tugged at Jefferson's heart. Oh, how he longed to say *yes*, that he would come to Alice and Theo's rescue. But he couldn't, not while he was trapped. "I don't know," Jefferson whispered, hating that he couldn't say otherwise. It would be a lie, and he wouldn't needlessly raise Theo's hopes. "But I intend to try."

Luci took Theo's hand, and together, they slipped out the door as the blonde girl held it open. Then the door swung shut behind them, and Jefferson and Blaise were alone once more.

Blaise let out a heavy sigh as the door closed. He turned and moved back to the bed, sinking down onto the thin mattress.

"Well, that was certainly an unexpected turn of events," Jefferson remarked, trying to keep his tone light.

Blaise nodded slowly. "Unexpected, but not unwelcome. At least we know Luci and Theo are relatively safe for now." His mouth twisted unhappily. "Though I don't like the idea of Luci putting herself at risk for us."

Jefferson put an arm around him. "She's clever. She'll be fine, I'm certain."

Blaise exhaled softly, resting his head against Jefferson's shoulder. "I know. It's just hard, knowing the risk she's taking."

They sat like that for a moment, drawing strength from one another. So much remained uncertain, but they would face it together. Jefferson was glad for that.

"Are you okay?" Jefferson's question was as quiet as a falling feather. Even with Luci's news that Zebulon didn't intend to harm Blaise...this was still not a situation in which he wanted to be trapped. Blaise was a novelty. An experiment. And so was Jefferson.

Blaise swallowed. "No. Later, when I can think clearly, I want to start planning a way out of this. But what about you? Are you okay?"

Jefferson smiled. "To uphold my vow of transparency, no, I am *not*. But seeing Theo, knowing he's unharmed—it's a small beacon of hope. And being here, with you, brings its own peace. So, while circumstances are dire, there's comfort in these small graces."

"That was a very complicated answer," Blaise murmured.

"Transparency will do that." Jefferson chuckled, then cleared his throat. It was time for a change of topic. "So, what would you like to do to take your mind off things? I have another idea for a card game."

Blaise groaned. "I don't think my head can handle that right now." He pursed his lips. "If I could lose myself mixing batter for muffins, I'd feel better."

"And it's a great tragedy that you can't." Jefferson grinned, the faint aroma of a fresh bake wafting in his memories. "You with flour on your face, lost in your art. There's an image to cherish." His eyes grew distant, reminiscing. "You know, this confinement reminds me quite a bit of the hurricane parties we used to throw back in Ganland."

Blaise arched a brow. "Hurricane parties? Why would you celebrate something like that?"

A wry smile played on Jefferson's lips. "It wasn't really about the storm. Think of a band of spirited youngsters gathered in a cozy shelter, waiting out nature's fury. Imagine the mix of excitement, tension, food, willing partners, and perhaps an unhealthy amount of alcohol. The storm outside creating a backdrop for... well, let's say various *indoor activities*."

"Aside from the food, I'm not seeing the draw," Blaise said, though his eyes danced with amusement. "Or how this is anything like that."

Jefferson shrugged, leaning back. "The essence wasn't the party but the closeness, the intimacy of it. Being confined with someone special, like we are now, has its moments." He offered a soft smile, thinking about their closeness despite the adversity they faced.

Blaise's lips twitched. "So about these *willing partners* you mentioned…"

Jefferson's laugh was soft and teasing. "Feeling possessive, are we?"

"I would have hated that party." Blaise gave Jefferson a look he couldn't quite discern.

"Probably," Jefferson agreed.

"But I would have liked being with you." Blaise closed the distance between them with a kiss.

CHAPTER TWENTY-NINE

Violent Violin

Alice

The gentle resonance of violin music rolled over Alice, the instrument an extension of herself. In this circular chamber, with its high-domed ceiling adorned with gorgeous frescoes, everything else melted away.

Each note she played seemed to rise, flutter, and dance, echoing in the vastness before settling back around her like a comforting embrace. This piece was her ode to Theo, her precious son; an anthem of love she hoped would reach his young ears wherever he might be.

In her periphery stood Phillip, his usually sharp and discerning gaze now tinted with unease. Shadows from the gas lamps played on his face, emphasizing the deep furrows of his brow. Alice felt reassured by his presence, drawing strength from it. But why did he look so troubled when they were cocooned in this moment of musical solace?

Lost in the swirling emotions of the piece, Alice barely noticed the door ease open. A young woman with chestnut hair, probably a student, entered tentatively. Drawn in by the spellbinding music, her eyes were wide with admiration as she edged closer, captivated by the poignant tune Alice produced.

In the intimacy of her music, Alice sensed the newcomer like a ripple in a tranquil pond. The soft murmur of conversation between Phillip and the young intruder threatened the harmony she was striving to maintain. Annoyance prickled at her, but she was determined to keep her focus.

Phillip's voice, deep and soothing, conversed in muted tones with the girl. Alice recalled the conversation she'd had with him: he had mentioned using the music as a sort of camouflage for activities in a nearby building. She would do anything for Phillip, and she intended to play the song he desired.

But the presence of the young woman, engaging with Phillip, ignited a spark of jealousy within her. The irrational feeling momentarily skewed her concentration, causing a disruption in her melody.

No, she chided herself, forcing her focus back to the strings under her fingers. This music, this emotion, wasn't for Phillip; it was for her precious Theo. She took a steadying breath, closed her eyes, and channeled her maternal love into the bow's gentle strokes on the violin's strings. With each note, she envisioned her love traveling like bees flitting from flower to flower before finally reaching Theo. The girl's presence faded back into the periphery as Alice played on.

However, the girl's voice pierced through once more, rising above the cascade of notes. "I've never heard such beautiful music before," she remarked, the sincerity of her admiration clear in her tone.

A tremor ran through Alice's fingers as they touched the

violin's strings. The girl's compliment felt threatening, as if she were trying to ingratiate herself to Phillip. Alice's tempo increased ever so slightly as irritation flickered through her. She couldn't allow this girl to disrupt what she'd been tasked to do. The notes coming from her violin transformed, taking on a subtle but unmistakably dark edge. Where the song had once been filled with her love for Theo, hints of malice seeped in like corruption. Every note she played seemed to challenge the girl, to mark Alice's territory. The violin's voice, which had once sung a lullaby for Theo, now emitted a protective growl, warning off any who might threaten Alice's place in the world.

Alice barely registered Phillip saying something to the girl, urging her away. She was too focused on the music swirling around her, on eliminating the disruption the girl's presence caused.

The girl's eyes widened as the sinister notes washed over her. She took an instinctive step back, one hand rising defensively. "I-I'm sorry. I didn't mean to intrude," she stammered.

But Alice was ensnared in her own creation, determined to weaponize it. Every draw of her bow intensified the room's electric atmosphere, amplifying the emotions she felt. With an almost primal satisfaction, she felt the pull of the music, its darkness spreading like vines strangling a tree. Alice was a predator, preparing to pounce on her prey.

The girl backed further away, the blood draining from her face. Like a startled deer, she pivoted and made a hasty exit, her hurried footsteps receding to faint echoes in the distance.

A gentle hand on Alice's arm drew her back. She blinked, the room coming back into focus. Phillip stood before her, concern creasing his brow. "Alice?" he asked, his voice hesitant. "Why did you do that?"

She quirked an eyebrow, genuine confusion seeping through. Alice allowed herself a momentary break. "Do what, my love?"

Phillip's expression tightened, a furrow forming on his brow.

"Your music—it took on a life of its own. You frightened the girl away with it. She meant no harm. She was only a student, come to admire your talent."

Alice tried to make sense of the blurring line between her music's intent and her own emotions. Had she done that? Was she so lost in the music that she'd forgotten its power? The memory felt hazy now, lost in the euphoria of playing for her husband.

"I...I don't know," she said slowly. "Phillip, I wanted my music to be an echo of my love for you." A flicker of memory jolted her. "No, not just for you—for Theo, as well!" A rush of conflicting emotions washed over her, making her feel unsteady. The room whirled before her eyes like a top pivoting on its axis.

Phillip studied her intently, his gaze grounding her once more. Alice preened under the warmth of his attention. "Alice," he whispered. "That music—what it did to the girl—that wasn't you. I know your heart, and this..." His eyes, always so full of certainty, seemed to search hers, seeking an answer to the riddle of her recent behavior. "This isn't right."

Alice frowned. That wasn't the Phillip she knew. He enjoyed having power over others. Surely, he understood. He was possessive, and now, so was she. Alice blinked rapidly, grasping for clarity. "I don't understand," she murmured. "I thought the music would please you."

Phillip sighed, raking a hand through his hair. "No, my dear. It does not please me to see you act with cruelty, especially toward an innocent. That's not...that's not you." He pulled out his pocket watch, checking the time. "You're past due for a break. Even a Songbinder needs her rest."

Alice's breath quickened, panic rising. "No, I can keep playing!" she insisted, clutching her violin tighter. Every fiber of her being clung to the rhythm of the melodies, terrified of the void they masked. The music and Phillip were all she had now. Without them, the haze would lift, and she would have to face...what? What else was out there? She couldn't remember.

Whatever it was, it didn't matter.

Seeing her struggle, Phillip reached out, touching her wrist gently. "Just for a short time," he assured. "You've been playing for hours without rest. Please, Alice, let us pause and regain our strength. The music will keep."

Alice hesitated, torn. But Phillip's voice was soothing, his touch the solace she needed. She exhaled slowly. "Very well. If you wish it. But just for a little while."

Phillip nodded, his features softening. He checked his pocket watch again. "We have time before the evening performance."

What other choice did she have? Phillip wanted a break, so they would have one. Reluctantly, Alice placed her violin back in its case. She straightened, wincing at the sudden tightness in her neck and shoulder, and the deep ache in her fingers. How long had she been playing? The hours had blurred together into an endless stream of music.

She stood in the center of the rotunda, frozen by the foreign thought that this...this wasn't *right*. She had been sitting for so long that even her tailbone throbbed. But she...she didn't usually sit when she played the violin. She was on her feet, moving. Dancing. This was different...but why? Why did it have to be so different? If she could figure out why, Alice was certain she...what?

Alice shook her head, trying to clear the strange fog that had settled over her mind. Whatever was amiss, Phillip would know how to make it right. He always took care of her.

"Shall we go find some dinner?" she suggested brightly, linking her arm through his. Food and drink would help revive her depleted strength.

Phillip regarded her with an inscrutable look, his sharp eyes searching her face. "Dinner would be welcome," he said at last. Was that a note of relief in his tone? He patted her hand where it rested in the crook of his arm. "You must be famished after such an extended performance."

Alice smiled, leaning into him as they left the music hall. "I could eat a whole roast chicken!" she declared dramatically, stirring an unguarded chuckle from Phillip. She was pleased to have lightened his mood, even if only for a moment. Something troubled him deeply, that much was clear. But she would remain firmly by his side, offering comfort and companionship until the shadow passed. She would make sure he was happy and loved.

For now, they had earned a reprieve from...whatever it was someone had tasked them with. Alice pushed aside the bothersome questions that pecked at the edges of her mind. Phillip was here, leading her to dinner. That was all that mattered.

Despite that, the wrongness clung to her, and she wondered.

CHAPTER THIRTY

Pegasus Plans

Emrys

As the stablemaster walked down the aisle with another man, they paused before Emrys's stall. The stallion paid no mind, opting instead to catch some much-needed rest. Recent nights had been taxing, with him and Seledora sneaking out of the barn. Their wings carried them over the city, searching relentlessly for clues to Blaise's whereabouts. However, their quest was always thwarted whenever they approached Cheswell, repelled by a peculiar melody that sent them retreating.

"That is indeed a fine stallion, as you've said," the newcomer remarked, studying Emrys with a spark of admiration. "When might he be available?"

Available? Emrys's ear flicked at the word. They couldn't possibly be referring to him.

The stablemaster, with a sweep of his hand, pointed out the stalls flanking Emrys. "These three have been left here unpaid for several days now. Should they remain unclaimed and the dues unpaid by week's end, the law grants me the right to sell them."

Upon hearing this, Emrys swiveled around, his nostrils flaring with indignation, ready to offer them a piece of his mind and perhaps a taste of his hooves, too.

<Hold off,> Seledora cautioned from the stall to his right. <Everything he says is accurate.>

<That doesn't mean I'm going to stand here and allow it!> Emrys shot back, shaking his mane.

<I didn't say we'd allow it,> Seledora interjected, a fiery spark in her tone. <Just lay low like Naureus here.>

<I wouldn't call it laying low. I'd call it conserving energy for when it actually matters,> the buckskin chipped in matter-of-factly.

Emrys huffed. Perhaps Seledora and Naureus had a point. It might be wise to conserve his energy. But he couldn't help the wave of irritation that swept through him when the men entered his stall, running their hands over his legs to check for soundness and then opening his mouth to peer at his teeth. It was unspeakably *rude*.

The men stood in the stall aisle, engaging in a lengthy discussion about potential pricing once Emrys was deemed *available*. Their casual appraisal stoked the fire of resistance within him. At last, they walked away, their voices echoing down the aisle as they left.

Emrys turned to Seledora, the urgency clear in his stiff-legged stance. <Fine, I didn't kick them into next week. What do you propose? I will not stand by and let them sell me out from under Blaise!>

Seledora lifted her head so that he and Naureus could see her over the partition. <We've stayed here long enough. I think we can all agree that Blaise is not coming back imminently.>

<Do not say that!> Emrys snapped, ears pinned flat to his skull. The mere suggestion that Blaise wouldn't return was *unacceptable*.

<Let me finish.> Seledora swished her tail in agitation. <I am not suggesting our riders are lost to us. But we cannot just sit here and eat oats and play at being horses.>

<Oh.> Emrys bobbed his head, the light of understanding dawning in his eyes. <On this, I agree.>

<I propose that when we make our flyover tonight, we do not return,> Seledora continued. <There's enough shelter and grazing outside of Greylight to sustain us. I think that it's best if we remain close, Emrys.> Her gaze then shifted toward Naureus. <But I think you should return to Fortitude.>

The buckskin stallion flicked his ears forward and then back, showing his uncertainty. <For what purpose? I came here with Luci.>

<And she is stuck inside the university, too.> Seledora sighed. <None of this is ideal. But we need help. Blaise suggested Nadine and his mother. I think that is a sound plan.>

Naureus shifted his weight, his hooves making soft thuds against the straw-covered floor of the stable. His gaze settled past the wooden beams into the distance as if visualizing the path back to Fortitude. <I can do that. Alone, I can fly back to Fortitude quickly. It will take longer when I have others with me.>

Emrys sighed. <What if we need more than Marian and Nadine? They are only two.>

Seledora's dark eyes gleamed. <A Leech-Healer and an alchemist with her children in danger? I would not stand in their way.> Her words held a certain confidence, cutting through Emrys's doubts.

Emrys chewed on that thought. Seledora had a point. <Nadine and Marian, then. The sooner we get our riders out of there, the better.> His hide twitched at his withers, as if he were shooing a horsefly.

<Then we agree,> Seledora said coolly. <We do this tonight.>

<Tonight,> Naureus echoed.

Emrys blew out a long breath. Twilight couldn't come soon enough.

CHAPTER THIRTY-ONE

A Tall Order

Luci

*L*uci bent over the table, studying the pages of research notes laid out before her. Her fingers trailed across the paper, carefully turning each sheet as she searched for clues. Formulas and arcane symbols covered the pages in Professor Woodrow's meticulous script, detailing experiments on catalyzing magic through alchemy.

Around her, the murmur of voices drifted in the background. The other graduate students spoke in hushed tones about their own projects, heads bent together over bubbling vials and strange contraptions. The cramped laboratory hummed with scholarly purpose.

Luci traced the painstakingly precise design of an alchemical circle, each symbol and line intertwining into an intricate web of intentions and effects. The case study it accompanied painted a dark portrait of experimentation. The young victims, all orphans, had been subjected to a potion's cruel trial. Most of the test subjects had died.

Only one survived.

"Oh, Blaise," she whispered, shaking her head. Did he know? He had to. It explained why, for a while, there had been a deep rift between him and their mother.

How had he hidden this secret pain, this childhood trauma masked by an alchemical designation? Subject Zero—the dehumanizing label assigned by Marian Hawthorne, their mother—had been Blaise.

How could you do this to him, Mom? Luci's gaze flicked to the surrounding students, fixated on their tasks. The newfound knowledge felt suffocating, an unspeakable horror inflicted on someone she loved. Bitter tears threatened to spill, blurring the inked pages.

And now, here she was. How could Luci follow in her mother's footsteps? Luci would become a great alchemist, that she vowed. But not like this. Not by losing her heart and soul.

Closing the worn journal, Luci took a deep, fortifying breath. While the past remained unchangeable, mired in its grim choices and repercussions, she still controlled her future. All she could do was move forward and try to make things right.

The clink of glass caught her attention. She turned to find Josh, a tall, dark-haired graduate student, meticulously arranging tubes and wires around the glass tank containing the deceased woman. Her skin was an ashen grey, her eyes recessed, lending her face an eerily hollow look. Even in the dim light, Luci could make out the sheen of perspiration on Josh's forehead. His hands might be steady, but the lines creasing his brow and the way his lips pressed tightly together spoke volumes. He was deep in concentration, as if his academic life depended on the task.

It was possible that it did.

For a moment, their gazes connected. Luci quickly turned her attention away, discomfort growing. She still didn't know what they intended to do with the dead woman, but whatever *this* was—her gaze drifted back to the lifeless body suspended in viscous fluid—felt wrong. Unnatural.

Luci rose from her seat, smoothing her hands over her trousers. She needed to get out of this room, with its cloying air and looming sense of wrongness. "I think I left something in the storage room. I'll be right back," she announced to all in earshot.

No one even looked in her direction. The lab's door whispered shut behind her as she ventured down the corridor. The storage room door loomed ahead. It was more like an ice box than an actual room, the temperature inside frigid.

Inside, countless jars and vials occupied rows of shelves, their labels a record of countless experiments and subjects. A faint glow emanated from some, casting eerie luminescence. Luci idly scanned the labels, eyes widening when she came across a vial with the words *Jefferson Cole* followed by *Subject One.*

"No way," she whispered. When had Professor Woodrow taken a sample from Jefferson? Luci shook her head. The only thing that *really* mattered was that Woodrow had it, period.

Balancing on her tiptoes, she stretched, the tips of her fingers brushing the cold glass. As she grasped the vial, the edge of her sleeve accidentally nudged another. She made a grab for it, curling it in her palm and ensuring it didn't topple. Breathing a sigh of relief, she was about to slip it back into place when she read the name on the label.

Blaise Hawthorne. And then, in Professor Woodrow's hand, *Subject Zero.*

Luci's breath caught in her throat. Blaise? When had Professor Woodrow gotten this? Certainly not at Cheswell, or Blaise would have mentioned it, she was sure.

She shook her head. The how and when didn't matter. The simple fact remained: Professor Woodrow had Blaise's blood. And after what she'd read, it made her extremely uncomfortable.

Clutching the samples, she slipped out of the storage room, securing the door behind her. She paused at the echo of approaching footsteps.

A door swung open, revealing a tall figure bathed in the light from the corridor. The man's eyes—a clear, piercing gaze—locked onto Luci for a brief second. That face. She'd seen him before.

It was the man from the rotunda. The one who had been with Alice.

Luci's mouth went dry. She clutched the vial to her chest like a protective amulet. The man's gaze flicked to her briefly, then seemed to dismiss her as unimportant. Just another student.

With a commanding air, he moved into the lab, the squeak of his leather shoes punctuating his arrival. "Zebulon!" he called out, every syllable drenched with a sense of purpose. Gone was the concerned gentleman from the rotunda; in his place stood someone who exuded dominance and expectation.

Professor Woodrow, lost in a sea of papers, looked up, his eyebrows knitting in response. "Ah, Phillip," he commented in the kind of tone one might use when remembering a vaguely familiar acquaintance from a social gathering years ago.

The man—Phillip—leaned in close, lowering his voice as he spoke. Still clutching the vial, Luci nonchalantly strode past to reach her workstation, which was conveniently close to the pair.

"I can't do this anymore. Seeing her like this... That woman isn't Alice. The spark, the fire I loved...it's gone." The pain in his voice was like an open wound. "What you've done to her...it's not right. She's a stranger to me. This supposed Love Potion stole the woman I love!"

Luci set down the vial and masked her eavesdropping by organizing her supplies. *What? A Love Potion?* But that was something for stories, wasn't it? Yet, given the very real concoctions around her, she couldn't deny the realm of possibilities. In this lab, tales and reality blurred seamlessly.

Meeting Phillip's gaze squarely, Professor Woodrow

responded with his normal placid demeanor. "You came to me with a specific request. You wanted Alice's unwavering love and affection. And, in my own way, I provided exactly that."

A visible tremor ran through Phillip, his once confident stature now diminished. "But not like this. Not an Alice robbed of her spirit and essence. She's little more than a conjured illusion."

"Well, Phillip," Professor Woodrow began in his signature drawling tone, "the potion, as I explained—or at least, I *thought* I had—does a little rearranging in the noggin. It...enhances the rosy feelings and dims down the, oh, let's say *less favorable* memories. Remove the elixir, and you might just bring back all those less-than-stellar moments you two shared."

"She has no feelings for me beyond this...this mindless devotion!" Phillip hissed.

Raising an eyebrow, Woodrow continued, "You came to me with a problem, a little hiccup in your romantic narrative, if you will. And I provided a solution. A fresh canvas for you both. Sounds pretty straightforward, right?"

Phillip's face tightened, a muscle twitching in his jaw. "I didn't want a blank canvas. I wanted the colors back, the passion, the fire. Now, all I see is a faded portrait of Alice. I sought reconciliation, not a puppet."

Luci's heart ached at the raw pain in the man's voice. She thought of the vacant look in Alice's eyes, the disconnected way she had played her violin when Luci had found her in the rotunda. What had they done to her?

Tilting his head slightly, Woodrow responded, "Well, it's always tricky with emotions, isn't it? Can't really order them from a catalog. But remember, I only provided the brush. *You* chose to paint."

Phillip paled, swaying as the professor's soft words struck him as surely as a bullet. His last words, a hushed promise or threat, were reserved for Woodrow alone. Then, Phillip turned on his heel and strode for the door, anger radiating from him in waves.

Luci's mind raced as she watched Phillip storm out. How could she help Alice? Confronting Professor Woodrow head-on felt risky. But inaction wasn't an option either.

She rose, her chair scraping against the wooden floor, and approached a nearby bookshelf. The lamplight glinted off the old tomes, revealing the gold-foiled titles embossed on their spines. She skimmed over the titles, selecting a dusty book that seemed unrelated to her actual intent. As she feigned interest in its pages, her thoughts remained anchored on Alice's plight.

A Love Potion. Luci hadn't known such a thing existed until now, so she couldn't even imagine how to formulate a counter for it.

Blaise, though...his magic was the perfect counter. He'd proven before that he could break alchemical effects just as handily as he could break physical materials. But Blaise might as well have been on the moon. Luci couldn't see a way to get him to Alice.

Unless...

Luci considered the large amount of alchemical reagents she had access to. She could do a lot of damage with them, could potentially create an acid to eat through the door. But the reagents needed for that were so vastly different from what she was meant to be researching, someone would uncover her intent in no time.

How can I get Blaise to Alice?

Wait. A distant memory, a fragment of a story Blaise had shared about his time in Itude, jolted Luci's mind.

The collapse of the original windpump had been linked to a potent alchemical mixture—Breaker's Touch. A thrill laced through her. She had seen the recipe in her mother's notebooks. Luci closed her eyes for a moment, summoning up an image of the page in her mind. She could almost see it clearly. Snatching up a pencil, she jotted down notes of her recollections.

"Maybe there's a way to harness something like your magic

after all, Blaise." She hesitated, aware of the precarious situation she was in.

Alice's face, so vacant and cold, flashed in Luci's mind. Blaise and Jefferson, relegated to little more than specimens. Yes, it was worth the risk. She couldn't stand by while Alice was being controlled and her family was held captive.

She paid another visit to the supply room, gathering the components required for the volatile potion. None of them were even vaguely useful for feigning work on alchemical mages. She shielded them against her body as she approached her workspace. Luci took a quick survey of the lab, relieved to find her peers deeply engrossed in their own experiments. Professor Woodrow had his back to her as he prepared a set of vials at a workstation.

She cleared off an area to begin her work, pulling out a journal to record observations and document her work. At the top of the page, she wrote ALCHEMICAL MAGES, then drew little flowers and hearts around it. Let anyone who thought to check her work think she was vacuous.

Tapping the end of the pencil against the page, Luci blew out a long breath. There was no doubt in her mind that the things she was considering doing...they were a tall order. *Figure out a way to make a universal counter for that Love Potion with Blaise's blood. Craft Breaker's Touch from an old memory.*

These were things her mother would have done easily, of that Luci had no doubt. *Time to walk in Mom's footsteps.*

Blaise

THE STILL AIR OF THE ROOM WAS STIFLING. BLAISE STARED AT THE ceiling, then briefly scrunched his eyes shut. His mind took him to the sun-bathed canyons of the Gutter, where the wind carried reminders of freedom with each hot breath. He could almost feel the bustle of his beloved bakery around him, the comforting rhythm of kneading dough beneath his practiced hands, and the sugary aroma of fresh pastries painting the morning air with the promise of a new day.

But reality was starkly different. The cramped room felt like a cage, a cruel reminder of a past he fought to keep at bay. The old fears tried to sneak in, but he held them at arm's length. It was an old battle, one he had become adept at fighting, though the scars were never too far beneath the surface.

Beside him on the narrow bed, Jefferson toyed with his silver pocket watch, his fingers tracing the delicate scrollwork on the case. "Do you think they'd give me a razor if I asked for one?" He scratched at the dark blond stubble along his jaw. "This is really not a part of the Jefferson Cole aesthetic."

The whimsical complaint brought a soft, almost imperceptible smile to Blaise's lips. It was a small semblance of normalcy, a brief escape from the quiet tension that hung around them.

"I doubt they would," Blaise replied, the ghost of a chuckle in his voice. His hand went absently to his own beard, the bristles rough under his fingers. It was growing scraggly—another reminder of the unforgiving reality they were in. "But don't worry, it makes you look dashing."

Jefferson's eyes glinted with amusement at the compliment. "While I appreciate the aesthetics of a bit of stubble, I prefer to keep my grooming impeccable." He gave a theatrical sigh, embodying the mock despair with a tilt of his head and a rueful smile. "Alas, such standards are hard to maintain when one is being held captive by an unhinged alchemist." Then he paused, his gaze suddenly intent. "Do you really like it?"

Blaise chuckled. "Like I said, it's a good look for you." Though, to be fair, Jefferson would probably look good after riding across the Untamed Territory through a windstorm. "But you know I love you no matter what you look like."

Jefferson beamed. "I'll be sure to remember that when I'm old and grey, with a hunched back and only two teeth."

Despite their predicament, Blaise huffed a quiet laugh at his husband's dramatics. "Thank you."

Jefferson arched a curious brow, the action so familiar and endearing. "For what?"

"For distracting me. Your knack for finding minor inconveniences in the face of doom is weirdly comforting," Blaise admitted, a small, warm smile playing on his lips, softening the worry lines that had made a home on his face.

"Oh, are we at the doom level now?" Jefferson glanced toward the door, as if a monster or a battalion were about to parade through at any moment. "I didn't get the memo."

Blaise shook his head, his smile growing a little wider at the easy banter. "I'm just feeling antsy. I don't like…" He trailed off, the words catching in his throat like thorns. His fear of their predicament attempted to claw its way back into his mind, but he pushed it away. Blaise didn't like feeling helpless and trapped. And while Jefferson's presence was a steadying rock, every passing hour seemed to peck at Blaise's soul a little more than the last.

"You've never told me about yours, you know," Jefferson said, the statement serving to not only knock Blaise out of his spiral but also confuse him.

"What?" He blinked.

Jefferson grinned. "Your beard. Why do you prefer it? I've only seen you without it once."

Blaise decided to pointedly ignore the Confederation-related trauma of that occurrence. Maybe it had been a secret mercy that his beard had regrown in the time he'd been trapped within his own body by Lamar Gaitwood's cruel magic.

He cleared his throat. "If you saw me without, it's pretty obvious."

Jefferson tilted his head. "Perhaps obvious to *you*."

Ugh. Jefferson was really going to make him say it, wasn't he?

Blaise wanted to be annoyed at him, but it was difficult with the earnest way Jefferson was peering at him.

Blaise pursed his lips. "Because without *this*—" He stroked his fingers over the facial hair in question. "—I look like I'm twelve."

Jefferson's eyes danced. "I didn't think it made you look that young. I thought it wasn't a bad look for you, though I agree that it's not a part of your charming..." He paused, eyeing Blaise appreciatively. "Aesthetic."

Blaise huffed at Jefferson's assessment, rolling his eyes for good measure. Reaching into his pocket, Blaise's fingers closed around the cool metal of the spoon he'd tucked away earlier that morning. He pulled it out, spinning it deftly between his fingers. The scant sunlight from the small window flickered briefly on its surface.

The motion caught Jefferson's eye, prompting him to sit up straighter on the bed, now attentive to Blaise's nimble movements. "Is that a...? Oh. I thought you'd somehow magicked a razor into being. I doubt a spoon would work very well. Unless I get truly desperate."

Blaise chuckled. "You sound as if you're *almost* that desperate."

Jefferson studied Blaise as the spoon continued to dance between his fingers. "I know that look," he said, leaning closer, his eyes narrowing with anticipation. "You've got an idea brewing, don't you?"

Blaise met his husband's keen gaze, giving a slight nod. "I might. But I'll need your help."

The casual humor in Jefferson's expression shifted to a serious resolve. He swung his legs over the side of the bed. "Anything you need. What's the plan?"

"It involves moving the bed," Blaise began. When Jefferson's eyebrow quirked up in a suggestive jest, Blaise rolled his eyes, but couldn't suppress the amused smile that curled at the edge of his lips. "Not like that. Here..."

He motioned for Jefferson to stand, which Jefferson did, rising gracefully to his feet. Together, they shifted the bed away from the wall, the screech of the legs against the wooden floor sounding out of place.

Jefferson glanced between the bed and Blaise. "Color me intrigued. What's next?"

This was the part Blaise wasn't entirely certain about, and the last thing he wanted was to foster a sliver of hope that could be squashed. "I'll tell you in a moment," he murmured.

He sat on the thin mattress, the old springs sighing beneath his weight. With a cautious glance toward the door, ensuring they remained unobserved, he began scraping at the newly exposed section of wall behind the bed with the spoon. The metal rasped against the rough plaster. Each stroke seemed to ring through the silent room, a slow, rhythmic chipping away at their prison.

Tiny flecks of translucent material came away under the determined scrape of the spoon. Blaise's hand moved with a steady, meticulous determination, his focus dagger-sharp on the small but significant task before him. Each strip he removed felt like a minor victory, a step closer to reclaiming their stolen freedom.

Jefferson hovered over Blaise's shoulder, watching the progress with unbridled interest. His eyes widened as realization crept in. "Is that...?" he began, his voice a low, cautious whisper.

"The null paint," Blaise confirmed with a terse nod, not pausing in his efforts. It felt *good* to be doing something that might help. Zebulon's preparation of the room had been thorough. The clear alchemical paint covered not only the obvious spots like walls and door, but every inch of the window, floor, and likely the ceiling, too, effectively snuffing out their magic.

Understanding lit Jefferson's expression. "But if we remove some of it..."

"We might be able to use our magic," Blaise whispered. He glanced up, meeting Jefferson's earnest gaze. "It's a long shot, but worth trying. If I can just get enough scraped away..."

Jefferson settled on the bed beside Blaise, close but not crowding him. "That's brilliant," he said, a note of admiration in his voice. "What can I do to help?"

Blaise's lips quirked into a faint, grateful smile. "Do you have a spoon? A fork would work, too."

Jefferson patted his pockets in mock-seriousness. "Alas, I'm fresh out of flatware at the moment." His eyes darted around the sparse room, searching for something that could aid their efforts. Coming up empty, he turned back to Blaise with a rueful shrug. "I suppose you'll have to be the spoon wielder for now. But let me know if I can assist in any other way. Maybe a light shoulder rub?"

Blaise chuckled softly at the offer. "Your company's enough." He resumed scraping, slowly and methodically removing more of the null paint.

After several quiet minutes, Jefferson spoke up again, keeping his voice low. "Wouldn't the door make more sense?"

Blaise halted, spoon mid-scrape, and met Jefferson's inquisitive gaze. "The door is too obvious. This way is more subtle. At least, I hope it is." He cast his eyes downward. "I don't want to risk jeopardizing Luci or Alice."

As realization dawned, Jefferson's face softened, and he nodded slowly, appreciating the wisdom in Blaise's method. "You're right. That's rather savvy of you." His next question carried a thread of cautious hope. "What exactly is your plan here?"

Buoyed by Jefferson's support, the rigid lines of Blaise's shoulders eased slightly. "I was hoping we could use your Dreamer magic once I get enough scraped away."

Jefferson hummed thoughtfully, his fingers unconsciously drifting to his chin. His expression soured for a moment as they grazed against his growing stubble. "Mine, and not...oh." The realization clicked, and with a snap of his fingers, a knowing grin emerged. "You hope to speak with Luci."

Blaise nodded. "And maybe Alice, if we can manage."

The Dreamer's eyes widened at the suggestion, the gears in his mind visibly turning as he pondered the new realms of possibility. "Oh. Oh yes, that would be..." His voice trailed off, his gaze drifting to the small gap Blaise had created in the null paint. "Do you really think it'll work?"

With a tentative hope, Blaise pressed the tip of his index finger against the scraped sliver of wall. He closed his eyes, urging the dormant magic within him to stir. It resisted at first, weary from the suppressive effect of the null paint. The effort felt like trying to wake a hibernating bear, coaxing it gently. His power felt dull and distant, but as his fingertip touched the freed section, Blaise sensed the familiar pulse of Breaker magic, tingling beneath his skin, hinting at the freedom it sought.

His breath hitched. "Yes."

Jefferson leaned over and kissed him, his eyes alight. When he pulled away, the Dreamer sighed and said, "And here I am without a spoon."

CHAPTER THIRTY-TWO
Cruel and Unusual Punishment

Luci

As Luci made her way to the alchemy building, she strode past the music hall. Aural tendrils of Alice's melody seemed to reach out, trying to reel her back in. The sweet notes clung to her, a ghostly whisper echoing within the chambers of her mind.

Several times, she felt a pull to return to the music building, momentarily forgetting her original destination. Bowing her head, she forged ahead, pushing against the song's enthralling grip, reminding herself of her purpose.

As soon as she pushed open the creaking doors of the alchemy building, a veil of silence surrounded her, severing the magical tendrils that chased her thoughts. The enchanting music no longer demanded that she retreat, that she forget all her reasons for going there. She paused, briefly wondering if this was the effect Alice's music had on everyone, or if it was solely a whisper meant for her ears. And if so, what was the purpose?

That was a knot she'd have to untangle later. For now, she had to attend another special session with Professor Woodrow. After last night, she'd been tempted to skip it, but…she couldn't. This was her best opportunity to learn something that might help.

As she approached the door to the lab, Luci steadied her nerves with a deep breath. Despite Blaise's assurances, every step felt like a betrayal. He was a mage, and she was an alchemist. They were supposed to get along as well as cats and dogs. But that wasn't the case, not within their family.

She closed her eyes briefly, rubbing her temples as if she could smudge away the doubts. *I'm not cut out for this. Someone else should be here doing this.* There wasn't a gallant hero waiting in the wings. It was her.

With a breath meant to fuel her resolve, she set her jaw, letting a ghost of courage guide her as she pushed open the door.

The interior was full of students working on various projects. Luci caught a glimpse of a group huddled around a large, intricate machine. They were busily attaching wires and gears, their focus intense. It struck her as odd—wasn't that the purview of the engineering school?

But she had no time to ponder the oddity. Professor Woodrow stood by the door as if ready to greet her. "Ah, Miss Mason. Right on time."

Luci nodded, her hands instinctively clasping behind her back to hide the tremble of her fingers. The use of her pseudonym, a paper-thin shield, didn't escape her. It was a game of veiled truths, one she was ill-equipped for.

"Of course, Professor." Her cheeks flushed. She tried to be early to events if she could. But Alice's music had slowed her down. "I'm excited to see what we'll be working on tonight."

Woodrow turned fully toward her now, and she noticed a worn leather satchel clutched in his hands. "There will be a slight delay before we begin work tonight. An...excursion of sorts is in order. Follow me, if you would." His words were an enigmatic invitation, one she knew she couldn't deny.

With a furrow between her brows, Luci fell into step behind Professor Woodrow, who moved with a determined stride through the quiet hallway.

"Where are we going?" Her gaze still on the satchel, a thought occurred to her. Her mother had a similar satchel, and Luci knew about the implements stored within. "I assume we'll be collecting samples?"

"Oh, right on the nose, Miss Mason." Woodrow's face twitched into a semblance of a smile. "Indeed, we have an important errand to attend to." His next action caught her off guard as he paused, extending the satchel toward her. The unspoken expectation in his eyes was clear. Luci accepted the satchel, slinging it over her shoulder, before following him again.

As they navigated the dimly lit corridors, an uneasy realization slowly dawned on her. They were making their way toward the dormitories. Her breath caught in her throat. No, it couldn't be. But the further they walked, the tighter her chest became. She recognized this path. It was the same she had taken to reach the dorm complex.

They were heading to see Blaise and Jefferson. It was a cold, prickling certainty that crawled up her spine like a spider.

Luci's palms grew clammy. She wiped them discreetly on her trousers, hoping Professor Woodrow wouldn't notice her unease. What could he want from them? Had he lied about not hurting Blaise? And why was he bringing her along, of all people? Was it a test of her loyalty?

Before she could spiral further, they arrived at the familiar wooden door. Professor Woodrow pulled a key from his pocket and unlocked it swiftly.

The door swung open. Inside, Blaise and Jefferson leaped to their feet. Luci only glimpsed them from around Professor

Woodrow's shoulder, but she saw her brother and his husband standing shoulder to shoulder, as if prepared to face a threat. In all her time around Blaise, Luci had never seen him look...well, *fierce*. But in that moment, he did.

Professor Woodrow stepped into the room, ignoring Blaise and Jefferson's defensive postures. "Gentlemen, please relax. We've only come for a brief visit." His voice was smooth and calm, as if he were greeting old friends.

Luci hovered in the hallway, peering around Woodrow to get a better look. Blaise's jaw was clenched, his eyes narrowed with distrust. Beside him, Jefferson watched the professor warily.

"Yes, well, we're not prepared to receive any visitors, so please do come back another time," Jefferson said, every word razor-sharp, etched with a courteous disdain that thinly veiled his displeasure. "Or, you know, perhaps never."

Professor Woodrow chuckled, looking from Jefferson to Blaise. "You know, the idea of 'preparedness' always intrigued me. Did you know that in certain regions, it's considered improper to arrive unannounced? And then there are others where spontaneity is celebrated. Funny, isn't it? All about perspective." His words flowed smoothly as he casually made his way further into the room, disregarding the unwelcome air. "Speaking of perspectives, the dynamic between you two... It's as if you're two elements in a rare synthesis, creating a bond more profound than any transmutation I've witnessed in my studies."

Luci hesitated, uncertain what to do while the professor prattled on. He had shifted into full lecture mode.

Professor Woodrow continued, "The depth of your connection, the intensity of your bond—it's almost tangible. It got me thinking: can the essence of love be distilled? Turned into a solution? Like how we turn grapes into wine. Is love the wine of emotions?" His gaze shifted over his shoulder toward Luci, eager to pull her into his philosophical musing. "Miss Mason, would you say that's an apt analogy?"

"Uh..." Luci stammered, caught unawares. "I...I'm not sure about love being a type of...wine." Her gaze shifted around, landing on her brother's tense stance for a fleeting moment before returning to the professor's expectant face.

Woodrow's eyes narrowed, thoughtful. "You're right. That's not what we're after, anyway. No, perhaps it's more like an energy source. Like coal or steam." His head bobbed, pleased with this redirection of thought. To him, his musings likely bordered on revelations. Luci didn't understand his genius, but there was no denying the keen intelligence that lay within the man.

Shaking off his whimsical detour, the professor gestured vaguely with a hand. "I've been sidetracked. That's an investigation for later. There's a purpose to this visit." His gaze settled on Jefferson with a pointed intensity. "Miss Mason, please proceed with retrieving a blood sample from Subject One."

Jefferson's eyes met Luci's, his expression like a veiled fortress. But it was the taut line of his shoulders, the subtle shift of his stance, guarding Blaise, that spoke volumes.

"Do what you must," Jefferson said softly, his gaze never leaving hers.

Drawing a shaky breath to steady her jittering nerves, Luci inched further into the room until she stood before Jefferson. She lowered the satchel onto the floor, crouching to retrieve the necessary tools with deliberation.

Blaise's presence was a solid weight at her back. It occurred to her that Professor Woodrow might use this scenario to glean some reaction from Blaise. Luci was well aware of the grim history Blaise had with blood extraction. The professor's watchful eyes were trained on Blaise with an interest that felt almost predatory, making her wonder if this was merely an extension of his ceaseless experimentation.

Maybe it was.

Her hands shook as she prepared the needle. Luci took a deep breath, attempting to root her thoughts to the task at hand.

However, the room's atmosphere, thick with veiled anger, made it hard to focus.

The soft scrape of soles against the floor was a sure sign that her professor was on the move. Luci shot a furtive look over her shoulder to see Professor Woodrow stealthily sidling up to Blaise. Woodrow's posture was deceptively relaxed, arms folded casually, but his gaze held a gleam of mischief.

"You know, Subject Zero," Woodrow said, his voice taking on that unmistakable inflection that heralded a long-winded lecture. "I recently read a fascinating article about the history of alchemical symbols. I can't recall where I put it now, but it discussed how certain symbols used by alchemists and wizards overlapped. Rather intriguing, don't you think?"

Oh no. I think that's almost worse than taking blood from Blaise. Luci glanced over to see Blaise tilt his head back, eyes rolling skyward in clear exasperation.

Woodrow, ever oblivious to such cues, or perhaps delighting in them, pressed on. "And speaking of overlaps, the Elves of Eskala believe there's an overlap between life and death, a sort of liminal space between where the soul waits. Now, in the village where I grew up, there was an..."

Jefferson hissed out a soft breath as Woodrow droned on. "I thought you said he had no plans to harm Blaise."

"I did," Luci whispered back.

"I think, at this point, Blaise would rather offer a blood sample." Jefferson eyed the needle she held.

Luci bit back a laugh and refocused on the task at hand. As she carefully slid the needle into Jefferson's arm, she pitched her voice low. "I found Alice. In the music building rotunda." Luckily for her, Professor Woodrow's ongoing lecture proved to be a useful cover.

Jefferson's eyes sharpened, attention zeroing in on her. "Did you? And were you able to speak with her?"

She cast her eyes downward, focusing on the steady fill of the vial. "No. Something's off about her. She was playing her music, and then I spoke to a man who was there with her. As soon as I spoke with him, the song became...malicious. I can't explain it, but it made me flee."

Luci risked a glance up to see alarm flicker across Jefferson's face. "That doesn't sound like Alice at all," he whispered. "Her magic comes from the music, and she can use it to influence others, but..." His green eyes flicked to the filling vial. "Oh, Fortunes of Tabris."

"What's wrong?" Luci asked, her voice a soft veil of worry.

Jefferson's brow furrowed. "They're using her magic to influence people. But who, and why?"

Luci frowned. "Would she work with someone to do that?"

Jefferson seemed torn, his eyes a turbulent sea. "Maybe under duress, but not willingly—not the way you described. You have to find out more. Please, Luci. Perhaps they plan to use Theo as leverage against her." His voice trembled, an undercurrent of fear breaking through before he averted his gaze.

Luci felt a pang in her chest at the tremor in Jefferson's voice. Gently pulling the needle from his arm, she placed a small bit of gauze over the puncture, her touch as tender as her words. "I'll find out what's going on," she promised softly. "Alice, Theo, all of it. I know there's more to this."

Jefferson gave a tiny nod. "Blaise and I are working on something, too."

She slid a glance his way, raising a brow, hoping he would sate her curiosity. But he was clearly reluctant to do so, likely because of Professor Woodrow's presence. She didn't blame him.

With careful movements, Luci labeled and nestled the vial snugly in Professor Woodrow's worn leather satchel. As she did, the professor wound down his one-sided conversation with Blaise and turned toward them.

"Oh, stellar execution, Miss Mason," he remarked, a placid smile on his lips. "You certainly have a knack for this, don't you?"

Luci managed a tight smile in response. "Thank you, Professor."

With a gracious sweep of his hand, Woodrow gestured towards the door. "Ah, the fruits of our labor nestled safely in that satchel. A brief but successful excursion, wouldn't you agree? Now, the path of enlightenment beckons us back from whence we came. Shall we?"

Nodding, Luci swung the satchel over her shoulder. As she ambled behind the professor towards the exit, her eyes sought Blaise and Jefferson one last time.

Blaise gave her a subtle nod, his blue eyes troubled, while Jefferson mouthed *thank you*. Their faith in her fortified Luci's resolve. She would sort this out, no matter what it took.

Squaring her shoulders, Luci followed Professor Woodrow down the stairs and to the exit. Though outwardly compliant, inwardly, her thoughts churned with questions. She had to learn more about Alice's situation and quickly. The answers were out there somewhere.

She just had to find them.

CHAPTER THIRTY-THREE

Dreaming

Jefferson

*T*o think *that small patch of wall, scraped free of its paint, might be our key to freedom.* The night had settled around them, with shadows stretching across the room, tamed only by the modest glow of the oil lamp on the desk. Jefferson supposed that the null paint would keep even a mage-light from functioning here.

Jefferson studied Blaise's profile, his eyes on the window. Blaise glanced at it often, as if reminding himself that there was a world beyond the walls of the dormitory. Jefferson patted the mattress gently, breaking the stillness. "It should be late enough, don't you think?" Jefferson asked.

Blaise's gaze swung toward him, and he nodded. "Yeah." The soft word was loaded with fears and uncertainty that this plan might not work. That Blaise's efforts were in vain.

But he came and sat on the bed, waiting for Jefferson to situate himself facing the wall. The bed frame creaked as Blaise lowered himself to the mattress, his chest warm against Jefferson's back.

With a slow exhale, Jefferson cautiously pressed his palm against the scraped section of wall behind the bed. It was a challenge, crammed as he was between Blaise and the wall. Normally, he was quite fond of the concept of a single bed forcing them into intimately close proximity, but sometimes, there was much to be said for the ability to stretch oneself.

"Do you have enough room?" Blaise asked.

"Yes," Jefferson whispered. The truth was, if Jefferson took up any more room, then Blaise might find himself an unwilling guest on the floor.

"Transparency." His husband murmured the reminder.

With a soft snort, Jefferson retorted, "Some lies are harmless, darling. How could you possibly create more room?"

"Like this."

To Jefferson's great surprise, Blaise's arm shifted, sweeping around him, coaxing him into a half-embrace. He leaned against Blaise at a cozy angle. A comfortable, warm, sweetly intimate angle.

"Oh." The simple syllable carried an ocean of appreciation as Jefferson nestled his head against Blaise's shoulder.

Blaise shifted beneath him. "Your face feels like sandpaper."

"Told you I need a shave," Jefferson groused, the words shaking with restrained laughter.

"You weren't kidding," Blaise murmured. The banter between them was comforting.

That was something Jefferson could remedy in the dreamscape, at least, though it had no bearing on the real world. He sighed, settling the palm of his hand against the wall again. The anticipation before the touch felt like a stone in his chest, a reminder of the numb emptiness that his magic had become in this null space.

But this time, as his fingers grazed the rough surface, a gentle wave of energy cascaded into his fingertips. It was faint but undeniable. His breath hitched, his eyes widening as he turned toward Blaise.

"I can feel it," he whispered, a note of disbelief dancing in his words. "It's weak, but my magic...it's there."

A spark of hope flashed in Blaise's eyes. He favored Jefferson with a smile. "Let's see if I can help with that."

The Breaker scooted over an inch, taking Jefferson with him. His fingers found their way beneath Jefferson's, twining together in a tender weave of unity while maintaining contact with the wall.

Blaise had lent Jefferson power before, and it had never been a difficult thing for the younger mage. He had an aptitude for it. But now, Jefferson felt Blaise's muscles strain, as if he were bearing a physical load. The magic flowed into Jefferson, but it was sluggish. It was there, though, and it was enough.

Jefferson closed his eyes, focusing on the magic now thrumming through him. Even with Blaise's boost, it was weaker than he was accustomed to, but it would have to suffice.

He reached out with his power, grasping at the threads of the dreamscape. It came slowly, images swimming hazily before him. But then the scene solidified into view—the familiar landscape of his magical domain.

Jefferson opened his eyes to find himself and Blaise standing hand in hand on a sandy beach, the waves lapping the shore. The purple and orange hues of sunset tinted the horizon. A warm breeze ruffled their hair.

After days trapped in the confines of that tiny dorm room, the sheer openness was dizzying. Each breath of salt-laden sea air that Jefferson inhaled seemed to lessen the oppression they had been living under.

"Sunrich Isle?" Blaise's voice bordered on incredulous as he took in the familiar vistas around them.

"What can I say? I enjoyed my honeymoon with you," Jefferson admitted, a wistfulness coloring his words. He turned to meet Blaise's eyes, allowing the suppressed tide of his emotions to surface momentarily in the safe harbor of the dreamscape. They were free, however briefly.

Jefferson turned to Blaise, tugging him close, wrapping an arm around him. "I'd like nothing more than to kiss you here, on this beach," Jefferson whispered, feeling as if it were a defiance of their captivity.

Blaise grinned at him, his eyes alight with momentary happiness. The breeze tousled his hair, making it unruly. "We have a task, but one kiss never hurt."

No, Jefferson intended to use the kiss to give them both the strength and hope they desperately needed. He pulled Blaise close, one hand tenderly cradling Blaise's cheek, the caress a counterpoint to the ferocity of the kiss. Blaise responded with a soft sound, as if his soul needed this as much as Jefferson's.

As they parted, a contented smile played on Blaise's lips while he brushed his index finger across Jefferson's clean-shaven cheek. "Nice and smooth," he noted with a chuckle.

"See? Even you prefer it." Jefferson laughed softly, the sound a warm resonance amidst the serene beauty of the isle. For a moment, they merely stood together, forehead to forehead, savoring the peace, the world beyond momentarily forgotten.

But they couldn't delay much longer. Reluctantly, Jefferson drew back, though he kept their hands entwined.

"Right. I need to find Alice." The responsibility hardened Jefferson's expression.

Blaise gave his hand an encouraging squeeze. "I'll be here."

"Beside me, as always," Jefferson whispered. He was with Blaise, and together, they were a force to be reckoned with. It was a belief he had to cling to. To think otherwise would herald a slow slide into despair, and Jefferson was glad that thus far, he and Blaise had steered clear of that.

With a nod, Jefferson closed his eyes and felt the wisps of his magic stretch out into the dreamscape. Here, distance meant little if he knew someone well enough. He needed only to home in on the essence of the one he sought.

There—a familiar flicker of life: Alice's bright signature, though it seemed muted, like a moon wreathed by clouds. He focused his will and tore through the gossamer-thin barrier, navigating to the essence of his sister.

His dream split to reveal a warped rendition of what he thought must be the music building rotunda. Shadows shrouded the airy space, the columns twisted into gnarled, thorny vines. Alice sat ramrod straight on a stone bench, her violin held like a weapon as she played. She didn't seem to notice his arrival.

"Alice?" he called over the ominous tune, advancing cautiously. "Alice, it's me."

As his voice pierced the veil of her music, her head snapped up. Her eyes widened momentarily, her face a blend of confusion and suspicion.

"What is this? Where am I?" Alice remained where she was, still holding the violin like a lifeline.

Jefferson eased closer. "This is my magic. The dreamscape." Jefferson glanced over his shoulder. "Well, technically, this is your dream." Nightmare, he supposed, but he didn't want to say it aloud. "I intervened."

Her brow furrowed. "So you can just...wander into people's dreams?"

And so much more. "Yes." A sigh of relief escaped him as Alice's posture relaxed. "We don't have much time, and there's much to discuss. May I?"

"May you what?" Her frown deepened.

"Use my magic." He gestured to the eerie surroundings. "Take us away from here."

She nodded, bending down to place her violin and bow into its case. With a final click of the latch, both the case and the instrument within vanished into a mist. She turned toward him. Standing beside her, Jefferson focused, invoking his magic to transport them to the serene beach where Blaise awaited.

The Breaker sat on a log, watching the sunset, though he turned when Jefferson and Alice reappeared.

Jefferson observed Alice as she absorbed their new surroundings, still wary but also intrigued. "This is incredible," she murmured, her toes sinking into the soft sand.

Blaise rose, moving closer to Jefferson but keeping a polite distance from Alice. The Songbinder hesitated when she registered Blaise's presence, her eyebrows lifting.

"Well, I was hoping this would happen under happier circumstances, but here we are," Jefferson said, circling an arm around Blaise. "Alice, I'd like you to meet my husband, Blaise."

With those words, ease rolled over Alice. Her eyes, brimming with curiosity, took in Blaise. "So, you're the one who tamed my brother from his wildcatting ways? How did you manage that?"

"By not even trying." Somehow, Blaise kept a straight face as he spoke. Maybe he didn't mean it as a joke. Jefferson supposed there was a fair amount of truth to it.

A chuckle broke from Alice. "Typical of Mal—Jefferson, I mean—to fall for someone with no interest to him."

Blaise cocked his head, impressed. "How did you figure that out?"

"Because I know my brother." For a moment, Alice relaxed, and the atmosphere between them was pleasant. Familiar.

Jefferson wished their conversation could remain on such benign topics, but the urgency of the situation nudged him forward. His gaze found Alice's. "Are you okay?"

She turned back to him, mouth opening as if to say she was fine, but quickly snapping shut. Alice swallowed. "I..." Confusion clouded her eyes. "I don't know."

He shared a swift glance with Blaise, then flicked his gaze back to Alice. "What do you remember?"

Tucking her arms, Alice began pacing along the beach, her footprints etching thoughts into the soft sand. "We were captured. By...by college students, of all things! But I didn't figure that out until later. You were taken away..."

Her pacing stilled as she sifted through the fragments of memory.

"Phillip." The name slithered out of her. "They brought me to Phillip. Gods!" Frustration flared as her hands shot up before wilting again. "He said...I don't remember exactly. But Theo was there. He was hungry, and a student took him to find food. Then I had an argument with Phillip."

Jefferson froze at Phillip's name, eyes narrowing. A rumble filled his chest, a deep growl of rising anger. *Phillip Dillon.* He was the one behind this. And he had come to Jefferson, beseeching his help. Like a fool, Jefferson had listened, had considered that maybe, just maybe, he might change, too.

"Jefferson." Blaise's voice was a soft murmur, his hand finding its way to Jefferson's arm. "Save the rage for later."

With a jolt, Jefferson realized storm clouds had encroached upon the dreamscape, laced with veins of lightning. "Ah, right. Sorry," he managed, clearing his throat. "Go on."

Alice inhaled a shaky breath before resuming. "Then I was...I was taken to a laboratory."

Her expression turned fierce as she delved into the memories. "They seated me in a chair, strapped me down, then forced me to drink something vile. Phillip walked in later. I had to look at him." Her hands curled into fists at her side. "He drugged me. That bastard drugged me!"

Jefferson reined in his mirrored fury at her words. "What happened after that, Alice?"

"I...I don't know." Alice hugged herself as if to ward off a chill. "Things become blurry. But I remember my violin...music...and Phillip." Her voice shredded the air, reducing Phillip's name into nothing but a venomous whisper.

Blaise gently tapped Jefferson's elbow, his gaze on Alice, brimming with empathy. "There's someone we can bring in. My sister, Luci, is here as an alchemy student. If you don't mind, she may be able to help."

Alice wiped tears from her eyes, but she nodded as she fought back a sob.

Jefferson nodded, his expression softening as he regarded his sister. "Of course. Let's bring Luci in."

He grasped Blaise's hand, extending his magic through the connection they now shared. Blaise aided in guiding it, honing in on Luci's essence. They found her in proximity, and soon, Jefferson was navigating through a dream teeming with cryptic alchemical equations and an unending lecture by Professor Woodrow.

No, not just that, he realized. The scenario shifted abruptly, showcasing Luci sprinting into the lecture hall, tardy, her face a blend of mortification and panic as she clutched a book and journal to hide her unclothed form. *Ah, the classic* late and bare *nightmare,* Jefferson realized.

"Luci!" Jefferson called, and at the same time, sending out a pulse of his magic to shatter her nightmare. Like breaking dawn, the gloom of the lecture hall dissolved. With a ripple of his magic, sensible attire draped over Luci, freeing her from the clutches of the uncomfortable dream.

Blaise's sister visibly startled. Jefferson shifted them to the beach, where Blaise and Alice waited. The young alchemist peered around them, her expression relaxing when she saw Blaise. "Oh!" She rubbed her forehead. "Is this what you told me about? The dreamscape?"

Blaise moved to hug his sister, relief in his eyes. "Yes."

"But how?" Luci's gaze bounced between Jefferson and Blaise. Her expression crumpled. "Or am I dreaming that you've reached out to me? What a letdown!"

"This is not a dream…um, well, it sort of is, but…" Blaise stumbled on his words, glancing toward Jefferson.

"Magic. It's magic," Jefferson supplied with a hint of amusement. "As for how, let's just say Blaise had a good idea involving a spoon."

Alice frowned. "Are these two always this strange?" She gestured to Blaise and Jefferson.

"You get used to it," Luci said, then turned to face Alice. She did a double take, then edged backward. "You're the violin player from the rotunda!"

Alice's brow furrowed, bewildered. "The rotunda? I don't…"

Blaise stepped between the women, his expression serious. "Luci, you were right. That was Alice. She was dosed with something and needs your help."

As Blaise spoke, Jefferson's mind was already whirling, examining everything Alice had said. The connection between Phillip and Zebulon Woodrow…there was something there. Then, with a pit growing in his stomach, the pieces fell into place.

Blaise nudged him, stirring him from his thoughts. Jefferson shook his head. "What?"

His husband exhaled a sigh of exasperation. "Didn't you catch what Luci said about knowing what they used on Alice?"

Realization hit him like an icy wave. He turned toward Luci. "Apologies. Please, continue."

"*A love potion,*" Alice snapped, each word clipped with anger.

"I heard Professor Woodrow talking about it with a man. Phillip," Luci explained.

Jefferson sighed. He wasn't sure if he should rejoice that his mind had gone down the right track or feel frustrated because this surely didn't bode well for them. Raven Dawson had planned to use a love potion on Vixen, but had been thwarted. Tara Woodrow's fingers had been all over that scheme, and she was Zebulon's wife. The pieces all fit together.

"That bastard," Alice whispered, the words loaded with fury

she didn't even attempt to conceal. "Is there any way to break it? To...to reverse the effects?"

Jefferson and Blaise both turned to look at Luci. The young alchemist hesitated, uncertainty written across her face. "I don't know," Luci admitted, a trace of doubt shadowing her words. She bit her lip, then with a hint of resolve, added, "But...I'm going to try. I have some ideas on how to neutralize it." She turned to look at Blaise, a glint of promise in her eyes. "And to help you with that null paint."

"If anyone can do it, it's you." Blaise smiled at his younger sister.

"Something more advanced than a spoon would be lovely," Jefferson chimed in.

As Luci opened her mouth to respond, a peal of thunder overtook her words. Jefferson jolted; that was not his doing. The surrounding dreamscape trembled, its veil tearing at the seams. Luci and Alice swirled into the chaotic ether, swept away to the recesses of their own dreams or nightmares.

Jefferson's eyes snapped open to the reality of the room. Blaise was right there, flush against him, blue eyes wide as they met his.

"What was that?" Blaise's whisper carried the tremors of the transient realm they just left.

"Reached the limit." Jefferson sighed. He squeezed Blaise's hand in his. "But we did it. That was something, wasn't it?"

"Yeah, it was." Blaise nestled against him. "I need some proper sleep. Lending you power took a toll on me."

Had Blaise been channeling magic to him all along? No wonder the dreamscape held as long as it had. "Get your beauty sleep while you can," Jefferson whispered tenderly, planting a kiss on Blaise's cheek.

A chuckle escaped Blaise before he drifted into a peaceful sleep, his breath steady and comforting against the rhythm of the night.

CHAPTER THIRTY-FOUR

Alchemy

Luci awoke with a start, remnants of equations and formulae twirling in her mind. The dreamscape was still vivid, etching the faces of Jefferson, Blaise, and Alice into her memory like engravings on glass.

"Blaise," she whispered, shutting her eyes for a breath. She had seen her brother. Luci had made promises in the dream that she wasn't certain she could uphold.

But she would try.

She rose and began her morning routine, but her thoughts kept drifting back to her encounter in the dreamscape. Her movements were certain as she dressed and gathered her books, but her mind swayed to the tune of last night's encounter.

Luci hurried through her morning classes, barely hearing the professors' lectures. Her mind whirled with ideas of ingredients and methods capable of neutralizing a love potion. Unconcerned with the lectures, her pen danced across the margins of her text-books, sketching half-formed ideas and snippets of solutions.

When the lunch bell finally rang, Luci sprang from her seat and raced out of the classroom. She headed straight for the library, weaving through the maze of shelves until she reached the alchemy section. Running her fingers along the leather spines, she searched for anything related to love potions, antidotes, or emotional alchemy.

Not finding what she needed, Luci cautiously approached the librarian's desk. Fortitude didn't have a library, so this was her first true experience with one. The librarian, a middle-aged woman with spectacles perched on her nose, peered at Luci over her glasses when she approached.

"Excuse me, do you have any detailed books on love potions, antidotes, or emotional alchemy?" she asked, trying to mask her urgency.

The librarian smiled. "Let me check for you." She rose from her chair and walked to a huge wooden filing cabinet with tiny drawers. Luci waited as the librarian searched through the cards. After a few moments, she returned to the desk, shaking her head. "I'm afraid the card catalog shows we don't have anything specific here. But we could request these materials through an interlibrary loan from the archives in Ravance."

Luci's heart leaped. "How long would that take?"

The librarian pulled out a piece of paper that appeared to be a form and a pencil. "Typically, it's a three to four months process."

Luci winced, disappointment washing over her. "That long, huh? I don't have that much time, but thank you for checking."

"Of course. I wish I could be of more help," the librarian said with a sympathetic smile.

With a resigned sigh, Luci trudged out of the library. As she walked, she heard the first haunting notes of the violin waft through the air. She paused, looking toward the music building.

"Wish me luck, Alice," Luci whispered, then continued walking.

Luci arrived at the alchemy building just as the last hints of sunset were fading from the sky, casting eerie shadows on the ancient, ivy-clad stones of the edifice. She hurried inside and down the hallway to Professor Woodrow's laboratory. Even from down the corridor, Luci could hear a commotion coming from within.

As she drew nearer, she saw several students clustered around the large glass tank. Luci edged closer, her curiosity rising despite her disgust with whatever experiment was at hand. A few students were busy disconnecting tubes and wires from the tank. Others were hauling in planks of wood, dropping them nearby while ensuring they were out of the way to prevent accidents.

Luci tapped the shoulder of the nearest student, Josh. "What's going on?" she inquired, her voice barely above a whisper. "Why are you moving her?"

Josh turned to her with a shrug. "Professor Woodrow wants his wife moved up to the roof."

Wait...his wife? Luci felt a jolt of disbelief electrify her veins. This woman, floating eerily in the glass tank, was Professor Woodrow's wife. It made a certain amount of horrifying sense.

Luci's gaze dropped to the woman's neck, where the grotesque scar marred her otherwise pristine skin. Of course, she had heard the rumors swirling around Fortitude—that Raven Dawson had savagely slashed the throat of a well-to-do Confederation woman.

Josh peered at her with a trace of concern. "Are you okay?"

Luci coughed to clear the tightness in her throat. "Me? Oh, yeah. I was just wondering why. You know, exposing the tank to the elements will destroy any chance of preserving her."

Josh shrugged again, the gesture exuding a hint of callous indifference. "Hey, I'm just doing what I was told. Same as you. My grade depends on it."

Luci wet her lips, feeling a cold draft creep along her spine.

She had to tread carefully. "What exactly is the experiment? I've been so distracted with my work that I..." She trailed off, hoping Josh would fill in the blanks.

He scrutinized her, his eyes narrowing slightly as if he couldn't believe she had been so absorbed in her own little world. "To resurrect her, of course." Josh gestured to the tank with a casual flip of his hand. "Why else would we have done everything we could to not only halt the decomposition but, in many cases, reverse it?"

"Uh..." Luci's breath caught in her throat. Resurrect? Surely he didn't mean... "Right. Yes. Um, thanks for the explanation. Now I'd better get to work...on my special...project." Luci turned away, feeling like an idiot. *Smooth. Real smooth there, Luci. Gods, you are not cut out for this!*

She drifted over to her station, fingers tracing the rough grain of the worn wood as she went. Luci sank down onto the stool, her heart a heavy thud against her ribcage as she stared blankly at the equipment in front of her.

Bringing back the dead. Creating alchemical mages. Professor Woodrow hadn't been exaggerating when he said he had many important experiments going on. Her gut clenched with dread. Resurrecting the dead—it seemed the stuff of myths and legends. Yet, here was Professor Woodrow, daring to tread the line between life and death right before her eyes. If he could accomplish something so audacious, so hubristic...then a simple love potion would be child's play for him. The realization settled heavily within Luci.

With the daunting challenge of creating Breaker's Touch and trying her hand at a counter to a love potion taking over her thoughts, she dove into action. She began gathering ingredients and equipment, her movements sharp and charged with urgency. The glass vials clinked together in a chorus as she assembled the components for the two distinctly purposeful potions she was about to craft.

Luci's fingers shook as she measured and poured, whispering to herself, "Two birds, one stone. Don't mess this up, Luci."

Each meticulous movement was a step toward achieving dual solutions to save her brother and free Alice. The delicate dance between hope and desperation fueled her precision, leaving no room for error.

The bustling activity of the lab faded into background noise as Luci focused singularly on her task. She tuned out the shuffling footsteps, the squeaking wheels of the tank being moved, the tinkling of glassware. Her world narrowed down to the workspace before her, the orderly line of vials, the bubbling mixtures, her trips to the alchemical furnace.

A yawn threatened to tear her from her task. Luci rubbed her eyes. This wouldn't do. She had a long night ahead of her. Luci's fingers fumbled with the pouch at her belt, pulling out a cotton-wrapped tube. She checked the label on it. Her mother's neat writing read *Crimson Cow*. Marian had sent along several ready-made potions, some for the event of injury or illness, and others, like this one, for the event she needed to study into the early hours of the morning.

With a sigh, Luci popped the cork and downed the liquid. A warm, feathery lightness filled her veins, sweeping away the crumbs of fatigue—for now. She dreaded the inevitable crash once the elixir wore off, but there was no other choice right now. The nagging thought buzzed at the corner of her mind, but Luci cast it aside, refocusing on the task at hand.

The solution began to roil and change color, shifting from clear to a pearlescent pink. Luci watched closely, making adjustments as needed. Her lips moved silently, reciting the steps and ingredients from memory.

Luci worked late into the night, long after the other students had left. The lab grew quiet, with only the occasional bubbling of mixtures or the scratching of Luci's pen on paper breaking the silence.

Fatigue weighed down Luci's limbs, but she pushed through it. There was too much at stake to rest now. Her eyes stung from staring at ingredients and procedures for hours on end, but still, she pushed on.

At last, as the small hours of the morning approached, Luci carefully decanted two vials. One cradled the luminescent green Breaker's Touch, a potion designed to mimic Blaise's power, albeit with a deliberate delay. Its partner housed Luci's brave venture to counteract the love potion, shimmering a serene blue as it sparkled under the soft glow of the laboratory's lamps.

Luci held up the two vials, gazing at them with red-rimmed but determined eyes. So small, yet so much depended upon them. Her shoulders sagged as the long night's exertions caught up with her. But looking at the two vials renewed her sense of purpose. She had to succeed. This was alchemy, and she was good at it.

But was she good enough?

Blaise believes in me. I should believe in myself, too. With great care, she tucked away the precious vials into a soft, cotton-lined case. Her work here was done for now. But her mission had only just begun. The true test would be administering the solutions and hoping against hope that her antidote would be enough to break the insidious effects of the love potion.

As Luci prepared to leave, weariness and doubt crept in. Had she done enough? Was she truly ready for what was to come? Shaking her head, she banished her uncertainties. She had given it her all tonight. Now, fate would decide the rest.

CHAPTER THIRTY-FIVE

Subject One

"I can't believe we're doing this," Blaise muttered beside Jefferson. He still had his spoon in hand, diligently scraping away at more of the stubborn null paint.

"You said I could pick the game. And really, you know, I could have done far worse than this." Jefferson grinned back at his husband, his gaze tracing the muscles in Blaise's arm as it flexed with each painstaking scrape against the wall. The ongoing rhythm of Blaise's effort against the null paint was almost hypnotic.

Blaise sighed, an expression of resigned amusement crossing his face as he nodded, taking his turn in their playful game to lighten their moods. "I'm going on a picnic, and I'm bringing an apple pie, bacon, chocolate cake, daisies, Eskelan wine, forks..." His words slowed, and his scraping ceased for a moment as he struggled to recall the sequence. "Ginger cookies, horses, and icicles. Your turn."

"Our list for this game is making me unfairly hungry," Jefferson muttered.

"Don't look at me. You're the one who led with apple pie." Blaise flashed a grin back at him.

"Guilty," Jefferson chuckled, his thoughts wading through an assortment of items for his next selection. *Jam-filled pastries, juicy watermelon—no, no. Steer away from the food. Ah, Jackalope, that's good.* "Very well. I'm going on a picnic, and I'm bringing apple pie, bacon—"

The sudden knock on the door catapulted them back to reality, sending their light-hearted fantasies scuttling into the shadows. The blithe ambiance shattered as the door swung open. Startled, Jefferson jumped to his feet, instinctively moving to shield Blaise's handiwork from sight. If anyone discovered what they were doing, the consequences could be dire.

Blaise wedged the spoon between the bed and the wall and rose as well. They stood shoulder to shoulder, silent solidarity forged between them as Zebulon Woodrow appeared at the threshold.

Jefferson's eyes searched past the foreboding figure of Woodrow, hoping to see Luci by his side—but no. Instead, four young men flanked the professor. Jefferson heard Blaise's soft intake of breath as he noticed the same.

"If you've come for more blood, I'm going to have to charge a fee," Jefferson said, striving to cloak his unease with humor. He hoped his voice didn't quiver as much as his insides. "To what do we owe the displeasure, Zebulon?"

"Ah, Subject One," Zebulon began, his gaze briefly drifting toward the ceiling tiles before snapping back to Jefferson. "Have you ever pondered the nature of experiments? Their evolution? It's akin to...baking, really. Specific ingredients yield specific outcomes."

Jefferson rolled his eyes. "Can you perhaps skip the culinary lesson? I much prefer those from Blaise."

Undeterred, Zebulon carried on, "In the early days of alchemy, it was believed that a harmonious environment was key to a successful experiment. There existed an alchemist who serenaded his concoctions with a flute." He laughed to himself, seemingly adrift in a personal memory. "But reverting to the present—well, relatively—it seems that you, dear Subject One, might just be the...shall we say, pinch of salt that my most pressing experiment has been lacking."

Jefferson shifted uneasily at Zebulon's roundabout revelation. The full scope of the situation dawned on him. He was being singled out for something significant.

"*No.*" The word erupted from Blaise, resonating through the quiet room as a growl. He repositioned himself protectively in front of Jefferson, chin tucked in defiance.

"You can't fight them like this," Jefferson whispered into Blaise's ear, uncertain if his words found their mark. Blaise wasn't a fighter, not in the conventional sense. *But he'll always fight for the people he loves.* The thought formed a sour knot in Jefferson's throat.

Zebulon nodded, his expectation confirmed by their reactions. "Yes, this is why you're the most suitable, Subject One. You love deeply and are loved a thousandfold in return." The alchemist's gaze brushed over the young men flanking him. "Please neutralize Subject Zero. But be gentle, will you?"

Before the words fully settled in the air, Blaise was in motion, but not towards their impending threat. Instead, he lunged toward the bed, his hand outstretched. The goal was clear to Jefferson: Blaise aimed to reach that one spot on the wall through which he could channel his Breaker magic. Their eyes met briefly, sealing a silent pact.

Jefferson, no more a warrior than Blaise, knew his role was to afford his husband precious seconds. He bolted forward, making himself a barrier to the approaching brutes. But the young men, constructed much like battering rams, were hardly dissuaded. With alarming ease, they shoved Jefferson aside, and he collided with the opposite wall, a pained gasp escaping him as they descended upon Blaise.

Jefferson struggled to his feet, a sharp claw of pain raking through his ribs with each breath. But pain was an echo, faint against the screaming need to get to Blaise. One of the young men had already grabbed the Breaker, pinning his arms behind his back. His other accomplice unsheathed a syringe.

Blaise cried out against the painful hold, his eyes bulging when he caught sight of the needle.

"No!" The word roared from Jefferson's throat as he lurched forward. But like a wall of flesh, the first young man intercepted, locking his arms around Jefferson's middle, and with a casual toss, sent him crashing away.

The impact shunted the breath from his lungs as Jefferson hit the floor. Gasping, he lifted his head in time to see the needle burrow into Blaise's shoulder.

The gasp of pain wrenched from his husband's lips was a lance through Jefferson's heart. Blaise's fingers fluttered toward the wall, their hope disintegrating mere inches from salvation before going limp.

"Blaise!" Jefferson cried. He scrambled over on hands and knees as Blaise slumped bonelessly across the bed, his head nearly striking the wall. The quartet of young men moved to block him. Rising on shaky legs, a fury, untamed and raw, roared to life within Jefferson. "What did you do to him?"

The alchemist adjusted his spectacles. "Merely a sedative, I assure you. He will wake in a few hours, no worse for wear."

The reassurance was a blade of ice, cold and unsatisfying. Jefferson's hands trembled as they curled into fists, every ounce of his being screaming for retribution. But he had to keep himself together, for Blaise's sake. "If you've harmed him—"

"I told you, Subject Zero is unharmed," Zebulon replied, his sigh laced with cold indifference. "Now, you may either walk out of here with us under your own power or be carried. The choice is yours."

They would sedate me, too. Jefferson didn't bother weighing his options. "I'll walk. Thank you very much." And he would be ready, watching for any opportunity to turn the tables on these bastards. He spared a desperate glance toward Blaise, uncertain if he could trust Zebulon's claim that he would remain unharmed.

Jefferson held his head high as the quartet of young men ushered him out of the dormitory into the embracing arms of the late afternoon. As they moved through the thrum of the mundane, other students immersed in their routines surrounded them. Jefferson considered trying to call for help, but would anyone even listen? They made their way across the quad, advancing toward the structure prominently marked as the Rickson Building.

The haunting caress of violin music graced the air, weaving through the space between the rustling leaves. As if the tune beckoned them, Zebulon halted momentarily, a satisfied smile gracing his lips. "Ah, just in time."

The melody—it was Alice's. *But* just in time *for what?* Before Jefferson could untangle the web of implications, a forceful nudge on his back thrust him back to the grim march.

The threshold of the Rickson Building marked the divide between the familiar and the uncertain, the secure and the perilous. As Jefferson stepped over it, the pristine white walls loomed ominously, wrapping the silence around him like a cloak, broken only by the sterile scent that displaced the earthy aromas of the outdoors. He tensed, ready to bolt at the first chance.

At last, they reached an imposing door, its cold surface a keeper of what he was sure must be horrifying secrets. It swung open, revealing a sterile room. Its heart was an examination table, thick leather straps strewn across it like constricting snakes ready to ensnare. Jefferson's heart stuttered in his chest, and he tried to take a step backward.

Zebulon strode ahead and turned, gesturing imperiously to the table. "If you would be so kind as to lie down, Subject One."

Unyielding, Jefferson folded his arms across his chest. "I don't think so. And I have a name, by the way."

A flicker of annoyance passed over the alchemist's face. "I assure you, this is all for the sake of progress."

"Progress? Is that what you call kidnapping and experimenting on people against their will?" Jefferson shot back. His hands flexed, ready to summon his magic.

Zebulon sighed. "If you insist on being difficult..." He nodded to the men flanking Jefferson.

They closed in, preparing to seize him. Jefferson snarled, and his power burst forth.

The magic rose like a storm, potent and eager. He crafted a chain of nightmares and, with a thought, hurled it into their minds. Their faces twitched, eyes glazing over as the dreamscape engulfed them, dragging them into a deep, twitching slumber. They sank to the floor.

He whirled to face Zebulon and the remaining students. *Best to take care of the authority next.* "Sweet dreams, Zeb—"

Zebulon was swift, a syringe already in hand. He lunged forward, jamming the needle into Jefferson's shoulder before he could react.

Jefferson cried out, more from surprise than pain. Almost instantly, he felt the tendrils of his magic recoiling, the once-flowing connection abruptly severed. "What...what did you do?" he gasped, staggering backward, the floor seeming to tilt beneath him.

Zebulon calmly pocketed the now empty syringe, his voice as cool as the chill that danced across Jefferson's skin. "Merely a little concoction to suppress your abilities," he explained, his displeasure apparent. "I had hoped to avoid this step, as it may interfere with the procedure. However, I cannot allow you to assault my students, destroy my meticulously assembled equipment, or jeopardize the experiment I've dedicated countless nights to."

Jefferson's shoulders slumped as he realized his only chance at escape was gone. Zebulon's eyes, cold and detached, scanned him like a mere specimen awaiting dissection.

"Come now. Let's not prolong the inevitable," Zebulon commanded, his voice echoing with a chilling finality. He gestured to the students surrounding Jefferson. "Bring him to the table."

No. Jefferson summoned every bit of strength he had, hoping to pull away. To escape somehow. Raw fear spurred him on, instinct driving his struggle. His muscles strained against the students' iron grip. He kicked out, aiming for a gap in their defenses, hoping to find some leverage.

But the students were unyielding. Jefferson never had a chance against them, not without the equalizer of magic. They moved with practiced efficiency, countering each of Jefferson's moves with a grim determination. Their unrelenting hands held him tighter, forcing him step by step toward the table.

Jefferson knew if they put him on that table, he might not leave it alive. He redoubled his efforts, trying to twist from their grips, even baring his teeth, ready to bite anyone who came within his reach like a feral beast. He managed to slip an arm free, elbowing one of the students in the side. But the moment of hope was fleeting. Another student quickly filled the gap, and with a combined effort, they overpowered him.

With a force that knocked the wind out of him, they slammed Jefferson onto the table. His back smacked against the cold, unyielding metal. Leather straps, frighteningly supple from use, drew tight across his wrists, ankles, chest, and thighs, snaring him in a dread-laced embrace.

No. This couldn't be happening. Icy fingers of panic clutched at Jefferson as the reality of the situation sank in. He had failed, and now he was trapped. Completely at the mercy of Zebulon and whatever twisted experiment the alchemist had planned.

"Let me go!" he bellowed, writhing against the restraining straps. But it was all in vain. Zebulon only watched with a detached air as the students completed securing him to the table.

Once the last restraint was fastened, two students took position at either end of the table and wheeled him down a long corridor. His head rocked side to side with the motion as they escorted him further into the belly of the alchemy building.

As they turned a corner, a blur of motion caught his attention. Luci was there, peeking from a room down the hallway. Her eyes, wide with a mix of shock and fear, met his. A lump formed in Jefferson's throat. Had she witnessed his struggle? Did she know where they were taking him?

He teetered on the verge of calling out to her, but clamped down on the impulse. Her cover needed to remain intact. Blaise's little sister might be his only hope now.

Jefferson's pulse pounded in his ears. He had no idea what twisted experiment awaited him, but he knew no good could come of it. As they wheeled him deeper into the chilling core of the alchemy building, terror washed over him. He strained against his restraints once more, to no avail.

His fate was no longer his own.

CHAPTER THIRTY-SIX
A Canyon Full of Rattlesnakes

Luci

Luci's original intent was to make her way to the storage room, but the horrifying sight of Jefferson, confined to a gurney, rooted her to the spot. She flattened herself against the wall. A sick sensation grew in her gut at the realization that Professor Woodrow had promised no harm would come to Blaise.

He hadn't said the same for Jefferson. And he'd been *so* interested in him. Why? Although Jefferson was an alchemical mage, Professor Woodrow had seemed to dismiss his potential contribution to their research in that area, focusing his intense scrutiny on Blaise. If only she had a shred of understanding why Professor Woodrow had taken Jefferson, she might be able to help. But as it was, she was in the dark.

She glanced at the wall clock. She was early. If she left now, there might be enough time to free Blaise and Alice.

Nodding to herself, she hurried to her workstation and opened the case containing Breaker's Touch and the counter to the love potion. She wrapped them carefully in cotton before pocketing them. Luci also grabbed a pair of thin leather gloves and stuffed them into another pocket. Thicker gloves would have been better, but they'd be too conspicuous, and the last thing she wanted was to draw attention to herself.

Luci closed her eyes briefly, pulling in a deep breath to steady her nerves. *I can do this. There's no one else who can.* Though she had always portrayed a facade of confidence, especially around alchemical concoctions, doubt niggled at her now. It had been easy to feign knowledge back home, with a prodigious alchemist for a mother and the infamous Breaker for a brother. She tried to muster that farce of self-assurance now, but it fluttered away, elusive as a ghost.

With a shake of her head, she stepped away from her workstation. "Oh, no! Forgot something in my room. I'll be right back!" Luci announced to the room at large. A few peers in the laboratory cast brief, indifferent glances her way, evidently finding her outburst more of a mild nuisance than anything. Unfazed, Luci spun on her heel and raced for the door.

Outside, she dashed down the cobblestone path that led away from the alchemy building. Nearby, a group of young men laughed and called to each other as they tossed a ball back and forth, running the length of the quad in a game she didn't understand. The scene stung Luci with a pang of normalcy she sorely missed.

Upon reaching the dormitory building, Luci halted in the entry. She took a moment to catch her breath.

Then, Luci rushed to the staircase, her footsteps echoing in her ears. She sprinted up the stairs, a sigh of relief escaping her as she reached the floor where Jefferson and Blaise had been held.

Glancing over her shoulder to make certain she was unobserved, Luci halted outside their door. Her heart pounded in her ears as she eyed the worn wood. Behind that door could be Blaise, if he was still here. She needed to get him out.

"Blaise?" Luci called softly, uncertainty coloring her voice. "Blaise, it's me!"

She had hoped for a stealthy rescue, but with every passing silent second, panic nibbled at her composure. Luci bit her lip, fear knotting in her stomach. Was he even in the room?

Get it together, Luci. She had seen Jefferson but not Blaise. He might still be in the room, though the silence from within was unnerving. But she had crafted a plan, made a potion. *Stick to the plan.*

Decision made, Luci pulled out the gloves from her pocket and slipped them on, flexing her fingers for a better fit. Then she fetched the small vial of Breaker's Touch. Carefully, she opened the vial, pulling out the tiny brush she'd attached to the lid. Luci winced. The bristles were disintegrating, a clear sign that the slow-acting corrosive potion was effective.

Luci scrutinized the door, then, with a steady hand, she used the brush to coat the clear potion along the door's edge where it met the frame, hoping the corrosive substance would reach the hinges on Blaise's side. Afterward, she dabbed some on the doorknob for good measure. There wasn't enough time or potion to cover the entire door, but she was thorough with what she had, trusting that Breaker's Touch would penetrate and counteract the null paint on the opposite side.

Or maybe the door would simply fall off the hinges. Right now, she'd welcome either outcome.

She hastily stuffed the brush back into the now empty vial, securing it closed. Off came the gloves. She tugged out a small notebook. Tearing off a sheet of paper, she found a pencil stub in her pocket. It would do. Luci braced the paper against the wall and scribbled:

Blaise,

Door!

Jefferson lab!

She folded the paper as tightly as she could and slid it under the door. Now, it was up to Blaise to find it and wait for the potion to work. Leaving even this cryptic message was risky, but she had no choice. It was a chance she had to take.

Luci stashed the notebook, halting for a beat to ponder her next step. The potion for Alice was secure in her pocket, but a fresh worry occurred to her: she hadn't seen Theo for several days. The dorm where she had watched him was the next building over. She could risk a quick check on him, then rush to the music building.

It was early evening; the sun was just beginning to set over the campus. In the distance, a thunderstorm brewed, the dark clouds roiling against the dimming sky, laced with intermittent lightning. Luci wondered if it was rolling their way as she observed students in scattered clusters, navigating the pathways, some heading for a meal, others heading to their rooms or other entertainments. She blended into the crowd, her presence unnoticed as she maneuvered through the throng.

Arriving at the door to Theo's room, she rapped on it briskly. Silence answered. She tried the knob, and the door opened, revealing an empty room. However, the resident stuffed animals left scattered across the floor were proof that Theo had been here. Swallowing, she stepped back into the hallway.

Just then, Jules, another undergrad assigned to keep tabs on Theo, trudged down the hall. His arms were loaded with textbooks, face reddening from the strain. He nearly bumped into Luci.

"Oops! Sorry, didn't see you there." Jules angled to glimpse her around his mountain of books.

Luci waved off the near collision. "It's fine. Hey, Jules, have you seen Theo?"

Peering over the precarious stack, Jules shook his head. "Not since earlier, when Professor Woodrow came and got him." He blew out a breath as he adjusted his heavy burden. "Can I get by? Sorry, I have a paper due tomorrow, and I haven't even started on it." Jules edged around her and started down the hall again.

Luci stared after Jules as he hurried away, her mind blank. Theo was gone. Professor Woodrow had taken him. What did that mean for the boy?

Icy fear pooled in the pit of Luci's stomach. If Professor Woodrow had Theo, chances were the boy was tucked away somewhere in the alchemy building. She stood rooted, a torrent of indecision ensnaring her. As much as she wanted to make sure Theo was unharmed, she had to stick to her plan. Besides, she'd head back to the alchemy building soon enough, and she could pretend like nothing was amiss and snoop for Theo.

"Alice," she whispered, her resolve transmuting to steel.

Once outside, Luci broke into a run, sprinting toward the music building. She took the stairs two at a time, an impromptu race against time. But the brisk ascent left her lungs searing with the effort, gasping for breath by the time she reached the top.

Bending over, hands braced on her knees, Luci sucked in gulps of air. Stars danced before her eyes from the exertion. A distant rumble of thunder echoed through the open space, heralding the approaching storm she'd noticed earlier.

With a deep inhale, Luci straightened, still wheezing. She shook her head to clear it, her eyes regaining focus.

Alice sat in the same upholstered chair as the last time Luci had seen her, her fingers dancing across the strings of her violin with practiced ease. The music flowed effortlessly from her, filling the rotunda with its acoustic embrace. Beside her, Phillip stood, hands clasped behind his back as he gazed out the large windows lining the curved walls, lost in the melody or perhaps the stormy horizon that lay beyond.

Luci's eyes narrowed as she assessed the scene. Phillip Dillon, the husband Alice had spoken of with such disdain in the dreamscape. The one who dared to chain her to him with a love potion. Luci hadn't realized exactly who he was during her first visit to the rotunda. Rage simmered in her chest.

But then...she recalled him from Professor Woodrow's lab. This man had spoken against the love potion, had disliked what it had turned Alice into. That didn't absolve him. He had still been complicit in the potion's use.

But her options for allies were rather limited. She approached Phillip with the intent to sway him to her side, but after witnessing Alice's automaton-like movements, a surge of anger swelled within her chest. "How could you?" she demanded.

Phillip spun around, startled by the sudden intrusion. His eyebrows knit together, perplexed. "I'm sorry, do I know you?"

"No, but I know you," Luci bit out. She jabbed an accusing finger toward him, the action releasing a fraction of the storm brewing within her. "You're the one who did this to Alice. Your own *wife!*"

Recognition dawned in Phillip's eyes, widening as the realization set in. "You—you're one of Zebulon's assistants," he said, his voice now carrying a wary edge as if he trod upon the ice of a thinly frozen lake.

Luci crossed her arms over her chest. "No. I mean, yes. I mean...I don't have time for this!" Her frustration simmered in her words, boiling to the surface with each syllable. She stamped her foot, impatient. "What matters is that you've trapped your wife here with a love potion."

Phillip's gaze drifted over to Alice, who, despite the confrontation, continued her serenade, though she had turned to observe their conversation, her eyes narrowing. Phillip's jaw tightened.

"It's complicated," he said in a low voice. "I didn't...it wasn't supposed to be like this."

Luci scoffed. "Oh, please. You don't get to play the victim here—"

"Little girl," Phillip interrupted, cutting through her words like a scythe through ripe grain, "I don't need to explain myself to you. If Zebulon sent you here, then you should leave. Now."

Little girl. His tone made her hackles rise, and Luci held her ground. "I'm not here for him. I'm here for Alice...and Theo."

At the mention of Theo, Phillip's shoulders tensed, eyes widening. For a fleeting moment, Luci thought she caught a flash of fear cross his face. "Theo?" Phillip rasped. "What's happened? Where is he?"

"I don't know," Luci admitted, her honesty a bitter draught to swallow. "But I suspect Professor Woodrow has him."

"I need to go to him...gods, who knows what Zebulon might do to him?" The words tumbled out, each one a stone chipping away at his composure. Phillip spun in a frustrated circle. "But I can't. I can't leave Alice. She won't let me out of her sight." His voice warbled.

Luci set her mouth in a determined line. "I can fix that." *I hope.*

Taking a deep breath, she approached Alice, whose once entrancing music had ceased, leaving a silence that spoke volumes. A scowl warped her porcelain features, eyes flashing with jealousy and suspicion.

"Alice," Luci began gently, "do you remember me?"

Alice's scowl deepened, her expression full of hatred. "Yes. You came here the other day! You want to take Phillip away from me." Her voice was high and thin, the fragility of glass echoing with a tinge of mania. "But he's not yours. I love him. He's mine."

Luci raised her hands placatingly. "No, I promise that's not why I'm here." She took another measured step closer, the space between them feeling much like traversing a canyon full of rattlesnakes. Alice's grip on her violin bow tightened, knuckles whitening against the aged wood. The mage looked as if she was considering using it as a weapon.

Gods, the love potion had sunk its hooks deep into the tender flesh of Alice's mind. Luci swallowed the knot of worry nesting in her throat. How could she earn this woman's trust in this state? Alice had been reasonable in the dreamscape, but that sliver of rationality seemed to be buried beneath layers of alchemical infatuation.

"Do you remember your brother, Jefferson?" Luci asked softly. "And your son, Theo? They need your help."

As the names *Jefferson* and *Theo* brushed against the walls of the love potion, a jolt of confusion and recognition flickered across Alice's features. Had that cracked the armor of the love potion? Luci hoped so. "Jefferson is in trouble, Alice. And Theo…" She glanced at Phillip, the shadow of worry sculpting his face further. "Theo is missing. We need to find him."

Alice blinked rapidly, seeming to struggle internally. For a fleeting moment, Luci saw the spark of reality brighten in Alice's eyes. But then Alice's features placidly settled once more into a gaze of undying adoration toward Phillip.

"I don't care about any of that," she said breezily. "Phillip is all I need. And the music. Oh yes, I'm supposed to be playing. I play every night." As if shutting the door on the plea for sanity, she lifted her violin to play again, drawing the bow across the strings.

Phillip stepped forward, lowering himself to crouch in front of his wife, desperation etched across his face. "Alice, please listen. I know you're…confused right now. But Theo needs you. Our son needs you. And you need him." His voice cracked on the last words.

But Alice merely smiled, a tranquil look washing over her. "You're so silly, darling. I only need you."

Phillip's shoulders sagged in defeat as he dropped his hands.

He turned helplessly to Luci. "I don't know what to do. She's completely under the potion's thrall."

Luci bit her lip, her mind racing. This wasn't going as planned. She needed an alternative approach, and fast. Jefferson and Theo were depending on her. "Who told Alice to play music?" she asked, her voice sharp.

Phillip shifted uncomfortably, his expression drawing closed. "I did. But it was at Zebulon's command!"

"I don't care about that part." Though, Luci *did* wonder why Professor Woodrow was so insistent about the music. It would have been a lot less trouble to just use a regular violinist attending Cheswell, wouldn't it? That wasn't something to worry about now. "You told her to play, so she did. If you tell her to do something else—besides listen to me—maybe she will."

His brows leaped at the suggestion, but he nodded. "I can try."

Luci pulled out the counter potion. "She needs to drink this."

Something swept across Phillip's face, a brief ripple of revulsion, as if the sight of the vial churned up an uncomfortable memory. But then he turned back to Alice, his movements tender as he gently took the violin from her hands and set it aside. Alice made a small sound of protest, a soft note of loss, but he squeezed her hands reassuringly.

"Alice, my love, I need you to do something very important for me." He spoke slowly and clearly, as one would to a child. "Our friend Luci has a special drink she wants you to try. It will help you feel better. Please, take the drink from Luci and swallow all of it down."

Alice's eyes widened in alarm, and she visibly recoiled. "A drink? No, I don't think..."

Phillip cupped her face in his hands. "Trust me, Alice. This will help. Just a small drink, that's all I ask."

Alice searched his face, then relaxed. "Well, if you want me to, then I will."

Luci sighed with relief. She uncorked the small vial of blue liquid and handed it to Alice with an encouraging smile.

With Phillip's hands still cradling her face tenderly, Alice accepted the vial. She swirled the sparkling liquid, eyeing it suspiciously. Then, with a deep breath, as though gathering courage from the depths of her being, she tipped her head back and drank it all down in one go.

Yes! A surge of victory coursed through Luci. Finally, something was going her way. She turned to Phillip. "I think—"

"Luci Mason!"

She froze at the voice. Slowly, Luci turned and found that Josh, the graduate student who had been tinkering with the deceased woman's tank, had reached the rotunda. He clutched the railing as if the climb had sapped all his strength.

Luci mustered a faint smile and lifted a hand in a weak wave. "Uh, hi Josh. What's up?"

The graduate student cast a suspicious glance her way. "Professor Woodrow is looking for you. He's all worked up since we're attempting one of his grand experiments tonight. If I were you, I'd hurry."

One of his grand experiments. The phrase curled in Luci's stomach like a cold serpent. She turned to Phillip and Alice, brandishing a feigned smile. "Thanks for talking to me about the music! It's really lovely!" Then she swung around to join Josh. "Sorry, I got distracted. I'd heard this music for so long I wanted to see who was playing." She ducked her head, as if embarrassed.

"Whatever." Josh shrugged nonchalantly. "Let's go."

As Luci walked away, she heard Phillip murmur to Alice, "I need to check on Theo, but I'll be right back."

"I'll keep playing," Alice chirped brightly. "Hurry back, or I'll come looking for you!" Her laughter tinkled through the air, light as a daydream.

The soothing notes of the violin wove through the space as Luci followed Josh out of the rotunda. She sighed. The counter potion should have worked almost instantly, according to her calculations. Something was off in her mixture. Some error from which she couldn't recover.

I did my best, and it wasn't enough. Now Luci feared that she'd made some critical error with Breaker's Touch, too.

But she could do nothing about it now. Professor Woodrow was waiting, and she dared not keep him any longer.

CHAPTER THIRTY-SEVEN

Especially You

His tongue felt like a rough piece of cotton. Blaise smacked his lips, then slowly coaxed his eyes open. He expected to see the familiar trappings of the room he shared with Jefferson over the bakery, but the ceiling overhead didn't belong to the loft. This wasn't their bed. Too small. He pushed himself up on his elbows, frowning at the plain walls and sparse furnishings. Nothing here echoed the comforting familiarity of home.

His eyes darted frantically around, seeking something, anything he recognized. But the room was barren of personal effects. Just a bed, a stern-looking desk, a solitary chair, and a partially open door that revealed a glimpse of a lavatory.

For a moment, panic seized him, his heart pounding. How did he get here? And where was Jefferson?

At the thought of his husband, memories flooded back, so intense and awful that they sent him flat on his back atop the bed once more, covering his face with his hands. *Zebulon came. He wanted Jefferson. I wasn't going to let them take him.*

"Jefferson," Blaise whispered into the stillness, eyes squeezed shut to ward off the reality.

They had drugged him, ripped Jefferson away from him. *Jefferson!* Blaise pushed himself upright and scrambled out of the bed, nearly tumbling to the floor in his haste. His head spun from the lingering effects of the sedative, but adrenaline pushed back the fogginess. Jefferson was in danger.

The rest of Blaise's body wasn't primed for action, however. With a grueling effort, he hauled himself into the chair at the desk, leaning heavily against its solid surface. Blaise tried to shift in the chair, the movement nudging the top drawer of the desk open. He moved to close it, but a glimpse of familiar handwriting on a piece of paper caught his eye.

Jefferson's handwriting. Fingers trembling, Blaise pulled a few half-folded sheets of paper out. He unfolded them, spreading the pages before him. The compelling need to rise and act jarred against the jelly-like feebleness of his legs.

Breathe. Calm down. Blaise knew acutely that he teetered on the brink of a panic attack. It wasn't something he could risk right now. Swallowing, he focused on the writing.

The first time I ever laid eyes on you, Blaise, was in that quaint bakery in Fortitude.

What was this? Blaise scanned the page, discovering that Jefferson had penned his musings about him. All of his thoughts, memories—all laid bare on these sheets, recounting how Jefferson felt about their entwined lives.

Remember the first time we shared a bed?

"Yeah," Blaise whispered, a pit opening in his stomach.

That was when I understood there was more than physical need. I needed you on an emotional level.

Blaise tenderly brushed the page with his fingertips, as if he could feel the warmth of Jefferson through the ink.

He stretched his right leg cautiously, testing. The muscles still felt fuzzy and partially unresponsive. The sensation was fading, but slowly.

He carried on reading to distract himself.

Do you know that your unwavering need to save your friends made me jealous? I didn't want you to go, even though we both knew you must.

"I'll always try to help my friends," Blaise murmured. "And you. Especially you."

He couldn't wait any longer. Blaise collected the pages, folding them into a neat square before stowing them in a pocket close to his heart. He maneuvered in the chair, gripping the surface of the desk with one hand and using it to hoist himself upright.

His legs wobbled like those of a newborn foal, but he didn't stumble. And after a moment, the sensation of unsteadiness passed.

Blaise was up, but what could he do now? He couldn't use his magic, aside from on that small portion of the wall. What good would that do? He blew out a frustrated breath…and then a slip of paper on the floor caught his eye.

He moved over to it and gingerly snatched it up, surprised to see his sister's familiar scrawl. Luci had sent him a message. His pulse quickened as he read the cryptic words:

Blaise,
Door!
Jefferson lab!

The part about Jefferson made sense. But what did she mean about the door? He stared at it in bewilderment. His sister clearly thought the door was important, but he didn't understand.

Blaise approached the door cautiously, remembering how the young men had burst in to take Jefferson. He rested his hand against the doorknob, half expecting to feel the numbness from the null paint. But to his shock, there was no numbness. Instead, he felt a tingle of magic come alive in his palm. His breath caught. What did this mean? Eyes wide, Blaise ran his hands over the rest of the door, seeking similar sensations. In several places, the null paint's effects had faded, and along the hinges, it was gone completely.

Hope surged within Blaise's chest. Luci had weakened the paint somehow. Just enough magic was returning that he could use his abilities.

Blaise pressed his fingertips against the hinges, lips pursed, as he summoned his magic. There was a grinding crunch as the metal began to fracture and crumble under the invisible force. Brittle cracks spider-webbed along the surface, deteriorating the once sturdy iron. The hinges and lock disintegrated from the inside out.

"*Yes.* Come on," he whispered. Blaise reached to touch the doorknob. As soon as the first wisp of magic met it, it fell away from the door, shattering into tiny shards when it hit the floor.

With a deep breath, Blaise pulled at the fragile door. It came free with a scraping sound, warped and riddled with cracks. He stepped over the threshold into the hallway, magic rushing back through his veins.

Blaise stood in the hallway, magic coursing through him once more. But he hesitated, unsure which way to go. The need to find Jefferson pressed him, but he had no clue where to even begin looking on the sprawling campus. Blaise headed for the stairs and began his descent.

He eyed the sparse students passing by warily. None seemed to pay him much mind, but he shrank back against the wall, anyway. If anyone realized he had escaped, they might try to recapture him. Blaise had no way of knowing who was a friend or a foe. He wasn't willing to risk asking someone he didn't know.

Blaise took a few cautious steps through the dormitory's common room when the faint, melancholy strands of violin music drifted to him. He paused, listening. The playing spoke of sorrow and longing, yet possessed an ethereal beauty.

Alice. That had to be Jefferson's sister. He followed the melody across the quad toward an ornate building with the words *Castor Building of Music* carved into the facade. Blaise looked up, noting the dome atop it. Hadn't Luci mentioned finding Alice in a rotunda? Blaise straightened with renewed conviction. If he could find Alice, he might be able to use his magic to free her of the potion. He had used his magic against alchemy before.

Blaise hurried up the steps and slipped inside the music building. The lobby was empty, but the violin's song echoed through the halls, drawing him onward. He located a spiral staircase and ascended, his footfalls quiet on the plush carpet.

As he climbed higher, the music swelled in volume but took on a slower tempo. Blaise imagined Alice pouring her conflicted feelings into the notes—her devotion twisted by the love potion.

At the top, Blaise found himself under an ornate domed ceiling covered in a fresco of clouds and dragons of every color. Large windows lined the rotunda, and though it was dark outside, flashes of lightning intermittently illuminated them.

A black-haired woman sat on a chair, her back to Blaise as she played the violin. The woman rolled her shoulders, making a soft groan. She was alone. Blaise hoped he was right, and that she was Alice. He approached, his boots far too loud on the marble floor. The woman didn't seem to hear him.

"Alice?" Blaise called, approaching her slowly and carefully, as one might a wild animal.

She didn't stop playing, but she acknowledged his presence with a fleeting glance. Blaise didn't like the way she looked at him. There was something very wrong with her; something that didn't match the woman he'd met in the dreamscape.

"Go away. You're interrupting my music," she said, and the tune shifted to match her words. Blaise felt it like a physical force trying to urge him away. Magic—Alice's magic. His own Breaker power reared up to meet it, allowing Blaise to remain rooted in place.

"No, we need to talk," Blaise said as her music washed around him.

Alice hurled more magic at him, another melodic command for him to leave. The music became aggressive, reminiscent of a hulking monster with gnashing fangs, summoning every scary tale ever told.

Blaise gritted his teeth. He'd been through far worse, and as long as she didn't have a way to tap into his specific traumas, he could weather her storm with the shield of his magic.

"Go away!" Alice shrieked. "Why won't you go away?" Outside, distant thunder rumbled, echoing the tumult inside.

"Because I'm here to help you," Blaise said, taking another step closer. He had hoped Luci might have broken the love potion, but that must not have succeeded. He hoped he was up to the task. "You know me. We've met."

She rose abruptly, knocking her chair back so that it tumbled over with a clatter. Her eyes widened as she gazed at the toppled chair. Then she turned back to Blaise, her face pale. "This is wrong."

Blaise paused, unsure what she meant. "Let me help you."

Alice's eyes flicked between the fallen chair and Blaise, as if trying to piece together a puzzle. "Wrong. This is wrong. I never sit. I don't sit when I play." She blinked, and it was as if a veil of confusion lifted from her face. Alice set her violin in a nearby case with trembling hands, then moved to right the chair.

"Here, let me help." Blaise stepped forward to grab the chair, too. But he didn't stop with the chair. His palm brushed her arm long enough for him to send a wisp of Breaker magic into her.

Alice shivered, then plopped down in the chair. She didn't reach for her violin, though. Instead, she stared at Blaise, her eyes clouded with confusion and traces of distant memory.

"I saw you in my dream, didn't I?" she finally said. "Only it wasn't a dream."

Blaise felt a tiny bubble of his own tension burst. She remembered. "It was a dream," he said carefully, "but it was also real."

With cautious optimism, Blaise reached out, offering his hand. She took it, her eyes widening as more of his power coursed into her. This time, Blaise guided it delicately, tearing away the thick webs of the love potion that had ensnared her mind. The potion was an awful, sticky thing, reminding him of a heavy syrup. It threatened to cling to everything it touched, including him, though his magic repelled it.

Blaise spoke as he worked, his words offering a tether to reality. "We met in a place called the dreamscape. Jefferson's magic brought us there. My sister, Luci, was there, too. We were making plans. Do you remember?" He cleared away the last of the potion's influence, though it tried to cling to Alice like a suffocating vine. "But now Jefferson's in trouble." He hesitated, the words heavy on his tongue. He hated to ask more of her when she had already suffered so much. Alice sucked in a deep breath, as if this were the first time she was breathing of her own volition in ages. "Can you help?"

"I was a prisoner in my own mind," Alice whispered, her words carrying a heavy anguish. The statement felt sickening in its honesty. Blaise swallowed hard. He'd had more than his share of trauma, and he understood, to some extent, the ghostly shadows that now lurked in her eyes.

"But you're free now. I was...I was captive, too." Blaise's voice trembled, a reflection of haunting memories. He realized that later, when the world was not resting on their weary shoulders, he would have a lot to unpack. But not now. He took a breath to steady himself. "And I know how you feel—"

"How can you?" Her words were a hostile snarl, eyes narrowed.

Blaise closed his eyes, momentarily retreating from the raw gaze that bore into him. "The Confederation held me in the Golden Citadel. Abused me. Dosed me with a potion intended to kill me and everyone around me, including people I love." The words tumbled out of him in a rough cascade, and he shook his head to dispel the visuals that accompanied them.

He heard the whisper of her skirts as she rose. "Blaise Hawthorne. The Breaker." Her words were soft, delicately laced with recognition, as if she were sifting through the fragments of her memory. And then, "My brother-in-law."

Blaise hadn't expected the last. And somehow, it was a safe harbor, pulling him out from the pit of memories that had threatened to submerge him in despair. He opened his eyes to find Alice standing in front of him, her posture less guarded, a flicker of understanding lighting her features.

"Yeah," Blaise agreed, voice hoarse.

"My son, Theo. Do you know where he is?" Alice's tone was oddly calm, as if she were steadying herself. "I remember something about him..." Her gaze drifted away, finding solace in the view beyond the windows.

Blaise swallowed. Her son. Jefferson's nephew. *My nephew*. The connections between them seemed to tangle further with each passing moment. He shook his head. "I...I'm sorry, I don't. I just got free myself."

She nodded her understanding, though her eyes carried a faraway look, likely scouring the remnants of her memories for clues. Then she turned back to him, returning to the present. "You said my brother's in trouble?"

"I think so. They drugged me and took him away." Blaise chewed his bottom lip. "And I don't think I can help him by myself." He didn't even know where Luci was or if she could help.

Alice regarded him for a long moment, her countenance like a still lake, bereft of any hint of the thoughts beneath the surface. Blaise felt anxiety wind tighter in his gut. What if she refused? He was depending on her knowledge of this place.

But then she gave a single nod. "Tell me what you need."

Relief swept through Blaise so strongly that his knees nearly gave way. She would help. His voice carried a shaky note of hope as he asked, "Do you know where the laboratories are?"

At the mention of the laboratories, Alice's face lost color. She dropped her gaze, her eyes now on the violin nestled in the case on the floor.

"I know it," she said finally, her words a fragile thread of sound. "I've been there."

She shuddered, and Blaise could only imagine the horrors she must have faced in that place. He chose not to pry.

As if shaking off the ghosts of her past, Alice turned abruptly, her eyes steely. "We have to hurry." Alice bent over, strapping her bow securely into the case before closing it. She picked up the instrument case, striding toward the spiral staircase. "Follow me."

CHAPTER THIRTY-EIGHT

Alchemical Mage

I was used. That bastard turned me into a mindless sycophant. I can't believe he did that.

Alice's steps carried a new, unforgiving cadence as she marched toward the looming edifice of the alchemy building, with Blaise keeping pace off to her left. Her mind raged like a hurricane. Not that Phillip's betrayal was beyond belief. He had always been a man who seized what he desired. But that recollection warred with a fuzzy memory from her time under the potion's sway. Her husband peering at her, concern in his eyes. *Regret.* Phillip, murmuring that she was not the woman he'd married. Saying she had lost her fire, her essence, the spark that made her Alice.

She shook her head, uncertain if that memory was even true or a hallucination from the potion. Whatever it was, it didn't matter. Phillip had wronged her, shackled her very will. And she was going to make certain he paid once all this was done.

The rhythmic beat of Blaise's boots against the cobblestones pulled Alice from her vengeful thoughts. She cast a sideward glance at him, her curiosity about this man who had captured her deceitful brother's heart growing. Though their acquaintance in Jefferson's dream realm had been brief, there was an air of sincerity about Blaise. And the anguish that had etched itself across his features during his raw recollection of his own tormented past was undeniably real.

Alice turned her gaze back to the path ahead. She couldn't change the past, but she could ensure they had a future where no one would suffer as they had.

As they approached the alchemy building, thunder rumbled overhead, punctuating their mission. Alice tightened her grip on the violin case. Rain wasn't good for the instrument, but she felt like she needed it near as protection. The source of her magic. And she would use it, if it came to it.

The heavy oak door to the building loomed before them, a silent gatekeeper to what lay ahead. Gathering her resolve, Alice pulled it open and gestured for Blaise to enter first. He did, cautiously scanning the new surroundings.

They found themselves in a hallway devoid of people. A sterile, clean scent permeated the air—the faint hint of bleach. The hallway was painted a bright white with black accents along the walls and floor. It was so clean, Alice could see her reflection on the floor. Doors lined the corridor on both sides, each labeled with names and titles that were nonsensical to Alice. Blaise, however, paused at each, examining them with a furrowed brow.

Alice glanced back, her impatience flaring. She opened her mouth to call for Blaise to hurry, but snapped it closed when she saw the troubled crinkle of his brow and the worry bright in his eyes. He had been patient with her. Alice needed to give him the same courtesy. She thought about asking if he was okay, but dismissed it as an empty question. Of course, he wasn't okay. She wasn't, either.

The name on the plaque outside the next door caught her eye. *Woodrow*. Alice had only hazy memories of the room they had brought her to when she first arrived, but knew it was nearby. "Blaise, over here." She pointed to the name.

Blaise's jaw tightened, his hands clenching and unclenching at his side. Was it her imagination, or did Alice spy a sheen of silver wash over his palms? Whatever it was, she didn't have time to worry about it. Alice tried the door, but it didn't budge. "It's locked," she said, shaking her head.

"Not for long." Blaise stepped up, and in that brief instant he seemed to shed his fear and worry, replacing it with confidence.

He laid his hands against the door—and *oh gods*, Alice hadn't hallucinated the silver motes. She scooted backward as the heavy wood cracked beneath the might of Blaise's magic. And then it did more than crack, the wood falling to splinters, to sawdust.

Blaise stepped inside, his hands held before him, as if he expected to be met with resistance. But no one came. He glanced back at her. There was a glint of fear in his eyes, but it lifted, replaced with determination.

Alice stepped over the ruined door. She'd heard that this man had taken down an airship—and more—but it had always sounded like an exaggeration. He really was as potent as the stories claimed, and now she understood exactly why he'd faced those abuses. Alice knew only too well that the powerful among the elite would have either wanted to use Blaise or to trap him. She swallowed, then shook the thought away. Blaise was on her side, and they had a task at hand.

With a wary gaze, she scanned the room, half-expecting Woodrow himself to spring out like a ghoul from a bedtime story. But the lab was empty. The workstations sat tidy and undisturbed, equipment neatly arranged. Notes and books lay open, as if their owner had just stepped away momentarily.

Alice moved farther inside, senses heightened. Where was everyone? This sterile room felt like a trap about to be sprung.

Alice turned in a slow circle, taking in every detail of the lab. Too pristine. This didn't feel right. "It's empty," she said aloud, her voice echoing off the walls and floors. "There's no one here."

She glanced back at Blaise. His shoulders slumped, and his eyes scrunched shut. "That can't be right," he insisted, a note of desperation in his tone. He strode past her, tugging books from shelves and rifling through the papers on the nearest workstation. "I was told he'd be at the lab. Jefferson has to be here somewhere. Or...or some clue to lead us to him." His voice cracked. Alice imagined soon he would start peering under the desks to see if Jefferson might be crouched there, ready to jump out, as if it were a surprise party.

"I'll help you look." Alice set her violin case down on a nearby stool. She joined him in searching the room, opening drawers and cabinets. Her fingers skimmed over vials and containers, seeking anything out of place.

Most of the laboratory's contents were unfamiliar to her, but she hoped she'd know if she uncovered something useful. Alice worked quickly but thoroughly, driven by an unfamiliar protectiveness. She had to find something to help Blaise save her brother.

Alice eventually halted at a workstation nestled in a far corner. Her eyes landed on the journal that lay open. As she leaned down to study the open page, she faced a hauntingly familiar sketch. It was a portrait of Blaise, his features captured with surprising accuracy despite the crude pencil strokes.

"I found something," she said, striving to keep her tone neutral.

Blaise hurried over to Alice, his footsteps echoing in the empty lab. As he approached, Alice held up the journal so he could see the sketch.

He stilled, astonishment flashing across his face. It was undeniably him. The words inked at the top and bottom sent a shiver down Alice's spine. She didn't know what they meant, but she suspected it was nothing good.

Alchemical Mage.
Subject Zero.

Blaise let out a shaky breath, reaching to take the journal from Alice's outstretched hand. He studied it for a long moment before his eyes drifted to the margins.

"This...this is my sister's handwriting," he said, tapping his finger against the hastily scribbled words:

Up Up Up.

Alice followed his gaze, frowning. "Your sister? What does it mean?"

Blaise shook his head, clearly as baffled as she was. "I don't know. But she wrote it for a reason."

He looked up toward the ceiling. Following his lead, Alice tilted her head back, inspecting the unremarkable surface above.

"There's nothing there," she said. Unless Blaise's sister meant they should literally go up higher into the building? But why?

Blaise ran a hand over his beard, looking disturbed. "Something's wrong. She wouldn't leave a cryptic clue like this unless it was important." His face had gone pale, and he had the look of a man growing sick to his stomach. Alice couldn't imagine how he felt after viewing that foreboding sketch. Did he know what it meant?

Alice pressed her lips into a thin line as she weighed their options. Staying here in this deserted lab would get them nowhere. And fretting over a vague clue without context wouldn't help, either. They needed more to go on.

"Zebulon wanted me to draw people away from here," she said after a moment. "He didn't want anyone digging too deep." Her eyes narrowed, her mind working furiously. "But there's nothing on this floor. Maybe we should keep looking. Higher up, like your sister suggested."

Blaise blinked, some of the sickly pallor fading from his face. "You're right," he said, straightening. "We can't stop now."

Alice nodded briskly, glad to see a flicker of dedication reigniting in Blaise's eyes. "Let's keep moving then. We'll find him." Her words were steady, or so she hoped.

But doubt eroded her optimism. And while the situation looked grim, giving voice to her outlook wasn't an option, especially when Blaise clung to every shred of hope. And frankly, she needed to cling to it, too. Taking a deep breath, she picked up her violin case.

Blaise took a moment to fold the Alchemical Mage paper before tucking it securely into his pocket. His jaw set, perseverance reflected in his eyes as he turned to follow Alice out of the room. She led the way into the hall, searching for a stairwell.

Suddenly, Blaise halted in his tracks. A soft breath escaped him, followed by a muted curse. "The roof. They're on the roof."

Alice frowned. "You figured out the note?"

Blaise shook his head. "No. I mean, well, it makes sense *now*. My pegasus just flew into range and told me."

Pegasus? What...? Oh. That was right; many of the outlaw mages rode pegasi. Alice nodded. "Right. So, let's figure out roof access."

CHAPTER THIRTY-NINE

Unnatural

Jefferson

"I never want to ride in a freight elevator again," Jefferson muttered, wishing he could shake off the memories of his harrowing ascent.

As if being trussed up hadn't been bad enough, Zebulon had instructed the students to take him to the roof. He could still feel the sensation of the gurney being jostled by the freight elevator, powered by students turning an oversized crank. The creak of the ropes, the strain clear in the faces of the students, and the slow rise had all combined into a nerve-wracking journey upward.

And now…well, he was on the roof. He didn't know what that meant. Storm clouds boiled in the distance, their dark bellies ribbed by lightning.

Wonderful. Strapped to a metal table on top of a roof with a thunderstorm blowing in. This could not possibly get any better. Jefferson gave another tentative tug against the restraints, but the leather still cinched him in place. And the earlier injection still numbed his magic.

The students shifted his gurney. Jefferson angled his head. His breath hitched as his eyes fell upon a towering machine. It was an amalgamation of engineering and alchemy, that much was clear. At its center was a complicated heart made of valves and gears, resembling the inner workings of an engine, all encased in a web of brass and iron. It appeared to be the driving force of the contraption, pulsing steadily amidst the metal framework. Extending from this central mechanism were two tentacle-like metal arms, each lined with intricate joints and ending in an array of delicate tools and sensors. They hovered over the roof like the limbs of an iron giant, poised and ready for some unknown operation.

"What is that thing?" Jefferson demanded of the nearest student, only to find himself ignored. All around the rooftop, students scurried around like a colony of ants, each one striving to avoid eye contact with him. They must have heard about his magic and were wary. Others clustered around Zebulon, hanging onto his every word before bustling off to carry out his instructions.

Another group of students worked to pry wooden planks from around a long, rectangular box. Jefferson watched as the planks fell away, revealing a glass tank in which the lifeless form of a woman floated in a fluorescent greenish liquid that emitted an eerie glow. They docked the tank to the heart, scurrying to attach various tubes and filaments or...whatever they were. Jefferson didn't know. Didn't care, really.

Soon, a pair of students approached him, wheeling his gurney closer to the mechanical beast. They positioned him beneath one of the large mechanical arms that extended from the core, hovering above him like a harbinger of doom. The arm branched out into many smaller appendages, each adorned with tubes, wires, and vials of liquids that shimmered in the pale moonlight.

He barely noticed the cold bite of metal as the students began attaching the wires to him. Couldn't tear his focus from the arm looming above, its appendages trembling with a sinister anticipation. By the time he realized the wires were sinking into his flesh, melding into his very being, it was too late.

"No!" Jefferson growled, tugging once more. His muscles screamed against the restraints, each pull a bid for freedom that fell on uncaring ears. The students were unmoved, their faces detached as they ensured everything remained in place before moving away. Jefferson heaved a defeated sigh, head sinking back against the table again, gaze drifting to the side.

Then, a student moved a wooden cart full of supplies, and Jefferson saw another gurney opposite his position on the roof. His breath snagged in his throat as he recognized the small, still form lying atop it.

"Theo!" he cried out. A fresh wave of terror surged through him. He fought against the restraints binding him, shrieking his fury, but to no avail. Theo remained motionless, not a flutter of response to his name being called. Sedated, Jefferson hoped. *Gods, Theo.* Jefferson fixed his eyes on the closest students. "That's a little boy over there! I don't know what you're planning, but this is wrong!"

The abrupt outburst from Jefferson momentarily interrupted Zebulon's string of instructions. The older man glanced toward Jefferson, a contemplative expression molding his features. "Ah, *wrong.* Now there's a term that's seen its fair share of interpretation throughout the ages. What is *wrong* to one society is a celebrated tradition in another. It's all quite subjective," he mused, stroking his chin. "For instance, in the ancient city of Veridial, they believed it was *wrong* to consume any form of root vegetable. Can you imagine? No potatoes!"

"This isn't the time for a history lesson! It will always, *always* be wrong to harm a child," Jefferson snapped.

"But isn't it always the time to ponder morality and ethics?" Zebulon replied, then turned back to his students. "Especially in such a...charged environment."

Jefferson swallowed. The bastard was taunting him now. Another flash of lightning overhead accentuated Zebulon's attempt at humor. His mind raced, scrambling for a way out, for anything that might save them from this dire situation. It was not only his own predicament that clawed at him, but Theo's, too. Jefferson's eyes were drawn once again to the glass tank. The woman floating inside seemed vaguely familiar.

With a start, he realized exactly who she was. "Tabris's sweet golden ass," he murmured. Tara. Could he use that to his advantage? It was worth a try. "You know, Zebulon, most people prefer having fish in an aquarium. This seems a bit...unconventional, don't you think?"

The alchemist didn't miss a beat of his preparations. "Ah, aquariums. A delightful concept, yet what we have here is far beyond the mundane." His gaze turned toward Jefferson, sinister amusement playing in his eyes. "You'll see its remarkable purpose soon enough."

"I'd rather not," Jefferson retorted, but his attempt to veer Zebulon off his chosen path fell flat. He strained against his bindings, futile as it was, his mind darting in every direction for a solution. Blaise was still back in their room, drugged into unconsciousness. Alice was...

Wait. I don't hear the violin. I think I would hear it where I am, wouldn't I? A shimmer of hope sparked amidst the dread tightening around his chest. Perhaps this was a good sign. Though, by this point, he was painfully aware that it would take more than hope to untangle them from this mess.

"Professor Woodrow, I found her," a male voice announced.

Jefferson couldn't see the speaker, but he saw Zebulon turn, his smile patient and just a touch condescending. The alchemist lifted his hands, fingers spread in a pseudo-dramatic fashion. "Ah, Miss Mason! The celestial bodies must have truly aligned for us tonight because here you are, right on cue. Or perhaps a tad late, but who's watching the time?"

Oh gods. Luci was here, too. Jefferson wished he could adjust his position to see if she was in the same sort of trouble as him. But he quickly realized she wasn't bound in any way when she moved into his line of sight.

Blaise's little sister ducked her head in apology. "I'm sorry, Professor. I lost track of time."

Zebulon leaned in, his eyes bright. "Time! Such an elusive construct. Often dances away when we're engrossed in certain...clandestine activities. Like crafting some *very specific* potions. Not exactly standard curriculum, hmm? But, of course, some of the best discoveries lie outside the syllabus. Or so they say."

Luci's face turned ashen. Jefferson silently cursed. Zebulon was on to her.

Zebulon tilted his head with an almost benign smile that had nothing kind in it—akin to a cat toying with a cornered mouse. "You know, Luci, it's quite impressive, your initiative. Really. Though, did you assume I'd be oblivious to the clandestine pursuits of Marian Hawthorne's offspring? Oh, the audacity!" His soft chuckle curled through the air like smoke. "But you see, you're still budding, green, like unripened fruit. Yet your potential! Oh, it's tantalizing."

Luci's eyes flicked to the glass tank, wide with horror. "What you're doing is wrong. It's unnatural."

Jefferson raised his brows. Had she had some forewarning of Zebulon's grim intentions? No...she would have warned him. Wouldn't she?

Zebulon's expression turned contemplative, his head canting, as if her words carried fresh insight. "*Unnatural*? My dear, aren't we always pushing the boundaries of what's considered *natural?* Candles gave way to gas and electric lights. Horse-drawn carriages to steam-powered vehicles." His sigh held a trace of whimsical nostalgia, his gaze softening momentarily. "Tara... she was taken before her time. An unexpected plot twist in our shared narrative. Isn't it only fitting to try to rewrite that chapter? For both our sakes."

Jefferson froze. Zebulon had planned some madcap process of resurrecting his deceased wife? That was impossible. Necromancers...they could raise the dead, but what came back was a husk. The soul of the person had moved on to Perdition and beyond to Paradise, or so Jefferson had been taught. Then Jefferson snorted to himself. *The person would need a soul for that. Maybe Tara never had one.* Still, returning the dead to true life was impossible.

But so was creating mages from nothing. And I'm living proof it can be done. That was an uncomfortable truth that Jefferson decided was inconvenient at the moment.

Zebulon adjusted his glasses, peering at the cloud-marbled sky with a bemused expression. "You know, I had a little chat with one of those up-and-coming professors in meteorology. Quite an intriguing subject, isn't it? Predicting the weather. Makes me think of those little barometers people put in their parlors. But I digress. He seemed fairly convinced about the potency of this impending storm. Seems it might provide just the right...ambiance for our experiment."

A student raised her hand. "Professor Woodrow, isn't it dangerous for us to be up here with that storm?" She glanced toward the ominous clouds, her fear apparent. "My uncle was struck by lightning when he was plowing his field a few years ago. He fell down dead, right there!"

The professor angled his head, offering a small nod of acknowledgment. "Ah, Madeline, life does indeed come with its...electrifying moments. But, as with many things in alchemy, there's a certain spark required for success. Though, if you feel this spark isn't for you, perhaps it's an opportune moment to reconsider your academic path?"

Madeline's face flushed, but she shook her head adamantly. "Oh, no, Professor, I'm fine."

With a satisfied nod, Zebulon turned to address the rest of the hushed assembly. "Very well. Before we dive in, let's ensure we're all on the same page, shall we?" His gaze swept across anxious faces before resting on the glass tank. "In essence, we're aiming to welcome my cherished Tara back to the world of the living. My working theory, which I must say is rather intriguing, is about concocting just the right blend of vital essences." Zebulon meandered over to Theo, giving him a studious look. "And our sprightly young friend here? He's central to the process. His youthful exuberance, I believe, might just be the key to giving the cold shoulder to death's seemingly final say."

"You're a monster!" The words erupted from Jefferson, his eyes blazing with anger.

Zebulon, unfazed by the outburst, leisurely made his way over to Jefferson's gurney. "Ah, Subject One, always brimming with fervor." He shot a brief, cold smile in Jefferson's direction. "You might think I've overlooked you with all the commotion, but truly, you're right up there on my list of crucial components." He waved a dismissive hand, yet his eyes bore into Jefferson with a disconcerting intensity. "Perhaps even topping the list. This project...well, let's just say it's a passion project. Your profound affection for your husband—it's something to behold. Would you, maybe, die for him?"

"*No.*" Jefferson's voice was as sharp as the razor he sorely missed. "I would *live* for him, every single day."

The simplicity and conviction in Jefferson's voice seemed to strike a chord, even with Zebulon, who regarded him with a nod. "That's just the sentiment I was hoping to hear. Dying? Oh, that's a fleeting gesture. But choosing to live for someone? Now, that's *dedication.* And it's that very essence, the profound depth of your feelings, that could be the keystone for our little experiment here."

Jefferson shut his eyes, the sick feeling swarming in the pit of his stomach. Now, the alchemist's ramblings about love made sense. *He didn't want me because I'm an alchemical mage. He wants me because of how strongly I love Blaise.* Tears stung his eyes as he heard Zebulon continue to instruct the students. It was the most twisted thing imaginable.

<Jefferson! There you are!>

The unexpected warmth of Seledora's voice within his mind jolted Jefferson. His eyes flashed open, searching the skies for Seledora. But it was dark, aside from the lightning and the few lights that Zebulon's alchemy students had set up on the roof so they could see their work. Their glow barely pierced the darkness, leaving the expanse above a mystery.

<There was a strange barrier that turned us away every time we came to look for you and Blaise,> the mare continued.

There, in a flash of lightning, he caught her silvery form far overhead. How he wished for a way to communicate the danger he was in. To relay the twisted web Zebulon had spun around them, or to strategize an escape from this horrifying predicament.

As if sensing the flurry of his anxious thoughts, he felt the gentle touch of Seledora's consciousness against his. <You're stressed.>

Oh, stressed, am I? Jefferson almost laughed at her observation.

The telepathic connection went silent for a heartbeat before Seledora's voice resonated once more within his mind. <I think I've narrowed down where you—oh Mother of Mares, Jefferson, what have you gotten yourself into? And why is there a dead woman in a water trough…wait—there's the boy from Starvation!> Jefferson felt her brewing anger when she saw Theo. <Hold on. We'll figure something out.>

Jefferson swallowed. Seledora had found him. Perhaps there was hope after all.

Zebulon brought his hands together with a soft clap. "Right, let's see...everyone should be on the same page about our methodology now, correct? I'd suggest—no, I'd *strongly recommend*—that each of you finds your respective spots. Prepare to play your roles." He took a deep breath. "Oh, and don't forget the potions and other *entertainments* I've handed out. If we, by any chance, find ourselves in a predicament or an unforeseen interruption, do use them. We really mustn't let any hiccups derail our proceedings here."

There was the sound of a machine rumbling to life. Already bound by wires to the heartless monstrosity, Jefferson felt a subtle shift in the surrounding atmosphere, a tightening in the air that preceded the unknown. The wires attached to his flesh seemed to twitch, ever so slightly, in rhythm with the machine's newfound heartbeat.

Jefferson's world exploded into a bright flash as lightning struck nearby. Students shrieked.

And then Jefferson felt as if the bolt had struck him directly. White-hot pain lanced into him, crackling through every point the wires touched. He screamed, distantly aware of the sickening aroma of burned hair. His muscles seized, his entire body aflame with pain.

Seledora battered against the barrier of his agony, trying to get through to him, but her voice was lost in the tide.

CHAPTER FORTY
The Thunder Rolls

Blaise

*H**e was right. I was wrong.* Blaise repeated the words over and over to himself as he and Alice raced down the long corridor in search of the roof access they knew must exist. After seeing the sketch of his own face in that alchemical journal, Blaise couldn't shrug off the sickening feeling. Jefferson's methods might have been questionable when it came to ending potential threats, but it was frustratingly clear that he was right. Blaise wasn't safe. Might never be safe.

Emrys's commentary kept Blaise moored. The stallion had been ridiculously happy to find Blaise and now kept up a one-sided dialogue as he soared over the campus.

<They have him on a table,> Emrys told him. <There's a bunch of people up there, too. I don't know how much longer Seledora

and I can stay in the air. The wind is picking up, and there's so much lightning.>

The last thing Blaise wanted was for the pegasi to be struck by lightning. He was certain Emrys was aware of the danger, but his loyalty and worry for his rider kept him skybound.

<Blaise, Seledora says there's a child up here, too. She seems to recognize him.>

The news made Blaise wince. He slowed, turning to Alice, who was just a couple of steps behind. "Alice, I think Theo is up there."

Her eyes widened. "Oh, gods. Theo!" She stopped abruptly, setting down her violin case. Opening it with swift fingers, she pulled out her violin and bow. "Rain and humidity aren't good for this, but I'm ready."

Blaise raised his brows. "What are you going to do?"

"Whatever it takes."

He shook his head. While Blaise admired her grit, they needed to go on more than that. "No. I mean, I need to understand how your magic works."

At his explanation, she nodded, though they both continued their search. "With my music, I can influence emotions, sway a person's frame of mind." She pointed ahead of them. "There's a staircase."

That reminded him a little of Vixen's Persuader magic. But it wasn't something he could see as being useful if it came down to a fight. And with each step they climbed, Blaise had the sinking feeling there was going to be one. But maybe that wasn't fair. He'd used his own power for more than simple destruction.

Finally, he asked, "Can you fight with it?"

Alice tucked her chin. "We're going to find out. My child and brother are up there, and only Tabris knows what's happening to them."

That was all the answer he needed. They reached a new floor. Turning, Blaise scanned the hallway. Something caught his eye:

the words *RESTRICTED ACCESS* and *DO NOT ENTER* painted on a door. Alice saw it, too, and without a word, they sprinted toward it.

Alice wrestled with the doorknob and even tried to body-check the door, but it didn't budge. "Damn thing's locked." She peeked through a small window in the door, but years of grime obscured the view. "Can your magic bust it open, like you did earlier?"

Blaise nodded, but his hand hovered hesitantly over the door. A faint murmur seeped from the other side. Voices. "I can, but..." He paused, an idea taking root. "Let's try the less destructive approach first." He rapped his knuckles against the sturdy wood, the knock reverberating down the desolate hallway.

Blaise's patience was a thin veneer, ready to crack as the silence stretched between the knock and any response. But just as he considered unleashing his magic, the door hesitantly opened, revealing a boyish face Blaise remembered all too well. It was one of the young men who had drugged him. The undergrad's eyes widened as he made the same connection.

"The Breaker!" he squeaked, any bravado he had lost at the realization that he faced a potentially dangerous situation. He scrambled backward, bumping into someone else.

"Hey, what's the big—?"

"Out of the way! We need to warn the professor! And get help!" The urgency in the youth's voice echoed down the corridor as their footsteps hammered against metal stairs in retreat. Blaise grimaced.

"Do you get that a lot?" Alice asked.

"It depends," he mumbled, stepping into the dimly lit room the young men had occupied. The air was stale with a scent of mold touched by a hint of alchemical reagents. "His fear is justified, since he helped drug me. I'm not thrilled about that."

"You're pretty calm," Alice pointed out, clearly impressed.

"The undergrads aren't my enemies. And I just want Jefferson back." Ahead, Blaise saw a steep stairwell leading to what he hoped was the roof.

"Anyone standing between me and my child are enemies," Alice murmured.

"Fair enough." Blaise started up the stairs. The fleeing students had shut the access hatch, but it was going to take a lot more than that to stop him. The wind whistled through the cracks of the hatch. He sucked in a breath, then glanced down at Alice. "Ready?"

"What are you planning to do?" she asked, clutching her violin. Her voice carried a hint of awe mixed with apprehension. "With your magic, I mean."

"Whatever it takes," he said, purposely echoing her words from moments before. With a hefty push, he forced the hatch open, a gust of wind aiding his effort. It slammed against the roof with a resounding *bang*.

As quickly as he could, Blaise scrambled onto the roof. A young man turned to gawk at him. "Professor Woodrow!"

Alice was beside him a moment later, violin against her shoulder, bow ready.

Blaise scanned the scene to orient himself. A metallic behemoth crouched in the middle of the roof, huddled beside a glass tank, while the storm boiled overhead. Flanking this setup were two steel tables. On one, a little boy lay slumped with a pair of nervous-looking students standing guard. On the other...

"Jefferson!" The shout tore from Blaise's throat before he could stop it. A tangle of wires snaked from the metal monster's arm, connected all over Jefferson's body. Jefferson's eyes were squeezed shut, his face twisted in agony, oblivious to Blaise's cry.

Zebulon exhaled a weary sigh, the exasperation clear in his voice. "Subject Zero, your knack for disruption is as predictable as it is inconvenient." He shook his head, feigning disappointment. "But let's not dwell. Students, remember the tools I equipped you with? Now's the time to employ them. Let's keep our experiment on course, shall we?"

"Theo, hold on!" The urgency in Alice's call pierced the tumultuous air as she positioned her bow over the strings of her violin.

The students' momentary hesitation was as brief as the lightning that forked overhead. Hands delved into the depths of their garments, emerging with an assortment of alchemical tools and potions held at the ready. A few held vials containing swirling, luminescent liquids, their colors pulsing with potential energy. Other students grasped devices that hummed with contained power, reminiscent of the awful machine overhead. Several students drank from potions. Their bodies responded instantly: one's frame began to shimmer with a translucent sheen, while another's muscles tensed visibly, veins coursing with the glow of a growth potion. There was no immediate violence, no instant aggression, just a show of unity made by the students—a promise of an alchemical tempest that could be unleashed in defense of their work. The young alchemists stood as ominous sentinels, their readiness to use these items a dark portent hanging as heavily in the air as the storm itself.

Blaise paused, eyes narrowing in a quick attempt to assess the threat level of each student. They were *all* a danger to him and the people he cared about—and that was what mattered.

Alice's bow glided against the strings. "I don't know what that's all about, but I think it's time to fight my way."

Zebulon turned back to his work, seemingly confident in his students. Blaise's gaze flicked to Jefferson, so far out of reach, flanked by a pair of students. The young man on the left held a pistol-like device that seemed to ripple with lightning. The woman at his side tucked an empty potion bottle into the pouch at her belt, leaving her capabilities a mystery. But none of the students advanced on Blaise or Alice, obedient to Zebulon's advice to stay at their stations unless bothered. Was that something they could use to their advantage? Blaise wished he had more time to think, but the storm was growing overhead, and he didn't know how much longer Jefferson and Theo had.

Alice seemed to have the same thought. She glanced at him, then stepped forward. "Sorry. This will probably hit you, too."

She played.

The somber tune that emanated from her violin engulfed them like a fog of sorrow, echoing the deepest misery dwelling within their souls.

Blaise faltered, his body almost buckling under the intense feeling of desolation that washed over him. He stumbled, his knees meeting the cold stone of the rooftop. Tears welled in his eyes, blurring his vision, but not enough to erase the sight of Jefferson in distress. Grief was an old friend, a familiar foe, but it dug deeper. Every name that flashed through his mind—*Jefferson, Emrys, Mom, Luci, Brody, Jack, Emmaline, Flora*—carried with it a torrent of longing and loss that threatened to drown him.

Nearby, Alice, too, struggled, a sheen of tears glistening on her cheeks. Her chin trembled, but her hands were steady, the mournful tune her offering of defiance in the face of the threat before them. The melody seemed to have an impact on the students, who sniffled and wiped away tears, their shoulders shuddering with the emotional onslaught the music brought on.

Jefferson. Oh, gods. He...wait! Jefferson isn't dead. Not yet. But he might be if I can't get to him. Blaise lifted his head, and through bleary eyes, he saw Jefferson, *still alive* but still in terrible danger. He heard the muffled sobs of the nearby students, wailing as if they, too, were heartbroken. Even Zebulon had been impacted by the song.

Zebulon dabbed at his eyes, then rubbed his nose on his sleeve. "My goodness, Alice," he mused, voice quivering. "That's quite the poignant melody. Takes me right back to the sunlit parlors where I read aloud lengthy alchemical texts, hoping they'd spark a certain...appreciation in Tara." He sighed at the memory. "I thought I was moments away from truly capturing her heart with those readings. But then, in a rather untimely manner, she departed. I've been trying ever since to bridge that gap." Wiping away a stray tear, he lamented, "How can one concentrate on groundbreaking endeavors with such depressing background music?"

Blaise tried to fight through the emotional barrage, but his body refused to cooperate. "Alice, I...I can't move in this state," he choked out, overcome by the artificial sorrow.

<Neither can we,> Emrys's voice echoed through the bond, faint and filled with despair. <It feels like...like I've lost you, Blaise.>

Alice clenched her jaw, resolution carving through the emotional fog. "Right. I can't do this alone. Especially not while on the verge of tears." She sighed as a large raindrop splashed nearby. "Okay, trying something else. Theo, Mama's coming!"

As if shaking off the sorrow with each stroke of her bow, the tune transitioned from mourning to a fiery defiance. Blaise's head snapped up, eyes narrowing as he focused on Jefferson. But he wasn't the only one given a reprieve by the change. The students sniffled, some of them wiping runny noses on their clothing, though they remained in their defensive positions.

Zebulon, momentarily intrigued, raised an eyebrow at the audacity of hope carried in the new tune. As Alice's bow danced ferociously across the strings, he murmured with a flicker of appreciation, "Ah, a change in tune. Always enjoyed a bit of variability in my background music while engaging in alchemical pursuits. A little crescendo here, a diminuendo there. Makes for a lovely auditory experience." His gaze then sharpened as he gestured around, a sliver of anticipation coloring his words, "Josh, engage the Etheric Resonance Capacitor for the Crucible of Life. Let's add a dash of vigor to this experiment, shall we?"

At his command, the contraption buzzed to life. Streams of lights chased along its structure like shooting stars.

Whether the machine was born of alchemy, magic, or a breed

of science native to this realm, Blaise didn't know. Didn't care. His mind, fueled by the rallying cadence of Alice's tune, was set on a single goal: reaching Jefferson.

"Maintain your posts, students! Ensure the sanctity of this experiment remains undisturbed!" Zebulon called out.

Breaker magic dusted from Blaise's fingertips as he strode toward the waiting students.

CHAPTER FORTY-ONE

Warrior's Dance

Alice

I can't do this. I'm going to lose my baby. I can't do this.

The terror of the unknown loomed over Alice as she played, an edge of panic threatening to capsize the resolve carried in her music. She was no traditional warrior clad in armor, but she was versed in the art of Vientoza, the dance of battle. The rooftop, bristling with mechanical contrivances and students poised with alchemical curiosities, was her unconventional stage.

Theo, her world, her son, was out there—vulnerable and ensnared by the mechanical beast's ominous hum. That thought alone steeled Alice's resolve. Her child would not suffer if she had any say.

The thought of Theo in danger almost blew her loosely gathered courage into the wind. But Alice inhaled deeply and focused on her art. On her music and magic.

She advanced, the rain beginning to patter against the rooftop, a reminder of the world's indifference to her inner turmoil. Her violin, precious as it was, mattered little compared to Theo's safety. She'd bear the loss of a hundred violins for him.

Lightning split the sky. The fierce clap of thunder that followed made her jump, but she gritted her teeth. *I will see this through.*

With a defiant crack of thunder as her overture, she moved ever closer to her son, Alice's resolve as unyielding as the music that poured from her instrument.

The students didn't attack but watched her intently, their hands clutching at the potions and devices they bore. Alice sensed the potential violence crackling in the space between them, a prelude to the storm of conflict that awaited.

One student, emboldened or perhaps unnerved by her approach, uncorked a vial, downing its contents in a swift gulp. His body began to blur, movements becoming swift and erratic—a potion of speed. He lunged toward her, but Alice was ready.

Her music faltered, a dissonant wail echoing her shock. But Alice found grounding in that moment of discord. This was her stage, her performance, and she'd not falter in her Warrior's Dance.

She resumed her melody, letting it guide her movements. She spun, a whirlwind of grace and fury. Her foot lashed out to connect with the hastened student, sending him staggering back, his speed now a hindrance as he struggled to correct his overzealous momentum.

Another came at her, gadget in hand, as Alice's violin sang a tempo of urgency. The young alchemist hurled an egg-shaped object at her. She leaped, the device exploding in a flash of light where she had just stood. Her dance carried her through the chaos.

The rooftop became a stage of war, with students advancing, each armed with an alchemical concoction or device. Smoke bombs rolled across the ground, their smog attempting to obscure her vision, but her music was her guide, a beacon through the mists of war. As the vanguard encircled her, Alice's melody soared into a crescendo of desperation. She danced through them, her bow a baton of leadership, conducting her feet in a ballet of evasion and attack.

An assailant lunged, a syringe with some concoction in hand, but with the poise of a prima ballerina, Alice spun, her elbow connecting with the unfortunate student's face with a grace that belied its strength. The impact sent the student howling and the syringe clattering away.

Her music was a storm, her body its eye. Each step, each note, was both defense and offense, a symphony of survival. She swept a leg, toppling a student who had hurled a flash powder in her direction, his own tool now the instrument of his downfall.

But the alchemist's attempt distracted Alice from a new foe. The girl was nearly invisible, her outline only betrayed by the strange deflection of raindrops and the play of light around her form. Alice tried to dodge as the invisible student plowed into her, tackling the Songbinder to the ground.

Instinctively, Alice wrapped herself around her violin, her top priority to shield the source of her magic from harm. Though her tumble was graceless, she managed to cushion the instrument with her body. It scraped the rooftop with a heart-stopping sound, but by some fortune, the damage was minor — a few scuffs on the varnish, perhaps, but nothing that compromised its melody.

"You have to stay out of this!" the mostly invisible girl called, her words almost a plea. "Our grades depend on it!"

"No way in Perdition." Alice scrambled out from the girl's grasp, sweeping her violin and bow up with her as she moved.

More students approached, their faces lined with new desperation as Alice glanced around. She was so much closer to Theo, but at the same time, so very far away. Tears prickled her eyes. They were too many. Every step she took was countered, every note she played met with an equal force.

Her gaze flickered across the rooftop, searching for Blaise, for any aid. And there, emerging from the shadows, was Phillip, his eyes wide with the same fear that clawed at her heart. "Alice!" he called, though his eyes were wide with horror at the scene before him. "I'm coming!"

"Not me!" she shrieked at him. "Theo! Get to Theo!"

Phillip shifted, uncertain. She saw purpose snap onto her estranged husband's expression as he turned to survey the scene. The brisk wind lashed against him, his coat billowing around him like dark wings. He froze when he, too, saw Theo strapped to the table. Whatever their past, their love for Theo united them in this moment of peril.

"Zebulon!" Phillip bellowed, fists balled at his sides. "What have you done?"

Zebulon adjusted his glasses, squinting as if trying to understand what had Phillip out of sorts. "Phillip? How timely. You, of all people, should understand the lengths one might go to for a touch of romance. I'm merely trying to stitch together a love story with my dear Tara once again."

"Just get Theo!" Alice's scream was a blade of panic cutting through the chaos.

As Phillip dashed toward their child, Alice turned back to the fray, the music from her violin a rallying call, even as the odds mounted against her. She needed to stand, to fight for Theo, until her last note was played.

Her violin wept and wailed, the notes the aural embodiment of her desperation. With every draw of the damaged bow, she dodged and struck, the dance of survival a frantic ballet.

There, in a break, she caught sight of Phillip. He'd reached Theo, fingers flying to unstrap the unconscious boy. Zebulon cried out in alarm, running over to intervene. With a snarl, Phillip whirled and smashed a fist into the alchemist's face, sending Zebulon reeling.

Above them, the menacing machine whirred louder, its lights frenzied. Nursing his swelling eye, Zebulon scrambled to a control panel, slamming his hand down with a manic resolve. "It's now or never, my sweet Tara!"

Luci

LUCI STOOD AT HER POSITION ON THE ROOF, THE ONLY STUDENT not taking advantage of a potion or device. Josh had given her a potion, but she had tucked it away in her pouch. She refused to be one of Professor Woodrow's minions.

She stood, unable to decide on a course of action. Blaise struggled toward Jefferson. Alice was fighting off a horde of students with her music, though Luci couldn't hear it all that well. After her other encounters with Alice, she'd taken to carrying soft wax in her hip pouch and had stuck it in her ears as soon as the musical mage had made an appearance.

But what should she do? The calculations, the risks, the lives at stake left her frozen, unable to take any action at all.

Then she heard Blaise's anguished cry, and Professor Woodrow's victorious whoop as the resurrection engine—no, he had called it the Crucible of Life—began in earnest.

Someone screamed Theo's name.

Theo. The thought of that sweet, funny boy who loved dogs and cherished a lucky rock broke the ice of fear encasing her heart.

Decision made, she abandoned her position, sprinting to his gurney. His eyes were closed, his face waxy, though he appeared to be just asleep. Sedated, probably. She hoped. Like Jefferson, a myriad of wires were attached to his slight form.

No, not *wires*, she realized with a start. They were more like tubes, hollow on the inside. Conduits. Professor Woodrow planned to drain Theo and Jefferson of…something. She didn't know what, but figured it wasn't good with a machine called the Crucible of Life whirring nearby.

Phillip was already tearing the conduits free. With each he removed, it flailed like a living thing, a leech seeking purchase. Some of them clung to him, but he ignored them, solely focused on the child.

Luci joined him. She pulled out a pair of gloves, quickly tugging them on. Phillip didn't glance up at her, simply gave her a nod of acknowledgement as they worked to free Theo.

The machine's engine hummed, changing its rhythm as if gearing up for a dark task. Phillip yanked the last conduit free, and together, he and Luci hurried to undo the leather restraints that bound Theo to the cold metal. The urgency in their fingers heightened with every passing second.

But as Luci worked on the final restraint, the conduits, as though infused with sinister life, lashed out at Phillip. They clamped onto him like vipers sinking in their fangs.

He yelped—a sound edged with shock more than pain—as they dug into his flesh. Through gritted teeth, he gasped, "Get Theo to Alice! Get out of here!"

Luci's voice failed her for a moment, the sight before her momentarily rooting her in place. But she nodded, scooping the unconscious boy into her arms as the conduits wrapped around Phillip like relentless serpents. She shot a look back, fighting an internal tug-of-war between helping Phillip and getting Theo to safety. But the urgency in Phillip's face propelled her forward.

Alice finally won free of the students who had hemmed her in. She raced to Luci, dropping her violin as she snatched the child from her. Theo's head lolled against his mother's shoulder, though his eyes fluttered, as if now that he was away from the gurney, the sedation was lifting.

Behind her, Phillip shrieked in agony.

She heard Blaise's wail. Luci turned to Alice. "I have to go to him."

Alice cradled Theo close, a maternal bulwark against the world. "Go. He's with my brother. I'll do what I can to buy you time. Help them!" She gently laid Theo at her feet, as if she were putting him down for a nap. Then Alice reclaimed her battered violin and bow.

Luci ran.

CHAPTER FORTY-TWO

The Crucible of Life

Blaise

Students stood as a barrier between Blaise and Jefferson, each armed with the dangerous fruits of their alchemy studies. Blaise's hands tingled with the readiness of his Breaker magic, a force potent enough to tear through stone and steel. But he knew better than to unleash it recklessly on the rooftop. It could bring the entire building down, especially with the gusts of the building storm.

Alice was hemmed in. Phillip Dillon had burst out of the roof access, then made a beeline for Theo, though he grappled with Zebulon, too. Blaise held onto a sliver of hope that this diversion might carve a path, but that hope dimmed as Zebulon turned his attention back to the machine.

The contraption sprang to life as an array of lights chased along the length of its arms. Jefferson, still in its grasp, convulsed with a sudden jolt. His eyes snapped open. Then the Dreamer's mouth twisted as he released a harrowing scream that seared Blaise's soul. In that gaze, Jefferson's pain was evident, a silent plea that pierced Blaise to his core. It was a call to action he could not ignore, his heart shattering with the agony in Jefferson's voice.

The thought broke Blaise, and he wordlessly screamed his grief. Alice's tune shifted into something aggressive, wild fury mirroring the storm that loomed overhead. It was a melodic summons to the darkest depths of Blaise's power.

Silvery motes of Breaker magic played across his palms as Blaise stalked forward, confronting the nearest student who dared obstruct his way. The young alchemist held a device that sizzled with electricity, a modern interpretation of a dragon's breath. The student lunged, confident in the gadget's power.

Anticipating this, Blaise channeled his magic into a more subtle form, creating a shimmering barrier just as the student's device discharged its arc of fire. The blast crackled against the magic shield, the backlash sending the student reeling. The device short-circuited in his grasp with a pop and hiss of defeat.

Blaise wasn't done. With Alice's belligerent music provoking him, he snatched up the device. He held it out from his body as he sent a bolt of power into it. The invention made a terrible shrieking sound followed by a dull boom as it fell to the roof in pieces. The student's eyes widened as he scrambled backward.

"You won't keep me from him," Blaise growled as he went after the young man, hands outstretched and ready to shatter every bone in his opponent's body.

"Blaise, stop!"

He whirled at the voice. No one would stop him, not while he was determined to plow a trail of devastation to get to Jefferson. With the alchemy student shrinking away from him, Blaise focused on this new opponent who was running at him. He lifted his hands, ready to give her a taste of his power, too.

"Blaise, it's...it's your sister." Jefferson's voice, ragged with pain, shattered Blaise's haze of anger. He twisted to stare at his husband. But before Blaise could process the words, another harrowing scream from Jefferson pierced the air.

The heartbreaking sound renewed Blaise's rage. His fists clenched, magic trailing over his skin.

Wetness splashed into Blaise's face. With a gasp, he shook his head, bringing up his hands to wipe at his now-stinging eyes. Whatever it was, it had the strong scent of vanilla and cinnamon. Clarity washed over him, even as he felt the strange pressure of someone doing something to his ears.

"It's me!" The familiar voice was faint, as was the violin music. Luci. She had come to stop him.

Blaise blinked at her, realizing she had doused him with a calming potion. "I don't want to fight you." He lifted a hand to prod one ear. She had stuffed wax into them. Why?

Luci's eyebrows quirked in confusion. "What?"

He swallowed. "Please just get out of my way. I won't fight my sister."

She rolled her eyes at him. "Just because I used a potion to knock sense into you doesn't mean I'm with them!"

Blaise stared at her. She wasn't against him? He was so relieved, he almost didn't know what to do. "Why the wax?" He nearly shouted the question, pointing to his ears.

"Because I already knew what she was capable of doing." Luci nodded to Alice. "Now, let's get to Jefferson!"

Blaise spun around, his attention snapping to the alchemy students who had created a barrier between him and Jefferson. Instead, seemingly inspired by Alice's music, the students turned on one another. Their tempers flared as confusion took hold, their devices sparking and potions sloshing in the chaos.

Seizing the moment of distraction, Blaise bolted toward Jefferson, with Luci keeping pace beside him. Jefferson spasmed as the machine above made a whirring noise. He tried to struggle against the restraints, but they were so tight he could barely move. Tears streaked pale paths down his cheeks, his eyes frantic and bloodshot.

"You're too late. Progress, once begun, can only be slowed, not stopped." Zebulon's voice was distant through the mire of wax in Blaise's ears. He glanced over his shoulder, ready to greet the alchemist with righteous fury if he approached. But Zebulon remained in place, turning dials on the machine as if they were having an idle conversation as he worked. "Miss Hawthorne, isn't it intriguing how your priorities are somewhat...divergent from the grand tapestry of alchemical progress? You know, in my days as a student, they often told us about the unexpected twists and turns of academic commitment. One might say, you've strayed from the syllabus. Such potential, wasted."

Luci glanced at Blaise. "Get Jefferson out of those conduits. I'll do what I can against Professor Woodrow."

Blaise didn't know what hope his sister had against a master alchemist, but he had to have faith that she could take care of herself. He nodded, stepping beside Jefferson.

"You found me," Jefferson whispered, each syllable streaked with pain. He groaned, eyes rolling before scrunching shut against the agony.

"I never lost you," Blaise told him, staring at his husband. Jefferson's eyes flashed open at his voice. The pain etched on his face shredded Blaise from within. Then, there was no more time for reassurances. Blaise turned to look at the wires—no, Luci had called them *conduits*—connecting Jefferson to the machine. They burrowed into his flesh.

Without hesitation, Blaise gripped the nearest conduit attached to Jefferson's wrist and yanked it free. A small bead of blood marked where it had been. The conduit seemed to come alive, twisting and writhing, aiming to re-embed itself.

"*No,*" Blaise growled, reaching out to snatch the wire before it could burrow into Jefferson again. The wire squirmed like a worm, then tried to sink into Blaise's skin.

It *hurt*. Blaise's Breaker magic rose against the intrusion, striking at the wire. It turned into a frayed, shredded thing, wilting beneath his power.

Jefferson's agonized gaze was on him. His lips parted, as if he were about to speak, but then his eyelids fluttered closed, his face growing slack.

"Jefferson!" Blaise swung into action, Breaker magic silvering his hands as he reached out, sending jolts of magic against each wire. They shrank back, retreating from Jefferson, leaving tiny puddles of crimson in their wake.

And then only the leather restraints stood between Blaise and his husband. He spared a single glance over his shoulder, if only to make certain no one was going to interfere. At the moment, he would tolerate no interruptions.

He grasped each strap with his hands, bypassing the buckles, and instead disintegrating the leather bonds with a burst of his magic. They peeled away under his touch, setting Jefferson free from their cold grasp.

The Dreamer lay too still, only the faint movement of his breath betraying any sign of life.

Thunder rumbled overhead.

"Jefferson?" Blaise nearly choked on the word.

He wrapped his arms around his husband. Gathered Jefferson up and gently, ever so carefully, lifted him from the metal table.

His muscles ached, his magic strained, but Blaise held on, easing Jefferson down to the rooftop. Settling down, he cradled Jefferson's head in his lap, the rain cascading around them. His gaze scoured Jefferson's face, the pallor of his skin, the frightening grey of his lips. A whimper of desperation escaped Blaise as he leaned down, his lips brushing against Jefferson's in a whisper of a kiss, a silent plea.

"Stay with me. Please."

Luci

THE CRUCIBLE OF LIFE MADE A RUMBLING SOUND. LUCI'S GAZE flicked to the grotesque dance of essences swirling in the tank alongside the lifeless form of Professor Woodrow's wife. Her alchemical intuition told her *something* was happening in there, and the wrongness of it soured her stomach.

She stepped away from Blaise, though it tore at her to leave him. She had once asked Blaise if he ever got angry, and now, seeing him with that wild look, she finally had her answer. Jefferson's capture, tempered with Alice's aggressive music, had pushed him into a force of nature Luci hardly recognized as her gentle brother.

But she had to leave him. In her gut, she knew she was the only one who could keep Professor Woodrow distracted long enough for Blaise to free Jefferson. Luci's gaze flicked to the machine. Maybe she could end this twisted experiment before it got further out of hand.

"I really am quite disappointed in you," Professor Woodrow said, though he continued to adjust the machine. "I offered you so much, and you would rather align yourself with our test subjects than with progress."

She was tired of him speaking about the people she loved like that. But was he baiting her? Luci bit her lip. Maybe she could bait him, too. Anything to buy Blaise more time.

"You'll never be half the alchemist Marian Hawthorne is!" Luci shouted over the wind and machinery.

Luci's words seemed to stir something within Professor Woodrow amid the chaotic blend of gusting wind and whining machinery. "Marian Hawthorne? You know, she struck me as one of those cautious artists afraid to dip into the fuller spectrum of her palette. Like, 'Oh no, I can't possibly use that shade of blue!' She's bounded by her...let's term them *ethical nuances*, which, to my mind, stifle real innovation."

Woodrow's eyebrows quirked as he glanced aside, noting the change of subjects on Theo's gurney. "Hmm, seems there's been a bit of a switcharoo. A younger subject might have been a tad more optimal, but Phillip has his...vitality, in his own way."

Luci followed his gaze, aghast when she saw Alice's estranged husband slumped against the table. The conduits cocooned him, pulsing like a heartbeat. Phillip hadn't gotten free. The sick feeling in her gut expanded.

She had to end this. Now.

Luci dug a hand into her hip bag. She didn't dare let down her guard, so she had to rummage and find what she needed by touch alone. The cool glass of potions swathed in cotton greeted her. But that wasn't what she needed, not right now. At least, not while she couldn't read the label on each bottle.

There! Her fingers connected with a metal cylinder, the same canister that had served as a quick way to create fire when she and Blaise had begun this ill-fated trip.

Professor Woodrow was still speaking. "I will give you a final opportunity to reexamine your priorities, Miss Hawthorne. This is your chance to return to the path your mother turned from. Join me here, or I'll have no choice but to consider you just another subject, which would really be a shame."

Luci closed her fingers around the canister, her mouth as parched as a desert in high summer. She heard Blaise's heartbroken cry.

"You'll end up like Subjects Zero and One," Woodrow said, his voice lacking even a shred of sympathy. "Is that what you want?"

"No," Luci whispered. With reluctant, heavy steps, she approached the Dean of Alchemy.

Professor Woodrow's face lit up. "Ah, I knew you would come around. You have a good head on your shoulders. As a show of good faith, I'll even allow you to observe the final stage of the experiment." His lips curled into a satisfied smile.

Luci struggled to fight the terrified shiver that slid over her body. "What are you doing?"

He slanted a look at her. "In time, I'll impart that wisdom to you. But for now, simply watch...and learn."

His fingers flew over a panel of arcane controls covered in alchemical symbols. From this distance, Luci couldn't tell exactly what they were or remember the order in which he activated them. This close, she noticed more about the Crucible of Life that she hadn't seen at a distance. Above the control panel, Luci saw a shelf on which a star-shaped pendant rested. It looked like gilded copper, with large, winking, oval crystals embedded within. The pendant had been placed beneath three huge, convex crystals. Light filtered through two of the crystals, harsh beams of light focused on the pendant. The third crystal had been installed in reverse of the others, directing the light that bounced onto the pendant back up into...the tank holding the woman.

Luci swallowed. Those weren't just crystals. They were some sort of magnifying lens or siphon. The crystals were connected to the two gurneys through the conduits. This was how Woodrow was collecting essence from Phillip and Jefferson to imbue in the woman! The pendant was more like an amulet than a piece of jewelry.

Professor Woodrow glanced back at her. "Now, observe the culmination of my work!" His fingers flew over a final sequence on the panel.

Luci pulled her hand out of her hip bag. She uncapped the canister, fire hissing to life despite the rain. Luci hiked back her arm and hurled the travel-sized alchemical furnace at the amulet and crystal set-up.

"No!" Woodrow howled, noticing her too late and diving to intercept. His hand clipped the side of the canister as it flew past, sending it off course.

Luci gasped. The bottom of the furnace struck the amulet, ricocheting off it, spinning upward. The contraption gouted flames as it went. Was it her imagination, or did the fire seem to interrupt the beam of light pouring into the crystal pointed at the woman's tank?

She didn't have time to ponder. The furnace's fire died, and it fell harmlessly to the roof with a loud clank. Woodrow's face contorted with rage. She had never seen him so angry. He moved faster than she expected, closing the distance between them as he clamped a hand down on her shoulder. His fingers dug in so hard that Luci yelped.

"You've jeopardized all my work!" he shouted, eyes wild.

Luci tried to duck out of his grasp, but she couldn't. She struggled to dig into her pouch once more to grab something, anything, but the professor grasped her hand before she could.

"This is the last time a Hawthorne will get in my way," he growled, dragging her toward the edge of the roof. Oh gods, he was going to throw her over! There was no way she would survive that.

"Leave Miss Luci alone!" a small, defiant voice piped up, followed by a yelp from Professor Woodrow as he spun, dropping Luci to the relative safety of the roof. A small, glistening rock clattered past Luci. Theo's lucky rock. She staggered to her feet.

Theo stared at the professor, backed by his mother's fierce melody. "Theo, run! Get away!" Alice yelled. He must have come out of the sedation and slipped away while his mother was distracted, determined to come to Luci's aid.

Woodrow beamed. "Perhaps it's not too late to use you, after all—"

The tank shattered. Shards of glass exploded outward. Some of the shrapnel caught Luci on her face and arms. She yelped, grabbing Theo to shield him with her body, afraid that the experiment's failure would only get worse. With alchemy, they often did. The fluid from the tank splattered the nearby students, turning their attention from their own squabbles.

Theo wailed in surprise and fear, clutching Luci close.

"*I LIVE!*" a voice rasped. The sound grated through the air like fingernails against a chalkboard. Every hair on Luci's body stood on end, leaving her feeling as puffed up as an alarmed cat.

Luci still held Theo protectively close but turned, shaking the hair from her eyes. She looked up and stared at a surreal sight. "*Oh, gods.*"

Hovering above the remains of the broken tank was a woman encased in an aura of raw power and frost. The drizzling rain shifted into sleet and hail around her. The woman's eyes, glowing an ethereal silver. They bore into the living world from the fringe of death. Luci had seen silver eyes in the living before, but never in...whatever this woman was.

It hit her then—this was Tara. Professor Woodrow's late wife.

Professor Woodrow beamed, eyes shimmering with joyous tears. "Oh, Tara! Just look at you! Here you are, making an entrance only you could pull off. Truly spectacular."

The woman's chilling gaze landed on the alchemist. "Zebulon? This is...you did this?"

The alchemist replied with an awkward enthusiasm, rubbing his hands together. "Oh, Tara! Indeed, it was me. You see, on that rather unfortunate day of your...departure, the idea of a final farewell just seemed so...pedestrian. So, I thought, why not turn this tragic setback into a, well, a project of passion? I simply had to ensure you weren't interred with the common masses. All in the hopes of, well, this exact moment. Our reunion!"

Luci yanked the wax from her ears as distant shouts pricked her attention. Moments later, a pair of Cheswell night watchmen barged through the roof access, pistols glinting under the dim light. They halted, eyes darting over the floating woman, the humming machine, and the transmuted graduate students. The scene before them was bewildering, and bewildered guards were a recipe for disaster in Luci's book. She raised her hands to show she was unarmed. Theo still hid behind her, quaking.

"Intruders," Tara whispered, malevolence in her eyes.

The night watchmen steadied their pistols at her. "You! Floating woman…get down and…stop floating," one of them stuttered, his command trembling in the icy rain.

Tara smiled and flicked a wrist. The night watchman who had spoken went sprawling backward, almost over the edge of the roof. His companion bellowed something incomprehensible and fired his pistol in a panic.

"No!" Professor Woodrow howled.

The undead woman remained unfazed. With a graceful sweep of her hand, a flurry erupted around her, masking her figure momentarily. The bullet seemed to vanish in the snowy shroud.

As the snow dissipated, she turned to the alchemist, her voice firm. "Come, Zebulon. We must leave." And with that, she swept down, cradled Professor Woodrow in her arms, and soared away into the stormy night.

Luci stared after them, losing sight of them quickly in the storm. Even the erratic flashes of lightning failed to catch their silhouettes again.

"What in the name of Garus is going on here?" the night watchman demanded.

All around them, the graduate students ended their squabbles, though some had clothing partially shredded or splattered by diabolical devices or caustic potions. Nearby, a faint voice asked, "Does this mean we passed the practicum?" Luci almost laughed, because what else could she do at this point? It was either laugh or scream.

A sudden pang of helplessness engulfed Luci. A glance behind her gave her a worrying view of Jefferson, utterly limp in Blaise's embrace, her brother sobbing over him. Phillip's body was as wilted as Jefferson's, though he lay draped across the table. He looked as if he were asleep, but in her gut, Luci knew he wasn't.

Alice looked up at the watchmen, plaintive. "We can explain later. But we need help." She gestured around at the students, each one bearing the toll of the night's unforeseen havoc. "All of us."

Seeing the guards soften at Alice's appeal, Luci seized the chance. She was glad an adult had taken command of the situation. Licking her dry lips, she looked down at Theo. "Stay with your Mama, okay? I need to check on someone."

Theo nodded, running over to Alice.

Luci rushed over to Blaise, falling to her knees beside him on the damp, cold rooftop. Her brother was shaking as if he might fracture into a thousand pieces. "Is he alive?"

Blaise held Jefferson protectively close, tears trailing down his cheeks before getting lost in the bristles of his beard. Luci wasn't sure if Blaise had heard her because he didn't respond. She took the initiative, extending her hand and cautiously grabbing Jefferson's wrist. His pulse was there, though it was faint and sluggish.

Luci reached up and pried the wax from Blaise's ears. He didn't even respond to that. Her fingers flew to her pouch, pulling out vials from within. She held up a potion.

Chill of Death.

"We can use this," Luci told Blaise, hoping that he would give her an answer. "Do you want me to?"

His eyes flicked toward the potion, reflecting the shimmering liquid for a moment before they met Luci's. He knew well what it entailed. The potion could buy some precious time for Jefferson, but at a steep price. Blaise had been through the icy grasp of the Chill of Death before, its cold tendrils a reminder of how close the dance with death was.

Blaise's throat bobbed. "Do it," he whispered.

CHAPTER FORTY-THREE

Cold's Cruel Bite

Jefferson

*I*ce.

Cold.

The frigid breath of oblivion nipped at Jefferson's consciousness, settling into the marrow of his bones. It seemed to seep into the core of his very being, burying his soul in a sheath of frost. A piercing, never-ending brightness surrounded him, as if he were a snowflake illuminated by a sunbeam.

He shivered—a shiver that seemed to echo through the realms of his thoughts. Far away, beyond the bright, he heard a medley of sounds. Among the echoes, there was a voice—a voice that seemed to carve through the cold, a voice he knew, a voice he cherished. Along with it, the tender strains of a violin offered a soothing warmth against the cold's cruel bite.

Where am I? Jefferson's mind fluttered like a candle flame in a breeze, straining against the chill that sought to extinguish it. His memory was a fleeting shadow, there on the fringes, but hazy. He only knew that he wanted more of the warmth promised by that voice, by the melody.

The voice held an edge of sorrow, of heart-shattering misery. The music was a stirring counterpoint, a ballad of hope, of promise. Jefferson relaxed, feeling as if the rising notes enveloped him, like a pegasus riding a thermal.

But then the distraction tore him back to his reality...or whatever this was. He was walking, his feet seeming to move of their own accord as he followed a mist-shrouded trail.

"Where am I?" Jefferson whispered, willing his restless feet to halt as he spoke. They didn't.

The surrounding area reminded him of the dreamscape, but some deep instinct hold him that this was not his realm. The mist drifted, patches of it revealing parched bones. There, the spine of some massive creature, with ribs partially attached. Just ahead to the left, the bleached, horned skull of a Knossan.

"No." Horror gripped Jefferson as reality crashed upon him.

This was the long walk to Perdition.

The music and the familiar voice nudged at him again, breaking through the boundary between life and death. The sweet medley belonged to Alice. And the voice...Blaise. Jefferson didn't understand the words, but he felt the desperation. The love. The heart-wrenching pleas.

This wasn't right. Couldn't be right. How could he leave Blaise now, when they finally had a chance at happiness?

"This is a mistake!" Jefferson called, his voice echoing around him as if he were in a canyon. "I need to go back!"

No one responded. The only sound was the steady, muffled thud of his shoes against the desolate ground.

"I want to speak to whoever's in charge!" Jefferson pulled on all his old haughtiness, if only to grant himself a little courage.

"Tabris! Garus!" He paused. As a mage, it would only be right to beseech the goddess of magic. "Faedra!"

Still no response.

Jefferson brought both hands to his face, massaging his forehead and cheeks to ward off his growing desperation. He knew what was happening. He was dead, or dying. Jefferson wasn't sure which. Whatever it was, it was unfair—not to him. But to his husband.

"I'm sorry, Blaise." Jefferson twisted to peer back in the direction he'd come, though the looming mist hid the trail.

"There you are," a voice announced.

Jefferson was startled, though his stubborn feet never stopped moving. At first, he thought a savior had come for him—but then he saw Tara Woodrow striding toward him. She looked as she had in life. Well, not as she had at the end, when Raven had slashed her throat. Tara was whole and beautiful, her obsidian hair gathered atop her head in a regal updo.

"Come to join me on a stroll?" Jefferson asked, wary. There was something about Tara that he couldn't remember at the moment. Something very important.

Her eyes gleamed with mischief, and she glanced in the direction Jefferson was inexorably headed. Tara walked alongside him, though she seemed frustratingly free of the compulsion. "Oh, I've already been there." She waved a hand. "Did I really hear you calling for the management like you'd found a fly in your soup?"

Jefferson huffed. "I need to get out of...wherever this is."

Her lips twitched with amusement. "Always so dramatic. But I agree. As much as you *deserve* to make the long walk to Perdition, you need a bit of a detour."

Sweet Tabris, Jefferson was right. This was the long walk to Perdition. But her last words grabbed his attention. "You're going to help me?"

She linked her arm through his, and at her touch, Jefferson's feet stilled. "You can't die yet. We're still bound, you and I." The corners of Tara's lips twitched into a very concerning smile. "And I'd rather not be drug back to Perdition so soon."

Tara pivoted, turning Jefferson away from the trail. He tried to balk in her grip, but couldn't. "What do you mean, *bound?*"

She shrugged. "I'm not exactly sure. I just know that my husband is quite insistent that you need to live." Tara's eyes gleamed. "At least a *little* longer."

"Why?" Jefferson demanded. Gods, he *really* wished he could pull away from her.

Tara paused and reached up to give his chin a condescending pat with her free hand. "We're almost at your stop."

"My stop? What is this, a hackney cab?" Jefferson glared at her.

She had the audacity to laugh. "Not quite. Just making sure you find your way back to your body is all." Tara drew him to a stop. "And look, here we are."

Jefferson saw nothing different about their surroundings. He didn't trust her.

Tara beamed up at him. "And before I send you on your way, you have something I need."

She plunged her hand into his chest, her flesh somehow both spectral and far too solid. Jefferson gasped, the renewed sensation of ice washing over him.

Tara curled her icy fingers around his heart.

CHAPTER FORTY-FOUR
The Path to Desolation

Marian

The door swung open with a resounding creak as Nadine barreled through, Marian close on her heels. Exhaustion dogged them both—they had flown to Greylight nearly nonstop once Naureus had returned to Fortitude with his dire news.

The room they entered was well-lit and smelled of antiseptic and a strange sweetness Marian couldn't place. No one looked up at their entrance. Nadine made a beeline for the bed in the middle of the room, where Cheswell medical staff were seeing to Jefferson.

Seledora had intercepted their group, telling them of Jefferson's dire condition. Marian swallowed a lump in her throat when she saw Blaise hunched over in a wooden chair, his face in his hands, shoulders shaking with silent sobs.

My baby. Marian spied another chair and dragged it over beside Blaise. There were too many people already working on Jefferson—and besides, she was an alchemist, not a healer or physician. For the moment, she would tend to the one she could.

"Blaise," Marian whispered. He didn't respond, but she hadn't expected him to. She had spoken simply so he would know he wasn't alone. She swept an arm around him, and he responded to that, slumping against her shoulder.

Blaise buried his face against her, sobbing as if his world was being torn away from him. Marian stroked his hair, her gaze falling on Jefferson. Perhaps his world *was* being torn away. She caught glimpses of her son-in-law as the physicians and Nadine worked. Jefferson's skin was milky pale, as if he were covered in permafrost—*oh*.

Marian swallowed. Chill of Death. She had sent the potion with Luci for only the most severe situations.

Small divots pocked Jefferson's body, the impressions weeping scarlet. Marian couldn't even imagine what had caused those. Branching red patterns crossed his chest like an arcane tattoo. She frowned. Had lightning struck him? No wonder Blaise was falling apart.

"I'm here," she murmured in her son's ear, holding him close.

He paused in his heartbreak to pull back just enough to peer up at her. The agony in his watery blue eyes shattered her. "He was right," Blaise whispered, his voice cracking. "And now I'm going to lose him."

It took Marian a moment to figure out what he meant. Then she recalled their quarrel. Jefferson's desire to protect them using magic, which had clashed with her son's peaceful inclinations. It made her heart ache for him.

And even more than that…Marian was a widow. She knew the pain of losing the other half of one's heart. Her gaze fell on Jefferson's form again. She hadn't liked him at first, afraid that he was using Blaise for his own ends. But in time, she understood that

Jefferson truly loved Blaise. And she finally thought that her son had a chance at happiness, at sharing his life with someone who treasured him as much as she did. Blaise didn't deserve to be a widower so soon.

She wanted to tell Blaise that he was wrong, that Jefferson would be fine. But she wouldn't lie to him. "Nadine is here. She's looking after him now." Marian wasn't sure if Blaise had seen the Healer come in. Probably not, in his current state. "Jefferson's under the best care."

Blaise turned to survey the scene with bleary eyes. He nodded, though the movement was mechanical, like he was a puppet on a string.

"Are you hurt?" Marian asked.

"I don't think so," Blaise said.

He had to be in shock. Marian noticed red lacerations on the palms of his hands, flaked with drying blood. He probably needed a thorough check, but she doubted he'd welcome that right now. She resolved to sit with him for as long as she could. Once the chaos around Jefferson died down, Marian would call for one of the physicians to tend to Blaise's wounds and check him.

What had happened here? None of the pegasi had known enough to give them a full picture. Marian only knew that, since Zebulon Woodrow was involved, it wouldn't be good.

She sighed. This was her fault. In Fortitude, she hadn't the contacts to access the staff directory of Cheswell. And it hadn't seemed like something that would matter, since Greylight was so far from Izhadell. But she had been wrong, and now people she loved were paying the price of her folly. Marian vowed she would do everything in her power to untangle the mysteries of Zebulon Woodrow's work. It was the least she could do.

She kissed Blaise's forehead, sealing the personal promise.

Luci

IT WAS NEARLY IMPOSSIBLE TO PRY OPEN HER GUMMY EYELIDS AT first. Luci groaned, rubbing at her eyes before blinking them open. Sunlight filtered into her dorm room through an open window, and just a handful of feet away at the desk in the corner sat...

"Mom," Luci whispered, jerking upright.

Everything came back to her in a rush. She had crashed hard after the events on the rooftop, the Crimson Cow potion finally calling in its debt. Luci had a hazy memory of her mother appearing, and then nothing after that.

Marian Hawthorne swiveled in the chair, an alchemical treatise in her hands. "I should never have sent you here."

Luci swallowed, pushing away the sheets to swing her legs over the side of the bed. "I think this would have happened even if I hadn't been here." And how would it have turned out in that case? Blaise and Jefferson wouldn't have had an ally on the inside. The thought of Jefferson's pale face flashed across her mind. "Jefferson..."

"Nadine is with him," Mom replied, her gaze falling back to the book as she paged through it. "The Chill of Death stabilized him."

Luci's shoulders sagged with relief. "Will he be okay?"

Her mother sighed, the sound carrying hints of too many unanswered questions. "I don't know. I've been trying to figure out what Zebulon did." Her sharp eyes flicked back toward Luci, digging for truths yet uncovered. "Do you know? Did you work with him on this?"

A queasy churn turned Luci's stomach as her mother's words hung in the air between them. She shook her head, attempting to fling away the unsettling thoughts. "No. But you can probably talk to some of the grad students." She squeezed her eyes shut for a moment. "He knew who I was. He wanted me to help him create alchemical mages." She hesitated before adding, "Like Blaise and Jefferson."

Mom nodded, as if that were the logical order of things. "So, you know."

Luci looked at her mother, trying to reconcile the woman who loved her, who raised her, with the same person who would use a toddler in an experiment. But…Mom loved Blaise, too. Luci knew that without a doubt.

After a pause that seemed to stretch thin the silence of the room, Luci murmured, "I didn't give Professor Woodrow much information. I was busy with other projects."

Mom's forehead crinkled, curious. "Like what?"

There was so much Mom didn't know. Sometime, Luci would fill her in. "Um, crafting Breaker's Touch. And trying to make a counter to a love potion, but I'm pretty sure it failed."

Mom's eyebrows arched, a hint of admiration shining through her stern facade. "Breaker's Touch isn't easy to replicate." Then she frowned. "A love potion?"

Luci sighed. "It's a long, long story. Is Blaise okay? And how did you even know to come?"

Mom closed the book with a soft thud, placing it gently on the desk. "Naureus flew into Fortitude several days ago and came directly to me, telling me there was trouble." Her lips twitched into a half-smile. "And he told me under no circumstances should I breathe a word of this to Jack Dewitt. Naureus rounded up Nadine, too, and then we came as quickly as we could." She exhaled a long sigh. "But not soon enough. Blaise is…I don't know, Luci. He's fragile right now."

Luci felt a pang, a dagger of ice at the unfairness of life. "I'll do whatever's needed to help."

Mom gave her a sad smile. "I know you will."

———

Alice

ALICE MASSAGED HER TEMPLES AS SHE CONTINUED HER WALK DOWN the scenic path that curled around the back of the Cheswell music building. The campus had lost its sinister veneer since Zebulon Woodrow and his resurrected wife had vanished. A haze of confusion and chaos had been thrust onto the shoulders of the administration.

She wanted to leave, but she couldn't—not yet. Her brother remained in the medical building, his condition tenuous. After everything they had been through, she wouldn't leave him like this.

Alice found a bench near one of the ivy-covered walls and sank onto it. Maybe she should have brought Theo along. His energetic chatter might have distracted her spiraling thoughts. But the girl, Luci, had appeared to check on Jefferson, too, and Theo had begged time with her. The sparkle in his eyes had made it hard for Alice to pull him away. She was reluctant to deny him time with a new friend.

She missed the humdrum life in Starvation. Alice had been happy there, had felt safe there. But safety was an illusion. *Everything* was an illusion.

And then there was Phillip—her emotions were a tangled mess when it came to him. She shook her head, a flare of anger rising. Alice recognized he had saved Theo, and in doing so, had doomed himself. She would be forever grateful for that. But Phillip...he had misused her from the start. But somehow, in his strange, twisted way, he loved her.

The knowledge festered within her; it felt like an unwelcome guest. It made a storm rise within, as if her own emotions were traitors. Alice shook her head. Maybe she needed to go back to the medical building and play the violin again. The battle and storm had ruined hers, but the one she had borrowed from the music department was serviceable.

The crunch of footsteps on the gravel path pulled her from her thoughts. As she looked up, she saw Blaise approaching. She studied him for any sign of a change in Jefferson. But his face was a mask, the redness around his eyes and nose a sign of his intermittent breakdowns and lack of sleep.

"What are you doing here?" The words left her lips before she could polish their edges, and they landed between them with a sharper edge than intended.

Blaise seemed to glide over her tone. He settled himself on the bench beside her, maintaining a respectful gap. "Nadine kicked me out."

Alice arched a brow. She thought no one could pry Blaise away from Jefferson's side, but Nadine, the silver-haired Healer, held a certain brand of harshness that bordered on intimidating.

Blaise reclined against the backrest of the bench, his sigh sketching his exhaustion in the cool air. "Not just that, though. Someone wanted me to talk to you."

Someone? She crossed her arms. "About what?"

Blaise's eyes avoided hers, as though the words he needed to say were found somewhere on the path. Alice could sense a reluctance in him, but the necessity of the conversation seemed to anchor him to the bench. "You probably feel hurt after..." His hand illustrated a vague dance in the air, a silent placeholder for the myriad of events that had transpired. "Everything. Betrayed." He fell into a momentary silence. It was not a silence seeking her words but a pause, giving room for him to gather his words. "You're not the only one who feels that way."

Alice's brow furrowed. "No, I suppose I'm not." What was he getting at?

"I was wondering if you'd be open to having a...friend. Someone who understands your feelings." His eyes, previously moored to the ground, now sought hers.

For a moment, Alice thought he meant himself. But something in his tone suggested otherwise. "Who do you mean?"

"A pegasus," he whispered.

The words hung between them for a beat, an unexpected gift. "A pegasus?"

Blaise slowly rose from the bench and offered her a weak smile. "I'll show you."

Casting a backward glance at the music building, Alice got up and walked beside Blaise, away from the campus. The memory of glimpsing the pegasi during the night of the rooftop skirmish fluttered in her mind. It felt like a brush with a dream, ethereal and distant.

Blaise walked in silence. Alice couldn't help but wonder about the man he was in times of joy, as Jefferson must have seen. But now, a marrow-deep sadness overshadowed the melody of his essence, a piece of music abandoned before it was finished. Each step he took was hesitant, as if he feared the path was about to open up and swallow him. She understood how he felt.

He led her to a wooded area outside the campus. A moment later, hooves crunched the ground, and four pegasi appeared. A majestic black stallion rushed over to Blaise, shoving his head into the young man's chest, nearly knocking him over. Blaise gave a half-hearted chuckle and hugged the stallion.

"This is Emrys, my pegasus," Blaise introduced, his hand affectionately stroking the sheen of Emrys's neck. His eyes then wandered to a stocky red roan. "That's Leorus. He's Nadine's mount." His expression tensed as he gestured to a graceful grey mare. "Jefferson rides Seledora."

<I'm also his attorney,> came a resonant voice that took a moment to register in Alice's mind. It was Seledora's voice, echoing within the quiet chambers of her thoughts.

Blaise gestured to a buckskin stallion who stood apart from the others. "And this is Naureus."

The stallion stepped closer, his head low, his hide the color of golden wheat. He stretched out his neck, nostrils flared as if reading her scent.

<I think we have much in common,> Naureus said, and somehow Alice understood his words were for her alone. <Someone who was supposed to care about me hurt me instead. This sort of betrayal...it cuts down to the bone.> He snorted, shaking his inky mane. <It is the sort that makes you think perhaps you should never give your heart to another living soul. That it might be better to leave everyone who could hurt you behind.>

"Yes," Alice whispered, the echoes of his hurt mingling with her own scars, resonating through her soul.

<But that is the path to desolation and loneliness. Pegasi and humans, we are social creatures. I thought that maybe, just maybe, our two broken hearts could form a whole.> The pegasus's huge brown eyes studied her, and Alice felt as if she were falling into their depths.

She swallowed, reaching out her hand, the palm outward. Naureus bridged the remaining distance; his forehead pressed against her palm, a gesture of trust as delicate as butterfly wings.

"I don't know anything about this," Alice admitted softly. Her gaze shifted toward Blaise. The warmth of Naureus against her skin felt reassuring, a soft balm to her aching heart.

He shrugged. "It's simple, really. It's all about love, if you're willing to embrace it."

Tears filled her eyes. She nodded, a whisper of hope fluttering in the space between her and the pegasus. It was a promise of healing and newfound friendship in a world that sometimes felt too harsh to bear.

CHAPTER FORTY-FIVE

Hope Reborn

Blaise

"You look like the Ghost Riders dragged you to Perdition and back. That cot over there is waiting for you, since I'm not foolish enough to believe you'll leave this room." Nadine stared at Blaise with her no-nonsense look, the one that usually cowed him.

Not today, though. He sat by Jefferson's side, clutching his husband's lukewarm hand as if he were the only thing anchoring Jefferson to the world of the living. The vibrant strands of violin music wafted through the room, played by Alice as she sat at the foot of the bed, hoping that her melody would help.

"I can't sleep," Blaise whispered, shaking his head.

The last time he'd caught his reflection in a mirror, he'd seen how red-rimmed his eyes were, both from exhaustion and tears.

Whenever he dozed, the same nightmare plagued him, relentless. Jefferson, limp in his arms. Dying.

"We have him stabilized." Nadine didn't drop her gaze. She knew Blaise hated stare-downs.

He wouldn't back down, though. Not this time. He tightened his grip on Jefferson's hand. "This...I don't call this stable." His words came out as a quaver, a harbinger of the tears he struggled to keep walled inside. His heart felt a thorny ache each time he blinked away the moisture welling in his eyes.

Nadine's stern facade crumbled, a sliver of compassion shining through. "It may not look like that to you, but I promise he is. He's not dying anymore. He's just..." Her words stumbled, her frown deepening. "Your mother and I are going to figure out what that insane alchemist did."

Blaise's throat tightened as he swallowed. The room seemed to shrink, the walls inching closer, suffocating him. He knew his mother was interviewing Zebulon's graduate students. But it seemed as if each only had a small piece of the puzzle, and it was taking time to put it all together. Luci was helping, combing through all the notes she could find.

Jefferson might not be dying anymore, but he *had* been. And now...he wasn't well. His eyes remained shut, his body motionless save for the rise and fall of his chest with each breath. Even Seledora, who paced outside the building, couldn't find his mind.

The cabochon ring on Jefferson's finger had suffered, too, its enchantment broken and drained. No longer did it hold the glamor that lent his hair a golden hue and altered the lines of his face. His true appearance emerged as the fractured magic dissipated: sleek obsidian locks replaced the golden blond, and the contours of his face returned to their natural, aristocratic state.

What if Jefferson was *gone?*

"You know," Nadine said, her tone shifting, as if she were adjusting her tactics, "I'm sure we could find a place for you to do some baking. That would help calm your mind, and then maybe you can rest without nightmares."

"No," Blaise whispered. Emrys had suggested the same earlier, and he had declined then, too. He could sense the stallion's distress, aching to help his rider but unable to find a way.

Alice's bow stilled on the strings, her tune fading. She settled the violin gently in her lap, her gaze wandering between Jefferson and Blaise.

Alice's voice broke the stalemate between Blaise and Nadine, her eyes focused on Jefferson's still form. "When you love someone, you don't give up on them. He was so annoying when he tracked me down in Starvation. I just...I wanted him to go away." A soft chuckle escaped her as she shook her head. "But he was frustratingly *stubborn*. He wouldn't back down. He came to every single one of my shows, hoping to talk to me."

Blaise's throat tightened at the recollection. Oh, how he wished he had gone along with Jefferson on that journey. His grip on his husband's hand tightened—a silent promise of holding on, of awaiting the moment when Jefferson's eyes would meet his again.

Alice's voice was tremulous, as she continued, "But he... Jefferson didn't give up on me. He was determined to set things right. I could never fathom why he went to such lengths— changing his name, his appearance...reinventing himself *completely*." She gestured toward Jefferson's still form on the bed. "I didn't understand, until one day, I did." A rueful smile graced her lips. "I was so damned certain he was going to be just like our father that I wrote him off. But he...he never wrote me off." Her eyes grew misty, and she brushed a solitary tear from her cheek. "I won't give up on him, either."

Blaise nodded, feeling some small comfort in their shared grief. But he couldn't ignore the yawning pit of emptiness he felt at the thought of a world without Jefferson.

Gingerly, he pulled the poppet from his pocket. Somehow, despite everything, he hadn't lost it. Blaise had considered sending one of the pegasi back to Fortitude with it, to pass it to Emmaline. To see if she could do anything at all for Jefferson. But he had dismissed the notion—if Nadine couldn't heal him, no one could.

Blaise leaned down, pressing his forehead to Jefferson's, his tears finding their way onto the cold, pale skin of his beloved.

"I read your letters. I don't know if you wanted me to find them, but I'm glad I did." Blaise paused, struggling against a lump in his throat. "Those memories…I want to make more with you. But I'm so scared that I'm going to have to face a life without you." The thought brought him up short, and Blaise was certain he was about to fall apart again. Hot tears gathered in the corners of his eyes.

Faint pressure around his hand startled him. Blaise jerked away, but he didn't let go of Jefferson's hand. The weak squeeze came again, somehow more insistent.

"Can't…have that." Jefferson's voice was a harsh rasp, so soft Blaise almost didn't hear. Slowly, ever so slowly, Jefferson's eyelids fluttered open, and a moment later, Blaise was the focus of his exhausted but warm gaze.

Blaise barely registered Alice's soft intake of breath, followed by a victorious shriek and Nadine's curse of surprise.

Nothing else mattered to him, in that moment, except the man lying before him. Blaise's eyes blurred with a cascade of tears that tumbled, unrestrained and unabashed, freely down his cheeks. He leaned down, pressing his lips to Jefferson's in a tender kiss, a gesture laden with hope reborn.

But Nadine shattered the moment, nudging him aside with a hiss of frustration. "I need room to work!" she huffed, her tone carrying an urgency that pricked at Blaise's topsy-turvy emotions. "Out of my way!"

A retort sat at the tip of his tongue, wanting to argue for his right to be near Jefferson. But Nadine was right—she needed to make sure Jefferson was okay.

He shifted to give her room, all the while his pulse thundering. He hadn't imagined it. Jefferson had spoken. Had awoken. Blaise traded looks with Alice, just to make certain he could believe his own eyes.

The Songbinder smiled, tears glittering on her cheeks, too. "He didn't give up," she whispered, the simple words carrying the weight of mountains.

Blaise slipped the poppet back into the sanctuary of his pocket, then sank into a chair in the corner and let Nadine work.

* * *

Jefferson

"RIDING A PEGASUS WAS NEVER SO DIFFICULT BEFORE," JEFFERSON murmured as they took another break on their trek back to Fortitude. Each mile seemed more exhausting than the last, accompanying a peculiar emptiness that he couldn't quite name.

Blaise settled beside him on the creek bank, close enough that their elbows brushed. Seledora and Emrys grazed nearby, neither letting their riders out of their sight. Nadine wasn't far, either, and she kept a keen eye on Jefferson, too. He was surrounded by a bevy of solicitous mother hens, but Jefferson didn't complain. Their concerns were justified.

Their group was almost a circus, really. When Naureus had returned to Cheswell, he'd brought Marian, Nadine, and a couple of riderless pegasi in case they were necessary. That had been smart, as it had allowed Luci and Marian to have mounts for the return trip, too. Theo rode aboard Naureus with his mother. Apparently, while Jefferson had been recovering, the buckskin stallion had warmed up to his sister. A bond forged by pasts full of betrayals, according to Blaise. Jefferson thought they were good for each other.

"You know why that is," Blaise said, his voice carrying a hint of unspoken worry.

The brush with death had shaken Jefferson. He wanted to forget, to move on, but he couldn't. Zebulon's use of him in the experiment that had raised Tara as...whatever she was...had left scars on Jefferson that he didn't fully understand.

Even worse, the glamor from his ring had been drained—Blaise said he didn't feel any remnants of magic within it. Jefferson had to bear his dark-haired countenance every time he ran across his reflection. For his part, Blaise seemed unbothered by the transformation, focused wholly on Jefferson's well-being.

There was a deeper loss that bothered him, something he struggled to explain to Blaise, Nadine, or even Marian. It was a hollow feeling, a missing spark. He couldn't quite grasp what it was, but he knew something essential was gone.

Perhaps with some time and distance from his trauma, when he felt more like himself, the missing piece would become clearer. For now, the fatigue was ever-present. His body felt sore, and his strength seemed to have dwindled away, leaving him as frail as a new-hatched chick. There loomed a fear, too, a niggling thought that, like Jack, the ordeal might have left him with lasting health issues.

"Yes, but I'd rather not." Jefferson sighed. It was a difficult thing, feeling like a shadow of one's self. Blaise slid a comforting arm around him.

Jefferson let his gaze drift toward the others. Alice stood by the stream, watching Theo as he looked for frogs. Marian and Luci were occupied with picking some buds from the nearby bushes, probably for their reagent supplies.

Theo broke away from his search, trotting up to where Jefferson and Blaise sat. "Uncle Malerson, will you help me find another lucky rock? I lost my new one when I threw it at the bad man."

Jefferson schooled his features to hide his reaction to the memories. The bad man. Zebulon Woodrow. The rooftop where Jefferson had almost died in a gruesome experiment.

"I would love to." He was proud that his words didn't quaver in the slightest. With a grunt, he rose to his feet, self-conscious of his weakness. But Theo paid him no mind, hopping from foot to foot as he told Jefferson all about the three frogs (one speckled, one with a blue stripe, and the third with golden eyes) that he'd seen so far.

"How will we know when we find your lucky rock?" Jefferson asked.

Theo paused to glance up at him. "You just know. It feels right." With those cryptic instructions, he set to the task of scouring the nearby rocks collected by the current.

"I don't know that I'll be of much help," Jefferson admitted. He wasn't sure if he could stoop down and get up again on his own. He was far too stiff from his time in the saddle.

"I just wanted you here while I look." Theo's words were simple, but they made Jefferson swallow with a roil of emotion.

He stood by as Theo trawled the bank of the stream, reminding Theo every few minutes that Alice didn't want him to get soaked. Then, with a triumphant whoop, the boy reached down and plucked a flat, smooth stone from the water.

He held his treasure aloft. "Look at this!" Theo dropped it in Jefferson's cupped hands.

Jefferson smiled at the speckled stone. "It's quite a remarkable lucky rock." He held out his hand to return it to Theo. "Here you are."

But Theo shook his head. "It's for you, Uncle Malerson. I think you need it more than me right now. You can give it back when you're all better."

Tears stung Jefferson's eyes. He closed his fist around the rock.

"I'll treasure it and keep it safe. Thank you." Then, Jefferson carefully tucked it into his pocket before going back to Blaise.

"A lucky rock, huh?" Blaise asked, warm amusement in his tone.

"It's quite the treasure," Jefferson said with a solemn nod. He groaned as he reclaimed his spot beside Blaise. "I hate that even sitting is a challenge."

"Be gentle with yourself," Blaise said, his words a soft caress. "Recovery takes time, especially after..." His voice trailed off, the unspoken words hanging heavily between them. "I know it's tough, but remember, I'm here with you."

<When we get back home, I'm sure Blaise will make you plenty of treats to strengthen you,> Emrys commented from nearby, his tone suggesting a hopeful share in the bounty.

Blaise chuckled. "He's not wrong. When we get home, I'll make you anything your heart desires."

At that, Jefferson managed a smile toward his husband. "I have what my heart desires right now." But even as he spoke the words, they seemed to echo emptily within him. They were the right words, the words he'd said before countless times, filled with love and gratitude. But now they felt rehearsed. He scolded himself mentally. *You're just weary and rattled. Blaise is right. The ordeal has left a mark, that's all.*

A gentle touch on his chin from Blaise pulled Jefferson back from his thoughts. "That's true. You got a razor so you could shave again."

"That's not—" Jefferson began, then he couldn't help but laugh a little. "Well, I will admit, that was a pleasant addition."

"I know what you meant." Blaise edged closer, his earnest blue eyes scanning Jefferson's face. It felt as though he was awaiting a sign, a reassurance.

"Are you trying to figure out if you should kiss me or not?" Jefferson asked, a playful lilt in his voice despite the hollow feeling that festered.

Blaise glanced away. "Uh…"

Oh, he was. Despite the melancholy that hung over him, Jefferson found this utterly endearing. With Blaise at his side, he was certain that, in time, even the most ravaged portions of his soul would heal. "The answer is you should always kiss me. *Always.*"

So, Blaise did.

Stay In the Know!

Sign up to my newsletter for sneak peeks, short stories, and more!
www.amycampbell.info

Soundtrack

Fight Song - Rachel Platten
Masquerade - Lindsey Stirling
The Reckoning - Halestorm
Queen of Swords - Idina Menzel
Breaking Inside - Shinedown
Sorry - Daughtry
I'd Come for You - Nickelback
All That I am Living For - Evanescence
The Arena - Lindsey Stirling

www.ingramcontent.com/pod-product-compliance
Lightning Source LLC
Chambersburg PA
CBHW011124190726
48289CB00012B/2889